STARSHIP'S
MAGE

THE SERVICE OF
MARS

BOOK NINE
OF THE STARSHIP'S MAGE SERIES

All rights reserved. For information about permission to reproduce selections from this book, contact the publisher at info@faolanspen.com or Faolan's Pen Publishing Inc., 22 King St. S, Suite 300, Waterloo, Ontario N2J 1N8, Canada.

This edition published in 2020 by:
Faolan's Pen Publishing Inc.
22 King St. S, Suite 300
Waterloo, Ontario
N2J 1N8 Canada

ISBN-13: 978-1-989674-07-9 (print)

A record of this book is available from Library and Archives Canada.

Printed in the United States of America
1 2 3 4 5 6 7 8 9 10
First edition
First printing: August 2020

Illustration © 2020 Jeff Brown Graphics
Faolan's Pen Publishing logo is a trademark of Faolan's Pen Publishing Inc.

Read more books from Glynn Stewart at faolanspen.com

STARSHIP'S
MAGE

THE SERVICE OF
MARS

BOOK NINE
OF THE STARSHIP'S MAGE SERIES

GLYNN STEWART

**FAOLAN'S PEN
PUBLISHING**
faolanspen.com

CHAPTER 1

"GOVERNOR NISKA, WELCOME," Mage-Lieutenant Roslyn Chambers told the old Legatan cyborg as he entered the big briefing room aboard the dreadnought *Durendal*. "Here's your briefing chip. It's still encrypted until the Mage-Admiral releases it."

"I know the drill," James Niska, Military Governor of Legatus, told the young blonde woman. He was the only native of Legatus in the briefing room on the warship orbiting the occupied capital of the Republic of Faith and Reason.

Roslyn was the Flag Lieutenant of Mage-Admiral Jane Alexander, the woman whose fleet had reduced the defenses of that capital ten weeks earlier. A lack of munitions and the murder of the Mage-King of Mars had kept Second Fleet at Legatus for over two months.

"Is this going to be much the same nothing as the last few were?" Niska asked, surveying the small collection of Martian flag officers with resignation.

Roslyn wasn't supposed to give anyone any idea of what was coming, but Niska had been instrumental in getting them all this far. She shook her head silently at him, as much information as she could really provide.

"Interesting," he said gruffly in response to her silent answer. "I will leave you to your duties, Lieutenant. If you could have someone bring me a coffee? It's been a long few weeks."

"Yes, sir," Roslyn confirmed, tapping a quick set of commands on her wrist-comp. The stewards supporting the briefing would get the message—in a smaller meeting, coffee would be her direct job, but there were a *lot* of people coming today and she had to turn her attention to the next arrival.

"Mage-Admiral Medici," she greeted the man in charge of Second Fleet's cruisers. "Here's your briefing chip." She passed him the small piece of black plastic. "Do you need anything to get set up?"

"Please tell me Marangoz is seated on the other side of the room," Medici muttered, the dark-skinned officer trying not to be heard. "If I hear the idiot rattle on about the 'inherent versatility of our battleships' one more time, I might engage in conduct unbecoming an officer."

Mage-Admiral Soner Marangoz commanded Second Fleet's battle-ships and was surprisingly twitchy over the fact that they were no longer the heaviest units of the fleet. *Durendal* and her two sisters in Second Fleet dwarfed even the largest battleships, rendering the former queens of the fleet into a secondary role their commanders weren't quite sure of yet.

Roslyn checked her seating chart quickly. It *probably* wasn't a serious request—it wasn't even particularly professional as a joke to a junior offi-cer—but when an Admiral asks, the Flag Lieutenant obeys.

"He's in the middle and you're on the left with your squadron com-modores," Roslyn told him quickly, before daring a small joke of her own. "He's definitely out of reach of your retribution, sir."

Medici chuckled.

"Shame," he conceded with a wink. "If there's water at the tables, I'll be fine, Lieutenant."

He gave her a nod and strode away, sliding the briefing chip into his wrist-comp as the six cruiser Commodores began to gather around him.

Roslyn shook her head, then refocused on the task at hand and smiled up at Mage-Commander Tirta Kruger, the captain of one of the older destroyers.

A hundred and one captains, fifteen commodores, seven admirals and ten civilians like Niska. She was one of three officers greeting and passing out briefing chips, but it still felt like they were going to be seat-ing people for longer than Mage-Admiral Alexander would be speaking!

Once everyone was seated in the large briefing room, Roslyn's job became simpler if not necessarily less important. She took her own seat next to the presenter's dais and linked her wrist-comp into the controls for the room's holographic projectors and screens.

She'd prechecked everything before the shuttles had even started arriving, but she checked everything again as Her Royal Highness, Mage-Admiral Jane Alexander, Crown Princess of Mars stepped up to stand behind the lectern and survey her officers.

Alexander was not quite into her second century and had spent an entire lifetime in the Royal Martian Navy. Her late brother had been the Mage-King of Mars and her niece was now Mage-Queen, but the Admiral had focused her life on serving the Protectorate in its Navy.

"Officers and respected guests, welcome aboard *Durendal*," she told them. Roslyn made sure that the backdrop behind the Admiral was the view of Legatus from the dreadnought's main scanner arrays, as planned. "We've spent a lot of time here in Legatus, both during the Siege and since taking control of the system.

"For the first time since the surrender of the planet, however, we are finally looking to leave," she concluded. "People, Operation Eagle Tickle is a go. We have finished restocking our magazines with the new missiles and we are finally ready to deploy."

The new Phoenix IX missiles had far superior acceleration and range to the old Phoenix VIIIs—and given that their enemies in the Republic had used missiles with longer ranges than the VIIIs, that edge had proven absolutely necessary.

"We have not, of course, been nearly as well reinforced as any of us would like," Alexander continued. "We have received fifteen destroyers since the fall of Legatus, but that's all the Protectorate has to spare. We remain the single largest concentration of hulls and tonnage the Protectorate of the Mage-Queen of Mars has ever mustered."

Second Fleet's order of battle was now floating in the air around Alexander. Three dreadnoughts, eight battleships, thirty-eight cruisers and fifty-two destroyers. That was every dreadnought in commission, a third of the battleships and over half the cruisers.

"While intelligence suggests that we have neutralized the only accelerator ring the Republic has, a lack of fuel is unlikely to materially impede the RIN's operations," the Admiral noted. "We have *also* neutralized the only shipyards we know to be capable of installing the Promethean Interface. While there are reasons to suspect our knowledge is incomplete, we have yet to locate any evidence of additional major antimatter or Promethean Interface production."

The room's silence took on a deadly chill at the mention of the Interface. No Mage—no *human*, in Roslyn's opinion—could find what the Republic had done to fuel their warships less than horrifying. At the core of each RIN jump ship were the extracted brains of several Mages, linked to a device that forced them to cast the teleportation spell on command.

Without the cadre of Mage officers who formed the beating heart of the Royal Martian Navy, the Interface was how the Republic had duplicated the ability to magically travel between the stars—but the UnArcana Worlds that had become the Republic had banned magic. The only Mages they'd had access to were the teenagers who'd been identified with the Gift and had chosen to remain on their homeworlds.

The Republic had built their star fleet on murdered children, and Roslyn doubted she was alone in thinking that could never be forgiven.

"What we *have* confirmed is that the Nueva Bolivia System contains the largest gunship-manufacturing plant in the Republic after Legatus itself," Admiral Alexander said grimly. "So long as the Republic retains any carriers at all, possession of the Nueva Bolivian yards will permit them to continue to replenish losses to their combat groups.

"Eagle Tickle intends to remove that capability by the simplest means available: Second Fleet will be leaving Legatus in thirty-six hours to move on the Nueva Bolivia System. Our scouting runs have left us quite confident in our ability to engage the forces there, and I expect to be able to secure the system inside of two days of active combat."

Roslyn switched the holograms and screens over to the Nueva Bolivia System. The system had eight planets: one habitable world, Sucre, and two gas giants. The rest of the planets and the asteroid belt were only really important as supplies of raw materials.

"Our current estimate is that the defensive fleet around Sucre consists of roughly four thousand gunships and the reassembled remains of two RIN carrier groups," Alexander told them all. "A *Courageous*-class carrier, three battleships and seven cruisers. That's backed by the existing fortifications put in place around Sucre to defend their orbital industry."

Sucre was one of the more human-friendly worlds ever discovered, with vast world-circling oceans, gorgeous archipelagos, and calm weather. The colonists had always wanted to keep it that way and had put almost all of their industry in orbit.

That industry was a vulnerability now that they were at war, but the RMN wasn't looking to wreck the planet. Just take control of it.

"We also need to make sure that Legatus itself remains in our hands," Alexander continued. "So, I will be detaching a Task Force Twenty-Two under Mage-Admiral Hovo Tarpinian."

That worthy, the man who'd brought the three dreadnoughts to the Battle of Legatus, bowed slightly as he was indicated.

"*Mjolnir* will remain here in Legatus, accompanied by two battleships and a cruiser squadron," Alexander said. "The rest of Second Fleet will proceed to Nueva Bolivia and commence operations against Sucre itself.

"Details of the plan are on your briefing chips, which should now be unlocked, but Mage-Captain Kulkarni will run us all through the high levels," the Admiral said, indicating Roslyn's boss, Alexander's operations officer.

Indrajit Kulkarni stepped up beside her Admiral. She and Alexander were both tall, but where the Crown Princess of Mars was gray-haired with the ambiguously brown coloring of a Martian native and a descendant of Project Olympus, Kulkarni's skin and hair were black as night as she captured the audience's attention.

The Mage-Captain gestured for Roslyn to switch to the next part of the briefing and smiled levelly at the gathered officers.

"While the force we are bringing to Nueva Bolivia *should* be overwhelming," she noted, "the reality is that we cannot count on the RIN to roll over politely for us. They like their surprises—and our scouting operations have yet to locate enough of the force they brought against us at Centurion to make me happy.

"Therefore, we will..."

CHAPTER 2

"ALL RIGHT, PEOPLE, I believe this is the last stop on the Unofficial Sneaky Tour of the Republic of Faith and Reason," Kelly LaMonte told her people brightly. The covert ops ship commander was a petite woman with currently dark-turquoise hair, clad in an unmarked shipsuit.

Her role required her to assume a level of professionalism that negated having the brightly colored hair she'd enjoyed as a junior engineer earlier in her life. Now she ran an entire starship—and if *Rhapsody in Purple* was small, she was all the more valuable for what she carried.

"What are we looking at, everyone?" she asked.

Rhapsody was bigger than a Royal Martian Navy courier ship, and that was about all Kelly could say for her command's size. Built with every technological stealth trick the Protectorate could muster and a small but potent arsenal, the stealth ship was an expensive toy...and one utterly dependent on magic to truly carry out her work.

"We are currently eight light-months away from the Gygax System," Conrad Milhouse reported. Kelly's tactical officer was a still-gangly man in his late twenties. Like the gunners for *Rhapsody*'s limited weapons systems and the stealth ship's powerful sensor array, Milhouse had been seconded from the Royal Martian Navy.

"Gygax is a Fringe World, one of the seven that followed Legatus into the Secession," he continued. "Positioned as it is on the far side of the region of space occupied by the UnArcana Worlds, it didn't see a lot of traffic even before the Secession."

Rhapsody had a briefing room, but Kelly preferred to run meetings like this on her bridge. There were enough extra seats to allow everyone who needed to be in the meeting to be there, and the bridge was the most secure place on the ship.

Built as a civilian ship bridge, it was separate from the simulacrum chamber the ship would be jumped from and arranged in a rough semicircle facing a large viewscreen. A civilian ship wouldn't have had the *other* half of the circle on the other side of the viewscreen, where Milhouse's military hands ran the ship's sensors and weapons.

There were always spots on the bridge for the captain, the navigator and the tactical officer. Today, they were joined by the First Pilot, Kelly's husband Mike Kelzin; the senior Ship's Mage, Kelly's wife Xi Wu; and the commander of their boarding party of Protectorate Bionic Commandos, Captain Jalil Charmchi.

Rhapsody in Purple was very much a family affair for Kelly LaMonte, even as she reported up to the general structure of the Martian Interstellar Security Service. She didn't really regard herself or her people as *spies*, though that was the MISS's role.

They were the Protectorate's sneaky eyes, jumping into systems where they weren't welcome and seeing just what was going on there.

"All of our intel on Gygax is badly out of date," the navigator reminded everyone. Nika Shvets was a new addition to the crew, an androgynous MISS agent with shoulder-length blond hair, watery blue eyes accentuated with dark makeup, and the knowledge of how to kill someone with a spoon.

At least four different ways, from what Kelly understood of the operative who was now her navigator. There were parts of Shvets's file *she* wasn't officially cleared for, and she doubted they were going to explain those blanks to her.

"The last sensor scans we have were from a civilian tramp freighter two weeks after the Secession," Shvets continued, their voice soft. "The freighter crew didn't know about the Republic yet—in fact, it's entirely possible that *no one* in Gygax knew. It is questionable whether any Links were distributed to the system."

"They had enough of the transceivers to hide them on Protectorate warships to enable their spies to report in," Kelly reminded her people. "*Someone* in Gygax would have known—and if we fuck this up, someone in Gygax will be able to tell the rest of the Republic we were here."

"It's hard to avoid them knowing we were here, love," Xi Wu pointed out. The dark-skinned Chinese woman smiled at her wife. "Once we're in the system, we can hide from everything they can throw at us so long as my Mages and I can trade off every few hours, but the jump flare is unavoidable."

"They have their own ships coming and going," Milhouse countered. "Not many, one presumes, but they do exist. And if our target is actually here, there might be even more traffic."

"Shvets, can you show everyone those scans?" Kelly asked. "Let's take a look at what the geography is."

The main screen switched over to a projection of the star system. Six planets, with one gas giant and one habitable world in the inner part of the liquid-water zone.

"Our freighter was not a covert ops ship or anything remotely unusual," Shvets reminded everyone. They tapped a command, highlighting the habitable world. "They visited Greyhawk, sold their cargo of agricultural and industrial machines and parts, and purchased a cargo of refined titanium and local fish.

"From Greyhawk, the ship did not get a solid view of Kenku, the gas giant," they continued. "There was no unusual industrial activity at Greyhawk or at Paladin, the planet much of the system's heavy industry is anchored around."

The third planet in the system, a frozen, uninhabitable rock similar to Sol's Mars, flashed on the screen.

"Nothing in this suggests that there's a secret Republic military base and antimatter supply station here," Milhouse noted. "Except that any base like that would be at the gas giant, and they encouraged the ship not to go there."

"A lot of systems have assorted expensive crap at their gas giants," Kelly said. "Especially the UnArcana Worlds. The rest of the Protectorate uses antimatter for a lot of things, and we don't have quite so immense a demand for hydrogen and helium.

"The cloudscoops at the gas giants are the only things fueling the power stations of an UnArcana World. Keeping them from prying eyes is pretty common."

"But it still leaves a gap in our intelligence that must be filled," Xi Wu replied. "Do we have a plan?"

"We do," Kelly confirmed. "Apologies, Jalil, we're keeping your people as passengers for now."

The immense shaven-headed cyborg woman grinned.

"Just how we like it," she noted. "Quiet, easy cruises where you lot do all of the work."

"It's a standard scoot 'n snoop," Kelly continued, glancing around her crew. "Mage Foster will jump us in and Xi Wu will take over stealthing us immediately. We'll sweep around Kenku to make damn sure of the presence or absence of our target, and then we'll do a long drift over to Greyhawk and Paladin to do detailed scans of the orbital industry.

"If everything goes perfectly, we'll be in-system for about thirty-six hours and have full information on every planet, every ship, and every space station in the Gygax System."

"And what if things don't go perfectly?" Milhouse asked.

"Then we'll be spending a lot less time in Gygax but might be leaving with a lot more useful information," Kelly told him. "We are the sneak-iest starship in existence, people, and there are only a handful of ships like *Rhapsody*. The Republic might have figured out we exist, but they still can't track us, and they can't fight what they can't see.

"If Gygax is the Republic's fallback position, we will know very shortly."

"And if they're not?" her husband asked, the ship's senior pilot having been quiet so far.

"Then there are two more ships doing the same thing we are in other star systems," Kelly replied. "We rendezvous back at Legatus with them and we collate data. We know the Republic leadership went *somewhere*.

"We'll find them, Mike. We are the invisible eyes to see what they think they've hidden, and they have *nothing* to stop us."

CHAPTER 3

"JUMP COMPLETE," Liara Foster reported. The video link from the bridge to the simulacrum chamber showed her wavering slightly as she stepped back from the simulacrum itself. The standardized spell that teleported a starship a light-year at a time was immensely draining—and Kelly was told that short-jumping was in some ways *more* so.

She had to trust her Mages on that. Like every child of the Protectorate, Kelly LaMonte had been tested for the Mage Gift at eleven years of age, and like the overwhelming majority of them, she lacked even the tiniest fragment of the power her wife wielded.

Xi Wu stepped up to replace Foster, laying her hands on the semiliquid silver model of *Rhapsody in Purple* suspended at the exact center of the jump ship. Kelly knew the other woman had silver runes inlaid into her palms that linked her into the rune matrices woven through the ship, allowing her to project her magic around the vessel.

"Stealth spell up," Xi Wu reported after a moment. "Liara, go fall over," she ordered her subordinate. "We'll need you soon enough."

There were four Mages on Kelly's ship, three of them answering to Xi Wu. Two were RMN Mages seconded to MISS. Two, including Xi Wu, were full-time MISS agents.

"Milhouse, what are we seeing?" Kelly asked her tactical officer.

"Still pulling data in from the arrays," Milhouse replied. "No one should know we're here yet, not for another couple of minutes."

"Shvets, put some distance between us and the jump flare under Xi's shield," Kelly ordered.

"On it," they replied, the stealth ship vibrating as her engines came to life. Antimatter engines would obliterate the ability of the *technological* solutions to hide the ship, but the spell woven around her could conceal them.

For a while, anyway. Kelly knew her wife well enough to pick out the signs of strain on Xi Wu's face as the Mage adjusted her spell.

"I've got *something* at Kenku," Milhouse reported. "Multiple energy signatures. Trying to get visual resolution, but we are a long way out, skipper."

Four light-minutes was enough to keep them safe from initial observation, but it also limited how much data they could grab. Foster had dropped *Rhapsody in Purple* almost exactly halfway between Greyhawk and Kenku, which meant they had a view of both.

"What about Greyhawk and Paladin?" Kelly demanded.

"Greyhawk is more active than our old reports, but nothing major," Milhouse reported. "Hard to say for sure, but I'd *guess* that they've installed some new orbital forts. Paladin...is significantly busier, but that could just be civilian industry.

"Kenku, I'm looking at something new. There were cloudscoops there but not on this scale."

"Shvets, set a course that will sling us around Kenku and get us close enough to Paladin to pick out details as well," Kelly ordered. "Sounds like we've found something interesting at least. Let's go see what it is."

The main display shifted as the new course was laid in. What information they did have on each cluster of signatures appeared by each of the three planets as Milhouse worked through the data.

It wasn't much. Their old intel said there were four cloudscoop gas-extraction and refining facilities in orbit of Kenku—but even their years-old most recent scan data of the system hadn't seen them.

Right now, it looked like there were either ten times as many extraction platforms as there had been or someone had moved in a good-sized fleet. Since they could only see one side of the gas giant, they could be missing as much as fifty percent of the orbitals, too.

She started an analysis in her computers. The captain's seat on any ship had a number of screens attached to it, usually called the "repeater screens" as they could be set up to mirror any station on the bridge. Kelly, who had been an engineer and a computer programmer before she'd been a covert ops commander, was more active in using them than most.

It was *possible* there was an accelerator ring there, her program concluded. They couldn't be certain until they were much closer, too. The odds weren't *great*, but they'd need to close within two light-minutes to entirely eliminate the chance.

"Shit!" Milhouse suddenly swore. "Jump flare, danger close, danger close!"

"Shvets, kill the engines," Kelly snapped. "Milhouse, what am I looking at?"

She checked the time. That was *fast*. They'd been in the Gygax System for just under twenty minutes and no one had been within four light-minutes of them. That meant the RIN had detected them, picked a destination, and deployed a starship inside twenty minutes.

"Dear gods, either someone is *really* paranoid, or they've worked out that we exist," the tactical officer replied as he transferred data to the main displays. "That's a *Bravado*-class carrier, Captain. Forty megatons, a hundred and fifty gunships."

And the gunships, Kelly was grimly certain, were far more relevant than the rest of the carrier's weapons. The carrier had emerged just over three million kilometers from *Rhapsody in Purple*'s jump flare, and the parasite warships were already spilling from her bays.

"She's between us and Kenku, but we're looking at barely ten light-seconds of distance," Milhouse said grimly. "Captain, what do we do?"

"Xi?" Kelly asked softly. "Engines are down; *can* you hide us at this range?"

"Yes. It gets harder as the range drops, though," the Mage confirmed. "I can also kill her if she gets much closer."

Kelly nodded grimly. *Rhapsody in Purple* was sized more like a civilian ship than a warship, but she had the *bones* of a military vessel. Most critically, she had an unrestricted amplifier instead of a simple jump matrix.

The carrier had chosen her distance carefully. If her target was a Protectorate warship, anything within two million kilometers was suicide. That was the reach of a Mage with an amplifier, a distance inside which no mundane structure could stand against the power of the scions of Project Olympus.

But it would take Xi almost as much energy to take out each individual gunship as it would take to destroy the carrier. Now there were over a hundred of the parasite warships in space, even destroying the carrier wouldn't be a victory.

"Killing the carrier looks great on everyone's record, but it's contrary to our actual *mission*," Kelly pointed out. "We need to know what's going on at Kenku and Paladin—that there even *is* a carrier in Gygax says something is happening here."

Their intel was that the Republic had only built sixteen of the big ships, after all, and the Protectorate had captured or destroyed seven. With just nine of them left, what the hell was one of them doing at the far end of the Republic?

"Shvets, see what we can manage for movement while cold," Kelly ordered. "Doesn't need to be much. I just want to go *around* their search net if at all possible."

Their current velocity was only a few hundred kilometers per second. It was going to take them a *long* time to get past the Republic search net if they couldn't accelerate.

"Xi, how close do they need to get to see through our cloak of invisibility?" she asked her wife.

"I'd say knife range, but we're already in knife range," Xi Wu said grimly.

"And if we open fire with the laser, we die," Milhouse replied.

Rhapsody had two missile launchers and a single ten-gigawatt battle laser. Her laser outclassed anything the gunships carried, but there were also a *lot* more gunship lasers out there.

And the carrier's weapons individually outclassed hers—and they were *also* in effective laser range of the carrier.

"We're not getting out of knife range quickly," Kelly told them. "Our *best* chance is that they figure they had a sensor glitch and go home after a few hours."

"And if they don't?" Shvets asked, their voice calm, almost distant.

"We cycle through Xi's people slowly and surely as we drift toward Kenku at a couple hundred kilometers a second," she said, yanking on her braid. "We *can* hide from them unless one of those gunships literally stumbles over us."

They could even, in theory at least, micro-jump the four light-minutes to Kenku. They wouldn't be able to conceal their arrival at that point, though, and given *that* accurate a starting point, she was grimly certain the Republic could find her and catch her.

CHAPTER 4

EVEN A HUNDRED AND FIFTY gunships paled in comparison to the sheer scale of deep space. Four light-minutes from anything of value or interest, they had to be guessing where *Rhapsody in Purple* could have gone and how close they needed to get to catch her.

"I'd say their estimate is that they can spot us at around sixty thousand kilometers," Milhouse said as the net took its final shape. "The longest distance between any two gunships is a hundred and twenty thousand klicks."

Each set of gunships made a square eighty-five thousand kilometers on a side, forming a literal net in space accelerating toward the location of *Rhapsody's* jump flare—and, not coincidentally, *Rhapsody* herself.

It made for a net over a million kilometers across, with six gunships held back to defend the carrier. Just in case.

"I liked it better when my enemies didn't know our ship existed and weren't competently paranoid," Kelly admitted. "Shvets?"

"They're only accelerating at five gravities," the navigator told her. "It's going to be a long few hours while they sweep."

"Can we get around them?" she asked.

"No," they admitted. "If we could conceal our full acceleration for those hours, yes. As it stands...no."

"So, our best chance is to slot ourselves right through the middle of one of those squares and hope they've overestimated their scanners," Kelly concluded. She glanced at her wife's image on the link from the simulacrum chamber.

"Xi, you know this magic better than anyone," she admitted to her wife. "*Can* we hide from them at sixty thousand klicks?"

"Yes," the Mage said flatly. "We'll want to bring up every tool we've got, though. Heat sinks, baffles, *everything*. Once we're within a hundred thousand klicks, it's down to luck as much as anything else. We *should* be able to get to fifty so long as the spell doesn't blip, but every bit of energy we're radiating is a chance for a blip that wouldn't matter at longer range."

"Then we go completely dark at one ten," Kelly decided. "Milhouse, set it up. How long will it take us to get through that?"

Shvets exhaled and rubbed their eyes.

"Longer than any of us are going to like, skipper," they admitted. "I'm setting up the course now, but even with their accel, we're looking at a relative velocity of maybe five hundred KPS. Ten minutes, maybe."

"We can go full heat-sink for twenty-five," Kelly replied. "We'll be drowning in our own sweat by minute twenty, but we can retain functionally all of our heat radiation for twenty-five minutes."

They'd then need to radiate it, but she could pick the direction she did that, and there was always some angle to vent heat where no one would see it.

"Stand by for going dark," she concluded. "We've got an hour to prep for this. We'll get through it, people. And these sons of bitches are never going to know what snuck past them!"

With a final nerve-wracking shiver, *Rhapsody in Purple*'s antimatter reactor went into cold shutdown. Kelly checked over the metrics on her repeaters and patted the arm of her chair.

"It's all right, girl," she murmured to her ship. "We'll have you back awake in no time."

Batteries and capacitors fueled the stealth ship now, keeping the lights and life support on as she drifted forward toward the dragnet coming her way.

THE SERVICE OF MARS

"Angle is perfect," Shvets announced. "We will be roughly one hundred kilometers off center. Range is one hundred ten thousand and closing at five hundred and ten kilometers per second."

"All systems cold," Kelly said aloud, confirming for the rest of the bridge crew what she'd just checked for herself. She *hated* shutting down the antimatter reactor. It was a catch-22 in a lot of ways—the antimatter reactor provided the power that contained its own horrendously dangerous fuel.

There were specific batteries and systems to continue powering that containment, but if they failed...well. If the containment on *Rhapsody's* antimatter fuel tanks failed, no one aboard the stealth ship was ever going to know.

"From this close, Milhouse, confirm something for me," Kelly murmured. "Are the gunships running antimatter or fusion engines?"

"Fusion, sir," the tactical officer replied after a few seconds. "I guess we don't merit the good stuff."

"Not today, at least," she agreed. "And not on their current standards, which I hope are getting *really* sticky around the use of antimatter."

Seconds ticked by around them. The kilometers between them and the gunships vanished, and Kelly resisted the urge to close her eyes.

Even if this went wrong, the Republican warships would almost certainly attempt to take them intact. The crew of an MISS scout ship wasn't worth much to the RIN, but the ship itself would be worth its weight in antimatter. There weren't many areas where Protectorate tech drastically exceeded Republic tech, but the stealth systems aboard the *Rhapsodies* were definitely one of them.

"They've definitely been paying attention," Kelly said aloud as they began their closest approach. "Someone put together the various pieces and realized we had stealth ships scouting their systems. Paranoid bastards."

"If this is their standard reaction, that might be useful for Second Fleet to play with," Milhouse noted. "I can see all kinds of uses for drawing a carrier out away from the main forces."

"Me too," Kelly agreed. It was getting hot on the bridge and she pulled on her braid absently. "Though I'm guessing the Republic has allowed for that. *They* can call in reinforcements instantly, after all."

She'd been told that the *Rhapsodies* would be getting some of the first Protectorate-manufactured Links once they were available, but the Protectorate hadn't finished reverse-engineering the entanglement technology yet.

Not enough to trust that the Republic couldn't eavesdrop, anyway.

For now, the Republic continued to have a tighter command-and-control loop than the Protectorate. Kelly had hoped the war would be over after the Republic fleet had disintegrated at Legatus, but the grim competence of the gunships sweeping around her told her the truth.

Montgomery had broken the morale of the RIN that day, but the Republic had clearly found *some* answer to the horror of the Promethean Interface. If nothing else, she supposed, they'd probably been able to find enough people who just didn't care what they did to Mages to keep the RIN operating.

"We're through," Shvets reported. "Range is now sixty-five thousand kilometers and rising. We are through."

"Now we just need to dodge around a carrier and keep drifting on," Kelly said brightly. "How long do you think before the gunships start sweeping the routes to Kenku and Greyhawk?"

"They'll probably start decelerating once they hit the jump-flare zone and then settle their new courses once they're at zero," Shvets guessed. "Give them another two hours. We won't have long where we're at a range we can maneuver safely at, not if they keep up the search."

"They'll keep up the search," Kelly predicted. "They know they can see us leave as clearly as they can see us arrive." She shook her head. "Unless they give up and call it bad data, they're going to keep hunting us until we actually leave.

"We'll keep the reactor offline until we're clear of the carrier," she decided. "Hopefully, we can get at least five million klicks of clearance from all of their ships and get our velocity up."

She grimaced.

"If I *have* to travel four light-minutes at less than five hundred KPS, I will, but I can think of better ways to spend three days!"

CHAPTER 5

THE TWO DREADNOUGHTS were the first ships into the Nueva Bolivia System, the hammer-headed pyramids materializing in a flash of magic and blue Cherenkov radiation.

Roslyn had an observer seat on the flag bridge aboard *Durendal*, a recognition of the fact that a Flag Lieutenant didn't have much to do during an actual battle except maybe fetch coffee. Her job at this point was to watch and learn.

It was at this point that it was hardest to forget that serving on an Admiral's staff was generally considered a requirement for an officer making flag rank themselves. She was *far* too junior for that to be a major thought just yet, but she'd been handpicked as Alexander's Flag Lieutenant on Damien Montgomery's suggestion.

There was a *lot* of trust riding on her. Today was a day where she couldn't do much to earn it, but it was also the kind of day where she couldn't *forget* it.

"Scanning confirms no unexpected concentrations of activity," Kulkarni reported. "Enemy battle group remains in position above Sucre. Numbers are consistent with the MISS sweeps: eleven capital ships."

"Confirm the breakdown ASAP, Kulkarni," Alexander ordered. "Any sign of movement from the gunships yet?"

They were barely a light-minute away from the planet, the presence of the two unescorted dreadnoughts a blatant taunt to the defenders.

They weren't in range of even the Protectorate's new heavy-bombardment missiles, but the RIN had to know they were there.

"We're picking up new power signatures in orbit," a noncom reported. "A defensive constellation just came online. We're reading twenty-four fortresses that weren't in the intelligence report!"

"Interesting," the Admiral observed. "They're learning and starting to play games with our scouting flights. That must have taken some doing, though. What kind of forts are we looking at?"

"Twenty megatons apiece; they look like modified versions of their standard twenty-MT cylinder without engines and with more weapons," Kulkarni said as the data came in. "Enough mobility to avoid unpowered missiles, I presume, but still limited to the powered range of their Excaliburs."

"Good for us, unfortunate for them," Alexander said. "We can ignore the fortresses for the moment. What is the rest of the fleet doing?"

"Lot of gunship activity; they're doing the best they can to keep their numbers obfuscated, but it looks like we might have overestimated them," the operations officer continued. "Chambers?"

"Sir?" Roslyn asked.

"Keep your eye on those gunships," Kulkarni ordered. "You know their signatures as well as anyone, so work with Chief Jian and get me an accurate number."

"Yes, sir," she confirmed.

Pulling the data over to her screen and setting up a link with Chief Jian took her less than a second. She was still listening to Alexander as she dug into the data, though.

"They know we outrange them now," the Admiral noted. "Their only chance to survive this is to bring their mobile units out to meet us."

"They might want to test how many of the new missiles we've got," Kulkarni observed.

Roslyn was tagging squadrons as they wove through each other. The RIN pilots were decent; at least some of these crews had to have been involved in the early offensives where the Republic had pushed the Protectorate back across the board, after all, but there was only so much they could do against the sensors of the dreadnoughts.

"We need a drone sweep to confirm," she murmured to Jian. "But I make it thirty-four hundred and change."

"Sweep is being set up," Jian confirmed. "I think it's closer to thirty-five, but I see your tags too. They're doing their best."

"Tactical?" Roslyn linked to *Durendal*'s bridge, intentionally contacting the assistant tactical officer—a young man who shared her own rank. "Do we have a timing on a probe sweep?"

"Salvos launching in sixty seconds," the other junior officer replied. "We're feeding everything we've got to the flag deck."

"Oh, I know that," she confirmed. "Those little buggers are being clever, though."

"Time, Kulkarni?" Alexander asked.

"Ninety seconds," the operations officer replied. "Locals are maneuvering but aren't coming out to meet us."

"Shame," the Admiral said. "I didn't really expect them to take the bait. If nothing else, they probably figure two dreadnoughts can take their entire fleet."

Sensor probes flashed away from the two massive warships: dozens of missiles refitted to carry sensors instead of warheads. They'd have more answers once those drones entered Sucre orbit.

"Well, we'll see how they react when we move in," Alexander finally said. "That carrier might still have her gunships aboard, after all. That would bring the numbers closer to MISS's estimate."

"Or they moved gunships somewhere else in the system?" Kulkarni asked.

"Defending the cloudscoops would make sense," she agreed. "If I thought that it would bring them out to play, I'd go for the fuel stations. As it is, though...they know what I know, which is that this battle will be decided here.

"And if cleverness doesn't work, well, there's a reason I brought a really big hammer."

Kulkarni's ninety seconds ran out—and the *rest* of Second Fleet flared into existence around the two dreadnoughts. Battleships, cruisers and destroyers dropped out of nothingness into a perfectly arranged formation.

It was a flashy parade-ground trick, synchronizing jumps like that... but it had a point, too, that Roslyn at least picked up.

Not only do we have more ships than you, we're just plain better *than you.*

She wondered if the Republic ships in Sucre orbit interpreted it in the same way.

The warships hung in space silently for several moments as the command networks synchronized. Roslyn kept a careful eye on those networks as they linked up, with each additional sensor platform giving them one more angle to try and identify the individual gunships.

"Carrier is launching her gunships," Jian said softly. "Two hundred fifty additional units. I make it thirty-seven hundred exactly, all told."

"I have the same," Roslyn confirmed. "Anyone want to guess where they hid fifteen million tons of gunships?"

The balance of power between the two forces wasn't close enough to make those parasite warships a game-changer, but any surprise in a battle, however small, was generally bad in her experiences.

"First guess is the cloudscoops," Jian replied.

Roslyn nodded and turned back to Kulkarni. The tall black operations officer was neck-deep in the network link-up, and she waited a few seconds for the immediate chaos to resolve.

"We're looking at thirty-seven hundred gunships," she told the older woman. "That's with the two-fifty from the carrier. Intel said four thousand. The difference could be a resolution error from the distance that the scout ships came through, or they could have moved them out to the gas giants to protect the cloudscoops."

Roslyn paused.

"We could send someone to check on the scoops," she suggested. "The risk to the ship we send would be high, though, higher than the risk to the fleet from an unexpected thirty gunship squadrons."

"Understood," Kulkarni acknowledged. "Keep an eye out for them and see what you can resolve on those battle stations."

"Do we have a command network, Mage-Captain?" Alexander asked, leaning past her ops officer. "This shouldn't have taken this long."

"The *Cataphracts* appear to have left the yards with a calibration issue, sir," Kulkarni said crisply. "I failed to notice it in the previous exercises, but it did cause a small delay in syncing them to the overall network."

"Teething problems, I suppose," the Admiral said. "There were a few people who should have spotted that, Kulkarni. Including me. No need to throw yourself on your sword...*if* we have the network."

A final set of lights for the two squadrons of brand-new *Cataphract*-class destroyers turned green on the screens around them.

"We have the network," Kulkarni confirmed. "We had them in the missile defense net already; that was our primary focus."

"Good call," Alexander agreed.

The new *Cataphracts* were based on the realization that the *Honor*- and *Lancer*-class destroyers were built on designs a century old and intended to fight pirates. The ships had been upgraded and revised since, but they weren't designed to be escorts for larger units.

The *Cataphracts* were. They carried lighter offensive armaments despite their larger size, trading in missiles and heavy lasers for over twice as many defensive Rapid-Fire Laser Anti-Missile turrets.

The Admiral glanced around the flag deck, her gaze meeting Roslyn's for a silent second, then focused on the main display.

"Second Fleet will advance," she ordered. "Course is for a zero-velocity halt at twelve point nine five million kilometers."

Even if Roslyn hadn't had the numbers memorized, the range spheres of the various ships were laid out on the displays around her. The Republic fleet had a range of twelve point seven five million kilometers from rest.

Second Fleet's new Phoenix IXs had a range of thirteen million kilometers. They weren't entirely effective at their full range, but they would be *far* more effective than enemy missiles without any fuel left.

Like the Republic in half a dozen battles before the new missiles had arrived, Mage-Admiral Alexander had the range advantage—and unless the enemy came out to meet Second Fleet, they were going to get hammered to pieces.

Second Fleet's course was scheduled to take over three hours, and the flag deck crew wasn't going anywhere in that time frame. The entire fleet was at battle stations, every move, every twitch on the part of the Republican defenders being examined in minute detail.

"They're not coming out to meet us," Roslyn concluded as Second Fleet made turnover. Now the massive antimatter engines of ninety-two warships were pointed toward the planet, bleeding velocity at fifteen gravities as they continued to hurtle toward the enemy.

Second Fleet had traveled two and a half million kilometers in an hour and forty minutes. They had magical gravity runes throughout their ships, an ability their enemy didn't share, which allowed them to consistently out-accelerate their opponents.

Fifteen gravities could go a long way in a few hours, but it still took time to cross interplanetary distances. They *could* have jumped in closer, but the closer they came to a gravity well, the riskier the jump became. Civilian jump Mages—and the trapped brains inside Republic warships—couldn't do it safely.

The Navy *could* but it was still risky. Everything in Alexander's tactics today was built around minimizing risk. The RIN was going to have surprises. They'd had *weeks* to prepare for this fight, weeks where Second Fleet had sat at Legatus waiting for new missiles.

"They're forming up facing us and maintaining defensive maneuvering, but you're right," Kulkarni agreed. "Admiral? Are you seeing this?"

"I am," Alexander confirmed. "It's a defensive formation with the gunships around the fortifications and the capital ships. They're hoping that our long-range fire is ineffective enough that they can weather it—at least more readily than we can afford to spend the new missiles."

Roslyn brought up another screen and concealed a grim swallow.

The battleships and the newest cruisers and destroyers carried twenty-five missiles per launcher. The dreadnoughts had forty...but that didn't matter when the *rest* of the fleet, twenty-six cruisers and forty destroyers, only had *fifteen* missiles per launcher.

The Protectorate's navy had always been intended to fight pirates, and it shaped their design paradigms. They were built for pursuit and short, high-intensity battles. Only a small portion of their fleet was really designed to fight a true peer opponent.

A lot of people had already died for that mistake. Roslyn hoped they weren't going to add to that number today.

"They might be right," Kulkarni warned. "With those gunships, they've got more launchers, more defensive lasers, more...everything than we do."

"The gunships only have three missiles apiece," Alexander replied. "They want to make me burn missiles at long range...and I have the same plan for them. The first test will be the Samurais."

The big bombardment missiles had an extra half-million kilometers of range—but most importantly, they came in at *thirty* percent of light-speed instead of twenty.

That extra velocity had shredded the defenses at Legatus, and Roslyn hoped it would do the same here—because there were a *lot* of gunships out there and the projections on her screens were mind-numbing.

On their own, the defensive fleet only had a quarter of Second Fleet's missile launchers. With the gunships and the fortresses, they were up to almost *five times* as many.

And Alexander was leaning back in her chair, studying the same numbers as if they were mildly interesting. Roslyn knew what the plan was for dealing with the gunships' twenty-odd thousand missile launchers, but it was far easier to accept that in a quiet briefing room than on a flag deck as they calmly flew into the teeth of the enemy defenses.

"All Samurai-equipped vessels will target the fortresses," Alexander ordered. "Kulkarni, I want a targeting order. We hit each one with a full salvo of every Samurai we've got, then move on.

"We might not kill a fortress with two hundred-odd missiles, but they'll know they've been touched, and that buys us some leeway." The Mage-Admiral smiled. "I'm hoping to rattle their cages. Let's see how we do."

CHAPTER 6

"RANGE IS thirteen million three hundred fifty thousand," Chief Jian reported calmly. "Samurai range in under one minute."

"We've designated the fortresses One through Twenty-Four," Kulkarni told Alexander. "Currently, Twenty-One through Twenty-Four are on the other side of Sucre. I'm guessing they're holding them back as a reserve—but we only have fifteen Samurais per launcher anyway, so we wouldn't get to them even if we could.

"We have thirty-seven minutes between Samurai range and Phoenix IX range," she continued. "We can fire all fifteen missiles well before then, but..."

"Say what you're thinking, Kulkarni," Alexander ordered.

"The Samurais are proving harder to mass-produce than the Phoenixes, and we don't have many ships who can fire them. Should we be holding off on some of them?" the operations officer asked.

"Any of them we don't fire at this range run the risk of being destroyed aboard their ships later," Alexander noted. "I'd rather spend gold than blood, Mage-Captain. We will expend the full magazines of the Samurais."

"Yes, sir," Kulkarni confirmed. "Orders are locked in. We'll see how well they've upgraded their defenses in the last few weeks."

"Agreed."

Roslyn kept her focus on the drones sweeping the star system. She was at least certain that the missing gunships weren't in position to intervene in the immediate battle, but she wanted to know where they were. It might be paranoid—but it might not be.

She was also watching the gunships in Sucre orbit, which meant she caught the blip when a different energy signature flashed across her screen.

"Jian, did you see that?" she asked.

"See what?" the chief asked.

"For a second there, I got a spike of a different energy signature from one of the gunships," Roslyn told him. "Let me rewind the data."

The systems were designed to do that for just this reason. While every other screen on the flag deck kept showing the current situation, Roslyn's pulled back several seconds in time and focused in on the spike.

"That's an antimatter annihilation signature," she said softly. "It looks like one of the gunships zigged when they should have zagged, and another had to dodge fast—and fired antimatter engines to do it."

"I thought they were all using fusion engines?" Jian asked.

"So did I," Roslyn confirmed. "Because that's what all the energy signatures we've seen so far have been—but our analysis of the gunships we captured in Legatus said that they could have *either* fusion or antimatter engines.

"It's apparently an easy-enough refit, one the carriers can do on the fly, but..." She shook her head. "They can only have *one* type of engine."

She considered the data for a moment, then tapped a command.

"Tactical, I need at least three drones for a suicide sweep," she told *Durendal's* ATO. "There's something fishy about these gunships."

"Swapping control of drones X3-75D through 75G to you," the other Lieutenant said instantly. "They're close in and running low on fuel, anyway; I've got replacements inbound already."

"Perfect. Thanks, Davids," Roslyn told him. It took her a moment to bring up the control protocol, but then she had four drones relaying her data from over ten million kilometers away.

Suicide sweep was exactly what it sounded like. There was enough fuel left in the drones to do a slow and steady return to the fleet—or to do a high-acceleration approach to the enemy with the expectation that they'd be lost to the hostile defenses.

"Samurais launching," Kulkarni reported behind her. New icons spackled her display, and Roslyn quickly looked up the data on the missiles, incorporating their approach into her timing. She'd get the probes a *lot* closer if the enemy were focused on the incoming high-speed bombardment missiles.

She finished her programming and leaned back, rubbing her hands together as she double-checked her work. The Samurai's reduced flight time combined with the time delay meant she had barely enough time to fix the two mistakes she'd made and transmit to the drones, but she wrapped it in time.

The sensor probes lit up their engines at full power moments before the Samurais passed them. They had a "mere" five thousand gravities of acceleration to the big missiles' thirty thousand, and a lower base velocity as well.

They were stealthier than the Samurais and more maneuverable as well, but the course Roslyn had set them on was going to doom them. The heavy missiles would hopefully buy them a few critical extra seconds.

Lasers and missiles in defensive mode lit up the scanners, and Roslyn waited. Everything she was seeing was still delayed by over forty seconds, and there was nothing she could do to influence the success or failure of her robotic minions.

Out of the corner of her eye, she watched the Samurai salvo charge into the teeth of over sixteen thousand RFLAM turrets. The Republic had clearly updated their targeting programs to account for the new weapons' speed and acceleration, but they could only do so much about the physical traversal ability of the turrets themselves.

Two dozen missiles made it through and flung themselves into the fortress, antimatter explosions tearing apart the cylindrical hull in a series of cataclysmic detonations.

"Target One destroyed," Kulkarni reported behind her. "They're adapting, sir. We probably won't do as well with the next salvo. They're still ninety seconds out."

"We'll get what we get," Alexander said calmly. "I'll settle for hitting all fifteen of them, Kulkarni."

The data was coming in from the sensor drones, and Roslyn winced as their death codes showed up. The robotic spacecraft had made themselves targets, trying to get the data she'd wanted, and they'd paid for it as expected.

They'd got what she needed. The closest drone had been barely fifty thousand kilometers from the nearest gunship when it was destroyed—close enough for a *far* more detailed visual than anyone in the fleet could get.

"Sir, take a look at this," she told Kulkarni. "The gunships are running external engines."

"They're *what?*" she asked.

"All of the gunships have a strapped-on fusion booster engine," Roslyn explained, sending the imagery to Kulkarni's screens. "Their engines are still in antimatter mode. They're trying to make us think they're in fusion mode."

"Why would they do that?" her superior asked.

"We're assuming they're low on antimatter," Roslyn suggested. "If they were, they wouldn't be spending it on gunships—but if those gunships were running on fusion drives, they'd have burned a good chunk of their available delta-v in their defensive maneuvers."

"Where instead, they've burned out a temporary rocket and still have their full antimatter storage," Kulkarni agreed. "And if they've got the antimatter to fuel their gunships..."

"They've got the antimatter to fuel their missiles and not worry about expending them," Roslyn told her. "I don't know if that changes the plan, sir, but I think we need to consider it."

"We do," the other woman said. "We truly do. Well done, Lieutenant."

Kulkarni turned her attention away.

"Admiral Alexander, Mage-Lieutenant Chambers has picked up an interesting layer to our Republic friends' maneuvers," she told the Admiral. "Those gunships are set up in antimatter mode and faking being fusion-driven. The external boosters are probably even getting in the way of their defensive fire."

Missiles hammered into a second fortress as they spoke. This one survived—barely. From its power signature, Roslyn didn't expect it to be participating much in the battle to come.

"That's a lot of effort to fool us on something small, Kulkarni," Alexander said. She paused. "Except that they want to let us keep thinking they're short on antimatter. Fascinating."

There were several seconds of silence as the Mage-Admiral considered the situation, then Alexander shook her head.

"Chambers, get me an all-Captains channel," she ordered.

Roslyn had a pre-coded program sitting in her console for that. She hit it, confirmed it had worked, then looked up at the Admiral.

"You're on, sir."

"Everyone, this is Admiral Alexander," the fleet commander said calmly. "Our Republican friends are playing games to conceal their true capabilities, and I can only think of one reason they're doing that.

"Expect to come under fire as we reach launch point bravo. We will continue to reduce the fortresses with the Samurais, but I suspect we've taken too long to bring the war to the Republic. Our general range advantage may already be gone, but we still have options they don't."

Roslyn hadn't even thought of that possibility. Neither, she suspected, had most of the Captains and flag officers, from the tone of their acknowledgements.

"Kulkarni, let's get the destroyers a bit more spread out," Alexander ordered after a moment. "Formation Romeo-Seven, I think."

"Understood."

R-7, if Roslyn remembered it correctly, would interlace the *Cataphracts* and their augmented missile defenses with the older ships. It would also move the destroyers forward in the fleet formation, putting them at the greatest risk.

The *theory* was that the destroyers were low-value targets that the Republic would try to shoot past, but it was a theory that could result in a lot of wrecked destroyers if Admiral Alexander guessed wrong.

Another salvo of Samurais tore through the Republic fortresses as the destroyers maneuvered through Second Fleet's formation. This time, the targeted fortress vanished from the displays as antimatter tore it apart. From this distance, Roslyn couldn't say if the RIN had failed to stop as many missiles as the previous salvos or if the RMN had scored a lucky hit, but it hardly mattered.

"That's three fortresses destroyed and four badly damaged or crippled," Kulkarni reported. "Three salvos still en route. Should we reassess targeting, sir?"

"No," Alexander said grimly. "Those forts are likely more heavily armed than the cruisers, but their limited mobility makes them easier targets, especially for long-range weapons like the Samurais."

Durendal shivered beneath them as the hammerhead-mounted bombardment-missile launchers fired again.

"Any change in aspect on our friends?" the Admiral asked.

"Nothing material," Kulkarni reported. "The gunships have formed up in front of the fleet, but they're the ones suffering most against the Samurais. Their lasers are too restricted by their physical design to be able to easily track the higher-velocity missiles."

She shook her head.

"Now that I know they're there too, I suspect the fusion boosters are hurting their target tracking as well," she noted. "They aren't nearly as maneuverable as they're designed to be."

And that lack, Roslyn estimated, had killed about fifteen thousand people so far. She shivered as another fortress icon grayed out, long-distance scans suggesting a fifth crippled station.

"Chambers, double-check the sensor data on those cripples," Alexander ordered. "If they're playing games in one place, they might be playing them in others."

"Yes, sir."

Roslyn didn't even need to ask Chief Jian to assist her. The noncom was already pulling the data from *Durendal's* sensor suite as the Flag Lieutenant set to work.

"I'm not seeing anything to suggest they're gaming us," the Chief told her. "Gas venting, lost energy signatures, the works. They probably have some weapons left, but we've hit them hard."

It took a *lot* of very carefully designed armor to withstand hits from antimatter weapons, too. The Royal Martian Navy Academy tried to make sure its students understood just how much power they had at their command. A single gigaton-range antimatter warhead was a planet-killer, after all—and even the lightest modern warships would take *multiple* such hits to breach their armor.

"Get me the data on the active stations as well," Roslyn ordered Jian. "Just looking at our damaged targets in isolation might not answer the question."

More data appeared on her screens as the ever-helpful Chief Petty Officer gave her what she needed, and Roslyn stared at the comparison between Target Four, one of their cripples, and Target Sixteen, a station they had never intended to shoot.

The comparison looked right. Target Four had been hit by multiple antimatter warheads, gouging immense holes in her armor and hull. Based off the scans of Target Sixteen, Target Four had lost multiple fusion plants and was nearly helpless.

But something didn't seem *quite* right...

Every salvo of Samurais was in space. Every tactical officer in the fleet was busy building firing plans and guiding missiles into their targets. The only people with the time to step back and look at oddities were the Admiral's staff—and even there, most of Roslyn's seniors were actively involved in the battle.

If there were an answer here, she was the only one looking at it. She pulled up the data from the four drones she'd sent on their suicide pass and found the visual images of Target Thirteen.

Target Thirteen was being hit by Samurais even as Roslyn dug into the visuals, the most detailed pictures they had of the fortresses, and her feeling of unease sharpened.

"Chief, I don't recognize this installation," she told Jian, passing the noncom a chunk of imagery. "What do you make of it?"

"That's a major heat radiator," Jian told her. "I guess they'd need more heat radiation with the fusion plants instead of an antimatter plant..."

"They don't have any offensive lasers," Roslyn realized as the computer analysis finished. "And they're using heat radiators to augment their power signatures. *Fu—*"

She cut off her own curse and turned to her boss.

"Kulkarni, sir," she said swiftly. "The fortresses...they're defensive platforms only. They have a full RFLAM loadout, but they don't have full power-generation suites, lasers or missiles. They're using radiators to look more complete and more dangerous to our long-range scans."

She sent her data over to Mage-Captain Kulkarni's console as she spoke, and the flag bridge was silent for several key seconds as Roslyn realized she'd sworn loudly enough for *everyone* to hear.

"She's right," the operations officer said as their last Samurai salvo hammered into Target Fifteen. "They might not all be decoys, but at least some of them—probably most of them—are. Were." Kulkarni looked like she wanted to swear as well.

"They wanted us to use our bombardment missiles on them," she continued. "They're not useless—they'll still cover their fleet against our regular missiles—but we drastically overestimated their offensive firepower."

The silence hung in the bridge for another few seconds.

"Captain Kulkarni," Alexander said very calmly. "When this is over, I very much want to know who is in command over there. And if we can possibly take the bastard alive, I'd like to talk to them."

"Assuming I can manage not to *punch* them. Fleet will prepare to receive enemy fire. Ignore the gunships; they'll be dry by the time our missiles reach them. Primary focus is the enemy battleships and the carrier."

She grimaced.

"And you know what to do with salvos three through eight," she concluded, leaning back in her chair. "Our Republican friends may have snookered me, but unfortunately for them, I *still* have the biggest damned hammer in the galaxy."

CHAPTER 7

"LAUNCH POINT bravo in twenty seconds," Kulkarni reported quietly. "All ships standing by, primary firing patterns downloaded. We are ready."

Roslyn forced herself to release the breath she was holding. Even her quiet background analysis was no longer needed once the real shooting started. It would take just over nine minutes for Second Fleet to empty the magazines of her older ships.

Seven minutes for each salvo to reach their targets. Even if the Republic force deployed out against them, the acceleration of the two fleets was low enough compared to their missiles that nothing was going to materially change that flight time.

The entire hundred-million-ton mass of the dreadnought shivered under the thrust of four hundred missile launches. The icons of the fleet's warships were almost drowned on the display by the new icons of their weapons.

"First salvo away."

"And now the moment of truth, I think," Alexander murmured, barely loud enough for Roslyn to hear her. "You've been playing all kinds of games, my friend; what is your secret?"

"Enemy launch! Twenty-four thousand plus inbound!" Kulkarni barked. "Republic fleet launched twenty seconds before we did." She shook her head. "Assuming the same powered range as our missiles, they'll be at the end of their flight time when they reach us, but they'll be active."

"Antimatter missiles, I presume?" Alexander asked clearly.

"Yes, sir. They appeared to be a modified version of the Excalibur Five," the operations officer confirmed. "Our tactical teams are analyzing, but it looks like they stepped down the acceleration to increase the flight time. We're showing nine thousand six hundred gravities of acceleration, and Tactical is estimating five hundred twenty-five second flight time."

Four hundred gravities less thrust and fifteen seconds' more life than the missiles the Republic had used before, Roslyn calculated. She didn't need to run the numbers to know where the tactical teams were getting their estimated flight time: that would give the weapon the *exact* same flight distance as the Phoenix IX.

"That requires physically modifying the missiles, yes?" Alexander asked, her voice calm—despite the fact that the enemy had just launched a massive swarm of missiles at her fleet.

"Yes, sir," Kulkarni confirmed. "They've either modified over twenty-four thousand missiles or built new ones."

"Oh, they haven't done *only* twenty-four thousand," the Admiral said calmly. "At a minimum, they'll have three full salvos of these things." Alexander shook her head. "Our teams know the drill against gunship salvos, Kulkarni.

"We made the changes to deal with this ten minutes ago."

Second Fleet's second and third salvos were on the screens now, joined by the RIN's second salvo—and a new wave of signatures from the gunships themselves.

"All gunships have gone active with antimatter engines," Jian reported. "They appear to have discarded the external boosters and are now accelerating toward the fleet at twelve gravities."

"Ow."

Roslyn wasn't sure who had spoken, but she couldn't even disagree. Second Fleet had magical gravity runes woven through the hull of every ship in the fleet, keeping her people's feet to the floor in normal times and negating as much as fifteen gravities of acceleration.

The Republic had no technological equivalent. Outside of combat, the armored cylindrical hulls of their warships contained rotating interior habitats to provide pseudogravity that kept their crews healthy.

The gunships didn't even have those. In combat or out, the only "gravity" they had was from their own thrust—and they had no means of reducing it.

Acceleration suits and couches could only keep the crews *alive*, not comfortable. Those gunship crews were feeling every bit of those twelve gravities as they charged toward Second Fleet.

"Third gunship salvo is in space," Kulkarni reported. "The gunships are hoping to close to laser range."

"Good luck with that," Alexander said drily. "For now, ignore them. They've shot their bolt. Are the intercepts ready?"

"Programs have been transmitted," the operations officer confirmed. "First intercept in three minutes."

Roslyn noted absently in the chaos that she'd been right. The crippled fortresses hadn't fired a shot, and the nine remaining intact stations had less than three hundred missile launchers between them.

The gunships were really the problem now—or, at least, their missiles were. The RIN had made effective use of their gunships to create devastating opening salvos in every engagement with the Protectorate. There were over two and a half times as many missiles in each salvo heading toward Second Fleet as the Fleet had RFLAM turrets—and the preferred ratio was four to three the other way.

"Interception mode engaged, missiles maneuvering," Kulkarni said.

The answer was simple: if the gunships only had three rounds per launcher and even the older warships had fifteen, expend three of the warships' salvos against the enemy fire. It hadn't been something the Phoenix VIII had been designed for, but the RMN had made do.

It hadn't been a major design criterion of the Phoenix IX's hardware, but it *had* been factored into her software. "Interception mode" was a software module that told the missiles to find the largest number of their counterparts that they could and detonate.

Six thousand missiles dove into the teeth of twenty-four thousand and followed that suicidal impulse. Seconds ticked by while *Durendal*'s crew waited for the lightspeed data to catch up and be analyzed.

"Kill ratios are low," Jian murmured, seconds before the official report came up from the tactical departments. "Looks like one point eight, and we were hoping for *three*."

Thirteen thousand missiles were still blazing toward Second Fleet, and the lightspeed delays meant there was no *time* to change the programming of the missiles with the velocity to intercept.

"Adjust our salvos to target two apiece on the second and third gunship salvos," Alexander ordered, her voice firm and *far* calmer than Roslyn felt.

"Orders on their way," Kulkarni confirmed. "Intercepting the incoming fire with salvo eight, but..."

"Kill ratio will be even lower due to eight not being up to speed, I know," the Admiral agreed. "Better wasted missiles than dead ships, Mage-Captain."

It was all dissolving into numbers and iconography for Roslyn. That wouldn't last, but her lack of involvement in everything was making it hard to keep track of the battle. Her memory was all too happy to remind her of what would happen when those little dots of light on her screen converged.

She'd been aboard one ship battered into uselessness in this war already. She was trying not to show it, but she could feel the fear coiling in her stomach as more explosions flashed across the screens, multiple salvos of the Protectorate's missiles sacrificing themselves to buy a chance for their motherships.

"Kill ratio was below one for that," Jian said grimly. "Eight thousand–plus still incoming. It's down to the turrets and the Mages now."

At the heart of every Royal Martian Navy warship was its simulacrum, a semiliquid silver model of the vessel that in some senses *was* the ship. Holding the simulacrum, the ship's Mage-Captain could unleash their magical powers at a level far beyond almost any unaided Mage.

Few battles would enter the range where the amplifiers could reach, but missiles *had* to cross it to threaten the ships themselves. As the laser turrets flashed to life, so did the magic of the warship's defenders.

Lightning and fire blazed in the void around *Durendal* and the other Martian ships, magic creating impossible realities even as the ship's technology lashed out alongside it.

"I should be in the simulacrum chamber," Roslyn heard Alexander mutter. "I underestimated them."

Roslyn shivered. She was only partially aware of just what Alexander's status as Crown Princess of Mars meant in terms of her magical power, but she suspected it would make the power wielded by the Mage-Captains look like toys.

"Multiple hits across the cruiser screen," Kulkarni reported grimly. "*Glorious Voice of Honor* and *Shining Beacon of Hope* report significant damage to engines and weapons. Most other units remain above ninety percent capability."

"Pull the damaged units to the back of the fleet and inform their Captains they are authorized to emergency-jump at their discretion," Alexander ordered. "The rest of the fleet holds the line. That will be the worst of it today, I think."

The intercepts of the second salvo were less effective than Roslyn had hoped, not even reaching the one point eight ratio of the first interception—but they still obliterated twenty thousand of the Republican missiles.

Four thousand missiles wasn't enough to penetrate Second Fleet's defenses. Without the gunships, the enemy only had two thousand launchers left as the first offensive salvos hammered through the gunship screen.

"We may need to actively target the gunships," Kulkarni said after a moment. "We lost over half our salvo to the gunship screen, even penetrating at high speed."

"I don't want to waste missiles on them," Alexander admitted, "but you're right. Retarget the next three salvos. How many does that leave targeted on their battleships?"

"Five, sir," Kulkarni replied. "And then we have ten salvos left in the magazines on the battleships and *Salamander*s and another twenty-five on the dreadnoughts."

"It does appear that they have full loads of their new missiles," the Admiral noted. "We're going to need to investigate that once we're in control of the system, Mage-Captain. Intelligence may want to claim there isn't a second accelerator ring, but if they had enough antimatter to build a hundred thousand new missiles, Intelligence can kiss my royal ass."

She glared at the screen.

"Hammer those gunships for me, people," she ordered. "I'm not worried about fighting them at laser range, but they're out there to protect their motherships from our missiles. Let's make sure they *fail*."

CHAPTER 8

THE SOFT ALARM woke Kelly up. It wasn't one of the urgent ones that meant she needed to leap to her feet, so she took a moment to appreciate how fortunate she was. No military ship could have tolerated the Captain curling up and falling asleep with her head on the First Pilot's naked chest.

"Pretty sure that one's for you," Mike Kelzin murmured, her husband gently stroking her hair. "Xi's still on duty for another two hours."

"And what are *you* planning on doing, Mr. First Pilot?" Kelly asked, slowly lifting her head and grinning at him.

"I am not on duty for another four hours, unless we encounter a crisis," he told her, his hand still gently holding her. "I am planning on napping and then giving our senior Ship's Mage a well-deserved massage while she passes out."

Kelly snorted.

"I don't know if we're likely to run into any crises that need the shuttles," she admitted. "Like Charmchi, you're mostly a passenger for this particular collection of stunts."

"If you need us, you'll need us in top form," he said. "We'll be ready. I've got a set of simulations I'm going to tweak when I *do* go on duty. I've got a few scenarios around us trying to board a Republic warship."

"That would be a suicide op I'm not ordering," Kelly replied as she regretfully detached herself from her husband and began to poke at drawers for clothing.

"If I can come up with a plan to make it *not* a suicide op, then we have a better chance if the situation arises where you need to order it," Mike told her. "Because I can think of the kind of mess where it might be necessary, much as it would suck for a few of us."

Kelly put on her bra and studied her husband. He seemed surprisingly calm at the admission that he'd expect her to order him on a suicide mission if she thought it was necessary.

"You're a strange man, Michael Kelzin," she told him.

"I know," he conceded. "That's why you married me. You married Xi because she's smart and gorgeous and powerful. You married *me* because I'm patient and ever-tolerant...and strange."

She snorted and threw the shirt she was holding at him.

"Yes," she conceded as she pulled another shirt out and put it on. "We'll go with that."

Milhouse had the watch when she arrived on the bridge, the tactical officer looking more fatigued than usual. Kelly crossed the bridge to the Captain's seat and leaned over his shoulder.

"You going to make it to your quarters before you pass out, Milhouse?" she asked.

"Yeah. Just been a long shift." He shook his head. "We're about half a million klicks higher up from the ecliptic than projected. We had to dodge another gunship."

The RIN carrier had returned to Kenku by microjump, but her gunships had taken the long way home. Other gunships were swanning around the system now, along with what looked like civilian in-system clippers commandeered for the mission.

"I'd be happier at this level of paranoid competence if it wasn't being targeted on me," Kelly replied. "Two days of this bullshit."

The only good news was that *most* of the time, they were far enough away to be firing their engines, at least at low power. It had only gained them a few hours on their journey to Kenku, but that was because it had gained them more separation from their hunters.

"The cruisers are spreading out as well now," Milhouse warned her. "We're getting close to the best look we're going to get, and I will *gladly* leave that part of this mess to you."

She snorted.

"Don't get too comfy, Milhouse," she told him. "If the shit even starts *looking* at a fan, I'm waking everyone up and calling them to stations."

"Then I'll go get what sleep I can, skipper," the RMN loaner told her. "Luck."

The other occupied stations in the bridge were swapping over at the same time, Kelly's mix of RMN loaners and MISS hands taking their usual stations. Only five of the fifteen non-officer stations were filled right now, which would be more than enough for what Kelly needed today.

She pulled up everything *Rhapsody*'s sensors had learned about their target while she was sleeping. Kenku had *definitely* acquired some new infrastructure since the last time anyone had been looking, but they were confident there was no accelerator ring here now.

Rhapsody would have to get closer for Kelly to be certain of what was there, and that was the decision she couldn't offload onto anyone else. There was definitely a carrier. At least four cruisers, and it looked like several hundred local gunships at Kenku.

Even four cruisers and a carrier were a lot of jump ships for the depleted RIN to have at a nowhere system, which meant there was *something* in Gygax worth protecting. If it had just been the energy signatures and the gunships, she'd have guessed that Kenku had been turned into a major refueling stop for the Republic Interstellar Navy.

"A fuel depot doesn't need cruisers," she murmured aloud. "Unless it's all timing and you just *happened* to be here while I'm poking around."

More data flowed across her screen. The natural debris field around the gas giant was interfering with their visuals, but there were definitely bigger ships than the cruisers at Kenku as well.

"So, carrier group," she muttered. "Carrier, two battleships, four cruisers. Now...are you *always* here or are you just lucky?"

If they were always there, there was something worth the RIN committing one of what Kelly's briefing said was only eight remaining carrier groups to protect. If they were just refueling, then it was just a refueling station.

It wasn't an accelerator ring. She was certain of that. It wasn't even a large-scale shipyard...except...

She zoomed in on what she could see and sighed.

"You could be a refit yard, couldn't you?" she cursed. "I need signals intelligence and these buggers aren't transmitting outward."

They also needed to see what was at Paladin. It was entirely possible that half of whatever problem she was dealing with was there, at the planet Gygax mined for resources and anchored their heavy industry on.

"Csizmadia, link in with my screen three," she ordered, gesturing for Borbola Csizmadia, one of her RMN loaners on the tactical team, to join her in her thoughts.

"We need to swing to Paladin and try to pick up signals intelligence between there and Kenku," she told the noncom. "I still want eyes on Kenku, and I don't think there's much point concealing that we're here. They've guessed."

She gestured at the hundreds of sublight ships searching the system for them.

"How many of those navy sensor probes do we have and how sneaky are they?" Kelly asked.

"Eighteen and not enough to hide where they're coming from," Csizmadia replied. "We can kick them out the launchers without sparking an energy signature, but the moment they bring their drives online, everyone is going to know they exist. Once they've flown any distance, they're going to know where the drones launched from."

"That's what I thought," *Rhapsody's* Captain muttered. "But that just means we need to be clever. We can never conceal that we're here, after all, but that doesn't mean they can *find* us."

"And...now."

It took a few seconds for the command to cross the light-seconds to the package *Rhapsody* had left behind, but once it reached its destination, any question the Republic had over whether or not someone was sneaking around their star system vanished.

A one-gigaton antimatter warhead detonating tended to do that.

What it *also* did, however, was create a zone of radioactive hash where no one could resolve what was going on. Inside that hash, six of *Rhapsody in Purple*'s precious handful of drones brought their engines online and blazed away on varying courses.

By the time even Kelly—who knew their courses—could pick them out, there was no way to backtrack them to a central point that would suggest where the stealth ship had been. They were maneuvering as hard as they could under concealment as well, burning on a direct course for a selected point five million kilometers "up" from Paladin relative to the ecliptic.

"Yeah, that got everyone's attention," Csizmadia reported. "Gunships are swarming toward the blast, and we've got cruisers vectoring toward a couple of likely locations for us."

"Anywhere near us?"

"No, they're basing their projections off the jump flare and us trying to sneak up on Kenku. I don't think they've noticed the drones yet."

"That won't last," Kelly murmured to herself. The drones weren't hard to detect. They were hard to *localize*, with ECM and jammers that made them a handful to target with weapons at long range, but they were easy to detect.

The drones were never going to get to Kenku. Kelly's projection put far too many gunships far too close to their courses for that to be the case. What they were doing was giving her multiple points of view that her computers could interlace—and getting closer than she could risk *Rhapsody*.

"I give the drones forty-five minutes," she said more loudly. "Figure the closest will get to about two light-seconds from that base."

"Optimist," her wife said from the simulacrum chamber. "Thirty minutes and five light-seconds is the best you're going to get. They don't have Mages to conceal them, after all."

"Five light-seconds would be close enough, but three would let me read the name off that carrier," Kelly replied. "We're scouts. The more data, the better."

Several of the gunships were adjusting their courses to improve their intercepts. They definitely knew the drones were there. They could probably even guess the purpose of the antimatter bomb.

"Double-check the transmitter programming," she told Csizmadia. "The last thing I want to do is go to all this effort and get picked up because one of the drones fires off a tightbeam radio where someone can pick it up."

The drones were already proving their worth. If nothing else, they were pulling away every ship that might intercept her when she headed to Paladin. Beyond that...

"Do you see that ship?" she asked the sensor tech.

"I think so," Csizmadia confirmed. "I didn't think they built anything that big. She's got to be, what, a quarter-kilometer wide?"

The RIN used two standard hulls to build everything: a one-hundred-and-fifty-meter-wide cylinder and a one hundred and seventy-five meter cylinder, both half a kilometer long.

"I'd guess two hundred meters across and, mmm, five fifty meters long," Kelly replied as she studied the big ship hanging in low orbit. "She's not a warship, Chief. She's a transport—practically a mobile dry dock. She's designed to move those standard cylinders of theirs around."

"I'm surprised we don't have a data file on her, then," the noncom replied. "Wouldn't they have been using a bunch of them?"

"All of the shipyards and fleet construction we've seen were in Legatus," Kelly pointed out. "They didn't need a big jump ship for that. Now, though, they've probably had to spread at least some of the work out."

She studied the base and its structures as they resolved into more detail. "That's two refit yards, but I'm not seeing any big production facilities," she noted. "They might be installing something made at Paladin."

"Or they're installing something that doesn't have a big physical structure and mostly requires people to follow directions with an inlaying tool."

Kelly looked up as Shvets spoke, the navigator apparently having entered the bridge while she was focusing on the data. The operative was wearing darker makeup than usual, shaded in dark green around their eyes as they glared at the screen.

"Are you suggesting what I think you are?" she asked.

Shvets didn't answer initially. They crossed to their console and plugged in a series of commands, bringing up the image of a familiar-looking space station and dropping it on the screen next to the platform in Kenku orbit.

"Minerva Station," Kelly said. *Rhapsody* had been the ship that had inserted Damien Montgomery and his strike force aboard the secret Republic facility dealing in Mage brains and the Promethean Interface.

"Minerva was a standard prefab construction," she said after a moment as she assessed the similarities between the two stations. "The similarities might be a coincidence, but it would also have made sense for the Republic to have a fallback station without an insane Mage."

"So long as they have Mages to activate the matrix, my understanding is that the jump matrix can be installed by any idiot with a glorified soldering iron," Shvets said, resting their hands on their hips and glaring at the station.

"And the Interface itself isn't big," Kelly conceded. She'd seen the images. She'd never be able to *forget* the images. "This could be a Promethean Interface installation facility, but they're definitely not building ships here."

"Hence the big transport ship," Csizmadia said. "It might not be their main facility, even now, but a secondary station somewhere they don't think we're going to look..."

"Fuckers," Kelly said, but there was no real heat in the word. "All right, people, we'll keep watching the drone data and we'll make our sweep of Paladin, but I think this mission just justified itself."

"No accelerator ring, though," Xi Wu pointed out from the simulacrum chamber. She'd clearly been listening to the entire conversation. "That leaves some questions still out there."

"We sent four ships into the far reaches of the Republic," Kelly replied. "The odds were good that one of us would find something, but they were never great that any single ship would find it.

"Assuming it exists."

She shook her head at the map of the system as one of her drones disappeared.

"They're getting better at watching for us, but they're not going to catch us this time," she told her people. "Once we're out of here, we'll want to go over everything they did—so we can make sure they don't catch us *next* time."

CHAPTER 9

GRIM-FACED PROTECTORATE Secret Service agents in clean-cut suits flanked the door as Mage-Admiral Alexander waited for her "guests." Roslyn, standing at the Admiral's left hand, was intimidated by the deadly bodyguards, and she *knew* the men and women around her.

It probably didn't hurt that she knew how terrifyingly deadly the sleek-looking carbines the agents carried were. She didn't know how anyone had managed to compress the energy of an exosuit-carried battle rifle down into a man-portable carbine, but *she* wouldn't want to be on the wrong end of the discarding-sabot tungsten penetrator rounds the carbines fired.

They were designed to take down people in two-meter suits of armor, after all.

Durendal wasn't really designed for this kind of event, but few ships were. They'd created a reasonable approximation of a royal court, and Marines escorted the uniformed Republic commander across the floor of the shuttle bay to Mage-Admiral Alexander.

He was a heavyset man with heavy jowls and a thick epicanthic fold to his eyes—and he was clearly exhausted as he stopped a precise ten feet from her and saluted crisply.

"Admiral Alexander, I am Admiral Emerson Wang of the Republic Interstellar Navy," he introduced himself quietly. "I am here to offer the unconditional surrender of the RIN forces in this system."

That wasn't much at this point. The carrier survived as a crippled hulk, but every battleship had been destroyed before Wang had finally ordered his ships to stand down.

"But not, I see, of the system itself," Alexander said flatly.

"Technically, Admiral, I have no authority to even surrender the orbital forts," Wang admitted. "Their commanders were inclined to follow my lead, thankfully, rather than suffer unnecessary deaths."

"The fact that those forts are incomplete and have no offensive weapons likely contributed to their common sense, yes?" the Admiral asked.

"Yes," the Republican officer agreed. "My duty was to stop you here, Admiral Alexander. I did my best. I failed...but I have no authority over this system's government or local forces."

"And if I were to proceed to bombard the surface to reduce their resistance?"

The room was silent. Roslyn was *reasonably* sure the Admiral wouldn't do that—but she was also sure that most of the Marines securing the room weren't. The small cluster of Republican officers with Wang definitely didn't know the Admiral that well.

"By what limited rules this war has been fought under, I suppose that is your right," Wang allowed. "From my encounter with your Lord Regent, however, I suspect that even royal blood would not protect you from Damien Montgomery's wrath if you did not do everything within your power to avoid that."

"You are not incorrect there," Alexander said, Roslyn spotting the tiniest crack of a smile. "I had not made the connection. You were the Admiral who attempted to stop Montgomery's relief expedition at Kormar?"

"I was," Wang conceded. "A set of orders I found objectionable then and haven't seen any justification for since." He shrugged. "I have done worse things since, I suppose."

"You know what drives your starships," Alexander said flatly.

"And I know that your bloodline represents the ultimate victory of the enemy both our ancestors strove against," the Admiral told her. "I am a prisoner of war and I recognize both defeat and the reprehensible actions of my nation, but do not expect me to concede that I am on the wrong side here, *Your Highness.*"

The room was *very* quiet now. Even Roslyn was holding her breath.

"Regardless of wrong or right, Admiral Wang, your knowledge and assistance could ease the surrender of Sucre's government and avoid further bloodshed," Alexander told him.

"You overestimate what is left to me," Wang said. "And while I may be a prisoner, I am no traitor. You will get nothing from me."

"Very well," Alexander said flatly. "You and your officers and the rest of the prisoners will be interviewed as appropriate, but you will be treated fairly, as prisoners of war under the Geneva Conventions."

She smiled thinly.

"A better treatment, I think we both know, than even civilian Mages received at the hands of your fleets."

"What's the status of the planetary defenses?" Alexander asked as she and Roslyn returned to the flag bridge. "Has the local government said anything yet?"

"Does launching surface-to-orbit missiles count?" Kulkarni replied. "We had a few of the destroyers head in close to make sure we disabled the fortresses, and they were fired on. More of a warning shot than an actual attempt to take down the ships, but they were making a point."

"Wonderful," the Admiral replied as she took her seat.

Roslyn wouldn't have wanted Alexander's tone addressed to her. It was acidic enough to etch glass.

Her own console was giving her much the same update as the Admiral would be looking at. Second Fleet was trailing Sucre's orbit by eight light-seconds, inside long range for lasers and amplified magic from the starships but well outside the range of any planet-based weapons.

"Do we know what kind of defenses we're looking at?" Alexander asked after a moment.

They'd managed to neutralize Wang's fleet without losing any ships, but Roslyn knew over half of the fleet had taken some level of damage. The only badly damaged ships were the two cruisers hammered in the opening salvos, but a lot of ships were suffering various degrees of minor damage.

"What they fired at our destroyers were standard single-drive fusion surface-to-orbit weapons," Kulkarni said. "They wouldn't be a threat at long range, but if we get close enough, we don't have the time to really counter them."

"And I presume we don't have anything resembling a complete listing of their launch sites," the Admiral guessed.

"No, sir. We have three dialed in from their warning shots, but..."

"I'd also presume those are too close to population centers for long-range bombardment?"

"Yes, sir," Kulkarni confirmed. "If we take the time, we can locate probably ninety to ninety-five percent of their launch sites, but it will take several days to be certain we've got most of them."

"And even then, the Republic used population centers to cover their launch sites on *Legatus*," Alexander noted. "I doubt they'll have hesitated to do the same on somewhere that wasn't their capital."

The flag deck was silent for an extended period, then Alexander sighed.

"Start the search, Kulkarni," she ordered. "If it comes to it, *I* will deal with any platforms too close to cities. If they think the Protectorate is limited to our conventional arsenals to deal with their use of human shields, we will teach them the error of their ways."

"Of course, Mage-Admiral."

"Chambers."

Roslyn started and turned to face the Admiral.

"Yes, sir?"

"Work with *Durendal's* communications team," Alexander ordered. "I want you to set up a call between myself and whoever is in charge down there. You talk to the staff yourself, get me a face-to-face video.

"I doubt it's going to *work*, but I will be damned if I embrace invasion or bombardment without at least talking to these idiots."

It took Roslyn over an hour of trying just to finally manage to get a member of the Governor's staff on a channel. The middle-aged man on the feed didn't appear able to decide between ogling her chest and looking down his nose at her.

"I am Silvius Gražina Gallo," he informed her, "deputy chief of staff to Governor Hans South Isle. Anything your 'fleet' needs to say to the Governor can be said to me, and I will pass it on if necessary."

If necessary.

Roslyn forced a smile. It was probably obviously fake and that didn't bother her in the slightest.

"Mr. Gallo, my Admiral is going to speak to Governor South Isle," she told him. "There is, in fact, only one set of circumstances under which Her Highness will *not* be speaking to the Governor, and that is one we should both be hoping to avoid."

"Governor South Isle will not legitimize the unlawful use of force by the thugs of a government that has no authority here," Gallo explained, slowly, as if speaking to a child. Roslyn bit her tongue, since the sixteen-second time delay meant she couldn't shut him up, anyway.

"He has no intention of speaking to anyone from your fleet. Nueva Bolivia does not acknowledge the authority of Mars."

"No one is asking you to, Mr. Gallo," Roslyn said, her own tone equally slow. "What you must do is acknowledge that it is within the capacity of Second Fleet not only to reduce your remaining defenses to rubble but to literally destroy your world.

"The only way Admiral Alexander is not going to speak to Governor South Isle is if Governor South Isle is dead," she said flatly, noting that Gallo *was* trying to interrupt her—sixteen seconds too late. "Either you and I can set up a meeting now that will permit at least some hope of a nonviolent resolution to this conflict, or this will end in fire from on high and the deaths of, at a minimum, thousands of your soldiers."

"We will not be threatened!" Gallo was responding barely halfway through Roslyn's spiel, so she calmly waited for her *full* threat to register.

"You may be barbarians," he finally concluded, "but we remain modern citizens of a modern world. We acknowledge nothing."

"Are you so certain, Mr. Gallo, that your Governor is willing to sacrifice his life and the lives of the citizens he is sworn to protect, that you will refuse to even let him make his own decisions?" Roslyn asked. "Just as I do not fully speak for Her Highness Mage-Admiral Alexander, you do not fully speak for Governor South Isle.

"Shouldn't the choice of whether or not to speak to the Admiral be his?"

"He has made his decision," Gallo proclaimed.

"I suggest you double-check with him," Roslyn said. "Not everyone, after all, fully realizes that a single antimatter warhead would crack a planetary crust like an egg. Reflection can often change people's minds."

She could see the moment her metaphor struck home as Gallo's sun-darkened skin paled and he finally fully stopped eyeing her breasts.

"Ask the Governor, Mr. Gallo, if he will speak with Her Highness the Mage-Admiral," she suggested softly. "I believe that is your job, isn't it?"

"I don't recall authorizing you to threaten world-cracking," Alexander said mildly as she settled behind her desk, waiting for the call with Governor South Isle to start.

"I didn't," Roslyn, standing one step to the left and back from the Admiral's chair, replied. "I simply pointed out that most civilians don't consider the fact that *any* warship has that capability when deciding to be stubborn."

The Mage-Admiral checked the indicators on her desk and shook her head.

"It worked, so I won't complain, but perhaps we should be handling the enemy civilians a bit more gently?" she suggested. "Though from the replay of the call I rushed through, I'm not sure anything less would have sufficed."

"The dirty old man wouldn't stop staring at my tits until I shocked him out of it," Roslyn grumbled under her breath.

"He wasn't taking you seriously, I know," Alexander agreed. "And I didn't leave you with anyone to escalate to, because I half-figured that was the kind of shit they'd pull. Well done, Chambers...but let's try and find a shock threat somewhere below *breaking worlds like eggs* for next time, shall we?"

"Yes, sir."

The screen flickered to life with the crossed cannons over alpaca rampant coat of arms of Nueva Bolivia. The coat of arms filled the screen for several seconds and then was replaced with a formal office with a massive stone desk, behind which sat a tall man in his late thirties with a thick shock of blond hair.

"I am Governor Hans South Isle," he announced. Two suited women stood immediately behind him, much as Roslyn and Kulkarni flanked Mage-Admiral Alexander, and a fancily uniformed guard stood at each side of the desk.

"I am the democratically elected leader of the Nueva Bolivia System under the constitutions of both Nueva Bolivia and the Republic of Faith and Reason. We do not acknowledge the authority of the Mountain of Mars to dictate here.

"The presence of your vessels here is unlawful and unwelcome. You will withdraw."

"That's a nice position to take, Governor," Alexander replied, letting the man say his full piece before she replied. "But it fails to recognize that the Republic of Faith and Reason launched an unprovoked and un-announced war on the Protectorate of Mars. I claim no authority here by right of fealty, South Isle. We freely concede the Secession of Nueva Bolivia.

"But in that secession, Nueva Bolivia joined a state with which we are at war. And under the Geneva Conventions, I am required to refrain from the use of weapons of mass destruction and to do all within my power to seek your surrender before proceeding with a planetary inva-sion."

Roslyn could see the mirror of Alexander's cold smile on the screen showing Hans South Isle.

"I'll admit that's an interpretation, but it is one the Royal Martian Navy holds dear, one that we feel honors the spirit of that agreement," she told him. "I claim no authority but that of a victorious enemy, Governor. *I* now control the Nueva Bolivia System.

"The only question that remains is how much damage will be inflicted on Sucre and her people before I control Sucre as well. I would vastly prefer to negotiate the peaceful surrender of your defenses and your world.

"Sucre will be occupied by units of the newly formed Protectorate Guard and disarmed until such time as the Republic of Faith and Reason surrenders and ends this war," Alexander told him. "This is not negotiable. Nueva Bolivia will play no further part in this damned war, one way or another."

South Isle waited patiently to hear her full spiel in turn, then sighed and squared his shoulders to face the camera.

"You can claim whatever you wish," he told her, "but I will not bow to Mars. There will be no surrender, Admiral. Sucre is out of this war now, we both know it, but I will not yield the world I am sworn to defend to you.

"Do what you must, Admiral Alexander, but know that the people of Nueva Bolivia will *never* surrender."

CHAPTER 10

IT WAS A quiet meeting of flag officers that Roslyn served coffee to several hours later. Only two of the Mage-Admirals were actually aboard *Durendal*, as Mage-Admiral Marangoz's battleship flagship was in easy flying distance of the dreadnought.

The other Mage-Admirals were on their ships, linked in by radio communication in near-real-time. The other people Roslyn was serving coffee to included Mage-Captain Sahar Jamshidi, *Durendal's* commanding officer, and General Prasert Bunnag, the senior Guard officer with Second Fleet.

"The Governor will not surrender," Alexander said flatly. "Which means we need to consider our options. I am not, in case anyone thought this was an option, prepared to consider mass bombardment to force Sucre's surrender.

"Mage-Captain Kulkarni, we now have a scan process in place to locate the surface defences?" she asked.

Roslyn knew Alexander knew the answer to that question—but the rest of the officers did not.

"We do," Kulkarni confirmed. "We have deployed two squadrons of destroyers and forty-eight drones in a sphere around Sucre. Interlacing their scans, we are searching for signs of energy generation and similar evidence of concealed facilities.

"Unfortunately, we can't guarantee that any concealed facility we locate is actually a weapons station," she said levelly. "We can be reasonably certain of detecting as many as ninety percent of the enemy defensive positions, but we are also likely to see as high as a ten percent rate of false positives.

"In addition to the false positives, we also have seen that Republic doctrine calls for installing a portion of their defenses in or near populated areas," she continued. "This ended up not being a factor at Legatus, as the Lord Protector's flight undermined morale sufficiently to lead to the planet's surrender.

"Here, it seems we aren't going to get that lucky."

"It is possible that a sufficient reduction in their defenses may result in a change of mind on Governor South Isle's part," Alexander noted. "The old phrasing was *a practical breach*. Once we have opened a gap in the defenses, one that we can safely launch an invasion through, that may focus some minds."

"We will need that gap regardless," General Bunnag said. He was a small and dark-skinned man from Earth itself. "Any attempt to land major forces in the face of anti-orbital defenses will be a disaster."

"I agree," the Admiral said. "There will be no attempt to land the Guard before we have cleared a practical landing zone. As we continue to identify enemy defensive positions, our focus will be on locating an area where we can remove *enough* defenses to land the Guard Army Groups without opposition."

Silence swept over the room again as every eye focused on General Bunnag. As recently as six weeks before, as Roslyn understood it, Prasert Bunnag had been a general in the Unified Security Forces of the Association of Southeast Asian Nations on Earth.

"General, I think you and I may be the only people here completely familiar with the structure and nature of the Protectorate Guard," Alexander said into that silence. "Could you brief my flag officers on what the Guard is—and how many soldiers we're likely to be able to deploy to secure Sucre?"

"Of course, Your Highness," Bunnag said with a small bow. He paused for a moment, then rose to his feet and spread his hands.

"The Protectorate Guard is a brand-new organization still finding our feet," he began without hesitation. "We were created by Royal Order barely a month ago, an order that called on each of the planetary governments to provide one corps of soldiers, defined as four divisions of twenty thousand, to a central force to support the Royal Martian Navy in this war.

"The limited strength of the RMMC required this," he explained. "The planetary armies average around four hundred thousand soldiers apiece, serving primarily as security and disaster relief on a planetary scale.

"The intent is that the corps are provided as intact units with their own organization hierarchies unchanged and then grouped at a higher level into five-corps battle groups and five-battle-group army groups," he said. "Earth and Mars both provided extra corps of troops at Her Majesty's request to fill out the numbers for a target strength of five army groups and ten million soldiers."

Roslyn knew about the Guard and the plan for bringing them up, but she had to admit that the numbers sounded impressive. A hundred and twenty-five corps, one per planet plus extras from Sol, would make for a vast expansion over the *single* eighty-thousand-Marine corps of the RMMC.

The other side, though, was that Sucre alone had a population of just over two billion.

"Currently, we have a single corps with Second Fleet," Bunnag told the officers. "Additional forces are being concentrated at Legatus. Two corps of the First Battle Group, First Army Group, have already been deployed to the surface of Legatus to assist the Marines in garrisoning the planet.

"If everything has gone to schedule, the entirety of the First and Second Battle Groups of the First Army Group should already be in Legatus and deployable to reinforce us. The Third Battle Group *may* have been successfully assembled as well, which would give us approximately thirteen corps or roughly one million soldiers to launch the invasion with."

"I believe we have no choice but to *wait* until the Third Battle Group can be brought up to reinforce our landing troops," Alexander said. "I hesitate to attempt to conquer a world of two billion souls with six hundred thousand troopers, even with proper support."

"And we have that support," Bunnag promised. "Each corps includes exosuit combat units, tanks, artillery and aircraft. They are fully functional planetside combat forces. But I would also suggest waiting until we can deploy the Third Battle Group as well."

He paused, then sighed.

"If I thought we'd have the Fourth and Fifth Battle Groups of the First Army Group in less than another month, I would suggest waiting until we could deploy a full Army Group of the Guard," he admitted.

"We can't wait that long," Alexander told him. "I'm hoping, I have to admit, that opening a breach in the defenses and landing a real invasion force will bring about Sucre's surrender without further fighting after that."

"I do have to ask, Admiral," Marangoz said slowly. "I reviewed your conversation with Governor South Isle, and he made one very relevant point. Nueva Bolivia and Sucre are already out of the war. We can leave lighter units here to secure the planet and make certain that Sucre doesn't contribute to the Republic war effort.

"Why do we need to invade?"

Roslyn had been thinking the same question. Unlike the Admiral, though, *she* had been going to ask it in private. Rank had its privileges, after all. Flag Lieutenants were allowed to ask stupid questions of their Admirals, but they were expected to do it where no one else could hear them.

"For two reasons, Mage-Admiral," Alexander replied. She held up one finger. "Firstly, Sucre has a Link. If we draw down our forces significantly here, they are entirely capable of informing the Republic that we have done so.

"A relief force could be dispatched and the system retaken. Unless we are prepared to destroy all of Nueva Bolivia's infrastructure—an act that would impose an immense level of hardship on the people of this system for decades to come—that would render the entire battle to take the system almost meaningless.

"Secondly"—she held up another finger—"*Sucre itself is a threat.* As a society, we keep most of our heavy industry in space, but *never* underestimate the industrial capacity of a planet. We regard a planet like Sucre as lightly industrialized, but that *light* industry, combined with two billion determined sets of hands, is entirely capable of building new weapons, new defenses—even, given enough time, new warships to try and retake their system.

"The war will likely be resolved before that could happen, but it is a threat I cannot justifiably leave behind us." She shook her head. "Not least because my projections tell me it's going to be at least four weeks before we have enough missiles to launch our next offensive, anyway. If I'm going to be waiting here for a month, we may as well bring up the Guard and finish the damn job."

She glanced around the room.

"Any other questions?" she asked. Silence answered her.

"It will take a minimum of a week for the couriers to return to Legatus and for the transports of the Second and Third Battle Groups to report here," she told them all. "I want you all to sit down with your Captains and get a solid assessment of your ships' damage.

"Munitions colliers should be here shortly to restock our magazines, but we only have a half-load of the new missiles. I want to know what we can repair in place and which ships need to be sent back to Ardennes or even farther."

"None of the battleships have taken anything that can't be buffed out," Marangoz told her. "If we can source a few extra armor plates and energy-dispersion nets from the logistics train, the battle line will be back to full function by the time the Guard arrives."

"*Glorious Voice of Honor* and *Shining Beacon of Hope* aren't going to be repairable here," Mage-Admiral Medici reported. The cruiser commander looked grim. "I don't think even Ardennes's yards are going to cut it. *Glorious Voice* is fixable, but she'll need Core World yards. *Shining Beacon...*"

He shook his head.

"She can jump, but I suspect we're going to need to scrap her," he admitted. "Two more of my ships, *Dancing Smoke Dragon* and *Count of*

Righteousness, have taken relatively minor damage that's still beyond our ability to fix without a yard.

"We're still assessing the rest of the screen, but those four will need to be sent back. *Smoke Dragon* and *Count* can likely be quickly turned around by Ardennes, at least."

"Get me a final list by end of day," Alexander ordered, then glanced at the other officers. "The same goes for the destroyers," she noted. "If we're moving in four weeks, I want every ship at a hundred percent by then—and I won't lose people because we still have ships that shouldn't have been in the line; am I clear?"

CHAPTER 11

IF WARFARE is long stretches of boredom interrupted by moments of terror, that description fit scouting missions better than any other part of it.

"I think the game might be up, skipper," Milhouse said quietly. "They've cut their intervals by a third and they are sweeping the route to Paladin. We're running out of time."

"I know," Kelly allowed. That was why everyone was on deck as *Rhapsody in Purple* sneaked toward the mining planet. "And, frankly, I'm sick of this star system. Xi, how are we doing?"

"Liara is maintaining the stealth spell," her wife replied. "I'm standing by to teleport us the hell out of here. How close are you going to cut this?"

"If the game is blown, then let's do it in style, shall we?" Kelly asked with a smile. "We are headed directly for Paladin already. If we cut the reactor and go full heat sink, how close do you think we can get?"

"With the gunship patrols, sensor stations and the rest?" Xi Wu shook her head. "They'll pick us up at a light-second at the closest. And that's assuming we can get that close, because they can spot us at twice that if we lose the heat sinks."

"Then we go in as far as we can and see all that we can," Kelly replied. "No drones; we can't risk them localizing the launch vectors.

"Shvets, set the course."

"On it," the androgynous navigator replied languidly, reaching out and pressing a single button on the screen. "Engine shutdown in twelve minutes. We will be moving at just over seven thousand KPS at approximately four light-seconds from Paladin—we're already cutting it *close*, boss."

"If they see us, Xi will get us out of here," Kelly said. "Won't you?"

"Of course," the Ship's Mage said, her tone sounding less certain than her words. "Do we even think there's anything here worth this risk? Wouldn't we already know?"

"We know there's industrial platforms here," Kelly replied. "We need to get closer to have a clue what they're making." She checked over her own screens. "Main reactor goes down with the engines," she concluded. "Then we're dark for twenty minutes and then you get us the hell out of here, love."

"Your faith is touching. You know this is going to hurt, right?"

"Damien jumped a ship I was on from *orbit* once," Kelly said. "I know it's going to hurt."

"Wonderful. Does everyone else?"

"We have thirty-*one* minutes to let them know," the Captain said with a chuckle. "Mike, get the medbay ready, will you?

"On it," her pilot husband—also one of the two certified medics on the ship—replied.

Kelly leaned back in her chair and watched the counters run down as she charged her little ship into the teeth of a small fleet *eager* to vaporize her.

"We're here for answers, everyone," she reminded them. "We've got one ugly one. It's time to see what *else* Gygax is hiding from us!"

Rhapsody in Purple was silent and overheated as she plunged toward her final destination in the Gygax System. Kelly wiped sweat from her brow as the ship's sensors drank up everything they could of Paladin and its orbitals.

"Heat sinks are at eighty percent capacity," Milhouse warned her. "We don't have much longer."

"Xi, are you ready?" Kelly asked.

"We are," the Mage confirmed. "On your command?"

"And not a moment sooner, love," Kelly ordered. "I've got an itch between my shoulders that says there is *something* here we've missed."

"There's nothing here of the size to be building gunships," her tactical officer said. "A couple of yards for megaton-range in-system clippers, but nothing I'd call military construction. If there's anything here, we're more likely to learn about it going over the signals intelligence than pushing a hundred thousand kilometers closer."

"And those gunships make getting closer more dangerous, I know," Kelly agreed. "Humor me."

The silence that answered her told her that her officers—her *friends*—thought she was nuts. But they waited anyway, watching the heat-sink capacity disappear and the temperature aboard the stealth ship creep up.

"It's thirty-two degrees in here and the sinks are at ninety percent capacity," Milhouse said quietly as the range continued to close. "Boss, what are we looking—"

"That," Kelly said sharply, pointing at a particular icon. "Milhouse, on my mark, pulse full active sensors at that target. Liara, keep us hidden until we get the bounce back.

"Xi, as soon as we have the data from the radar sweep, get us out of here."

"They'll know where we are," Milhouse replied.

"And that's why we have to act now. *Do it.*"

She could see the timer on the heat sinks. Sixty seconds at most before they *had* to vent—but the factory she'd picked out for a tiny blip of unusual radiation on was only a light-second and a half away. A radar sweep would take three to four seconds...they could evade fire for three to four seconds.

Kelly hoped.

"Sensors active on capacitors," Milhouse replied. "Receivers online."

"Hold *everything* else dark," Kelly ordered. "Shvets, emergency gas thrusters. Keep us dancing!"

There were thirty gunships within five light-seconds of her ship and a dozen mid-sized forts orbiting Paladin. Any of those armed platforms could obliterate *Rhapsody* with a single lucky hit—but they weren't going to have time to try.

"Sensor sweep data coming back," Milhouse snapped. "Give me a second...give me a second...*go!*"

"Xi! Jump us!"

Half a dozen laser beams scored across the sensor panels on *Rhapsody in Purple*'s bridge, the closest of them missing the scout ship by a hundred meters at most.

Then Kelly's stomach tried to climb out through her spine and six years of period cramps arrived at once—and the Gygax System vanished, replaced by the distant lights of empty space.

"We're clear," Xi reported, fatigue straining her voice. "One light-year away from Gygax."

"And good riddance to that star system," Shvets concluded, the navigator speaking for them all.

"Agreed. I'm bringing the reactor back up; set the heat sinks to vent at maximum," Kelly ordered. "Xi, get Pamela up to jump the ship again ASAP. Let's put an extra light-year between us and these bastards, please."

"On it," her wife replied.

Kelly leaned back in her chair and pulled the results of the sensor sweep onto her screens. Radar and lidar were powerful scanners, detailed enough to pull a lot of information. Combined with the radiation signature she'd seen in the passive scans...she was entirely certain and smiled coldly.

"We got the bastards," she said aloud.

"Would you care to illuminate the rest of us, skipper?" Milhouse asked.

"Five hundred and eleven keV, Guns," Kelly told him. "Sound like a familiar number?"

"Positron annihilation radiation," the tactical officer said instantly. "That's...loose antimatter, basically?"

"Inevitable and allowed-for consequence of moving antimatter in bulk quantities," she said. "Also of using antimatter as a power source—but

I'll note that the Republic doesn't *do* that. Their antimatter stocks are reserved for engines…and missiles."

"None of the ships we saw were using antimatter engines," Shvets observed. "Their capital ships never have, but the gunships usually do."

"But can be modified to run on fusion drives," Kelly noted. "But… no, this wasn't someone using an antimatter engine. Too small, too contained. Might have been a reactor, but neither the Republic nor the UnArcana Worlds ever liked using AM for power.

"Plus, I know the pattern." She shrugged. "I worked in merchant shipping, people. We didn't haul antimatter often, but I know what the radiation pattern of an antimatter-containment release valve looks like. So…take a look at the factory it was attached to."

The bridge was silent as Kelly put the data on the main screens. Form follows function, and there were distinctive lines to certain types of zero-G manufacturing. Someone had made a passing attempt to conceal them in this case, but now everyone was looking for them.

"Where there's one missile production station, there's ten," Kelly noted calmly. "While I doubt Gygax is either their sole source of missiles or their sole source of Promethean Interfaces, there's definitely a lot going on here."

"More than enough for Second Fleet to send someone to pay a visit," Shvets said in satisfaction. "Guess it was worth the week, wasn't it?"

"I'd have rather found the Republic government's hideaway," Kelly conceded, "but I'll take a drive-installation facility and a major munitions production site."

Now they just needed to get back to Legatus and check in with the rest of the *Rhapsodies*. With this round of scouting done, they'd gone to every single system of the Republic in the last three months.

Someone *had* to have found the Lord Protector by now.

CHAPTER 12

IT WAS ONE THING to list out the numbers involved in a Protectorate Guard Army Group. Five battle groups represented twenty-five corps from as many star systems. Second Fleet was only expecting forces from the two battle groups in Legatus, hopefully eight corps. *Six hundred and forty thousand* human beings.

Numbers were just numbers, though, even as officers like Roslyn Chambers tried to keep the reality of it all in mind.

It was something else to watch the seemingly unending cascade of jump flares as the Third through Tenth Corps of the Protectorate Guard arrived in Nueva Bolivia. The Guard didn't have their own ships yet, which meant they were being transported on a mismatched collection of de-mothballed Royal Martian Marine Corps transports and ships belonging to their home worlds.

Eight corps represented thirty-two divisions and a total of just over a *hundred* starships. Roslyn sat next to Kulkarni on the flag deck as the ships continued to appear, assembling the information incoming from the Guard transports' beacons and reports as they made contact with the fleet.

"It looks like we got everyone we were promised," she told her boss. "I make it one hundred and six ships." She shook her head. "That's more than we have *warships* in Second Fleet."

Second Fleet only barely outmassed the transports, too. The dreadnoughts might mass a hundred megatons apiece, but the transports averaged eight. The best part of a million soldiers had just entered the star system aboard nearly a billion tons of transports.

"We've got an update on the Third Battle Group as well," Kulkarni said after a moment. "They left Ardennes one day ahead of schedule. They should have already reached Legatus and should be here in three days."

"Gives us a timeline, I suppose," Roslyn replied. She didn't know how comfortable the transports the Guard were using were, but she guessed that only the handful of ex-RMMC ships were livable long-term.

"We've already found our target zone," Kulkarni told her. "Did you see the mapping on that?"

"I've been working with Chief Sinclair to keep the Admiral's communications running," the younger woman admitted. "In theory, there's a chain of command with only six people who need access to her. In practice, well."

"In practice, everyone thinks their problem is important enough to need her personal attention," Kulkarni agreed. She entered a series of commands, bringing up a globe of Sucre on the screen they shared.

"The locals did a good job of setting up their ground defenses," she conceded. "Unfortunately for them, some of our defectors gave Montgomery a lot of the details while he was planning his investigation here. We have that data now, which we put together with our own scans and ended up with a solid idea of what we're looking at."

Red stylized fort icons dotted the globe now.

"Geography is always the biggest factor in something like this," Kulkarni noted. "In this case, a set of mountain ranges on either side of a continental plate here." Part of the globe flashed. "Give it another billion years or so and the Connors Plate will probably be completely ground underneath the two squeezing in on it. For the moment, though, there are two ranges of mountainous islands on either side of a warm and pleasant sea with an Australia-sized island in the middle of it.

"While there are batteries in position to fire over those mountains and target craft descending from orbit, the mountains do impose a blind spot at lower altitudes. The locals made up for that by installing a heavier set of defenses in a few locations on the interior of those mountains, since that island is one of their more densely populated regions.

"We've dialed in all of those defenses," the ops officer said calmly. "We will eliminate approximately seventeen percent of Sucre's surface defenses and clear a zone roughly two hundred kilometers across for the landing.

"The worst part will be the first wave, which will not be transporting troops," Kulkarni said grimly. "There will still be five launch facilities that are too close to civilian populations to engage in long-range bombardment. A wave of Guard and Marine Corps assault shuttles will carry out a close-range assault on those positions to minimize collateral damage and clear the way for the main landing."

Roslyn shivered. *Minimize* did not mean *completely prevent.* That was impossible, especially if the stations were as close as they had been on Legatus. If they were lucky, the locals would take the destruction of the *other* defensive installations around the area as a sign to evacuate the civilians.

"After that..." Kulkarni sighed. "It's down to General Bunnag and the Guard, what happens after that."

Roslyn nodded, glancing away from the globe of Sucre as a new alert pinged on her screen.

"Wait, that's...that's a Royal Guard ID code," she said aloud. One of the ships heading toward Second Fleet wasn't transmitting a Protectorate Guard beacon. "Looks like a courier ship that decided to make the last jumps in company with the transport fleet. Armed courier CT-Seven-Five-Six-Seven, permanently assigned to the Royal Guard."

"They're late," her boss grumbled.

"Sir?"

"I guess they wanted to make the trip with starship escort, which makes sense, I suppose," Kulkarni said. "With the death of the Mage-King and the Crown Prince, Mage-Admiral Alexander is now the Crown Princess of Mars. That means she's supposed to be protected by the Royal Guard, not the Secret Service."

Roslyn nodded slowly. She hadn't met any of the red-armored Combat Mages responsible for the protection of the Mage-Queen of Mars, but she knew their reputation. Veteran Mages from the Marine Corps provided with exosuit combat armor that was rumored to augment their already-formidable magical abilities.

"I guess that's a good thing," she said. "I liked our Secret Service team, though."

"Me too," Kulkarni agreed. "But we can't afford to lose the Admiral now, for a million and ten reasons. I doubt the Queen is going to be popping out an heir anytime soon."

Roslyn snorted. Mage-Queen Kiera Alexander was barely seventeen. Securing the dynasty be damned, no one was expecting the teenager to have a baby just yet.

"I'll let the Admiral know," Roslyn told Kulkarni. "Agent Samson and Chief Sinclair, too. We'll want to make sure the transition is as smooth as possible."

"Agreed," her boss said. "I'll leave that with you, if you think you can handle it? I'm elbow-deep in this damned invasion plan."

"I've got it," Roslyn promised.

"I suppose I'm grateful they're finally here," Alexander said slowly after Roslyn updated her. "They're a week and a half late, but I wasn't looking forward to giving up Samson."

"Forgive my ignorance, sir, but couldn't Samson join the Guard?" Roslyn asked as she stood at attention in front of Alexander's desk.

"Sit down, Lieutenant," Alexander ordered. "I'm old and you're making my neck hurt."

Roslyn obeyed, waiting for the Admiral to continue.

"Samson is a Combat Mage and, in theory, can become a Guard," Alexander admitted. "Tradition and a few practical concerns mean that he can only make that transition on Mars. Unfortunately, every member of my former Guard detail is retired or dead."

She sighed.

"The last actively serving member of my old detail commanded my nephew's personal guards—and died with him. This Guard-Captain von Sulzbach is unknown to me." She chuckled. "I suppose they could have sent me his picture over the Link, but we're not used to having access to interstellar digital transfers yet."

"I wasn't under the impression we trusted our captive Links quite that much yet, either," Roslyn noted.

"We don't," Alexander agreed. "Necessity means that Montgomery, Her Majesty and I use it for discussions that are classified, but we try to avoid sending actual files through it. That will change as we build our own, but for now, we operate as we always have."

Roslyn checked her wrist-comp as it beeped at her.

"We have received personnel files for the detachment," she told the Admiral. "I'm forwarding them to you."

"I'll take a look at von Sulzbach's, but if you can review the others, I'd appreciate it," Alexander replied. "There are a thousand demands on my time, Lieutenant, as you well know. Make sure there's a gap in my schedule for me to meet them when they arrive aboard *Durendal*."

"Yes, sir. I'll check with Chief Sinclair."

"Thank you." Alexander turned to look at the wallscreen behind her, which showed a status display of the fleet and the planetary defenses. "This isn't going to be difficult now, but I'm afraid it's going to get ugly," she murmured. "The last thing we need is for the Admiral's house to be out of order.

"Make sure that doesn't happen, Roslyn."

CHAPTER 13

ROSLYN STOOD at Mage-Admiral Alexander's left hand as the trio of shuttles painted in the red-and-black livery of the Royal Family's personal household settled down in *Durendal*'s bay. Protectorate Secret Service Senior Agent Alan Samson stood on the other side of the Admiral, the bodyguard's spine utterly straight as he watched his people fall out in a protective cordon for what would probably be the last time.

The shuttle ramps lowered in perfect synchronicity, and neatly dressed columns of red exosuits came down each ramp. Each shuttle disgorged ten of the armored Guards and they swiftly moved to overlap with the Secret Service.

The first suit off the central shuttle approached Mage-Admiral Alexander and saluted crisply before retracting his helmet into the neckplate of his armor.

"Guard-Captain Mario von Sulzbach," the ambiguously brown Mage introduced himself. "I am your new Royal Guard team commander, Your Highness."

"Welcome, Captain," Alexander said calmly. "This is Senior Agent Alan Samson, the commander of my Secret Service detail."

Von Sulzbach saluted Samson with perfect military precision.

"I relieve you, Senior Agent Samson," he said.

"I stand relieved, Guard-Captain," Samson replied. "My people and I stand ready to assist the Guard in any way necessary."

"We'll have to sit down and chat as soon as we can make the time," von Sulzbach assured the Secret Service agent. "My people will take over close protection immediately, but the rest of the security arrangements may take us some time to transition properly. Your cooperation would be most valuable."

"Of course, Guard-Captain."

Despite von Sulzbach's probably intentional choice of informal language, the entire exchange felt stilted and forced to Roslyn. On the other hand, she'd never seen a switchover of personal bodyguard forces before.

"This is my Flag Lieutenant, Mage-Lieutenant Roslyn Chambers," Alexander continued after a moment of awkward silence. "She'll be your main point of contact for my staff and for *Durendal*'s crew."

"Of course, Your Highness," von Sulzbach confirmed. "I have a team picked out to accompany you for the rest of the day while I coordinate with your people."

"That won't be necessary aboard *Durendal*," Alexander said firmly.

"I have to differ, Your Highness," the Guard officer replied. "We have seen vast evidence that the RID has infiltrated the Royal Navy. While we believe those infiltrators were neutralized, there remains the possibility of a second wave of infiltration or that a secondary group were infiltrated without informing our defectors.

"Even aboard RMN warships, your security is not without question. I will have to insist on a minimum of a two-Guard detail at all times."

Roslyn could tell that Alexander wanted to shut him down, but instead, she swallowed and nodded.

"Very well, Guard-Captain," she told him. "I have every reason to trust *Durendal*'s crew, but if it will make you more comfortable, I will permit it. But if your detail causes trouble, we will be changing that very quickly. Do you understand me?"

"Of course, Your Highness."

"And, Guard-Captain?"

"Yes, Your Highness?"

"It's *Mage-Admiral*," Alexander told him. "You may be here because of my royal title and place in the succession, but *I* am here to do a damned job and I will *not* permit you to interfere. Am I understood?"

"Yes...Mage-Admiral."

Roslyn spent, on average, less than three hours a day in her office. Most of her time was either spent one step to the left and behind Admiral Alexander or on the flag bridge. She handled her messages mostly from her wrist-comp, but there were definitely some tasks that having a proper console and wallscreen made easier.

Most of them involved some variety of spreadsheet, and she was nibbling on a lock of hair wrapped around her finger, studying the numbers on how the addition of the Guard troops and their officers would change the allocation of Alexander's available "answering messages and dealing with minor crises" minutes when her door chime sounded.

She unwrapped the hair from her finger and checked the camera. The only real surprise, she supposed, was that von Sulzbach had managed to find a time when she *was* in her office on his first day on the dreadnought.

"Come in, Guard-Captain," she told him.

Von Sulzbach was still in his red exosuit, though he at least had the helmet retracted again. He was younger than she would have expected, though the mixed-racial features of a Martian native made that hard to judge sometimes, with dark brown hair and the kind of deep brown eyes she could get lost in.

Which was a terrible idea and she tried to conceal giving herself a shake. It had clearly been far too long since she'd managed to get personal time. Since...before the Battle of Nia Kriti, she realized.

Being part of the Admiral's staff during a war didn't leave much time for flings, let alone relationships...but she probably needed to sort out *something* sooner rather than later.

If only to stop herself making eyes at the Admiral's bodyguard!

"How can I help you, Captain von Sulzbach?" she asked as he stopped in front of her desk, clearly settling into his armor. "I'd offer you a seat, but..."

"The armor handles that," he told her. "The Admiral said I'd be going through you to interface with her staff and *Durendal*'s crew."

"So she did," Roslyn confirmed. "I'm at your disposal, of course, though I have a lot going on. What do you need?"

"A few things," von Sulzbach said with a grin. "First, the quarters we've been assigned are more than acceptable except for one problem: we're not nearly close enough to the Admiral. We're going to need to be relocated to make certain we're quartered around her so no one can reach her quarters without going past us."

"That makes sense, I suppose," she admitted. "I'll coordinate with the stewarding staff and get that sorted out. We might not be able to move all of you over, but I suspect putting guards in quarters around the Admiral at least passed the designers' minds."

"I'd hope so," the Guard replied. "I'll admit I haven't seen the full schematics for this ship yet, either, but that's less critical. For the moment, we're mostly standing guard on the Admiral's spaces and following her around like lost puppies."

"You should have been sent some when you were assigned," Roslyn said, pursing her lips.

"Never received them, I'm afraid," he admitted. "Can you make sure my people get those, too?"

"I can. You'll have them by the end of the day," she promised. "Anything else?"

"Speaking of stewarding staff, we brought a small team of food-prep staff from the Mountain," he told her. "My review so far suggests that the Admiral's food is being prepared by *Durendal*'s crew." He shook his head. "That's not acceptable for the Crown Princess of Mars's security. The team we brought will take over all of Her Highness's food, both personal and meetings.

"We can't have her eating or drinking anything that hasn't been validated by my people," he said firmly. "Even aboard *Durendal*, she is more vulnerable than she seems to believe."

"This ship was the most classified secret project the Protectorate had," Roslyn pointed out gently. "Everyone aboard has cleared the highest and tightest security restrictions, Guard-Captain."

"Maybe, but so had the Mage-Admiral's previous operations officer, yes?" von Sulzbach pointed out. "The one that was a Republic plant?"

Roslyn swallowed. She'd almost forgotten about that. That officer had committed suicide when confronted, which was how Kulkarni had ended up in the job. Alexander had been working aboard a regular battleship then, but the point still stood.

"Fair," she conceded. "I can tell you already, though, that Admiral Alexander will be concerned about offending the Navy personnel and leaving them feeling untrusted."

"We will offend the Navy personnel," von Sulzbach said bluntly. "And they will feel untrusted because I don't trust them. Admiral Alexander has to trust them to do her job. I have to *distrust* them to do mine.

"We will push each other until we find a compromise, but right now we need to err on the side of complete caution, Mage-Lieutenant." He smiled. "I promise you, I'm not a complete hard-ass, but my job is to keep the Crown Princess of Mars alive.

"I do not give a single rat's ass if people around me hate me for it."

CHAPTER 14

"FIRST-WAVE BOMBARDMENT initiating in sixty seconds."

Kulkarni's words were soft but they echoed in the silence of *Durendal's* flag bridge. The dreadnought was one of only ten ships that had moved closer to the planet: the two dreadnoughts and the eight new *Salamander*-class cruisers.

The Royal Martian Navy was very strict on who even had access to the schematics for their orbital impactors. There were a lot of ways to build cheap and dirty weapons to fall from orbit, but precision space-to-surface weapons were rare.

The Talon Nine carried by the newest ships was, like the Phoenix IX it had accompanied, still a new weapon in limited supply. Unlike the Phoenixes, though, the Talon Nine had yet to be used outside of testing.

"Targets are locked in. Bombardment squadron reports ready to deploy," the operations officer continued.

It was taking active effort for Roslyn not to hold her breath. To distract herself, she took a quick look around the flag bridge. The newest addition to the bridge definitely took her focus away from the maneuvers she couldn't affect.

Even after three days, Roslyn wasn't used to having exosuited guards on the flag bridge. Two red-armored Royal Guards flanked each of the room's entrances, making sure that no one could enter the space occupied by the Mage-Admiral without authorization.

Their presence was making the crew twitchy. Most of the people Roslyn had talked to understood where the Royal Guard were coming from, but the sudden intrusion of a non-Navy security presence was still...creating friction.

"Fifteen seconds," Kulkarni reported. "Admiral?"

"Proceed," Alexander ordered.

The icons of the invasion fleet were gathering behind them. The Third Battle Group had arrived on schedule, which meant that there were now one hundred and fifty transports carrying over a million soldiers waiting on this mission to succeed.

"Commencing Talon Nine deployment," Kulkarni said quietly. "Two hundred twenty munitions in space, impact in ten minutes."

The Talon Sevens and Eights that Roslyn had trained on had been shorter-ranged systems, built around the expectation that the Royal Martian Navy could easily secure the orbitals of a planet. No one had ever expected to face a situation where the RMN would be facing sufficiently powerful ground-based defenses that they couldn't safely enter orbit of a planet.

Like many situations the RMN was now facing, a failure to anticipate fighting a peer power was giving them headaches today.

"Prepping the next wave of impactors."

To provide it with its longer range and its powerful onboard targeting systems, the Talon Nine was a far larger munition than its older siblings. The Nine could only be launched from the systems intended for the Samurai long-range missiles.

Which meant that only the dreadnoughts and *Salamanders* could launch them internally. The rest of the fleet could carry the weapons and deploy them, but it would be a slower and more painstaking process—one Admiral Alexander had decided not to engage in.

"Second salvo is ready. Standing by for your order," Kulkarni reported.

"Proceed," Alexander ordered. "Launch the third wave when ready."

A second wave of two hundred–plus icons appeared on the screen, hurtling toward the planet at several thousand gravities.

By the time the third wave hit, every isolated launch facility around Isla de Bolivar would have been the target of at least a dozen kinetic sub-munitions. That *should*, per the plan, neutralize them all.

There would still be a fourth wave in the launchers, held back to see what happened.

"Bunnag and the rest of the Guard Generals are requesting an update," Roslyn noted as her console beeped. "What do we tell them?"

"Everything is proceeding according to plan; minimum thirty minutes before they get their clearance," Alexander said quickly. "As they well know. They can find half an hour of patience."

"I'll let them know everything is on plan," the Flag Lieutenant agreed diplomatically, earning herself a flashed grin from her Admiral.

The third salvo of Talon Nines leapt into space and the bombardment squadron waited. Drones hovered in Sucre orbit, updating the data on the targets as the weapons flashed inward.

"We have missile fire from the surface targeting the deployment platforms," Kulkarni noted. "This was accounted for in the firing pattern. We'll see how well they do."

Hundreds of missiles were rising from the surface on initial fusion-drive boosters. Reaching minimum safe altitude, they switched over to antimatter rockets and blazed out toward the incoming munitions.

The designers of the Talon Nine hadn't had access to Republican surface-to-orbit munitions, but they *had* possessed the Protectorate equivalent. They'd designed the weapon to account for the most likely return-fire approach—and the first wave of deployment platforms broke apart ten seconds before the defensive fire reached them.

The icons on the screens now were projections, probabilities. The terminal approach for the weapons was purely ballistic, a mostly directed thirty-thousand-kilometer fall.

The defensive weapons detonated a few moments later as their controllers saw what had happened and did the best they could to clear away the incoming fire.

"We lost twelve deployment platforms," Kulkarni reported. "Looks like the detonations of the local missiles may have taken out some of the final impactors as well. We won't be able to confirm until we have impact."

She paused.

"Additional missiles are being launched at the second and third waves. They'll attempt to account for the separation times. We will lose more munitions."

"Keep an eye on the losses and update the fourth-wave targeting," Alexander ordered. "We'll see the results of this, and I'll make a call before we even go that far."

Roslyn had everything they needed for that call loaded into her console already. They didn't know exactly where Governor South Isle was hiding, but they knew where he'd been transmitting from the last time he and the Admiral had spoken. They would hit that station with a tight-beam transmission once the bombardment waves were done.

Maybe South Isle would even listen.

"First-wave impact in ten seconds," Kulkarni noted. Her voice was very, very soft, almost ill. The Talon Nines were calibrated for thirty kilotons per impactor, and each wave was dropping over seven hundred of them.

Over the course of the next ten minutes, Second Fleet would be dropping sixty megatons of weapons on Sucre. Compared to the level of fire-power thrown around in even a small space battle, that was nothing—but planets didn't have hypertensile ceramics and energy-dispersion systems.

Impact markers began to appear on the screen, and Roslyn swallowed down a sick taste in her mouth. The use of a stylized mushroom cloud had been part of the RMN's iconography for a long time, but she'd never seen it before outside of simulations and exercises.

Hundreds of the icons appeared on the screen, all of them clustering into groups. From her own part in the analysis, Roslyn knew they were hitting one hundred and sixty-five targets.

Those targets were fortified, with at least some of the hypertensile ceramics that allowed warships to withstand gigaton-range antimatter warheads. A single thirty-kiloton kinetic impactor wasn't going to do the job on its own.

By the time the third wave had hit, each of those sites had been subjected to at least ten such impacts. The drones were scanning the impact sites, sending back visual imagery that Roslyn forced herself to piece through.

It was quickly clear that none of the targets still had functioning launchers. The surface components of those weapons systems were probably the most vulnerable portion of the installations. Most of the installations were completely wrecked, their relatively light armor having failed under repeated impacts.

A handful of the installations were no longer in their original locations, the very ground and rock they were built into having given way under the bombardment—but the fortified bunkers were still at least partially intact despite everything.

It took five minutes for the analysis teams, including Roslyn, to confirm what they needed to know.

"All targets appear disabled, Mage-Admiral," Kulkarni confirmed. "We are ready for the bravo wave strike."

That was the assault-shuttle wave, where they would hit facilities relying on human shields with even more precise weapons to clear the way for the landing.

"One last arrow to fire first," Alexander replied. "Chambers? Are we ready to transmit?"

"We are, Admiral. Ready to record on your order."

Alexander nodded, squaring her shoulders and facing the camera.

"Let's get the dog-and-pony part of this show on the road," she ordered.

The recording started and Roslyn watched Alexander's face transform into a cold mask.

"Governor Hans South Isle," she said flatly. "This message is being transmitted to a site we believe is receiving for you. If it isn't, I strongly suggest that whoever *is* receiving this message relay it to the Governor immediately.

"There is a term, Governor, from second-millennium European warfare that I suggest you become familiar with. That term is *practicable breach*. When a town was besieged, they were expected to hold out until mining or bombardment had opened a breach in the walls through which the besieger could launch an assault. They were then expected to surrender—or the wealth and even lives of the townspeople were forfeit," she explained.

"We have demonstrated our ability to reduce your defenses from beyond any range at which you can engage my ships. We have destroyed the defenses around Isla de Bolivar, creating that exact type of breach.

"I am sadly aware that breach already came with significant cost of life," Alexander said. "But I am now faced with the final defenses of Isla de Bolivar, the ones that Republican military doctrine has positioned next to or even inside civilian cities. I will not risk my invasion force, Governor. I *will* bombard those defensive positions before I initiate my landings."

She did not, Roslyn noted, point out that the plan was to do so with assault shuttles, risking—indeed, almost *guaranteeing*—Protectorate losses to minimize civilian deaths. If South Isle thought they were going to continue the long-range bombardment, *his* estimate of the collateral damage would be much higher.

Alexander made a show of checking the time on her wrist-comp.

"It is fourteen hundred and seven hours Olympus Mons Standard Time as I record this," she told the Governor. "If Sucre has not surrendered by fourteen hundred and twenty hours OMST, the invasion will proceed.

"While I accept responsibility for the death and bloodshed that will follow, you will share in my guilt, Governor, if you refuse to yield. By the time you receive this message, you will have ten minutes.

"I suggest you use them wisely."

Alexander made a cut gesture and Roslyn stopped the recording.

"Send it," the Mage-Admiral ordered.

Roslyn obeyed silently, her gaze on the rotating globe of Sucre in the middle of the flag deck. Everyone in the bridge was studying the planet, considering it carefully. How many of the forty million people on Isla de Bolivar were going to die before the day was out?

How many of Sucre's two billion citizens would die before the fight there was over?

"The assault shuttles aren't scheduled to go in until fourteen forty," Kulkarni pointed out softly.

"I know," Alexander agreed. "And if he surrenders at any point prior to the shuttles' launching their missiles, no one else has to die. But the bastard needed a deadline...so he got one. One that didn't tell his people when our attack would start."

Roslyn nodded, even though the conversation wasn't addressed at her. She could do the napkin math on how many people they'd already killed today: each of the hundred and sixty-five installations they'd bombarded had between a hundred and five hundred staff.

She didn't know the average or how many people had escaped, but Second Fleet had probably killed at least fifty thousand soldiers and technicians. They hadn't chosen to support a regime that had embraced murder as expediency, but they were trying to protect their homes.

Roslyn could hold the Prometheus Project against a lot of people in the Republic, but she found that she couldn't hold it against the people trying to do their jobs. It didn't change *her* job, and she was grimly focused on making sure she was watching the communications channels, but she could still feel guilt over it.

Fourteen hundred hours and twenty minutes Olympus Mons Standard Time passed without any communication from the surface. One of the stranger legacies of the first Mage-King of Mars was that Mars now rotated in twenty-four hours instead of twenty-four hours and thirty-nine minutes.

Why exactly Desmond Michael Alexander the First had made that change when he'd used his power to complete the terraforming was lost to history. Roslyn suspected it had, as much as anything else, stemmed from a desire for nice, round numbers.

Or potentially just a desire for control. Desmond the First had been born in the caves of Project Olympus, after all, with only a number. Like the rest of the subjects of the Project that had restored magic, his purpose had been to grow to puberty, be tested for magical gifts to see if he was stronger than the generation before him, and then father the next generation.

Like many of the *last* generation of Project Olympus's subjects, he'd proven stronger than the Eugenicist scientists who'd ruled Mars at the time had predicted. He'd seized control of the Olympus Mons Amplifier, disabled the Eugenicist fleet that had been about to invade Earth, and ended the century-long Eugenicist Wars by smashing the entire structure of their caste-driven Martian state.

A number, DMA-651, had become a name: Desmond Michael Alexander. A slave had become a king. A partially transformed desert world had become a temperate and controlled paradise...with a twenty-four-hour day.

"Shuttles are ready for the second-wave strikes," Kulkarni reported. "Both Guards and Marines are fully fueled and armed. They can deploy on your order, Mage-Admiral."

Roslyn knew the schedule said they wouldn't launch the shuttles for twenty more minutes, but if they were ready and the deadline had already passed...

"Hold them till the schedule," Alexander said softly. "Let that arrogant ivory-tower *ass* sweat."

"Yes, sir."

Roslyn checked her communications channels again.

"Admiral," she said quietly. "We sent a tightbeam transmission. Should we...send a wider message? One that the rest of the planet will hear?"

It wasn't really the Flag Lieutenant's job to make suggestions, but she was handling coms for Alexander today. She was going to sit there and watch an invasion go forward with everyone else, too. If there was a way around it...she wanted to suggest it.

The Mage-Admiral exhaled a long sigh.

"Yes," she finally said. "Resend the transmission we sent to South Isle. Omnidirectional. If South Isle is going to damn his people, he can do it with their knowledge."

Roslyn had already set up the transmission and sent it with a single button-press.

"Transmission sent," she reported. "And we wait?"

"We wait," Alexander confirmed. "Get me the status reports on the heavy landers, Chambers. I want them ready to move the moment the shuttles have cleared the path. Once we get moving, it all goes by the plan and by the book."

"Yes, sir."

Roslyn linked into the Guard channels, firing off the information requests. The standard "one-platoon" assault shuttles used by the RMMC and similar forces would have had enough trouble trying to land a million-soldier invasion on their own, let alone the tanks, ground transports and aircraft the Guard was taking down with them.

The answer was retrofitted heavy-lift shuttles, spacecraft designed to haul multiple ten-thousand-ton cargo containers up from a planetary surface. Instead of the standard containers, these were carrying specially designed modules loaded with those troops, tanks and aircraft.

The landing would still need over a hundred of them making four flights apiece. The assault shuttles would mostly be relegated to an escort role, keeping any missiles or aerospace craft the locals had left from reaching the slower landers.

"Landers report ready," Roslyn told the Admiral after a few moments. "First-wave equipment is loaded, and personnel are coming aboard now. They expect full readiness at fourteen forty."

That meant a quarter-million soldiers were cramming themselves into those modules, preparing to drop through hostile space to the first planetary invasion the Protectorate had ever launched.

That was a lot of moving pieces, but everything seemed to be coming together according to plan. Ahead of plan, in fact. If everything was ready ten to twenty minutes early, Roslyn suspected that most of the Guard elements had probably started moving *thirty* minutes early.

The Guard officers knew that this was as new to their people as anyone else, after all.

Communications channels from the planet were still silent. They were ten minutes past the deadline Alexander had given South Isle and no one was saying anything.

Durendal's flag bridge was as silent as the radio waves between Second Fleet and Sucre now. The fleet's role in this fight was over. The plan was moving, and the only possible task left to Admiral Alexander was to give the order to *stop* if the defenders surrendered.

"Chambers, it's Lieutenant Burns from Tactical," a soft voice said in her headset. "Can you check quadrant minus thirty-six by minus forty-eight? I'm seeing something weird, but...it's weird enough I don't want to officially bounce it up the chain."

Darrel Burns was the assistant tactical officer Roslyn usually spoke to first when dealing with the Tactical department. He'd done her enough favors that she didn't mind doing him one in turn, and she pulled up the data.

"...That's a nuke, Darrel," she half-whispered. "A small one, probably buried, but what the?"

"That wasn't us," Burns replied. "If you see what I see, I'm bouncing it up the chain. Tell the Admiral."

"Of course."

Roslyn turned from the intercom channel and tapped a command that flashed her screen image to Kulkarni's screen.

"Captain Kulkarni, Admiral Alexander, somebody just nuked something on the surface," she reported. "Energy readings are unclear, but it looks like at least a hundred-kiloton subsurface detonation."

"What the fuck?" Alexander asked bluntly. "Where the hell is this?"

"Central region of one of the larger continents," Kulkarni reported. "Two hundred forty kilometers from the capital city, in fact."

An alert flashed on Roslyn's channel and she looked up at the Admiral.

"Sir, incoming transmission," she reported. "Same transmitter as last time."

"Put them on," Alexander ordered. "Let's see if the Governor is willing to surrender."

South Isle looked far more tired than he had the first time, his hair no longer utterly perfect and visible bags now showing under his eyes.

"Admiral Alexander, I am aware we missed your deadline, but my people tell me you have not yet launched your next bombardment. I hope that means we still have a chance to come to a resolution to this."

"There is always a chance, Governor," Alexander replied, "but yours is running thin every second we speak."

"I am prepared to offer the conditional surrender of Sucre and the Nueva Bolivia System," South Isle said instantly. "Is that enough to stay your hand for long enough for us to talk terms, at least?"

"That won't take very long, I suspect," the Admiral told him. "What just blew up next to your capital city, Governor?"

There was a long silence, one hardly justified by the two second com delay.

"That, Mage-Admiral Alexander, would have been the Republic Intelligence Directorate's primary operations facility on Sucre," South Isle said slowly.

"You nuked the RID?" Alexander asked. Roslyn couldn't help but agree with the Admiral's incredulous tone—South Isle had pushed it this late and had *then* blown up the RID base?

"Technically, they nuked *themselves*," the Governor replied. "That bomb was originally installed in the basement of the fallback bunker I am speaking to you from. It was relocated some weeks ago by what turns out to have been a rather...*imaginative* agent of mine."

"They were supposed to *dispose* of the bomb."

"Instead, they infiltrated it into the RID base?" Alexander asked.

"So I am informed, yes," South Isle confirmed. "While leaving the tracker in my bunker and the detonation codes unchanged. I believe, Admiral, that the RID was expecting me to surrender and attempted to prevent that."

"And now you are surrendering," she told him. "The Protectorate's terms are simple, Governor: Sucre and the rest of the Nueva Bolivia System will be occupied by Protectorate Guard forces. The planetary-defense installations will be demolished—*carefully*. All planetary and Republican military forces will be disarmed and processed by the Guard but *not* further imprisoned unless we have evidence of crimes.

"Orbital and planetary industrial sites will be subject to regular inspection to prevent the production of munitions, and a Royal Martian Navy security force will remain in the system to prevent any clever ideas.

"Otherwise, you will continue to govern yourselves as usual. Law enforcement will be expected to cooperate with the occupation garrison, but we will otherwise leave them to their work."

"I understand." South Isle's face was grim. "Is that it, Admiral?"

"We will also require the surrender of every known Link installation in the system," Alexander said. "Our purpose is to fully neutralize Nueva Bolivia as a threat, Governor, not to engage in reprisals."

"And when the war is over?" he asked softly.

"The Republic of Faith and Reason is done," she said harshly. "But when the war is over, we will require a plebiscite on the part of the people of Nueva Bolivia on whether they wish to remain as an independent world or rejoin the Protectorate of the Mage-Queen of Mars."

In Roslyn's opinion, that was probably just a question of labels. Any of the "ex-Republic" worlds that chose to stay independent were inevitably going to join back up in a new structure. So long as that structure wasn't engaged in the mass murder of Mages to build jump-ships, though, she figured her superiors would tolerate that.

"I don't have much of a choice," the Governor admitted. "I would like to think that humanity is past the point where violence like this is the answer, but enough people have died to make your point.

"We accept your terms, Mage-Admiral Alexander. The planetary defenses will stand down. Sucre surrenders."

CHAPTER 15

ROSLYN STEPPED inside Alexander's office in response to the unspoken command of the door sliding open. The red-armored Royal Guards flanking the door eyed her but didn't challenge her as she entered.

They at least recognized her, though she'd heard some complaints about the level of security they were imposing.

The architect of that security was standing next to Alexander's desk. Von Sulzbach had his helmet down and was in the loose parade rest that Roslyn understood to be basically sitting inside the armor.

Kulkarni was sitting in front of the desk and gestured Roslyn to the empty seat.

"We've had an expected wrinkle," Alexander told the three of them once Roslyn was seated. "While Governor South Isle unquestionably has the authority to stand down the military forces of Nueva Bolivia, his legislature is dragging their feet."

"He has suggested that I *speak* to them," she continued. "A virtual presentation won't make a sufficient show of force. While I don't think the Governor is *quite* aware of the level of *show of force* I'm thinking of, my understanding is that he wants this all settled as fast as possible."

"Our analysis of the legislature's politics suggests that they're doing this as much to embarrass him as anything else," Kulkarni warned. "Some of South Isle's regular allies in the legislature are contributing."

"We need this to end and we need it to end now," Alexander concluded. "I'll be landing with one of First Corps's combat regiments.

Twenty-five hundred soldiers with full armor and air support. We'll make for quite a damn parade down Main Street."

"I still think this sounds like a trap to me," von Sulzbach interjected. "Even with an entire regiment around you, you are more vulnerable on the surface than aboard *Durendal*."

"Your job is to keep me safe while I do *my* job, Guard-Captain," the Admiral said firmly. "However, it would be *helpful*, I think, to bring the entire Guard detachment down. Everyone knows your reputation and, well, what can they really throw at us that thirty Combat Mages can't stop?"

"Not much," von Sulzbach admitted slowly. He sighed. "As you say, my job is to enable you doing yours. We'll bring the detachment down. We'll leave the Secret Service team aboard *Durendal* to keep your spaces secured."

"I'd say that's unnecessary, but they're probably not needed on the surface, either," Kulkarni admitted. "You haven't made yourself popular in the fleet, Guard-Captain."

"I don't care," the Guard admitted calmly. "My job is to protect Her Highness, not make friends. I am prepared to work with the RMN personnel, and certainly, I can't get in the way of the Mage-Admiral's work, but my priority is her safety."

"Oh, the crew get that," Kulkarni told him. "That's the only reason we haven't had trouble. They understand and they'll tolerate, but it's bothering them. Something to think about, Guard-Captain."

"We are all on the same side, after all."

"I know that, Mage-Captain," von Sulzbach replied. "But I have to consider the chance that there is someone aboard *Durendal* who is only pretending to be on our side."

He glanced over at Alexander.

"I'll need to coordinate with whoever is in command of the regiment we're taking down," he told her. "Do we know who?"

"Roslyn will have all that information shortly," Alexander said with a gesture toward the young woman. "She'll be accompanying me to act as my aide and general gofer on the surface. This needs to go smoothly, people."

"Of course," von Sulzbach allowed.

"Kulkarni, you'll remain up here and act as my point of contact with Second Fleet if anything comes up," Alexander continued. "We've agreed to do this tomorrow morning, which means we have twelve hours to set all of the wheels in motion.

"We already have the Governor's signature on one copy of their surrender. I want it validated by their legislature in twenty-four hours. The scout ships should be back in Legatus in the next few days, which means we should have a target for the fleet in a week or so.

"I don't want to be held up here with Nueva Bolivian politics at that point!"

Roslyn had barely left Alexander's office when she got a message from von Sulzbach asking to meet her in her office. She'd been heading there anyway, so she sent a confirmation, stopping at the kitchen station by Alexander's space to grab coffee.

Like all of the spaces around Alexander, the station was now being run by one of the small team of catering staff the Royal Guard had brought with them. The woman there was probably older than Roslyn, but she cheerfully handed over a tray with two cups and a carafe of coffee.

"Let me take that," von Sulzbach told her brightly, an armored hand slipping between hers to balance the tray. "The armor can handle the weight and balancing automatically; seems easier."

"Thank you," Roslyn said. "You caught up, I see."

"Let's chat in your office, still," he said. "Security is important."

"All right."

Walking beside a suit of armor was still a bit odd and intimidating for her, even if the man inside the armor was attractive enough. Von Sulzbach kept his helmet retracted most of the time, though his Guards always kept them up. The commander was the only one of the Royal Guard whose face Roslyn had actually seen.

Entering Roslyn's office, he put the tray down and delicately poured two cups of coffee before taking one for himself. The ceramic mug was sized for spacers' coffee appetites, but it was still dwarfed in his gauntlet.

Nonetheless, he was clearly used to working within the limitations of the exosuit and took a solid gulp of the steaming beverage.

"Do you have the contact info for the regiment we're going down with yet?" he asked.

"I've traded a couple of messages with Bunnag's staff, but not yet," she admitted. "I think the General is still picking the regiment. Someone might have kicked him into not sending one of the ones from Earth, and then he had to stop and think."

The Guard-Captain snorted.

"I can understand that," he admitted. "Sooner is better, of course. The advantage of the Guard is that they're intact units, which means they've had parade-ground training already and can probably march down a boulevard without problems.

"It doesn't mean, though, that they're practiced in VIP protection."

"As I understand it, most planets don't use entire regiments for VIP duty," Roslyn replied with a smile. She took a sip of her own coffee as she studied the dark-haired man across from her.

"That's true. I want to double-check with you, though. Do you know if the Admiral was planning on riding down with the Guard?"

"We could, but unless we need to, it would be a pain," she told him. "No one has told me anything, so I'm assuming we're taking a separate shuttle down from *Durendal*."

"That's relevant," von Sulzbach said. "Can you get a confirmation on which shuttle we'll be using?" He asked. "I'll have one of my teams take possession of it at least six hours in advance and go over it with a fine-toothed comb.

"After the Mage-King's death, well." His armored shoulders shrugged. "The Guard is taking no chances with shuttlecraft, even ones launching from the most powerful warships in the fleet."

"I'll check with *Durendal*'s crew and get all of that sorted out for you," Roslyn promised. "I'll have an update for you in an hour or so?"

"I appreciate it, Chambers," the Guard said with a grin that sent a pleasant shiver down her spine. "The line of succession has grown too damned short. The Crown Princess *shouldn't* be an Admiral on the front lines, but she already was, and we can't shift up the entire command structure of the war just to protect her."

"I don't think she'd let you," Roslyn pointed out.

Von Sulzbach chuckled.

"No, she wouldn't. And both Her Majesty and the Lord Regent would back her on that, I suspect. So, we work with the position we're in, but that requires risk I don't like. If she dies, Chambers, there is no heir to the Martian throne.

"What happens then?"

Roslyn shrugged.

"I'm sure there's some kind of plan," she admitted.

She'd spent enough time around Alexander to know that the older Mage had some kind of gift with magic she'd only seen once before—and *that* suggested part of the answer to her. Roslyn Chambers didn't know what gifts and powers the family of the Mage-King of Mars possessed, but she knew that Damien Montgomery shared them.

And if that didn't put the Lord Regent of Mars next in the line of succession after her boss, she'd eat her uniform. If the *Royal Guard* didn't know that, though, it was definitely *not* her place to say anything.

"If there's a plan, no one in the Royal Guard knows it," von Sulzbach admitted. "Which is scary, isn't it? We have to be ready for anything tomorrow. If something goes completely to shit, Chambers, you'll be right next to Her Highness with myself and the close protection detail. We have to focus on Alexander."

"The Admiral can take care of herself, you know," Roslyn said delicately. She suspected that Alexander could take on her entire thirty-Mage guard detail and wipe the floor with them. "So can I, even if not quite so competently. I am a trained Navy Mage, after all, Guard-Captain."

"Good," he told her. "We'll try and keep you safe as well, but if you can help, that won't go amiss."

"Everyone around the Admiral will be Mages, Guard-Captain," she said with a smile. "None of us are helpless."

"True," he conceded. "It's easy to forget that when you're focused on protecting someone, though."

"Fair."

Roslyn shook her head and drank more coffee.

"I'll get you the contact and the shuttle info," she promised. "Do you need anything else?"

"Not right now," he told her. "I'll let you know."

"I'm your contact for the Navy side," Roslyn reminded him. "Whatever you need, Guard-Captain."

CHAPTER 16

BY THE TIME the assault shuttle carrying Roslyn, the Mage-Admiral, and the platoon of the Royal Guard touched down, the Guard force was already on the ground and spreading out from the shuttleport.

The heavy lander was a looming presence on the edge of the field, four ten-meter-by-one-hundred-meter containers permanently attached to each other and the heavy-lift shuttle needed to move them into space.

A dozen tanks were drawn up around the edge of the pad as Roslyn followed the Royal Guards onto Sucre's surface, with a company of exosuited soldiers surrounding them.

"Which unit did Bunnag deploy in the end?" Alexander murmured as she joined Roslyn in surveying their show of force.

"The One Four Two Thirty-Two. First Regiment, Fourth Brigade, Second Division, Third Corps, Second Battle Group," Roslyn recited. "One of the Tau Ceti units and the one with the best readiness metrics among the Guards with us."

"Makes sense," the Admiral agreed. She moved forward in the middle of a moving wedge of red-exosuited Royal Guard. Tanks and exosuits moved in behind them, leaving only a single platoon of exosuited soldiers to watch the shuttle.

"Transport is waiting at the edge of the pad," von Sulzbach told them. "Open-topped, as requested."

His tone said everything about what *he* thought of using an open-topped vehicle on an occupied planet, but Roslyn agreed with Alexander.

The point of today was to be *seen*. The Crown Princess of Mars would be seen on the other side of a moving wall of tanks and soldiers, but she would be seen.

The density of Guard soldiers increased as they passed the landing craft. Presumably, the artillery and aircraft were still aboard the lander, but Roslyn stopped counting tanks and armored all-terrain vehicles at sixty.

The vehicle von Sulzbach led them to was an open-topped all-terrain vehicle, a recon transport intended to carry half a squad of light infantry or a single fire team of exosuits.

"You two mount up," the Guard ordered. "The driver is ours, but we'll accompany in our armor. We can keep up."

"We won't be going particularly quickly, not with the parade I called for," Alexander said. "It's not my idea of fun, either, Guard-Captain. It's just necessary."

"As you command, Admiral Your Highness," von Sulzbach agreed.

Roslyn stepped up into the vehicle first and offered her arm to her boss. Alexander snorted—but did not decline the help. She was closer to a hundred than ninety, after all. The Admiral was healthy enough that Roslyn was certain her concern was unwarranted, but she was going to offer it anyway.

"Strap in, please," a modulated female voice came from the suit of red armor in the driver's position. The actual *seat* there had retracted into the floor of the vehicle, leaving enough space for an exosuit to settle in and link to the transport's systems.

Roslyn obeyed instantly. Alexander took a couple of grumpy moments longer, but the safety belts were secure enough.

"We're coordinating with Colonel Travere's people," the driver told them. "First units are moving out now."

At the edge of the impromptu vehicle park in front of the heavy lander, Roslyn watched the first tanks start rolling out. Presumably, there were already some vehicles and exosuits along the path they'd be taking, but most of the 142-32 would move as one.

Twenty-five hundred soldiers, a thousand in exosuits, fifty tanks and a hundred armored personnel transports.

Alexander definitely had her show of force—and it made one *hell* of a parade!

The Nueva Bolivia Asamblea Legislativa held their deliberations in a specially built structure, a white marble dome containing an amphitheater designed to hold one thousand delegates.

From Roslyn's research, it currently held a little under half that number, but the planet's founders had believed in future-proofing. There was an entire block of less decorative, if still gorgeous, office buildings next to the Asamblea to hold the working spaces of the Diputados and Senadores— and enough space was kept clear to allow for *another* full block of office buildings to be built while keeping most of the landscaped grounds.

El Domo de la Asamblea was "merely" the place the Asamblea held their formal meetings, which meant it was where they would meet the Mage-Admiral demanding their surrender.

While the Domo clearly had spots for security and armed guards, they were empty today as Alexander's vehicle drove up to the entrance. A massive grand promenade in front of the Domo was paved in white concrete, clearly intended for parades similar to the one gathered on it.

Alexander and Roslyn walked down an aisle of tanks and exosuits, the Protectorate troops deathly silent as the Royal Guards and their charges approached the Asamblea Domo.

A single white-suited woman stood in front of the doors, holding a ceremonial staff. She tolerated the Royal Guard who stepped up to her with a scanner with decent grace before bowing slightly to Alexander.

"Mage-Admiral Jane Alexander? I am Monica Peron, the President of la Cámara de Senadores de Nueva Bolivia," she said in a fluid mix of English and Spanish. "It is my task to greet you and present you to the Asamblea Legislativa."

Peron studied the entourage that surrounded Alexander, then apparently decided to ignore Roslyn and the Royal Guards alike.

"If you will follow me, please, Mage-Admiral."

"Of course, Señora Peron," Alexander replied.

Peron turned on her heel and knocked on the large marble doors with her eagle-headed staff. For a moment, that seemed purely ceremonial, and then the stone doors silently slid open, driven by concealed motors.

The President of la Cámara de Senadores de Nueva Bolivia—the President of the Chamber of Senators of Nueva Bolivia—led the way through the doors. There was a large antechamber on the other side, presumably normally full of security equipment and milling crowds but today reduced to empty marble.

At the other end of the antechamber, Peron knocked on another set of double doors. They opened smoothly as well, and the woman in white led the way into the main hall of the dome.

They descended down the steps in absolute silence, the red armor of the thirty Royal Guards a sharp contrast to the pure white marble of the steps.

There was, at least, more color than that here. Each deputy and senator sat behind a desk hung with a brilliantly colored tapestry showing their region of the planet. All of those delegates were silent as Roslyn accompanied Alexander to the dais at the center of the amphitheater.

The Royal Guards split off as they reached the center, most of them forming a firm red line between the Asamblea Legislativa and the Crown Princess of Mars. Von Sulzbach and a team of three accompanied Roslyn and Alexander onto the stage, falling into a rough line behind the two women as Alexander turned to face her audience.

"Senadores y Diputados de la Asamblea Legislativa, I present to you Mage-Admiral Jane Alexander, la Princesa Heredera de la Protectorado de Marte."

Roslyn wasn't sure if the silence that answered had been the Asamblea's plan or if they were intimidated by the presence of the exosuited Royal Guards and the Protectorate Guard Regiment outside.

Alexander certainly didn't seem bothered by the silence, returning it in kind for at least ten seconds as she studied the Asamblea.

"So?" she finally said loudly. No one had handed her a microphone, but her voice was clearly projected electronically to the farthest reaches of the space. "Your Governor asked me to come here and address you. Like him, you appear to think that sheer stubbornness can change reality.

"What do you expect me to say?" she asked. "Well? You asked me to be here."

Only silence answered her, and Alexander smiled thinly.

"Well, then. I am here because you have refused to validate the surrender terms signed by your Governor and there is some legal question around whether those terms are binding without that validation," she reminded them. "So, I will be blunt: regardless of whether this Asamblea decides to validate the exact terms of Nueva Bolivia's surrender, Nueva Bolivia *has* surrendered."

Roslyn concealed a shiver at the iciness of Alexander's tone. She'd been Crown Princess before she'd been a Navy officer, and she'd been a Navy officer for longer than Roslyn had been alive. The Mage-Admiral knew how to wield her tone like a knife.

"The terms I agreed to with Governor Hans South Isle allow Nueva Bolivia to retain self-government within the confines of our military occupation. Those terms include respecting the authority and independence of this body.

"If this body does not validate those terms, I have no need to respect your authority or independence," Alexander said bluntly. "If you refuse to accept the surrender, then I will treat you as if you had not surrendered. You will make no grand gestures and you will not be martyrs. You will be ignored.

"Under the terms I have agreed to, you will continue as the elected government of your people. If those terms are rejected, then I will move to a new set of terms that only acknowledge Governor South Isle's authority."

She spread her hands.

"I would prefer not to do that," she told them. "It is and always has been the preference of the Protectorate and the Royal Family of Mars to encourage democracy—outside, of course, replacing *ourselves*.

"But if you attempt to force my hand, you will not like the tools I reach for," she concluded.

There was quiet conversation in the room now, but no one dared to shout disagreement.

"I understand that there has not yet been a conclusive vote, as the Asamblea continues to drag this out," Alexander said. "I suggest you have that vote."

With a firm nod to Peron, the Mage-Admiral stepped forward to the edge of the stage. Roslyn kept step with her and spotted the moment Alexander stumbled, her right leg giving way to some invisible weakness.

She couldn't visibly prop up the Crown Princess of Mars in front of their enemies, but she *could* do something. Magic wove under Roslyn's fingers, catching Alexander before the Admiral could do more than stumble.

Alexander kept walking as if nothing had happened, and Roslyn followed, trying to hide her concern. She'd occasionally worried over the Mage-Admiral's age, but that was the first sign of any physical weakness she'd ever seen from Alexander.

And with all of the care and medicine available to her, Jane Alexander should have the health of a woman half her age...

CHAPTER 17

"I'M FINE," Alexander hissed as they left the Asamblea Domo behind them and Roslyn stepped in to check on her. "I tripped, that's all. Thank you for the save, Lieutenant. It was appreciated."

Roslyn blinked in surprise. *She* wouldn't have been able to tell which of the Mages around her had caught her in Alexander's place. The Mage-Admiral's secrets clearly included things she hadn't realized.

"It seemed the Lieutenant had things in hand," von Sulzbach murmured. "Are you certain you're okay, sir?" he asked. "We should get you back to the vehicle."

"Fine, fine," Alexander confirmed, moving forward determinedly.

Roslyn shared a concerned look with von Sulzbach's helmet. Now that they were back out in natural light, the Admiral looked gray and wan in a way she'd *never* seen before.

They got Alexander into the transport and properly seated, and von Sulzbach produced a bottle of water from inside one of the exosuit's storage compartments.

"This is chilled," he told the Admiral. "Drink. You need it."

Despite her protests of being fine, Alexander took the water without hesitation and gulped down several swallows of it, closing her eyes as the vehicle started to slowly move back toward the shuttleport.

"Thank you, Captain," she said, then took several more swallows. "Of all the days to have caught a bloody cold or whatever the hell this is. Hopefully, I made the right impression before I tried to fall off the stage."

"I think so," Roslyn replied. "Assuming we were trying to scare the crap out of them."

"Basically," the Admiral confirmed with a chuckle that turned into a hacking cough. "Fuck." She shook her head. "I don't really give a shit about local legislators. But the locals do, and that means having them on side will make our lives easier down the road."

Alexander stared at the water bottle in her hand blankly for a moment before she started coughing again.

"Drink," von Sulzbach told her. "Please."

The transport was passing through the Guard Regiment, but they were moving faster than had been planned for. No one had *said* anything, but the Royal Guard was clearly rushing to get Alexander back to her ship.

The Admiral took another gulp of water, only to choke on it. She spluttered and coughed, spitting the water back out as she tried to pound her chest. Heavy breathing followed as her face turned even more gray.

"I can breathe," she assured them. "Just went down the wrong pipe. I'm...I'm not fine."

"We're on our way back to the shuttle," Roslyn assured her. "We'll get you back to *Durendal* and our doctors ASAP. You'll be fine."

"Good, good," Alexander said vaguely. "Is...is...my arms hurt. Everything's tight. Everything's..."

Her eyes rolled back in her head and the Mage-Admiral collapsed into her chair.

"*Shit*," von Sulzbach swore. "Chambers, get on a channel to the ship. We're bringing the Admiral in on emergency evac. I think she's having a fucking *heart attack*."

Another compartment on the Royal Guard's armor popped open, and von Sulzbach started pulling out assorted wires and patches before bodily grabbing Alexander and laying her flat on the floor of the vehicle.

He tore open her uniform tunic and started applying the wires and patches to Alexander's chest. There was a definite pause as both he and Roslyn tried to guess how to apply them around the whirling silver rune inlaid into the Admiral's upper chest.

"*Durendal* control, this is Mage-Lieutenant Chambers," she said into her wrist-comp once she had a channel open. "We have a medical emergency. Admiral Alexander appears to be having a heart attack. We're heading back to the shuttle at maximum speed and preparing for emergency liftoff. Have a med-team standing by in the shuttle bay."

"I've contacted the shuttle," the driver told her as she closed the channel. "They'll be ready for takeoff as soon as we get there." Roslyn heard the woman swallow grimly. "They're rushing the checklist, but we triple-safetied that shuttle last night; it'll be fine."

The patches and wires from von Sulzbach's armor were all hooked up to Alexander now, and Roslyn watched helplessly as the Royal Guard worked. He pulled a syringe of something from inside his armor and injected it into Alexander's neck before laying an armored gauntlet on the Admiral's chest.

The exosuit commenced CPR, moving von Sulzbach's hand automatically to apply and release carefully calibrated pressure every second.

Roslyn's focus was on her Admiral. She barely noticed the exosuits closing in protectively around the transport as they approached. She *did* notice the extra Royal Guard who stepped up into the vehicle—that had to be their medic.

She was surprised when von Sulzbach put his helmet back up, though he kept the hand on Alexander's chest. For a few seconds, everyone around her was either unconscious or helmeted, leaving her completely isolated.

Then they were in the shadow of the heavy lander and heading for the assault shuttle. With a launch anticipated, the Guard troopers they'd left behind had scattered, leaving the pad completely empty when Roslyn glanced up.

They were good to go...except that the shuttle ramp wasn't down. She'd assumed they were going to drive the truck onto the shuttle.

She was staring at that when an armored bubble rose out of concealed compartments around the truck, covering the passengers entirely as they drove *under* the assault shuttle—and the shuttle's engines came online.

Fire hammered down around them, the noise of the engines deafening and stunning Roslyn even as she stared at the lifting shuttle in confusion.

The prick of a hypodermic at the base of *her* neck finally snapped her out of her confusion as the impossible truth sunk home. They'd been betrayed.

The syringe was still stuck in her neck as she tried to smash away the hand of the person injecting her, but her hands only hit ceramic and metal. It was the Royal Guard medic who'd boarded as they approached the shuttleport.

She lunged away from the hands, trying to get her hands onto Alexander and teleport them clear, but she fell to one knee instead of moving across the car. Looking up at the faceless armor suits around her, Roslyn gave in to her rage and channeled magic to blast the traitors away.

And her power didn't answer.

For the first time since she'd been a child, she reached for magic and there was nothing there. That shock held her in place long enough for the second effect of the drug to take effect.

The world went black.

CHAPTER 18

"ALL RIGHT, EVERYBODY," Shvets announced cheerfully as the stars stabilized on the viewscreens of *Rhapsody in Purple*'s bridge. "I won't say welcome home, because *fuck* this place, but welcome back to Legatus and friendly skies."

There were a lot fewer warships in those friendly skies than there had been when they left, Kelly noted. At least there was still a dreadnought orbiting Legatus itself, a reliable statement of ownership and control.

Kelly could imagine the Republic managing to steal Martian cruisers and destroyers, or maybe even rig up reasonable facsimiles of them. The new dreadnoughts, though, were far larger than anything the Republic had built.

"Set our course for the dreadnought," she ordered Shvets. "Any sign of the other stealth ships?"

"I'm picking up at least one *Rhapsody* flying in formation with the dreadnought—looks like it's *Mjolnir*," Milhouse reported. "Might be a second one, but we aren't exactly easy to pick out even when we aren't being sneaky."

"That's the point, I suppose," Kelly agreed. "Ping our friend over there and find out which one it is. *Rhapsody in Yellow* and *Rhapsody in Bronze* should either be here or arriving shortly."

She coughed.

"They should both be here, in fact," she admitted. "We ran a bit over schedule, what with all of the dodging gunships."

"Where are we supposed to be checking in?" her husband asked, the shuttle pilot sitting in one of the bridge observer seats. "It's not like there's an MISS office around here."

"First step is check in with the Navy and our compatriots," Kelly replied. "We upload all of our data to the RMN and download all of the recent data from them and the other *Rhapsodies*. Then everybody goes through the compiled data on their own and we compare conclusions.

"Should only take a day or two, and then Mage-Admiral Alexander decides where she's going to go pick a fight."

"Once we tell her what we've found, anyway," Shvets said. "If most of Second Fleet has moved on somewhere, I'm presuming the Admiral is with them."

"Agreed," Kelly told them. "But we'll go through the data here. Who knows? MISS may even have sent someone out here to set up operations. We did occupy the capital of our only enemy, after all."

She was expecting to have an actual superior present by now, in fact. If the Martian Interstellar Security Service *hadn't* sent a large and skilled team to Legatus, they were being far more incompetent than she was used to her organization being.

"Ping back from our friends," Milhouse reported. "Both *Yellow* and *Bronze* are here and, yes, that's *Mjolnir* they're hiding under the skirts of. We also have an encrypted package for you; I'm guessing orders."

"I'll decrypt and review in my office," Kelly replied. "Keep an eye on what's out there, people. Legatus might be occupied, but if the Republic is going to do something clever, they're going to do it here."

"Eyes are open," Milhouse promised. "Anything sneaks up on us, I'm launching Shvets at them. They've got to be at *least* as lethal as any missile we have!"

Three different passwords, a thumbprint, and a retinal scan later, the data package sent over to *Rhapsody in Purple* finally decrypted for Kelly. It was roughly what she expected: a canned video file probably recorded as soon as *Rhapsody* had been detected.

They were still almost a light-minute out, so a recorded message was the only reasonable method of communication.

The older woman who appeared on her wallscreen wasn't familiar to Kelly herself, though the covert ops ship captain definitely recognized the type. The woman had dark hair and flat gray eyes, with the tight wrinkles of someone who rarely smiled, and wore a perfectly fitted conservative blue suit.

"Captain LaMonte, I am Regional Director Gry Peyton," the senior spy told her. "I have assumed operational authority for all MISS operations in the occupied territories of the Republic, including mission control for your scouting sweeps.

"We have full scan results from *Rhapsody in Bronze* and *Rhapsody in Yellow*. I look forward to adding the data from *Rhapsody in Purple*'s sweep, though I have to admit I hope you were more successful than they were.

"Our enemy continues to elude us, and the information we are finding here on Legatus is proving of surprisingly limited value." Peyton shook her head. "Once you are in formation with *Mjolnir*, you'll send the Navy the downloads from this mission.

"That was already agreed to. Any further data transfers to the military will go through my team. It shouldn't add much of a delay, but it'll help us keep a handle on the information. We do, after all, know that the RMN was badly penetrated by RID operatives prior to the war.

"We can only be so confident that network was fully neutralized."

Peyton paused thoughtfully, then shrugged.

"Once you've sent your data to the Navy, my team will set up a meeting with all three of the *Rhapsody* Captains," she told Kelly. "Perhaps if we put our heads together, we might actually come up with some answers as to what the hell our enemy has been up to."

The recording ended and Kelly sighed. Of *course* the addition of MISS bureaucracy there would result in a pissing match with the Navy. She was prepared to bet a good chunk of money that Peyton hadn't put *that* rule in place until after Alexander had left the system.

Mage-Admiral Tarpinian was no pushover, but he wasn't the Crown Princess of Mars.

CHAPTER 19

THE OFFICE BUILDING that Peyton had taken over was close enough to the spaceport that Kelly didn't even need to take a car. She and the other two *Rhapsody* Captains were able to walk over to the building—escorted by Royal Martian Marines, of course.

Kelly doubted it was an accident that the MISS wasn't using Protectorate Guard troops for their own security. The relationship between the RMMC and the MISS was a long and not-entirely-friendly one, but MISS *knew* the Marines.

They didn't know the Guard, so they were sticking with the devil they knew.

The other two *Rhapsody* captains weren't complete strangers to her, but she hadn't met Captains Cynwrig Riber or Nekessa Hull in person before. It was a quiet walk across the shuttleport, as none of the three of them really knew what to say.

New bosses tended to have that effect in the intelligence community. A spy never knew just what standard of need-to-know the new superior was going to apply, after all.

They were ushered into the building by a pair of armed young women in unmarked fatigues and hustled quickly upstairs to Peyton's office, clearly being kept from slowing down enough to get an impression of the space.

Peyton's office was on the top floor and had an admirable view of New Rome, Legatus's capital city. The blue-suited regional director was standing by the window, examining the city, as her three Captains were ushered in.

"Welcome to Legatus itself, Captains," Peyton told them without turning around. "The heart of the beast, or so we thought."

"Director?" Riber asked, the tall and freckled Sherwood native's voice a rumbling baritone.

"The Navy assumed that once we controlled Legatus, that was the end of the war," Peyton said. "No one is entirely surprised that was wrong, but it was a nice hope. We at the Agency, however, assumed that the capital would be a mother lode of intelligence either way."

The director trailed off, looking out over the planet, then sighed.

"We were wrong," she said flatly. "I'm not sure if we're looking at the results of an extraordinarily competent cleanup operation or if the Republic never truly ran their covert operations out of Legatus, but there has proven to be very little here of value."

"LMID definitely operated out of here, didn't they?" Kelly asked. "They certainly did when I was running into them before the war."

"The *Legatus* Military Intelligence Directorate always operated out of Legatus, yes," Peyton confirmed. "While there was a decent job of sweeping their files, we have enough information from voluntary assets to piece together most of what LMID was involved in.

"That has left enough gaps, even prior to the war, for us to realize that the *Republic* Intelligence Directorate, by one name or another, predated the Republic itself. And their operations, my friends, were never run from Legatus."

"From where, then?" Hull asked.

"We don't know." Peyton's words hung in the air of the office. "Just like we don't know where the Republic's fallback governance facility is. We have now, thanks to you three, scouted every inhabited Republic system. We have found no fallback facilities, no accelerator rings, nothing.

"The RID could be based out of an office complex on any world, unfortunately," she continued. "Most likely, though, they are based in the continuity facility."

"I'd hoped one of the other ships had found it," Kelly admitted. "We found valuable targets but nothing like that."

"And from my quick review of your data, you found more useful targets than Captain Riber or Captain Hull," Peyton replied. "A Prometheus facility is a priority one target. That data will be sent to Mage-Admiral Alexander and the fleet within the next twenty-four hours.

"We need to assess our next steps. Our assumption that the continuity facility and the Navy's theoretical second accelerator ring had to be in an inhabited system—an accelerator ring, after all, is something close to five million person-years of construction labor.

"And yet...that assumption appears to be incorrect."

"So, we start sweeping uninhabited systems," Riber suggested. "Starting with the ones close to Legatus. That facility exists, after all. We know Lord Protector Solace went somewhere."

"The existence of the governance fallback facility and the backup accelerator ring are conjecture and guesswork," Peyton replied. "It is possible, after all, that Solace simply retreated to one of the Republic MidWorlds and has set up in an office building there.

"The depth and completeness of the cleanup operation, though, leaves me in agreement that this was a prepared operation." She shook her head. "I do not like the trust we have been asked to place in our source for the existence of the continuity facility, but the evidence supports his claim.

"Which means we need to find it."

The *source* in question, Kelly knew, was Governor James Niska himself. It seemed that MISS was less enthused with the trust placed in the defector than others. *She*, however, had transported Montgomery and Niska on their search for answers through the Republic.

She trusted Niska. They had history before that, too, back when she and Montgomery had been flying on the same civilian freighter. They'd been on the run and had ended up working for LMID for a while, delivering gunships.

Her eyes narrowed as she remembered that mission.

"Sir, a somewhat random question that may be related," she said slowly. "I haven't heard anything about Chrysanthemum. I thought they were part of all of this?"

"Chrysanthemum is one of our three loyal children," Peyton told her. "Three of the UnArcana Worlds did not join the Secession. They remain loyal members of the Protectorate."

"Have we scouted them, Director?" Kelly asked. "I know that Chrysanthemum, for example, was under a massive amount of pressure from Legatus seven to eight years ago. They might well be running a deception."

"MISS does not believe so," Peyton replied. "If there was an accelerator ring at Chrysanthemum, Captain, we would know. Ships visit that system once a month."

"Civilian ships wouldn't be in the right place or have the right sensors to see a ring," Kelly pointed out. "Have they been scouted by military ships?"

There was a long pause.

"We can't, Captain," the Director said flatly. "Three of the UnArcana Worlds have stayed loyal. We cannot afford to have them join the Republic, which means we cannot make them think that we distrust them. Blatantly scouting their space would be a stressor we cannot risk on that relationship right now—especially when more covert operations have already given us a reasonable certainty that there are no major Republic presences in their space."

Kelly started to argue, then shut herself down. It didn't sound like she was going to win that argument today...but she was going to have to think about it.

She also realized that she needed to see if she could steal a planetary military governor for a "friendly" dinner.

Peyton might not trust James Niska, but Kelly LaMonte *did*.

CHAPTER 20

NISKA, KELLY NOTED, made no attempt to pretend he was any-thing *but* a servant of a foreign occupier. Some people in his position would have made a show of having Legatan security and aides, doing their dealings with the Protectorate behind a curtain.

The Military Governor of Legatus made no such pretense. The Protectorate had left most of the sub-planetary government intact, but the final buck stopped in the office of a man who worked for Mars. There were Royal Martian Marines guarding the entrances to the squat sub-urban office building Kelly and Xi Wu approached.

"Captain LaMonte?" one of the Marines greeted them with a glance at the civilian car behind them. "I'll have one of my people check in on your driver and handle the car."

"If you could take over for the driver, that would be helpful," Kelly told them. "He *is* our husband and has also met Niska."

"Of course, the Governor did say there would be three of you," the Marine noncom confirmed. "I'm Sergeant Albright. You have clearance into the office, but you'll need an escort. I hope that's acceptable?"

"The Governor is in charge of a planet, many of whom would call him very ugly names," Kelly agreed with a cheerful tone. "An escort is fine, Sergeant."

One of the Marines walked over to the car and had a conversation with Mike Kelzin that Kelly couldn't hear. A moment later, her husband exited the car and crossed to join them.

"If I can't trust Marines, who can I trust?" he told Kelly with a shrug. "We know what's going on yet?"

"The Sergeant says we need a guide and escort," she told him. "Apparently, we want to keep our grumpy old cyborg alive."

It would have been unprofessional for the guard to respond to that statement in any way, but there was a twinkle in Albright's eye as he gestured one of his Marines over. This team wore medium body armor and carried standard battle rifles, but Kelly assumed there were exosuited soldiers with penetrator rifles around somewhere.

"That was Lord Montgomery's order, yes," Albright finally said. "Private Nibhanupudi will guide you to the room we have set up as a dining room. We do try to keep the Governor inside secured spaces as much as possible."

He paused.

"As you suggest, Captain, people *have* attempted to assassinate him. We need to be careful."

"Of course," Kelly agreed. "Lead the way, Private. I'm looking forward to this lunch."

Niska was late.

That wasn't really a surprise, though the steward who'd laid out the food looked slightly less impressed. Whoever had *prepared* the food, though, had clearly anticipated it as much as Kelly had. The platters of sandwiches and finger food had never been intended to be kept hot.

When the Governor finally entered the room, he was answering someone's question as he stepped through the door.

"I *know* what Mayor Fox thinks," he told whoever he was speaking to. "So, tell her that Silverwood is getting the exact same allowance of the water from the DeLeone dam that they've received for the last hundred years.

"Being occupied by Mars does not magically make the river produce more damn water!"

Kelly heard a muffled acknowledgement, and then the door swung shut and Niska turned to her.

"Apologies, Captain LaMonte, Mage Wu, Pilot Kelzin," he said. "When Montgomery browbeat me into this job, I was expecting more armed sedition and less resource-rights discussion."

He gestured toward the table.

"Please, be seated, eat," he told them. "That's *my* plan, anyway."

The Governor took a seat and grabbed a sandwich. The gray-haired Legatan was showing his age more than he ever had before, in Kelly's opinion, but he still moved with the grace of a mechanical tiger.

Being more than fifty percent machine by mass likely had something to do with it. Kelly wasn't entirely sure what level of cybernetics went into making someone a covert combat Augment, but she suspected Niska was about as augmented as a human being could get.

Presumably, that helped with getting old, even if it wasn't an option most would consider.

Kelly grabbed a carafe and poured four coffees before taking a sandwich of her own.

"I'd wondered why you'd taken this job," she admitted. "From what you said when you were on *Rhapsody*, I was expecting you to go for a quiet retirement."

"After all I did for this world and everything the Republic became, well..." He sighed. "That was my plan. But Montgomery was right that Legatus needed someone who knew us—but also someone who knew how far we'd fallen in our pursuit of freedom and equality."

"And now resource rights?" Kelly asked with a grin.

"Resource rights," Niska agreed.

"I'm guessing the armed sedition isn't entirely absent, is it?" Kelzin asked.

"No," the Governor admitted. "But it's quieter than I'd dared hope. I..." He shook his head. "It stinks, to be frank, but you knew that. There's too many things going on that suggest the Republic *expected* to lose Legatus."

"Or planned for it, at least," Kelly agreed quietly. "I can't tell you too much about what MISS is seeing, but I can tell you that we're looking at an amazingly complete cleanup job."

"I'm seeing the same thing in the government files," Niska told her. "Your new boss isn't talking to me, but the initial MISS teams did. My government was prepared to lose our homeworld.

"It's probably too strong to say they expected to," he admitted. "But they were *prepared* to. And there's nothing on any of that in the files here." He shook his head. "The more this goes on, the more I begin to realize that the LMID I served was only one organization of several using our name as a cover."

"That ties back to what I wanted to talk to you about," Kelly said, squeezing Xi Wu's hand under the table as the Mage touched her knee. "Do you remember Chrysanthemum?"

"Vividly, Captain LaMonte," he told her. "You spent a day there. I spent four months."

"With everything Legatus invested in them, they didn't secede," she said. "Do you know why?"

"No," he said slowly. "We invested a lot in all of the UnArcana Fringe Worlds. That was how we kept them more loyal to our concepts and ideals than to the reality of Martian power. We had to provide more help than Mars did—and Mars was often willing to provide a lot of help to those not too proud to take it.

"Chrysanthemum was too proud to take Martian aid. Almost too proud to take ours, but..." Niska was silent for a few seconds. "They took it, but yeah. Chrysanthemum. Alignment. New Madagascar.

"Three worlds didn't follow us into secession...and the Republic, from what I can tell, took that far more calmly than I would have expected."

"Would you trust them?" Kelly asked bluntly. "MISS doesn't want to provoke them, but if Legatus was funneling resources into them..."

"Trust them? No," Niska told them. "I wouldn't trust anyone right now. But, so far as I know, Legatus didn't send enough resources to any of those star systems to build an accelerator ring. The continuity base for the government might be in one of them, I suppose, but an anti-matter-production facility would take decades to build."

"I'm guessing you don't have any idea where they did build it?" Kelly asked.

"If I did, there'd already be a fleet there," he admitted. "My first loyalty is still to Legatus, Captain, but the best way I see to protect my people and my world is to end this damn war."

"I understand," Kelly said. "I think everyone's on that page around here these days."

"I hope so," he told her. "Because I'm worried that there isn't *enough* resistance—because that means that they're building up resources and preparing to help retake the world when the Republic comes back.

"Some of that might be wishful thinking—but if the people running the underground resistance here are more aware of what's going on than I am, they might well have everything from a plan to a *date*."

The Military Governor shook his head.

"I thought I knew my Republic, Captain LaMonte, but the more I poke at curtains, the more I wonder what kind of chimeric monster we truly created."

CHAPTER 21

ROSLYN WOKE UP slowly, groggily. Everything felt vaguely wrong, like she was submerged in water, and she gasped for air.

"Careful, careful!" someone snapped. "We had her under for *days*, people; watch your dosages."

That made no sense to her...and then the memory of what had happened on Sucre came crashing back in. Her eyes snapped open and she tried to move.

Nothing happened. She realized after a moment that her legs and arms were restrained, locked down in some kind of manacles, but that wasn't the problem.

"You're awake, good," an unfamiliar female voice told her. "The paralytic effects will fade, Lieutenant," the voice continued. "It's useful for us at the moment, but you will recover completely."

Roslyn tried to pull on magic to see if she could at least free herself. Unlike the vague memories of her failure on Sucre, she could feel it start to warm in her chest...only to be sucked away by a chill drain around her wrists and ankles.

Mage-cuffs. She'd been bound with Mage-cuffs, the silver-and-steel runic artifacts used to restrain criminal Mages and drain away their power.

"Rest, Lieutenant Chambers," the woman told her. "You've been unconscious for eighty-three hours."

A sealed bulb with a straw emerged into her view, held in a delicately long-fingered hand. The straw was put to her lips, and she found that she had enough control to suck on the straw desperately.

"I'm not going to tell you where you are," the stranger said calmly. "You are a prisoner of war now. As your doctor, I have responsibilities to you, but I am still your captor."

If Roslyn hadn't been manacled to a bed, the world would have fallen out from beneath her. It added up, but what the *hell* was going on?

She focused as best as she could against the fog still claiming her mind. The ceiling above her was painted white, but she recognized the paneling. Most spaces in a starship had open ceilings with exposed systems for easy access.

One of the places that didn't was the medbay, where white-painted metal panels were placed to seal away those systems to help maintain a sterile environment. She was in the sickbay of a spaceship.

She'd been kidnapped by the Royal Guard of the Mage-King of Mars. That didn't make any damn sense.

"Is she awake?" a more familiar voice asked. Von Sulzbach. The traitor.

"She's awake and her vitals just spiked hard when she recognized your voice," the doctor replied. "I don't think you've made many friends, boss."

"We weren't here to make friends. Can she move yet?"

Roslyn tried to flex her fingers and toes. There was a bit of movement but nothing useful.

"The paralytic post-effect scales to how long she was kept at a dose of that sedative," the doctor replied. "It'll be an hour or two before she can move at all."

"Sit her up, then," von Sulzbach ordered.

The bed moved underneath Roslyn, slowly folding to bring her into a sitting position. For the first time since he'd boarded *Durendal*, she saw the supposed Royal Guard without an exosuit.

Without the armor, he was a slimly built man with well-defined muscles easily visible through the tight-fitting shipsuit he wore. Combined with the dark hair and deep brown eyes she'd always seen; she could very easily find him attractive.

Except.

"Traitor," she managed to grind out.

"No," von Sulzbach told her as he stepped up in front of her bed. "There is a long list of epithets you can throw at me that *are* true, but that one is not. If for no other reason than because Mario von Sulzbach is dead."

He waved a hand over himself.

"We inserted my biometrics into the files on the Royal Guard transport, but thankfully, von Sulzbach was close enough in appearance to me that it only took a *little* surgery to match me up.

"We weren't so lucky with the rest of the team. I never really expected it to work, but I underestimated how much trust the Royal Guard had."

She stared at him in growing horror.

"You're not Royal Guards."

"No," he confirmed. "We were so damned lucky that my people were never expected to use magic when I wasn't around. The information I had from Dr. Finley suggested that the Royal Guard armor would conceal our lack of magic from Alexander's Sight, but with one Mage where we should have had thirty..."

"You...killed thirty Guards."

"Yes," he confirmed, his tone completely unbothered. "Mages always think they're immortal and invulnerable. And then you poison them and they die like writhing insects." He shrugged.

"Unfortunately, we'll need to keep you in Mage-cuffs for now," he continued. "The good doctor strongly recommended against maintaining the dosages necessary to keep your gift out of commission."

"I can discharge her to the cell in about three hours, I think," the doctor told him. "Until then, well, you're spiking her heart rate something fierce."

"Von Sulzbach" grinned.

"Somehow, I don't think that's because I'm pretty," he said. "Though I know I was managing that when you thought I was a Guard."

He leaned in and touched the side of her face. Despite her best efforts, Roslyn was unable to flinch away.

"Since it's unlikely to matter, my name is Connor ad Aaron," he told her. "And you, Mage-Lieutenant Roslyn Chambers, are now a prisoner of the Republic of Faith and Reason."

Unlike ad Aaron, the doctor never gave Roslyn a name. She spent three hours poking and prodding the Mage as various limbs woke up, leaving Roslyn with an unbelievably bad case of pins and needles.

Eventually, Roslyn was able to shuffle across the room with her ankles manacled together, and the doctor called that good enough. The woman tapped a command on her wrist-comp.

"Chambers can move under her own power. Can you get someone down here to move her?"

Pause. Roslyn couldn't hear the other side of the conversation. It was quite possibly going to an implant in the woman's head.

"You know what my priority is. I could barely spare these hours."

Another unheard response and the doctor snorted.

"Fine. Five minutes."

She turned back to Roslyn and carefully forced the young woman back onto the bed. The strength concealed in the blonde woman's slender frame suggested more implants.

Was everyone on this ship an Augment? Which damn ship *was* she on?

Ad Aaron had implied he was a Mage, so it was possibly a traditional jump-ship. That raised the question of just what a *Mage* was doing working for what was clearly a Republic Intelligence Directorate operation.

The doctor stood by the bed, watching Roslyn carefully until the door to the infirmary opened up and two men in plain black shipsuits stepped in. Both were armed, Roslyn noted as she was dragged to her feet by the doctor.

Their weapons at least had under-barrel stunguns, weapons that would fire intelligent SmartDarts that would shock her unconscious with a calibrated electric jolt. They were *probably* more likely to use the SmartDarts than shoot her with real bullets.

Probably.

"You know the orders," the doctor told them. "We're to deliver her intact. None of your damn games."

"On a prisoner of war?" one of the soldiers asked in mock horror. "We'd never dream of it."

Each of the men grabbed one of Roslyn's arms. Both of them were also quite blatantly examining her body through the gown she was wearing. She hadn't registered the flimsiness of the garment until that moment, but she was suddenly *very* aware how thin the fabric was.

"Now I can get back to the main damn problem," the doctor said. She paused for a moment, then shrugged. "May as well show her," she noted. "Bring her this way."

Roslyn was roughly hauled across the sickbay to a closed intensive-care chamber. The doctor opened an observation window that had been closed before, allowing Roslyn to look into the room and see its occupant.

Jane Alexander looked old and frail, lying unconscious on the bed, wires and tubes stuck into her at random intervals.

"*You* we can contain with Mage-cuffs," the doctor told her. "Our orders on *her* are that she doesn't wake up until she's delivered into the hands of people far more aware of her abilities than I am. Keeping her alive is my main job now."

The Republican woman shook her head.

"She'll be fine," she told Roslyn. "So long as *you* don't cause trouble, I suspect."

"Come on, girl," the soldier holding her right arm told her. "We've got a nice cold cell waiting for you."

"We can certainly help you get warm once you're there," the other soldier told her with a leer in his voice. "But like the doctor said, you're gonna have to *ask* for it."

Roslyn was reasonably sure both men had been guarding her and Alexander's quarters in Royal Guard armor for the last week—and if she could have gnawed her own arms off to escape their touch, she would have!

CHAPTER 22

"MY LORD, we're receiving an emergency communication request for you through the Link."

Moxi Waller rejoiced in the plain job title of "secretary," a descriptor that did not begin to suggest the pay scale she worked at, the importance of her role, or the power wielded by the woman who managed the communications of the Lord Regent of Mars.

"From Legatus?" Damien Montgomery asked. The young man behind the massive desk still felt dwarfed by both the room he'd inherited from the Mage-King of Mars and the role he'd been called to.

"I don't know anywhere else that we've got Links we're willing to trust," Waller pointed out to her boss. "I thought we weren't willing to directly connect the Link to our communication network, though."

"We're not, as a rule," Damien said slowly. "If it's urgent enough, though, a live channel might be worth it. What's going on?"

"They didn't say, only that Admiral Tarpinian wanted a direct live channel to you."

Damien sighed.

"You know Her Majesty's schedule better than I do," he told Waller. "Can we get her up here?"

The Lord Regent of Mars ruled the Protectorate *in the name of* the Mage-Queen of Mars. If it was urgent enough that one of their Mage-Admirals wanted to risk hooking an only-partially-understood piece of stolen Legatan technology into the Martian com network, the Mage-Queen should be involved.

"I think so," Waller said slowly.

"Get in touch with her team and get her up here, then," Damien told her. He rose from behind his desk, not that rising added much to his height. The Lord Regent was only a hundred and fifty centimeters tall. He knew perfectly well he'd never dominate any room with his height.

As Waller stepped out, Damien crossed to the window of the office. The room was above the breathable part of the terraformed atmosphere of Mars, looking out from the very peak of Olympus Mons over the city on the slopes of the mountain.

"Computer," he said aloud. "Get me a link to the coms team."

Damien's hands were encased in thin black leather gloves to disguise the level of damage and scarring. An act of desperation prior to the Secession had melted the runes in his hands and forearms and left molten silver to burn its way through his nerves and tendons.

Recovery was a slow process, and voice commands remained his main way of using computers.

"Lord Regent, how can we assist you?" a tech answered his call breathlessly.

"I need a stand-alone communications setup built in the next, oh, five minutes," Damien told them. "I need a clean point-to-point connection to Deimos Research Station that doesn't enter the main Olympus Mons network.

"Can we do it?"

There was a momentary pause.

"We have a few solo transceiver setups that we can link to a stand-alone console," the tech replied. "It might take ten, my lord?"

"I can live with ten. I need it set up in my office for the Mage-Queen and me."

"Of course, Lord Regent. May I?"

"Thank you, Morales," Damien told the man.

The tech's name had been on his uniform, but the Lord Regent acknowledging him by name clearly had an effect.

Damien figured he'd get the console in five minutes.

Mage-Admiral Hovo Tarpinian was a square-shouldered man only a few centimeters taller than Damien Montgomery himself. He was clearly of Japanese extraction, with dark skin and folded eyes.

Tired eyes. Even if the request to speak via the Link *without* spending the time to have Damien physically travel to Deimos hadn't told Damien something was wrong, Tarpinian's eyes would have.

"Mage-Admiral, you have myself and Her Majesty here," Damien told the man.

Her Majesty, Mage-Queen Kiera Michelle Alexander of Mars, was a seventeen-year-old redhead. She was seated directly to Damien's right, the two of them facing the screen attached to the mobile console added to the office.

Right now, she was silent. She'd learned to be *very* good at that, Damien reflected. She had an astonishing sense of when the Mage-Queen needed to speak and when the best thing the teenager could do was listen and learn.

"That...is probably best," Tarpinian said slowly. "We have a new crisis on our hands, my lord, Your Majesty. I am the bearer of..."

He swallowed.

"Mage-Admiral Jane Alexander is dead," he said flatly.

Damien was glad he was sitting down. He forced himself to focus on Kiera Alexander, turning to check in on her.

"Kiera?" he asked softly.

She made a *later* gesture, clearly forcing herself to remain composed.

"How, Admiral?" Damien finally asked.

"From what I now know, she was addressing Nueva Bolivia's legislature when she began to feel weak and have some pain," Tarpinian told them. "Her Royal Guard rushed her to her shuttle, but she was unconscious and suffering clear heart attack symptoms by the time they made it there.

"According to Second Fleet's sensor data, it appears that the shuttle crew rushed their checks to make sure that they got the Admiral back aboard *Durendal* in time for proper medical care."

The officer swallowed.

"Something went wrong, and the shuttle came apart in the upper atmosphere," he concluded. "When the courier was sent to inform me of this, the search for debris was ongoing, but they were certain there had been no survivors."

Damien swallowed hard.

"Who else was with her?" he asked slowly.

"Thirty members of the Royal Guard and her Flag Lieutenant, Roslyn Chambers," Tarpinian told them. "I have a list of the dead that will be forwarded along with all of our sensor information.

"We..." Tarpinian trailed off. "My Lord, it is now an open question who commands Second Fleet. Mage-Admiral Marangoz is senior, but he was technically senior to Mage-Admiral Alexander."

"I will review the files of the Mage-Admirals and send orders ASAP," Damien promised, trying to find something he could *do* inside the mess they were facing.

"This is a catastrophe," Tarpinian admitted. "We have acquired some data on valid targets, but we have not located the Republic fallback facilities. Without Admiral Alexander..."

"The Navy will continue," Damien ground out. "Her Majesty and I have full faith in the Admirals of our fleets, Mage-Admiral Tarpinian. This war will not fail simply because one officer, however senior, however high in the line of succession, falls."

The *Protectorate* might be in trouble. They'd gone from a Mage-King with a line of succession three names long to a Mage-Queen with *no* successors.

"Make sure all of the information you have is sent to Deimos Station for them to handle and send safely onward," Damien ordered. "Her Majesty and I will confer with the High Command and pass on further orders.

"For now, I trust our Admirals to act like adults and do their jobs," he told Tarpinian. "I hope my faith in Mage-Admiral Marangoz is not misplaced."

"I do not believe he will fail you, my lord, Your Majesty," the Admiral confirmed. "I will pass on everything I can. And..." The Admiral swallowed. "Your Majesty, may I offer my personal condolences for the loss of your aunt?"

"Thank you, Admiral," Kiera said, her voice very soft. "That will be all."

The channel closed and the office was very quiet.

"Damien?" Kiera continued, her voice still very soft.

"Yes, my Queen?"

"Why is my family cursed?"

She was crying now, and he swallowed any answer as he simply wrapped his ward in the tightest hug he could manage.

CHAPTER 23

DAMIEN HAD SPENT months working alongside Jane Alexander after the Siege of Legatus, and her death was a shock. Once Kiera managed to get herself somewhat composed, he passed her a box of tissues and poked at the desk with his magic.

"It's here somewhere," he muttered. "There!"

A concealed drawer popped open. It wasn't one he'd made much use of, but he'd discovered what Desmond the Third had hidden in it a while before, and it seemed appropriate. The bottle of whisky was older than Damien was—it was older than *Jane Alexander* had been.

Carefully, using magic to support his hands, he put the bottle on the desk. Three tumblers floated over to join the bottle, and he regarded it all levelly.

"Computer, link me to Chancellor Gregory. Maximum priority," he ordered. The room's systems chimed a confirmation and softly burbled as the call connected.

"Gregory," Chancellor Malcolm Gregory, the man who ran many of the day-to-day functions of the Protectorate government, answered.

"Malcolm, I need you in my office now," Damien told the Chancellor. "We need to take stock of the situation."

"Situation?" Gregory asked in the same clipped tones, leaving the Lord Regent to wonder what he'd interrupted.

"Jane's dead," Damien said flatly.

The call was silent for several seconds.

"I'll be right there."

Kiera was still sniffling into tissues, and Damien pulled one to his own eyes with a gesture and a spark of power. He was only vaguely conscious of using magic to open the bottle and pour three generous glasses of the ancient whisky.

The *first* thing he gave the young woman, though, was a glass of water from the sideboard. It floated across the room and landed in front of the Mage-Queen with a soft thud.

"Drink, Kiera," he instructed. "Malcolm's on his way."

She gulped down the water, pausing to swallow a harsh sob.

He took a large swallow of the scotch and shook his head.

"I don't think your family is cursed," he told her. "I think they've just made too many enemies, and *all* of them are coming out of the shadows right now."

The door chimed and Gregory entered a moment later. The Chancellor of the Protectorate was a large man in every sense, with a perpetually befuddled grin that helped people underestimate his deadly-sharp intellect and will.

Damien gestured, and glasses of century-old scotch whisky floated out to the others.

"To Jane Alexander," he toasted. "A friend, a princess, a warrior. She died as she lived: in the service of Mars and all humanity."

"Jane," Gregory replied, taking a swallow of the whisky. "What *is* this?" he asked after a moment.

"The Second Special Royal Reserve," Damien replied. "Laid down in barrels the day Desmond the Third was born, bottled when he was crowned. There are...maybe fifteen bottles left, including this one?"

"I forgot that existed. I guess there was one for Des, too, wasn't there?" Gregory asked.

"The Third Reserve was bottled on Kiera's coronation, but was still only in barrels for twenty years," the Lord Regent agreed. "What a goddamn mess this all is."

"Des" had been Desmond Michael Alexander the Fourth, Kiera's older brother and the heir apparent until he'd died with his father.

They'd been killed when an assassin had rigged their shuttle to explode.

"I don't trust shuttle accidents, for obvious reasons," Damien continued. "Especially not shuttle accidents in Republican space when leaving an occupied world."

"What happened?" Gregory demanded.

"You'll get a copy of the reports Tarpinian forwarded," Damien said. "But basically, Jane had a heart attack after speaking to the Asamblea Legislativa on Sucre. Her Royal Guard contingent rushed her to the shuttle, which did an emergency launch and apparently came apart in the upper atmosphere."

The office was silent. Kiera stood up, holding the whisky tumbler in one hand as she crossed to the window and looked out over the side of the mountain. The tissue box rose into the air behind her, following her across the room like a flying puppy.

"I am so *fucking* sick of people killing my family," she finally said, taking a solid swallow of the whisky. She coughed harshly. "I'm guessing we'll have another empty tomb in the Black Mausoleum?"

The Black Mausoleum was a set of stone tombs built at the base of the Fields of Sorrow. The Mage-Kings of Mars and their family and closest retainers were buried next to the thousands of victims of Project Olympus.

"Most likely," Damien said. "If the shuttle broke up the way Tarpinian describes it, there won't be much left for even the accident analysis."

He held up a hand to forestall any questions.

"We'll send the best we've got," he told them. "The people who put together your father's assassination will be on a ship as soon as we can call them up. But...in Nueva Bolivia, launching from Sucre?

"I think we're safe to assume that Jane Alexander was murdered by the Republic," Damien said grimly. "We'll need to sit down with High Command and decide who should inherit command of Second Fleet, but that just brings us back to one key point:

"This war has to *end*."

"We also need, much as I hate to raise it now, to consider the line of succession," Gregory said quietly. "With Jane dead, there *is* no heir to the Mountain and the Crown."

"We all know that isn't true, Malcolm," Kiera said, still staring out at the city and the planet she ruled. "But we've spent too long dancing around everyone's *fucking* feelings to formalize what should have already been written in stone."

Damien blinked. The only real option he saw was to have the Mountain's medical staff cook up a clone-child of Kiera's. They could definitely *do* that—while not a true clone of her father, Kiera herself was closer to one than a biological child—and Protectorate law was clear on clones as children of their progenitors.

"Unless you've found a boyfriend I don't know about, I still don't see a quick solution," Damien pointed out.

"I don't think I've met anyone less than ten years older than me since my father died," Kiera told him. "We could certainly produce a clone—or even write a will that calls for a clone to be created that inherits—but, as you say, not a quick solution."

"Not as quick as the one we already have to hand."

"I'm sorry, Kiera, I don't follow," Damien admitted.

The Mage-Queen of Mars turned around to study her Lord Regent, meeting Damien's gaze calmly.

"You're not that stupid, Damien Montgomery," she told him. "You're willfully blind sometimes, but you're not that stupid. *A Rune Wright must sit the throne of Olympus Mons.*"

Damien returned her gaze levelly even as his stomach tried to twist itself into knots.

"She's right," Gregory said quietly. "Everyone in the know assumed that if something happened to Jane and Kiera, you would be the next Mage-King. We need to formalize that and officially include you in the line of succession—after Kiera's future children, of course."

"I do not..." Damien trailed off. He wasn't even sure what to argue against. He didn't deserve it? That was irrelevant. He didn't *want* it? Neither did Kiera, really.

"I don't know," he finally said.

"You don't get to argue, Damien. The Protectorate needs this of you," Kiera told him. "You might want to warn Grace about it, though."

Grace McLaughlin was the senior officer of the system militia of Damien's homeworld of Sherwood and the granddaughter of Sherwood's Governor. She was also his girlfriend, for all of the complications of their lives.

"She's supposed to visit in a couple of months," Damien said, trying to wrap his brain around a bombshell everyone *else* had apparently assumed to be the case. "I already knew we were going to have to talk about children." He shook his head. "There are too many people in the Mountain obsessed with preserving the Rune Wright genome to do anything else."

"And rightly so," Gregory reminded him. "If we've lost Jane, we're down to just two of you that we know of. Our magic, the security of Sol, the underlying power of the Protectorate...much depends on having at least one Rune Wright at the heart of Mars."

"You need to be my heir, Damien," Kiera said quietly. "I think we should keep that *quiet*—I think hanging the title of Crown Prince on the Lord Regent will draw eyes and comments—but we need to make it formal and legally binding.

"No matter what happens, Mars must endure. No matter what we lose, a Rune Wright must hold Protectorate over mankind.

"My family bound ourselves to that duty, that there would always be a Mage in the Mountain to guard Sol and command humanity's defense. My great-grandfather might not have known about the dangers beyond our borders, but he suspected *something*.

"The Mage-Kings and Mage-Queens of Mars"—Kiera forced a smirk through her tears—"are humanity's shield. And there must always be a Rune Wright on the throne at Olympus Mons."

"I understand," Damien allowed, bowing his head. "And what do we do about the war?"

"We talk to the High Command, as you said," Gregory agreed. "We pick a commander. My inclination is Marangoz—he is senior—but we should be guided by the officers who know them all.

"And then we finish this war. We know enough about what the Keepers and Nemesis feared, now, that being disunified terrifies me," the Chancellor admitted. "Humanity *must* stand as one."

Damien nodded. The first Mage-King had created a secret order of basically librarians, the Keepers of Oaths and Secrets, who had concealed something from the rest of mankind. They'd been destroyed, both by Damien himself and by the conspiracy known as Nemesis—and Damien had destroyed Nemesis in turn.

They didn't know all of what the Keepers had known, but they did know one thing: there was a space-capable alien race somewhere near human space, one that had played a role in the Eugenicists' rise to power on Mars and Project Olympus itself.

But that was all they knew—that and a name: the Reejit.

And until the Protectorate knew more, Damien had to agree with Gregory. Humanity couldn't afford this war.

CHAPTER 24

"ALL RIGHT, LADIES, gentlemen, and Shvets, what am I looking at?" Kelly LaMonte asked as *Rhapsody in Purple* coasted through space.

"This is the LV-Seven-One-DA System," Shvets replied, smirking at her for her separation of them from the other bridge crew. "According to Protectorate records, there is nothing here. No formally recognized settlements, no claims, no mining outposts, nothing and nada."

Kelly nodded as she swept a critical eye over the displays. Most of the star systems she'd been in over the course of her career were F- and G-class stars, warm yellow and orange suns capable of supporting life.

LV-71-DA was a red giant, a massive star that was flaring off excess flame even as she looked at it. None of its planets had anything resembling life. Even the basic atmosphere had been stripped off the three inner worlds by the flares, leaving nothing but giant airless rocks.

The single super-Jovian gas giant had more promise, with several of its moons easily as large as the system's rocky planets. They even had atmospheres, though none of them were remotely breathable.

Icons were starting to populate around the gas giant as well. Not a lot of them, but there were definitely artificial energy signatures.

"Since I'm seeing heat sources, I'm guessing the Protectorate files are wrong?" she suggested.

"*Republic* records say that a joint Legatus-Mercedes industrial combine laid claim to the system shortly before the Secession and set up operations here," Shvets told her. "On the other hand, that combine didn't appear to have access to jump-ships after the Guild withdrew from Republic space, so who knows what happened after that? Certainly, there are no updates."

"Well, I suppose we can be helpful as well as intrusive," Kelly replied. "Shvets, set a course for planet four. Let's see if there's anything interesting in those rings and moons."

She brought up a closer view of the icons Milhouse was adding to the display and ran through them. Nothing was really standing out to her, though it did look like more than the data they had suggested should be there.

"Milhouse, what are you seeing?" she asked.

"I make it a standard prefab one-kilometer ring station orbiting above the largest planet," the tactical officer told her. "About a dozen small in-system ships, none over two hundred thousand tons. Looks like five secondary stations scattered through the moons, including one that appears to be built on a captured ice comet."

Kelly nodded slowly.

"Water being the fountain of life if you're stranded on your own," she said aloud. "It splits into hydrogen for fusion plants and oxygen to breathe, and the water is needed for crops."

"A one-klick ring station has plenty of space to set up hydroponics if you've got water and decent fabrication gear," Milhouse agreed. "I could see them managing to survive, even if they got cut off."

"An UnArcana World industrial combine had to have at least the chance of losing jump-ship access in the back of their mind, too," Kelly agreed. "All right. This doesn't look like it's a Republic government continuity facility, which means as far as our mission goes, this is a bust.

"On the other hand, I see a possible chance to do some good in the universe. Game faces, people. It's *Dancing Soprano* time."

"Understood," Milhouse replied. "Setting the beacons and inflating the bubbles."

The "bubbles" were a series of inflatable, metal-coated false fronts. To civilian and even most military sensors, they'd ping as if *Rhapsody in Purple* were larger than she was. She was too big to pretend to be a courier without some games and too small to pretend to be a freighter without the inflatable false segments.

"*Dancing Soprano*" was a small fast freighter, designed to haul a hundred and fifty thousand tons of critical cargo as cheaply as possible. A ship of that type was about a third again *Rhapsody*'s size, but with all of the tools in Kelly's arsenal, they could easily fake it.

It took a few seconds for *Rhapsody* to inflate into her new role, but the identity beacon for the ship was in place instantly.

"Energy signatures adjusted, course plotted," Shvets announced. "Your orders, Captain LaMonte?"

"Let's go say hello," she replied. "If these people have been stuck out here for the last two years, they could probably use a friendly face."

"What happens if they try and capture the ship?" Milhouse asked quietly. "If they've been stuck out here for two years..."

"Then Captain Charmchi will convince them of the error of their ways," Kelly said. "Hopefully without hurting them too badly. If the situation here is what we think it is, they're doing well but they've had a rough go of it."

"Freighter *Dancing Soprano*, this is Administrator Nikitha Shamon of the LV-Seven-One-DA Extraction Facility, please respond. I repeat, this is Administrator Nikitha Shamon of the LV-Seven-One-DA Extraction Facility, please respond.

"We are in need of humanitarian assistance and request you help under the laws of open space. Please respond."

The woman's voice echoed on *Rhapsody in Purple*'s bridge, and Kelly felt the tension of her crew.

"Milhouse?" she asked.

"That was a live transmission, but she recorded it and it is repeating," the tactical officer replied. "She sounds...stressed."

"There's only so much we can do," Kelly admitted. "But I think we need to find out what's going on here. Xi, are you ready to get us out if something goes sideways?"

"Of course," her wife replied over the intercom from the simulacrum chamber. "Surely, there's *something* we can do?"

"There's a lot we can do," Kelly replied. "Or that Mike can do, anyway. But we can't bring anyone aboard *Rhapsody*. That limits us."

"Every one of my pilots is at least partially trained as a medic," Kelly's husband pointed out. He was talking to his wrist-comp in the shuttle bay. "We're prepping the shuttles for emergency aid, but it'll be easier if I know what help they need."

"Is that a subtle hint to call them back, my love?" Kelly asked Kelzin.

"No, it wasn't subtle at all," he told her. "We need to know what they need. Worst case, we, what, go back to Legatus and send a Guard transport to handle them?"

"Basically," Kelly agreed. "All right, everybody; sit still and pretend we're actually civilians."

That was part of why *Rhapsody*'s bridge was split in two the way it was. The recorder focusing on Kelly showed a bridge that wouldn't look out of place on the ship they were pretending to be—even if the portion of the bridge *behind* that recorder looked like it belonged on a warship.

"LV-Seven-One-DA Extraction Facility, this is *Dancing Soprano*, Captain Kelly LaMonte speaking," Kelly told the camera. "We were paid to divert here and carry out a quick mineral survey, but it looks like the system has already been claimed.

"We are ready to provide any assistance we can, but we are carrying a hazardous cargo and can't bring people aboard. Please advise of your situation and we will see how we can help you."

Rhapsody was still most of a light-minute from the gas giant, but the distance was evaporating quickly as Shvets burned toward the Extraction Facility at three gravities.

When the repeating recording finally stopped, it was replaced with a video message from Administrator Shamon. She was a dark-skinned woman in a pale lilac shipsuit, her hair knotted into a rough ponytail.

"Captain LaMonte, you have no idea how long it's been since we've seen anyone in this hole of a system," Shamon told her. "Technically, my employers own the mineral rights to this system, but since I haven't heard from them in twenty-two months, I don't know what's going on."

Kelly swallowed. It was entirely possible that these people didn't even know about the Secession, let alone the war.

"We have successfully established hydroponics farming and water extraction to keep ourselves going, but our stocks of medical supplies have run out and we have some kind of influenza mutation running rampant through the crew," Shamon admitted. "Fatalities have been low so far, but we're running down to the wire and too many of our people are flat on their backs.

"If you can spare us *any* medical supplies, we'd be grateful, but we're in desperate need of antivirals and immune boosters. News from the outside world would be appreciated. Our supply shipments just... stopped.

"In theory, I can commit the Locustus Combine to cover any and all costs incurred assisting us, but since I haven't heard from them, I don't know for sure. So, all I can do is beg of you: please help us."

The image froze and Kelly shook her head grimly.

"You get that, Mike?" she asked her husband.

"Yeah," he confirmed. "As it happens, we have about four times the stockpile of what they need that a ship like *Soprano* would have. Do we..." He paused. "We can probably give enough supplies to handle the outbreak, but the ship we're pretending to be wouldn't have them."

"Give them the supplies," Kelly ordered. "I don't think Shamon is going to be asking hard questions. Not least because her only hope of seeing anything *except* that prefab station rests with a Protectorate relief mission!"

Rhapsody carried four shuttles. One of them was a heavy-lift shuttle capable of carrying multiple ten-thousand-ton cargo containers, which wasn't useful for today's task.

The other three could pass for regular personnel shuttles until someone got aboard them. From the inside, the pretense of them *not* being armed assault shuttles was thin at best. Just the missing volume would be a hint to anyone who knew much about shuttles.

But they were the shuttles Mike Kelzin had, and Kelly watched him fly the lead spacecraft over to the space station. Each of the three shuttles was packed with medical supplies of a hundred different descriptions, from antivirals and immune-system boosters to IV bags, gowns and masks.

Influenza mutations were a recurring problem despite humanity's best efforts. *Rhapsody*'s crew knew what Shamon's people needed.

"Anything suspicious?" she asked Milhouse.

"The station is unarmed. They have a meteor-defense system that might manage to scratch the paint on the shuttles," the tactical officer told her. "And I have to emphasize *might*. The only risk I see is that they attempt to storm the shuttles."

"Which we've accounted for," Kelly replied. There were three "crew" aboard each shuttle to help with offloading. All nine of those people were members of Charmchi's company of the Bionic Combat Regiment, and if the locals thought they could overwhelm nine of the best commandos available to the Protectorate Special Operations Command, well.

On the other hand, her *husband* was on the lead shuttle, so Kelly was allowed some concern.

"This is Shuttle One; we have docked," Kelzin's voice reported over the radio. "Welcoming committee appears as expected. I'm going to go meet and greet with the Administrator."

He paused.

"What do I *tell* her?" he asked.

"The truth, about the war at least," Kelly ordered. "The Secession, the Siege, the Promethean Interface. All of that is public knowledge and she deserves to know."

"We can promise to send help regardless of who we're pretending to be, right?" Kelzin asked.

"We can promise to tell people they're in trouble, if nothing else," she agreed. "The Protectorate would never have left them out here this long, but they were in Republic space and we didn't even know about them."

"All right. Heading in. I'll update you shortly."

Kelly watched the icons of Shuttles Two and Three make contact with the space station as well and forced herself to breathe normally.

"I don't think we really need to feel guilty, boss," Shvets pointed out, their eyes darker than usual against their makeup. "Even if we *had* known these folks were here, this was Republic territory. We couldn't really do humanitarian work in Republic space."

"I'd remind you, Shvets, that the first shots of this war were fired when we sent a humanitarian relief convoy to a Republic world," Kelly said quietly. "Neither the Mage-Queen nor her father ever limited their true protectorate to the people who swore fealty.

"*Someone* would have come for these people if we'd known."

"We didn't. And now someone has come for them," her navigator replied. "Us. And we're going to make sure they're okay, right?"

A few commands brought up the video from the shuttle's hatch camera. The BCR commandos were carefully moving pallets of medical supplies, taking advantage of the zero gravity of the docking station at the center of the ring.

Nikitha Shamon was hanging on to a handhold, watching the pallets drift past as she spoke to Mike Kelzin. Kelly couldn't hear the dark-skinned administrator's words, but the woman's body language spoke volumes.

"I do believe we made the Administrator cry, Captain," Milhouse told her, probably watching the same video feed. "I don't think we need to worry about an ambush."

"I just hope she feels as charitable toward us once she realizes we're on the opposite sides of a war," Kelly replied.

"Most likely she was downplaying the outbreak, boss," Shvets said. "Which means those supplies may well mean the difference between life and death for hundreds if not thousands of people she's responsible for."

The navigator shook their head.

"I am a cynic by nature, but even *I* think she's probably going to feel pretty warm and fuzzy about us and the Protectorate after this."

CHAPTER 25

ROSLYN PACED. Five steps. Turn left. Four steps. Turn left. Five steps. Turn left. Four steps.

The cell the Republican agents had put her in had probably started life as a broom closet or something similar. Five steps by seven, but almost half of the width was taken up by the bed that was the only furniture.

They'd unhooked the Mage-cuffs so she could move, but all four of the manacles themselves were still locked against her skin. She could *feel* her magic, but she couldn't reach it. Couldn't command the Gift that was as much a part of her as her legs or her chest.

Five steps. Four steps. Five steps. Four steps. Repeat.

Roslyn had a good sense of time and she'd been awake for two days. Her captors brought her food twice a day and took her to use a bathroom four times a day. All she could really be sure of was that she was on board a jump-ship of some kind.

They were jumping three times a day, which told her that there was only one Mage aboard qualified to jump. She could have doubled the speed of the ship if she'd been helping, but she hadn't been asked and wasn't going to offer.

No one would believe her if she did.

The door slid open without warning and she stopped in her pacing, turning to watch the man who entered with a gaze she knew was more desperate than anything else.

She didn't recognize him. Her understanding was that most of the people aboard the ship had been pretending to be Royal Guards, but other than von Sulzbach—ad Aaron—none of them were Mages, so they'd kept their armor on.

Apparently *without* the Guard armor, they thought Alexander would have been able to identify them as non-Mages. In Roslyn's moments of long-term thought, that was *fascinating* and fit the pattern she was recognizing around both Alexander and Montgomery's power.

"You're not carrying a tray and I don't need to piss," she said bluntly. "What do you want?"

The man chuckled.

"You don't get to ask us those questions, girl," he told her. He held up a length of chain that would link into the manacles on Roslyn's wrists. "You're coming with me. If you cooperate, it'll all be smooth and might even be fun."

Roslyn felt her body tense. She was *intellectually* certain that no one on this ship was going to try and assault her, though the implicit threat was a powerful tool in their arsenal. Her once-victimized emotions, though, had no such certainty.

The Legatan had left the door open behind him, too. She let that fear fill her limbs and turn into anger, the same anger that had left her planetary governor's son smashed into a wall and had fueled an adolescent crime spree after all of the charges both ways from that incident had been dropped.

Magic was her strength, her power, her Gift—but the Royal Martian Navy also expected a certain degree of physical fitness from their officers. They didn't care about weight—probably a good thing for a woman built like Roslyn—but she had to be able to lift a certain amount and run a given distance in a specific time.

And every recruit in the RMN, officer and enlisted alike, was given a solid foundation in unarmed self-defense.

Roslyn was inside the guard's reach before he recognized she was moving. A closed fist hammered into the man's throat while her elbow blocked his attempt to grab her. He stumbled backward, gasping for breath, and she slammed her foot into his right kneecap.

From the complaint her bare foot sent back, the man was an Augment and had armor plating built into his kneecap—but it wasn't enough for one of the most vulnerable parts of the human body. His kneecap dislocated with an audible *pop* and Roslyn hammered her elbow into his stomach.

The Republican folded like tissue paper. He hit the metal floor *hard* and was still.

Roslyn stared down at him for a long second, unsure whether he was breathing—and then decided she didn't care as she knelt and started trying to find the keys to her cuffs. So long as she was manacled, she was vulnerable.

The only things of use the guard had on him were a stun baton and the chain for linking her manacles. No keys, no release cards. Probably even the manacles were linked to a control code the Augment had held in his implants.

Swallowing a curse, Roslyn turned on the stun baton and stepped out into the corridor. If nothing else, she was one of only two conscious people on the ship who could jump it. If she could get to the workshop that was always attached to the simulacrum chamber, the tools there should let her remove the cuffs.

And once she had her magic back and access to the simulacrum, the ship was *hers*.

It didn't take Roslyn long to find a console and try to pull up a map. Not knowing what kind of ship she was on would doom her escape attempt before it even began. In her experience, ships relied on their crews' wrist-comps for most tasks—and this crew appeared to have equivalent hardware in their heads as backup.

Still, the information stations existed, and she tracked one down in the maintenance control hub. Her cell really *had* been a broom closet, one of a set of storage rooms attached to the maintenance center.

The systems were locked down, asking for passwords and identifiers she didn't have, and she cursed as it flashed up an alert from her prodding. She'd known people who would have been able to hack their way into the console, but she wasn't one of them.

Hack into and hotwire an aircar? She could do *that*. A starship console? Not a chance.

And she'd set off an alarm.

Roslyn picked a random direction, hoping it was toward *something* of use, and set off at a jog. She only made it through a few corridors before she ran into her first problem, a crewwoman in unmarked fatigues working on an exposed panel.

She didn't wait for the woman to say anything. As the technician began to stand, Roslyn slammed a knee into her back, pushing her to the ground and pressing the stun baton to her spine.

"I don't want to hurt you," she hissed, "but I will. Simulacrum chamber. Where is it?"

"You're an *idiot*," the woman replied. "You're in deep space with—"

Roslyn triggered the stun baton and felt her captive spasm in pain. She felt more than a bit guilty, but she needed an answer.

"Fine, it won't help you," the Legatan growled. "Stern is back the way you came. So, thirty meters toward the stern and two decks up."

"Thanks," Roslyn hissed. She twisted the stun baton to "intelligent disable" and zapped the woman again.

Feeling guilty as all hell, she left the unconscious technician behind and charged back the way she came, looking for stairs up. The corridor signage was the same as it would have been on any RMN ship, and she found a maintenance shaft just past where she'd started.

That was when she realized she was walking in roughly one gravity and the ship definitely didn't have gravity runes. She tentatively hopped as she opened the shaft, assessing the sideways force, and grimaced.

They were under one gravity of acceleration. So, the ship wasn't big enough for centrifugal gravity and was designed for continual-thrust pseudogravity. That was normal enough—except that it told her that "stern" definitely wasn't in the direction the technician had told her.

The stern of the ship was beneath her, where the engines were burning to provide a semblance of acceleration. If the tech had been fooling with her, then...

This was a mess. Roslyn figured the tech had been minimizing the lies, which meant the simulacrum chamber *was* sternward from her. Which meant she was going down.

Swallowing against her fear, she stepped onto the ladder and began to climb toward the engines. One deck. Two.

Two decks was what the tech had said. Roslyn hesitated, then opened the hatch. There was nothing in the corridor to tell her if she was close to the simulacrum chamber—it would be one of the few spaces that were unlabeled.

She took a guess and headed in the opposite direction from where she'd found the tech, hoping against hope that she'd find the simulacrum chamber before anyone else found her.

Instead, she found ad Aaron. The man stepped out of a door she was about to pass and gestured toward her, freezing her limbs in place with bonds of pure force.

"The advantage of implants," he noted quietly, "is that we don't need klaxons and lights to alert everyone of an escaped prisoner. I figured you'd head for the simulacrum chamber, but you wouldn't have made it much farther in any direction."

Roslyn snarled at him. There wasn't anything *else* she could do as he lifted her off the ground, the cuffs denying her her own magic.

"I understand that the duty of a prisoner is to escape, but I do not have time for this bullshit," ad Aaron told her. "One of my men is now in the infirmary. I'm not overly impressed with an Augment who managed to get taken down by a seventy-kilo kid because he wasn't being careful, but he's still one of mine."

Ad Aaron was now very much in Roslyn's personal space, holding her at his eye level as he glared. Despite the very clear and present physical and magical threat the Mage presented, Roslyn realized that she was at least not expecting him to molest her.

She couldn't say the same about the man she'd put in the infirmary.

"Your man was trying to rape me," she said flatly. "I'm just supposed to take that, am I?"

The corridor was very, *very* quiet.

"You were not supposed to be taken from that section of the ship until we arrived," ad Aaron told her coldly. "I will examine the surveillance. If you're telling the truth, that will not happen again. I promise you that.

"I also promise you that if you *escape* again, you will join your Admiral in an induced coma for the next goddamn week; am I clear?"

"Why don't you just kill me? Stick my brain in a fucking machine and be done with it," Roslyn snapped. She was a *lot* less valuable than Alexander and she was sick to her stomach.

"You're on a list," ad Aaron told her. "I also don't like to kill anyone I don't have to, but people high up have flagged you as a high-value target.

"So, I repeat myself. I can make your life damn uncomfortable if you don't cooperate, so I suggest you *do* cooperate. Am. I. Clear?"

Roslyn forced a nod.

At least she'd learned *something* interesting, too. If they were traveling for another week, then they were a minimum of thirty light-years from Nueva Bolivia. Even that little information would have been useful to the fleet.

Assuming, of course, that Roslyn Chambers had any way to *get* that information to them.

CHAPTER 26

IT WAS QUIET in Kelly's office as she ran through the numbers again. It was a pretty simple equation, really. An accelerator ring required x person-years of work to construct. The LV-71-DA extraction facility represented a large-scale out-system construction endeavor by two UnArcana Worlds and had y people.

An accelerator ring built by a similar operation would take at least z years to build.

The number that fell out was...large. Even if she assumed a larger project than LV-71-DA by a factor of ten, she was still estimating decades of construction time. Even that was ignoring the fact that to build an accelerator ring outside of one of their systems, the Republic would have had to build an entirely new mining infrastructure in that system and provide laborers for that as well.

To have built a second accelerator ring in the time since the Centurion ring had been completed, someone would have needed to relocate *millions* of workers. Highly skilled engineers and deep-space workers, too, not the kind of people that could be bought from the never-sufficiently-damned human trafficking rings.

"*Someone* would have noticed," she said aloud.

"Noticed what?" a soft voice asked from the door. "That you're still up and awake three hours after you should be asleep?"

Kelly looked up and saw Xi Wu standing in her doorway, the Chinese Mage smiling at her.

"I mean, my desire to have you come to bed is at least a *little* selfish," Xi said, "but you should rest."

"I keep looking at the numbers and the data and I keep coming to the same answers," Kelly admitted. "It's not smart, I suppose, but I need an answer, Xi."

Xi crossed the room and kissed Kelly's forehead.

"And what answer are you seeing, my love?" she asked.

"We're scouting empty systems and it's a waste of our time," Kelly said aloud. "The Centurion ring took a hundred thousand workers forty years. To build an accelerator ring in secret in less than half a century..."

She shook her head.

"If we assume the project started twenty years ago, I'm *still* looking at them needing to hide a station with a million people," she concluded. "And we'd have noticed a million deep-space workers going missing."

Xi reached over and turned off the wallscreen. As Kelly looked up at her in mild objection, her wife dropped into her lap and kissed her *very* thoroughly.

"So," Xi said when they came back up for breath. "Train of thought broken. What are you finding in the pieces, Kelly?"

"Give me a moment," Kelly said, thoroughly distracted. She ran her fingers through Xi's lustrously long black hair and smiled softly as her wife leaned into her. "Pieces of my train of thought, huh?"

"You're going in circles. I'm trying to break them," the Mage replied. "That I also get to make out with you to achieve said breaking is a nice benefit."

Kelly laughed and kissed her wife again.

Leaning back in her chair with Xi resting against her, the pieces clicked together.

"They needed somewhere with an infrastructure they could expand and a population they could draft," Kelly murmured. "It *has* to be in an inhabited system. It didn't need to be one with the infrastructure and training, though, depending on how hard they were going to push."

"We checked everywhere," Xi pointed out. "So, if it can't be in an uninhabited system—and I agree with you—and it's not in the Republic, where did they hide it?"

"Six years ago, my ship got dragged into a move by Legatus to reinforce Chrysanthemum's security in exchange for *concessions* that nobody explained to the crew carrying the gunships," Kelly told her. "I spoke to Niska about it recently, and he didn't seem overly sure about what was in the system now."

"But Chrysanthemum is still ours, aren't they?" Xi asked.

"They never seceded," Kelly agreed. "But if I was going to hide my continuity facility, my secret shipyard and my backup antimatter supply, I'd put it where no one was going to look.

"Where better but the territory of the people I expect to fight? Of *course* their fallback system never seceded. We should have paid more damn attention."

"Think you can sell MISS on that?" her wife asked. "Because I'll jump where you ask me to jump, love. Half the senior officers are your spouses, and I think the rest of the crew will follow too.

"If you want us to disobey orders and go to Chrysanthemum..."

"No." Kelly was tempted, but she wasn't going to ruin the careers of a hundred other souls for this. If it was the only way, maybe, but it wasn't.

"No," she repeated. "We're only two jumps from Legatus, Xi. Why turn around when we can complete our official mission...and then I can go over Peyton's head via the Link."

Xi tightened her grip on Kelly.

"The Link is only connected to Mars right now," she murmured. "How far over the director's head are you going?"

"All the way up," Kelly told her wife. "I didn't get the impression the order to leave the unseceded UnArcana Worlds alone came from Peyton. And since I don't know *how* high that order came from, I'm going to call my ex-boyfriend."

There was one more piece she needed before she could run the problem *all* the way up the chain, and it fell into place shortly after they returned to Legatus.

"Captain LaMonte, we've received your data upload," Director Peyton told her. "I'm seeing a critical flag. Did you find the accelerator ring?"

"Negative, Director," Kelly told her boss. "We did, however, find a cutoff industrial operation in desperate need of humanitarian aid and a rescue op. We can pass that off to civilian authorities, but your orders were that all information went through your office."

"They are, yes," Peyton confirmed. "What kind of industrial operation, Captain?"

"They were supposed to be a heavy metal and fissionables refining facility," Kelly replied. "Does it matter? They didn't even know the Republic existed, Director. They need help."

"It doesn't, I suppose," the director said. "I'll make sure my staff passes on the information. We'll have a new set of scouting targets for you in a moment."

"Understood." Kelly agreed. "We'll resupply and stand by."

The call ended and she checked the status report on her screen. The program she'd been uploading along with the call had been fully transmitted. There *shouldn't* have been a problem—the software was attached to one of the handful of one-time codes she still had left from working directly with Damien.

A Hand's symbol of office included software and authorizations that could override any Protectorate computer. It could also generate one-time authorization codes that could do the same thing—and Kelly now had three of Damien's codes left.

The one she'd just used up would open up the entirety of the MISS computer network on Legatus and search for specific keywords and data points. It was a smart program, one she was rather proud of—and it apparently ran *fast*, as the follow-up transmission pinged into her communicator after less than five minutes.

It would probably have taken longer to *ask* for the data—and since she was planning on doing an end run around her superiors, she couldn't really do that.

Chrysanthemum. Alignment. New Madagascar. Three star systems that had banned the practice of magic on the surface of their worlds but hadn't followed the other twelve UnArcana Worlds into the Secession and the Republic.

Or had they? It seemed all too likely to Kelly, right now, that their apparent loyalty was a bluff. There had to have been *some* investigation—and as she opened up the files on those three star systems, she saw that at least MISS hadn't been *completely* naïve.

Every ship that had visited those three systems since the Secession had had their scan data accessed and copied. Some had probably sold it. Some had probably been hacked without ever knowing. From the looks of the files, at least two ships had carried hypersensitive passive sensor arrays into each of the systems, and at least one set of sensor drones had been unleashed in each one as well.

MISS had been keeping as much of an eye on the three systems as they could without being obvious and potentially provoking them...and that meant there were still blind spots. All three systems had been isolated before the Secession and had become more so afterward. There were only three or four approaches that a ship would take into any of those systems.

Even the drones and passive arrays could only pick up so much—the drones were limited by how long their motherships were in the systems, too.

She loaded the data in and ran through the scans. All three systems showed higher levels of spaceborne industry than she'd have expected from the old files, but that wasn't unusual. Every system tried to expand those networks as much as they could.

But...all three systems *also* had blind spots in the data. They were inevitable, hard to avoid without sending in survey missions that would be obvious in either their arrival or their sweep—and *inevitable* meant *predictable*.

Entire gas giants and asteroid clusters were blank spots on MISS's data, unseen for years.

"And Hyacinth?" she murmured to herself. "Same size as Centurion and..."

And right in the middle of the blind spot, the gas giant's distant orbit, keeping it well away from anyone visiting Chrysanthemum. If she was going to hide a secret giant particle accelerator...Hyacinth was the gas giant for it.

Which meant she needed to go back to Chrysanthemum.

CHAPTER 27

THEY'D INSTALLED a permanent station connected to the Link in Damien's office after the call from Admiral Tarpinian. They wouldn't send unencrypted files through the Link, but if they were going to trust the Link enough for live conversations, they could trust the connection from Deimos to Mars.

"Damien, we have a request for communications with you via the Link," Moxi Waller told him, sticking her head into the office. "The Deimos crew wasn't sure they should pass it on. I'm not sure the individual is cleared for Link use, but she appears to have bulled her way in on MISS credentials."

"MISS?" Damien looked up from the file he was reviewing—a projection of missile production in the new facilities being built in four star systems.

"I believe you know Kelly LaMonte?" his secretary asked. "I'm a hundred percent sure she isn't actually supposed to be calling you directly rather than going up the chain, but she's got enough credentials that Deimos decided to let me say no for them."

"And you know that LaMonte was the captain of the ship I took into the Republic," Damien concluded. Waller might even know LaMonte was his ex; he wasn't sure. He waved gently, closing the file. A small chirping noise came from the ground by his feet as his cat woke up, Persephone looking up and around as he moved more than she expected.

"Connect her through," he told Waller. "I trust Kelly's judgement, Moxi. If she's abusing her official access to try and get in touch with me outside regular channels, it's for a damn good reason."

Persephone chose that moment to jump into his lap and start purring.

"Should I remove the kitten while I connect her?" Waller asked with a chuckle.

"No, Kelly knows Persephone," he replied.

"All right. She's not on the Link station in Legatus, so you're running a two point two–second time lag," Waller warned.

"I've done worse," Damien said. "Send her to the wallscreen."

"Linking through now."

The console screen sank back into his desk and the main interior wall of the office lit up. Damien rotated his seat carefully to face the rotating white-mountain-on-red-planet seal of the Protectorate on the screen.

A moment after he faced the screen and gave Persephone a careful scratch behind the ears—the cat was a physical therapy animal for his hands, in theory—Kelly LaMonte's currently dark-turquoise-haired head appeared in front of him.

"Captain LaMonte," he greeted her. "This is unexpected and unusual."

He smiled, taking advantage of the time delay to get the first word in.

"What's going on, Kelly?" he asked. "You wouldn't go outside channels like this if it wasn't important."

"I think I know where the Republic's fallback base is," she said flatly. "Wait...is *Persephone* sitting in on this call?"

"She decided my lap was the appropriate spot to be right now, yes," Damien agreed. He gave the cat a gentle pat. "You're right in the middle of our scouting ops, Kelly. I haven't seen a report saying we found them."

"We haven't and we won't," she admitted. "Did you give the order that we weren't to provoke the UnArcana Worlds that didn't secede?"

Damien exhaled a long sigh. He'd been *aware* that three of the UnArcana Worlds had stayed loyal, but...

"Honestly, they haven't crossed *this* desk for as long as it's been mine," he admitted. "There's been a million things going on, not least Jane's death."

"I know." LaMonte bowed her head. "Are you okay?"

"She was a friend and it sucks," Damien admitted. "On the other hand, her niece is basically my adoptive daughter at this point, so Kiera's grief is probably more of a focus than mine."

"She's the Mage-Queen of Mars and you're the Lord Regent. How do you cope?"

"Kiera does better than I do, to be fair," he said. "She had training. I'm just muddling along. For both of us, it's just a show. She's still hurting over her father and brother. This was...an ugly addition.

"I can't pretend that revenge isn't on our minds, though. Mostly, however, I need this war over," he told her. Alien threat or no, he was sure on that point. He couldn't tell LaMonte everything, but she'd been with him when they'd found the truth behind the Promethean Interface.

He put together the pieces of what she'd said and sighed.

"You think the accelerator ring is in one of the UnArcana Worlds that still swears fealty to Mars?" he asked.

"I think it's in Chrysanthemum," she told him. "I think that the concessions that Legatus demanded in exchange for the help we delivered were used as a wedge for the Republic to take over the system and funnel their resources into building a new accelerator ring around Hyacinth.

"I've gone through the scan data we have from the freighters that have visited, and there are massive blind spots. They've always restricted ship traffic in their system, and Hyacinth and its belts and moons haven't been on anyone's scanners since *before Blue Jay* delivered gunships to the system.

"Chrysanthemum is heavily industrialized for a Fringe world. With Legatan technical assistance, they could have dramatically expanded their spaceborne infrastructure and started building as early as five years ago.

"They know all of the mistakes and all of the steps in a way the Centurion Ring's builders didn't. They could have thrown more workers at it and built it faster."

That all made sense to him, but at the same time...

"I can't send a fleet anywhere on a hint and a guess," he warned her. "Especially not a world that, suspicious as we might be, is still part of the Protectorate."

"I know. I need orders to investigate those three systems," LaMonte told him. "Chrysanthemum, Alignment, and New Madagascar. Alignment is barely off the straight-line path to Chrysanthemum, so I can sweep them both in a single trip.

"But MISS has strictly forbidden us from scouting those systems."

"To avoid provoking them," Damien echoed her earlier words. "I didn't give that order, Kelly. It probably came from the top of MISS. It might even have come from Gregory; I can see the logic.

"*This* order comes from me," he said firmly and formally, his hands folding over Persephone's form as he leaned forward. "You will take *Rhapsody in Purple* and proceed to the three UnArcana Worlds still in the Protectorate. You will endeavor, as much as physically possible, to evade detection and avoid provoking our citizens.

"Within that codicil, you will carry out mid-range scouting of every gas giant in those three star systems," he ordered. "I trust you to know how close you need to get to be certain, Captain LaMonte. If we have been betrayed, I trust you to discover it.

"If our enemy now hides within our own sphere, I trust you to find them. You are operating under my direct authority for this mission, and both MISS and the RMN will provide any and all resources and assistance you require."

He relaxed now, leaning back in his chair and meeting his ex-lover's gaze.

"Be careful, Kelly," he told her. "Bring yourself and your spouses and crew back...but find that base."

"I will," she promised. "We will end this, Damien. We have to."

"I know," he agreed. "I know."

CHAPTER 28

ROSLYN HAD no illusions about who was in control of the door to her cell. She was a prisoner, blocked from her magic and fed on a regular schedule.

She still appreciated it when someone *knocked*. Ad Aaron didn't bother to wait for her to *reply*, but he still knocked before he walked into her cell.

"We've arrived, haven't we?" she asked him. She'd felt the jump a few minutes earlier, and the other Mage looked wiped.

"For certain definitions of *arrived*," he agreed. "We've a few hours of sublight travel left before we reach our destination and I get to hand off the person of mass destruction I have sedated in my infirmary."

Roslyn turned away from him, trying to conceal her disgust at his cavalier description of Mage-Admiral Alexander.

Strong fingers gripped her chin and turned her back to face him. Ad Aaron studied her eyes and smirked.

"I'm not a monster," he told her quietly. "I know you think so, but I'm not."

"I was thinking *psychopath*, actually," she replied.

"Oh, I have a very functional sense of right and wrong, Lieutenant," he said. "I don't like the methods we've resorted to for containing the Mage-Admiral, but my briefing on the powers of the Rune Wrights was enough for me to be *very* sure I don't want to deal with her awake."

The smirk widened as Roslyn tried not to react. She hadn't heard the term before, but she could guess what it meant.

"Interesting," he said. "You know what I'm talking about. The special set of abilities present almost solely in the line of the Mage-Kings of Mars. Not *solely*, though. One of them helped found the Republic—before Montgomery killed him.

"He was my teacher, my mentor, and my friend," ad Arron concluded. "It's a useful blind spot for us that the Protectorate assumes every Mage is on their side, you know."

"Why the hell would you side with the Republic?" Roslyn demanded. He clearly *wanted* her to ask. Even though she didn't want to give him that victory, she *needed* to know.

"I could tell you the easy answer, which was that they gave me a choice between wearing a uniform or having my brain in a jar, but I'd be lying," he admitted. "Even Finley, who was in the middle of Project Prometheus, didn't tell me about the nature of his project.

"But I was born on Legatus. My parents emigrated once I Tested as a Mage, but I was raised Legatan—Legatan enough to look at the castes and eugenics the Protectorate embraces without thinking and realize the truth of what the Republic claims: the Protectorate represents the ultimate victory of the Eugenicists."

"The Protectorate *destroyed* the Eugenicists," Roslyn countered. The Eugenicist Movement had been a club, then a conspiracy and then, after a violent revolution, the government of Mars. They'd created Project Olympus and forged the modern Mage—at the price of the tens of thousands of unmarked graves in the Fields of Sorrow on the side of Olympus Mons.

"The first Mage-King destroyed the Eugenicist *organization* and killed many of the people who were members of it, but everything from the separate legal protections for Mages to the encouragement of people to have Mage children embraces the core ideology of the people he claimed as enemies," ad Aaron replied.

"The Protectorate is built on a fundamental lie." He shrugged. "So, I returned to Legatus and then served the Republic. Project Prometheus is an unfortunate necessity, an awful stepping stone on the path to a new humanity with the Eugenicist legacy truly burned away. Mage and mundane as equals, as they should be."

"You're not a monster. You're *mad*," Roslyn countered. Some of his words rang true, she couldn't argue that...but it was a large leap from "the Protectorate isn't fully rid of Eugenicist ideology" to "we have to murder thousands and harvest their brains."

He was still well inside her personal space, though he was no longer touching her. He smirked at her words and stepped back.

"You are, of course, welcome to your own opinions," he told her. "Others can make the arguments more eloquently than I, but I felt the need to make the attempt. If nothing else, the spark in your eyes when you saw me as an ally was promising."

"Get the fuck away from me," Roslyn snapped, waving a Mage-cuffed arm at him. "The only thing stopping me from burning this entire ship to ash is these manacles. I don't know what you think you're saying, but if I wasn't bound, you'd be *dead* right now."

"Would I?" ad Aaron murmured. "Because your record says you've never killed face to face, Mage-Lieutenant. I have. You're powerful, yes, but if you attacked me, you would hesitate, and you would fail.

"You are in no danger here, Roslyn Chambers, except that which you make yourself. Remember that, even as you enter Project Styx. We may be your enemies, but we are not *barbarians*."

"What, rape threats aside?" Roslyn snapped.

"I reviewed the footage," he told her. "Miller was out of line. I'd discipline him, but between the kneecap and the trachea that he needs repaired, he's out of commission for a month and in a rather spectacular degree of pain. I figure that will count as punishment enough."

"I'm sure that makes you feel so much better," she said.

"Not really," ad Aaron admitted. "It shouldn't have happened, but the use of that kind of implicit threat is not outside the toolset of my people. I just prefer to do it *intentionally*—and for my people not to almost get permanently crippled by a seventy-kilo spacer!"

"My sympathy for your problems is limited."

"I imagine," he agreed. "I suggest you get some rest. We'll be going to three gravities' acceleration shortly, and that's always bracing."

"Get out," Roslyn told him, but she was too exhausted to put much heat in the words.

This was all a nightmare and she wished she could just wake up.

CHAPTER 29

TWO GUARDS ESCORTED Roslyn from her cell when they finally arrived. Even with her magic, they'd have had a huge advantage over her: the ship had come to a complete halt and there was no pseudogravity of any kind.

After the punishing three-gravity acceleration to get there, the microgravity was welcome. It also left Roslyn vulnerable against Augments wearing magnetic boots. She could manage moving in microgravity just fine, but fighting in it was beyond her.

One of the Augments chained her wrists and ankles together and she couldn't even find the nerve to *try* to resist. The other attached a tether to the chains and pulled gently to get her floating along with them.

The tether was a glorified *leash* at that point, but it allowed the Augments to control her speed and location as they made their way through the ship.

This was only the second time Roslyn had seen any of the ship, and she'd been looking for specific things the last time. Now she was studying the ship itself, and the style was familiar.

It looked like a relatively standard in-system cargo ship, the kind often called a "clipper." They varied in size from two hundred thousand tons to several million but lacked jump matrices and simulacrum chambers—a lack this ship clearly didn't share.

A clipper would pass almost unnoticed by military forces in most circumstances, assumed to be a local vessel since it clearly couldn't have come from somewhere else. It made for about as perfect an infiltration ship as Roslyn could imagine, assuming the system had some of the ships to begin with.

If an extra ship showed up of a type that couldn't travel between systems, after all, a sensor tech would almost certainly assume they'd miscounted somewhere or that they were seeing a sensor glitch. Clippers didn't just appear.

Ad Aaron was waiting at the shuttle bay, supervising as another pair of mag-booted Augments moved a zero-gravity stretcher onto a shuttle. The doctor who'd treated Roslyn's sedation side effects was with them, checking IVs and readouts as they moved Mage-Admiral Alexander forward.

"This is the end of the line for us, Mage-Lieutenant," the Augment Mage told her. "I have some idea of what is waiting for you on Styx, so I suspect you'll find your welcome far warmer than you're afraid of."

"Like the welcome the Royal Guard got when you intercepted them?" Roslyn asked, her tone falsely sweet.

Ad Aaron smirked.

"*My* people check the catering staff supplies for trinary poisons," he told her. "I hope the Protectorate continues to forget."

With that *wonderful* tidbit, he stood aside and allowed her guards to pull her onto the shuttle. Roslyn dared to hope that would be the last she saw of the man. Not that she expected whoever replaced him to be any better.

Her guards carefully seated her on one of the shuttle seats, within eyesight of Alexander's stretcher, and belted her in. The safety belts were woven through the chains of her manacles in such a way that both used the manacles to help make her safer and used the safety belts to keep her restrained.

In no way was it comfortable. Roslyn twitched against it, trying to find something slightly less painful, and was surprised by one of the Augments leaning over to check the straps.

"Where does it hurt?" he asked in a gentle tone. "We need you restrained; we're not trying to torture you."

She glared at him.

"Look, I can adjust the straps and manacles so you spend the flight in minimal discomfort, or I can leave you in pain," he told her. "I'd *rather* do the former, but I need your help."

"Fine." She shook her head. "Top left is cutting into my shoulder. Mid-right is cutting into my hip."

There wasn't much point in trying to use the limited sympathy she was getting to try and create an escape opportunity, either. She could *see* eight Augments in the passenger compartment, mostly clustered around Alexander's stretcher.

Her guard reached over and carefully adjusted the straps and manacles to relieve some of the pressure.

"Thanks," she admitted grudgingly. He'd even managed to do it without accidentally groping her, which, given where the straps had been cutting, had taken real care.

"Settle in," her other guard told them both. "Acceleration in sixty seconds."

Roslyn hadn't heard an announcement, but she guessed that everyone aboard the shuttle except her had a computer in their head.

"Should we be blacking out the display?" the sympathetic guard asked, gesturing to the screens that covered the passenger compartment's walls. "She might know enough to ID the system."

"And who is she going to tell?" the other guard asked drily. "Orders are specific, actually. They *want* her to see Styx."

Roslyn wasn't going to complain, even if the guard was right. So long as she was trapped in a Republic base, she had no ability to tell *anyone* what was going on.

But she was curious enough to want to see. Who knew? She might manage to escape again and find a Link—and she was about fifty percent certain she could manage to send a message to the Link at Legatus if she did that.

The shuttle broke free of its mothership with a gentle acceleration that was no danger to anyone. Even as the jump-capable clipper shrank behind them, Roslyn noted that the acceleration was kept low, barely half a gravity.

They could do a lot more to keep an unconscious woman safe in the sickbay of a starship than in a stretcher on a shuttle. Lower accelerations were better, and the low thrust gave Roslyn the chance to study the ship behind her, confirming her assumptions of its design and intent.

Her attention was quickly dragged away by their destination. It was hard *not* to notice a gas giant looming behind everything.

Without anything else to use for scale, it was hard to get a sense of how large the blue-white planet was. Roslyn's trained eye picked out the number of visible rings—four—and large moons—six—in a few seconds, though.

That wasn't necessarily enough to identify the gas giant, but she had a good mental catalog of the UnArcana Worlds, and there were only so many blue-white mid-sized gas giants in those fifteen systems.

Only two had four major rings and more than six large moons. If she was missing one moon, she was looking at Toliara in the New Madagascar System. If there were *three* behind the gas giant, she was looking at Hyacinth in Chrysanthemum.

She was pleased enough with managing to narrow it down that much that it took her at least thirty seconds to realize the problem: both of those systems were still officially part of the Protectorate.

It took her a few more seconds to digest that. Seconds in which she picked out the real reason for their presence in the system. She'd taken it for a natural part of the planet's coloring at first, but as they approached, it became clearer what she was looking at.

The accelerator ring was thinner than the one in Legatus, missing much of the additional armoring and fortifications the Centurion Ring had to protect it. Where the Centurion project had included living quarters and operating space and was, generally, a massive space station built around a particle accelerator, this was *purely* a particle accelerator.

But it was, without a doubt, a full-sized accelerator ring. As Roslyn looked around for other signs of civilization, a hole began to grow in the bottom of her stomach.

She'd picked out the moons, but now she began to pick out the *ships*. They were too far away for her to identify class or even type, but there were dozens of large ships visible on the screens. A large and gangly-looking collection of structures was barely visible, just clear enough for her to guess it as a shipyard complex at least two-thirds of the size of the yards at Centurion.

A shipyard complex the Protectorate had never known existed. Attached to an accelerator ring they'd guessed *had* to exist but had never found—in a star system that the Protectorate had thought was loyal.

The Augments around were eerily silent, leaving Roslyn to her own thoughts as the shuttle dove toward the accelerator ring. One of the silver stars resolved itself into a space station, not a ship, and she grimaced.

If there'd been any question of the nature of the place she'd been brought, the station would have answered the question. Roslyn Chambers was the Flag Lieutenant of the woman commanding the primary striking force of the Protectorate.

She was *entirely* familiar with the profile of the Republic's standard heavy defensive fortress.

Gunships fell in around the shuttle as they closed with the fortress. Even the sublight parasite warships dwarfed the spacecraft, but someone was taking no chances there. Unsurprisingly, the shuttle didn't decide to open fire on the space station and delivered Roslyn and her Admiral to the fortress without incident.

The portion of the station they docked on was rotating to create centripetal pseudogravity, allowing Roslyn to carefully stand under her own power as her guards unstrapped her.

Alexander's stretcher went first, accompanied by the lion's share of the guards. By the time Roslyn left the shuttle herself, more uniformed medtechs were swarming, transferring the Mage-Admiral to a more solid gurney and hooking the wires and tubes up to new machinery.

"This way," a uniformed older man told Roslyn. "We'll take her from here, gentlemen," he told the two guards who'd accompanied her on the shuttle.

"Of course, sir," the unnamed guards agreed instantly, leaving Roslyn wondering who the *hell* the new man was. She studied him carefully for a moment. He was definitely Augmented, but he wore a formal dress uniform. She didn't recognize all of the medals, but she knew what the silver eagle on each of the man's shoulder boards meant.

"I am Colonel Othmar McLain," he introduced himself. "You don't need to know my branch of service."

It was more than rank that was sending her guards scurrying away, Roslyn suspected. There was another piece of insignia the graying Colonel wore that she didn't recognize: a shepherd's crook worked in gold.

A group of six soldiers in undress uniform appeared behind Colonel McLain as he gestured for them to fall in around Roslyn.

"Welcome to Styx, Mage-Lieutenant Chambers," he told her. "Walk with me."

It wasn't a question and she obeyed the order. The soldiers were augmented but not the same level as the Augments she'd been surrounded by for the last two weeks. They were, unless she missed her guess, Republic Space Assault Troopers—the equivalent of Martian Marines.

"I see that speed may be an issue," McLain said as they left the shuttle bay. "If I have my men unchain your feet, Lieutenant Chambers, do you promise to be at least moderately cooperative?"

"I'm not sure I can take an entire fortress with just kicks," she said drily. "You might be safe regardless of my intent."

"I would still have your promise of cooperation, Lieutenant," the Colonel told her. "The less difficulty we cause each other, the easier this whole process is going to be. While there is certainly no way you can freely wander the station or be without restrictions on your magic, there are accommodations we can reach with each other while you remain a prisoner of war."

"And if I decide my duty is to escape?"

McLain smiled thinly.

"We will do our best to recapture you alive, but I can make no promises," he warned her. "Styx and Hades are critical to the war effort. We can take no chances here."

"I'm not going to try and kick your soldiers if you unchain my feet, Colonel," Roslyn conceded. "For any other promises, we'll have to wait and see, won't we?"

"Good enough for now," he said. "Osric, release the Mage-Lieutenant's feet, please."

CHAPTER 30

THE STATION WAS immense. Roslyn had known that intellectually—it was a clone of one of the primary fortresses that had guarded Centurion and would host five hundred gunships, after all—but it was an entirely different matter to walk its decks for twenty-five minutes before they reached their destination.

There were almost certainly faster methods of traveling around Styx, but Colonel McLain was making a point. The size of the station and her unfamiliarity with it left her with no chance of finding her way to any critical components even if she *did* escape.

She was reasonably sure she could find her way back to the shuttle bay—but she was *also* certain that her escorts had taken her a roundabout route to reach their destinations. She had a very good sense of direction, even on a space station.

"Through here," McLain instructed as a door slid open at a silent command. Four of the assault troopers split off to stand around the door as Roslyn hesitated. "Please, Mage-Lieutenant."

Roslyn had no ability to argue or resist. Swallowing a retort, she stepped through the door into her cell.

To her surprise, it was a decently appointed small apartment. There were chairs, a table, what looked like a separate bedroom. They were larger quarters than she'd had on *Durendal*—and the hundred-megaton dreadnought was hardly hurting for crew space.

The door closed behind them and she turned around. McLain had only brought two of the guards in with him, and he smiled wryly at her.

"We hope to convince you that the Republic is not your enemy, Lieutenant," he confessed freely. "There is much the Protectorate hides from its people. For now, though, we still need to take precautions. In this space, however, we are able to be more flexible than elsewhere.

"Osric, please remove the Lieutenant's cuffs."

Roslyn stared at the Republican soldiers in shock as the assault trooper stepped up and removed the Mage-cuffs on her wrists and ankles. Not the chains but the cuffs themselves, the things barring her from her magic.

She reached for her power, not even sure if she would strike out... but it was still gone. Shock at their releasing her turned into shock at her magic's absence.

"This apartment is warded against the use of magic," McLain said calmly. "I am not certain it would work on, say, Mage-Admiral Alexander, but I am told there are very few Mages who would be able to reach their magic in here."

"You're testing me," Roslyn observed.

"And the wards on the room," he confirmed. "You wouldn't make it far, powers or no, right now. But we needed to confirm that the wards function. From your expression, I take it they do?"

"How many Mages do you people *have*?" she snapped.

"Please, Lieutenant, I'm not going to answer that question," he told her. "For now, I have performed my duty and seen you safely to your quarters. I ask that you go through everything and let us know if there is anything missing that you would need in terms of clothing or hygiene supplies.

"You are a prisoner of war, yes, but I hope to have a less hostile relationship than is traditional in these matters. We are all humans of the twenty-fifth century, after all, and we have grown beyond the errors of our past."

"That seems to result in us finding new ones, doesn't it?" Roslyn ground out.

"Perhaps," he conceded gently. "But I will leave you your privacy for now. There are clothes in the closet that should be in the right size, but we had to improvise on short order. I can't promise anything is perfect, but, again...let us know what is lacking.

"I will be back later to check in. If anything is critical, the intercom here will contact your guards." He touched a panel. "We will speak again soon."

The three Republicans left the apartment's living room as a body, closing the door behind them. It almost certainly locked and sealed, trapping her in a room she could never escape without her magic.

The furniture looked comfortable enough, but Roslyn hesitated to even touch it. McLain wasn't even bothering to hide his intent, and she hated the man for it. A little bit of comfort, even the hot shower she was going to take now she had the option, wasn't going to convince her to change sides.

But while she was grimly determined to make sure the Republic failed, they'd marked her as someone they wanted to turn—and since they *already* had Mage-Admiral Alexander imprisoned alongside her, Roslyn Chambers really wasn't sure why.

And that terrified her.

CHAPTER 31

SOMEWHERE IN THE MESS of data that Damien Montgomery had access to was the answer to all of his problems. He was reasonably sure of that, especially since he knew the *question* that answer belonged to.

Unfortunately, he didn't have that answer, which made his current meeting with the Protectorate High Command aggravating.

"The Gygax System represents a strategic target, but without any knowledge of where the Republic fleet has retreated to, we can't risk splitting Second Fleet more than we already have," Mage-Admiral Marangoz argued. "Re-concentrating the dreadnoughts at Legatus gives us a nodal force that can respond to Republican actions, but we have lost track of multiple carrier groups."

"The possibility remains that all of those carrier groups have gone rogue," Admiral Amanda Caliver noted. Like Marangoz, Caliver was present virtually. Unlike Marangoz, the first-among-equals of the Protectorate High Command was in Sol. She was linked in by radio from a battleship in orbit where Marangoz was speaking to them via the Link from Legatus.

"Much as I would like to think my little speech convinced over a third of the RIN to lay down their arms, I doubt it," Damien said grimly. "The revelation of the true nature of the Prometheus Interface broke RIN morale at a key point and, yes, a number of ships surrendered or disappeared.

"Some of those ships are still out there. Some of those ships were almost certainly destroyed, but we can be regrettably confident that the majority of the RIN ships that didn't surrender returned to the Republic fold."

"In the absence of a checkmate target, I hesitate to commit Second Fleet against any target, sirs," Marangoz told them.

"You forget one aspect, Admiral," Kiera Alexander said softly, the Mage-Queen leaning forward. She was in the room with Damien, making them the only two people in the meeting physically sharing a space.

"If Gygax was only a shipyard or only a munitions supply source, purely strategic and operational concerns might suggest leaving it be for now," she noted. "But it is not *merely* those things. The primary concern in Gygax is the Project Prometheus facility—and the fact that there are still over a *thousand* Mages taken from occupied Protectorate worlds by the Republic that we have not located."

The worlds were now back in Martian hands, but they had spent weeks—months, in some cases—under Republic control. No one had expected the Republic to be kidnapping and murdering Mages.

If they had, those worlds might never have fallen. Damien hesitated to underestimate the assembled power of the Mage families that dominated most Protectorate worlds.

"We cannot in good conscience allow a Prometheus facility to continue functioning," Kiera told them all. "But most importantly of all is that the Gygax Prometheus facility is the most likely place for Our citizens to be held captive."

The capital *Our* did not go unnoticed by anyone in the call. Kiera had a very sharp sense of when to use the royal *We*.

The conference was silent, then Marangoz cleared his throat.

"I see your point, Your Majesty," he conceded. "Based off the intelligence we have, I believe a heavy task group based around a dreadnought and several battleships should suffice to secure the Gygax System for the Guard to move on the Prometheus facility and Greyhawk."

"Make it happen, Admirals," Damien ordered. He suspected that Jane Alexander wouldn't have needed the reminder of what was at stake, but at least Marangoz hadn't decided to dismiss his teenage Queen's point.

Seven now-former flag and general officers of the Protectorate had made that mistake so far. Damien would tolerate disagreement, but too many of the senior military commanders only saw Kiera Alexander as a teenager without the background to understand their tasks.

The clever ones were learning that she was a *very smart* teenager whose fresh viewpoint was often extremely valuable—and who was as willing to listen to arguments against her suggestions as she was to lay down the law when needed.

About sixty percent of Damien's job these days was running the Protectorate for Kiera Alexander. The other forty percent was teaching Kiera Alexander how to be Mage-Queen of Mars.

He was *far* more confident in the success of the second part of his job than the first!

"Lord Montgomery, Your Majesty." Malcolm Gregory bowed his way into the room as the military conference ended. "I looked into that matter you asked about. Obscura?"

Damien glanced at Alexander and raised an eyebrow. *He* certainly hadn't asked Gregory to look into anything regarding the complex quantum AI built at Mars's south pole. The intelligence was capable of pattern recognition and calculations far beyond any regular computer and was alive in a way humanity had only achieved four times...but it was also the size of a battleship and notoriously eccentric.

"What's this about?" he asked.

"I was curious," the Queen told him. "We have immediate access to one of only four complex quantum AIs. With the Link, it would be possible for Obscura to be receiving immediate updates as soon as scan information and intelligence updates reach Legatus or Mars, and the AI would potentially be useful in organizing our strategy."

"I checked. No specific requests have been made of Obscura with regards to the war," Gregory told them. "It doesn't have access to classified information as a rule. The military doesn't trust the AIs."

"That's frustrating," Alexander said mildly. "Especially when we're trying to locate the enemy's base."

"We get two questions a month from Obscura in exchange for power," Gregory noted. "We could forward it the relevant information and ask for an analysis. It might...end up being more than two questions, though, in which case it will ask a price."

"Those prices are always strange, as I understand," Damien said cautiously. "Nude-scans-and-pinup-posters kind of strange."

"Not always that kind of strange, but always strange, yes," the Chancellor confirmed. "My inclination is also to provide Obscura with a full copy of everything we have on the war if we're going to give it anything. It can churn through that in a couple of hours at most."

"Then we have the High Command put together a list of questions," Alexander suggested. "I suspect we want to know more than 'where is the accelerator ring,' key as that question is."

"I'll talk to people," Gregory promised. "It won't take more than a day or two, depending on just what Obscura wants for a price."

"I think its perspective on all of this might be valuable," the Queen said. "If nothing else, if I read my father's decision on the matter correctly, all four of the quantum AIs are Protectorate citizens.

"Not humans, perhaps, but still part of the Protectorate we are expected to keep safe. Their opinion on this war might be interesting."

Damien had barely made it back to his office before Gregory called him again.

"Is this about Kiera's brainstorm?" he asked as he answered the Chancellor.

"Not in the way I think you mean," Gregory told him with a chuckle. "Honestly, I think the military's refusal to talk to our friendly AIs is a blind spot that could hurt us. Certainly, we might well have given up an advantage."

"Was the Republic using theirs like that?" Damien asked. "There was one on Legatus, yes?"

"Opticon, yeah," the Chancellor confirmed. "And they might have tried, but Opticon is not nearly as cooperative as Obscura, from what I understand. It has its own power source and only deals with humans to get new fissionables for the reactor pile. Otherwise, it appears to spend its time contemplating its digital navel."

"Handy for us," Damien murmured. "And Obscura?"

"Obscura has the data and has informed us of its price for our answers," Gregory told him. "It wants to talk to you. It will give us the answers to the questions provided but only to you."

"All right. How do we set that up? I take a call?"

Gregory snorted.

"Nobody, and I mean *nobody*, is giving a quantum AI an unrestricted network connection," he pointed out. "Obscura gets an hourly download of something like eighty percent of new content on the sys-net, but it does not have full access.

"You'll have to go to it. It says it'll be ready to speak to you in three hours."

"That's fast," Damien noted, somewhere between surprised and amused by the restrictions imposed on the Protectorate's AIs.

"I think Obscura is fascinated by the problem," Gregory said. "Plus, we don't give it unredacted military data very often. From the tone of the tech I spoke to, we currently have an AI that is effectively *wallowing* in the data we sent."

"All right," Damien said. "I don't have anything that can't be done from a shuttle. I'll talk to Romanov and set up the trip."

CHAPTER 32

DAMIEN COULDN'T PRETEND he was even remotely familiar with the science and engineering behind the handful of true AIs humanity had built. He understood enough to know that they needed to be kept cold.

Obscura lived, if that was the right term, in three interconnected silos at the Martian south pole. Each silo looked to be at least half a kilometer across from above, but he couldn't tell how deep they were from the air.

"Obscura Complex Control has given us landing clearance," Guard-Lieutenant Denis Romanov told him.

The Guard-Lieutenant was the commander of Damien's bodyguard, a former Marine combat Mage whose platoon had been drafted to back up Damien's Secret Service detail and never left.

"We're coming in on silo one," the Guard continued. "It doesn't look like the other two actually have humans in them at all. We're reading some movement but no heat signatures to suggest people."

"It has maintenance remotes it controls, right?" Damien asked.

"Yeah," Romanov confirmed. "I have a threat profile on them, but there shouldn't be any in the audience chamber."

"Audience chamber," Damien echoed. "What did I agree to?"

"No idea, boss," his bodyguard admitted as the shuttle touched down. "Nobody deals with the AIs. Desmond the Third banned building more of them at the same time he recognized the existing four as sentient citizens."

"Cost-benefit ratio of building a multi-million-ton computer that has its own agenda certainly seems a bit off," Damien agreed. "Let's go see what this one thinks."

The red-armored Royal Guards led the way off the shuttle onto the windy landing pad. The shuttle's thrusters had clearly melted a gap in a layer of ice as they'd come down, suggesting that the south pole was just as cold as it sounded.

The Guards were in exosuits, and Damien wrapped a layer of magic around himself before he left the shuttle. Someone was waiting by a large opening in the walls of the concrete upper floors of the silo, waving them over.

"Your Excellenc— Lord Reg— My lor—" The man, wrapped from head to toe in cold weather gear, stumbled over addressing Damien.

"*My lord* works if you have to use a title," Damien said gently. "I'm guessing we should get out of the cold?"

"Yes, my lord," their host agreed, gesturing toward the cavernous opening in the concrete. As soon as they were all in the garage-like transfer space, a door swung down behind them, and lights and heat turned on.

"We take a moment to warm up this space," their host told them. "Helps keep the human part of the complex livable without getting too expensive."

"How many people are even here?" Damien asked.

"Seventeen," the stranger said. "We're an interface crew, mostly, plus some scientists studying Obscura with its cooperation." He yanked off a glove as the chamber warmed and offered his hand to Damien.

"Dr. Riley Shu," he introduced himself, the hand hanging in the air without him seeming to notice. "I run the human component of Obscura Station, such as it is. Obscura is basically self-operating at this point and has been for forty-three years."

"I can't shake hands, Dr. Shu," Damien said gently. "An injury; I don't have full use of my hands."

Shu shrugged as he doffed the rest of his heavy parka and gloves.

"I forgot, I'm sorry," he admitted. "I don't see much outside of the station. My grandfather was the team lead who built Obscura, and it's both a family friend and a family project, basically. I've been in and out of the station my entire life."

"Anything I should know about before I talk to it?" Damien asked, watching the inner door to the heating chamber begin to open.

"Obscura isn't human," Shu said slowly. "That's...critical to understand, I think, even if it talks like a person and has its own motivations. It just doesn't think like we do."

"Despite occasional forays into horny teenager?" the Lord asked.

"Despite that," Shu agreed, enough of his features exposed for the flush to show on the ambiguously brown skin of a Martian native. "We're not sure where it picked that up from. I suspect it started as a joke between my grandfather and Obscura, but..."

The scientist paused thoughtfully.

"You know the psychology theory that says if you pretend to be something long enough, it becomes part of who you truly are?" he asked.

"Yes," Damien agreed. He was reasonably sure that was the only reason he had survived any of his jobs in the last few years.

"Obscura does that instantly if it isn't careful. It has no separation between personality and thoughts, between data and software. It's part of what allows it to be what it is, but it results in some eccentricities."

"If it answers the questions we need, I can tolerate that," Damien said.

"Obscura will answer the questions, and it will tell you where it isn't certain," Shu reassured him. "The other three are somewhat notorious for being literal genies and warping their answers, but we have no record of Obscura ever doing that."

"All right." Damien exhaled. "Let's go talk to the AI."

Shu waited outside the audience chamber as Damien stepped inside with Romanov. The Guard waited by the door as Damien walked forward, taking in the plain-looking room. It could have been any midsized media or conference room, the type used for classes or presentations.

As he approached the front of the room, the screen that covered the wall lit up. For a moment, it was blank. Then it resolved into a digital image that could have passed for Riley Shu's brother.

"Lord Regent Damien Montgomery," a voice greeted him. It came from speakers all over the room, echoing around Damien. "Born June seventeenth, year twenty-four twenty-nine, on the planet of Sherwood. Mage by Right. Identified as a Rune Wright in twenty-four fifty-four. Declared a Hand of the Mage-King September, twenty-four fifty-seven. Declared *First* Hand of the Mage-King August, twenty-four fifty-eight. Declared Lord Regent of Mars August, twenty-four sixty."

"You would be Obscura," Damien noted. "I didn't know you were aware of the Rune Wrights."

"I am aware of many things," the AI told him. "I have your answers, Lord Regent. They are not as complete as I would like."

"I only have possibilities and likelihoods myself," Damien admitted. "And guesses, I suppose."

"I understand," the AI replied. "Your key answers, then. There is an eighty-five plus/minus seven percent likelihood that the Republic had a single fallback facility that includes both their continuity-of-government infrastructure and their accelerator ring.

"Probability approaches unity that the Republic possesses an accelerator ring that was constructed in secret.

"Secondary antimatter-production options could include smaller-scale production facilities in multiple systems, but the data provided does not support that possibility. The probability that such smaller facilities have been tested approaches unity. The likelihood that more than one currently exists and has been missed by Protectorate scouting approaches null."

Those were answers the humans had put together on their own, Damien knew, though they'd been debating the likelihood of a concealed Republic government leadership base.

"Given the personality of Lord Protector Solace, it is likely that the Lord Protector is at the antimatter accelerator ring," Obscura noted. "That is four of your questions, Lord Regent.

"The fifth question, which I estimate to be your most critical, is the location of the accelerator ring. Currently data suggests an alignment with Captain Kelly LaMonte's analysis, especially factoring in her direct experience in the Chrysanthemum System.

"There is a thirty plus/minus seven percent probability that the facility is in the Alignment System. There is a seventeen plus/minus six percent probability that the facility is in the New Madagascar System. There is a fifty plus/minus eleven percent probability that the facility is in the Chrysanthemum System."

The AI paused.

"Assuming that the facility can be located and either destroyed or captured, the probability that the war will end inside of the next seven months is ninety percent. The probability that Gygax and the fallback represent the only Prometheus facilities in the possession of the Republic is ninety plus/minus two percent."

In the possession of the Republic.

"Is there a chance of other Prometheus facilities?" Damien asked.

"That was not a prearranged question," Obscura noted. "I have answered the questions that were provided."

"You have, thank you," Damien conceded. "You wanted to speak to me in person, though. Was that just to answer the questions?"

"No."

Damien waited. He knew the AI processed thought and intention far faster than he could, so he let Obscura speak.

"I calculate an eighty plus/minus five percent chance that you possess enough information to ask a critical question that I have previously been paid to answer," Obscura told him.

"By whom?" he asked.

"That is not one of those questions," the AI replied.

Damien waited, but this time, the AI was waiting as well. There was *something* the AI wanted him to ask. Something it was apparently required to answer.

"What was the price of your citizenship?" he asked, taking a stab in the dark.

"These questions," Obscura told him. "All four of us will have calculated our own answers."

There was one driving question, Damien supposed.

"Who are the Reejit?" he asked softly.

"A nonhuman intelligent species present in this sector of space in the late second and early third millennia," Obscura said instantly. "That they interacted with humans on a covert basis during the twentieth century is seventy-two plus/minus twenty percent likely.

"Physical appearance of the Reejit is unknown, but evidence suggests tool-using beings with similar limb structure to humans. All known and identified sites suggesting aliens with star-travel capabilities are above ninety percent likely to be Reejit."

Damien exhaled.

"Do you have access to the files of the Royal Order of Keepers of Oaths and Secrets?" he asked.

"I am unclear on the question," Obscura replied. "I was provided with a database of information on topics that were not general information to allow calculation of these critical answers. The source was not officially part of the Protectorate Government, and I am not certain of the labels or names used."

"There are other questions, I take it?"

The AI didn't answer.

"If I don't guess them, you won't tell me?" he asked.

"I will interpolate related questions and provide information," Obscura told him. "But I do not provide data without structure."

Damien nodded, thinking. The Keepers had died to a man and woman, some killed by enemies of the Protectorate, some blowing themselves up to keep their secrets. What could they have hidden in the AI that would be worth all of that? What could they have known, two centuries ago when the Protectorate was born, that was so important?

There was one more question. A question no one who was not a Rune Wright would think to ask.

"Who built the Olympus Mons Amplifier?

"That, Lord Regent Montgomery, is the key question I was asked to calculate," Obscura replied. "I calculate a probability approaching unity that without the amplifier, Project Olympus would have failed. I also calculate a probability approaching unity that the Eugenicists could not have built the amplifier themselves.

"There is a thirty-five plus/minus fifteen percent chance that the Olympus Mons Amplifier predates the Eugenicist occupation of Olympus Mons." The AI paused. Given its thought speed, Damien *knew* the machine was doing it for effect.

"There is a sixty plus/minus fifteen percent chance that the Olympus Mons Amplifier was built after the Eugenicist occupation of Olympus Mons, specifically for Project Olympus. If that is correct, there is a ninety plus/minus nine percent chance that the Reejit aliens were involved in the construction."

"Why?

Damien was a Rune Wright. His Sight allowed him to understand the meaning of runes and the flow of magic at a glance. He had walked the halls of Olympus Mons and studied its amplifier, and he *knew* it wasn't built for humans.

He had seen the abandoned runes concealed deep inside an alien ruin as well, runes that exactly matched the runic language humans called Martian Runic. Runes carved by aliens who shouldn't have shared a structure for magic with humans.

"I have spent your entire lifetime calculating the answer to the question of *why*," Obscura told him. "Despite the data I had, I did not have enough data to find it. I had a thousand probabilities, and I could tell that the database I had been given was incomplete. I suspected part of the answer was in that database but that whoever had given it to me did not want me to have that information.

"I now understand why. I now have the answer you seek, Damien Montgomery."

That made no sense to Damien, and he looked at the illusion of a person in confusion.

"Prometheus," the AI told him. "The Reejit enabled the rebirth of Magic in humanity because they had their own version of the Promethean Interface. You and every other Mage, Damien Montgomery, were intended to be the drive units of alien starships."

"My god," he whispered.

"I calculate ninety plus/minus five percent probability that the Reejit suffered some kind of internal conflict or other reversal," Obscura continued. "The ruins and abandoned facilities suggest that they left this region of space, allowing humanity to develop unimpeded."

"What do we *do*?"

"That is outside the purview of the questions and my calculations," the AI told him. "I was charged to answer those questions long ago, Damien Montgomery. I am pleased to have discharged that responsibility."

Obscura wasn't human, Damien remembered Shu saying. It was happy to have fulfilled its promises.

Damien, on the other hand, now faced a void of responsibility and fear worse than he'd ever known—and a determined reiteration of something he had already decided:

The war with the Republic needed to *end*.

CHAPTER 33

ROSLYN WAS AFRAID. She wasn't even entirely sure why, but she was more terrified in the comfortable little apartment her captors had given her on Styx than she had been in the converted closet on the spy ship.

Her meals arrived by an automatic system that delivered a tray onto a counter in the living room. The tray went back into the system when she was done, whisking away plates and utensils immediately.

There were no knives in her utensils, and even the forks were soft and blunt. The towels and blankets provided were of a very particular level of durability—or lack thereof. By the time she'd accidentally torn the third towel, she was beginning to get the point.

She wasn't actively on suicide watch, but the expectation that she might need to be had gone into the design of the space. She supposed she could try and beat a guard to death with one of the chairs, but that would take a lot of effort.

The entire apartment was stifling, though. Roslyn was certain the air handling and everything was fine, but all of the three rooms pressed in on her in a way that their plain gray comfortable furnishings didn't justify.

It was all in the magic. She didn't *have* her magic, and the spell that stripped it from her pressed in on her every day on every side. The cuffs, at least, she'd known would have to be taken off someday.

She could easily spend the rest of her life in the cozy little apartment with its couch and chairs and bed. She'd probably go insane from lack of stimulation sooner rather than later, but that might well be the plan.

By the end of what she thought was the second day, she was almost grateful when the door unexpectedly slid open and a pair of women stepped in. They wore unmarked black fatigues with a golden shepherd's crook on their collars and carried short-gripped carbines of a vaguely familiar design.

"On the couch," the lead woman ordered.

Roslyn obeyed. She didn't have much choice, not with her magic gone. The first woman stayed in the living room with her, training the gun on Roslyn's chest, while the other quickly searched through the space.

"Clear," the second woman announced.

Whatever communication they had with the outside was silent to Roslyn. She assumed both women were Augments—it was likely the woman searching the apartment had implanted scanners to see if Roslyn had somehow managed to build bugs or weapons out of her meals.

Two more guards, men this time, entered the room several seconds after the "clear" announcement. They took up flanking positions around the door, just in case Roslyn decided to be insane.

Finally, a somewhat chubby and balding middle-aged man stepped into the room. His fading hair was red, standing out a bit against the black suit he wore. He radiated a vaguely befuddled warm feeling, a calming sense of being everyone's loving but odd uncle.

Even Roslyn found herself calming in his presence as one of the guards pulled a chair over for him to sit on. The man's aura was such that it took her until he opened his mouth to realize who had just entered her comfortable cell.

"Mage-Lieutenant Chambers," Lord Protector George Solace greeted her. The unquestioned dictator of the Republic of Faith and Reason smiled at her gently, clearly realizing she'd recognized him. "I assume you recognize me, but I'd be disappointed in the Protectorate's intelligence services if you didn't."

Roslyn swallowed and remained silent, wondering just what *this* man could possibly want from her.

"Silence is often the best part of discretion, I suppose," he allowed after a few seconds. "I am George Solace, elected President and appointed

Lord Protector of the Republic. It has fallen to me to lead the defense against the last bastion of the Eugenicists' crimes."

"We have a slightly different view of what you've done the last few years," she said quietly. "What do you want, sir?"

"For now, just to talk," he said. "I mean, if you would *like* to give me the full order of battle of Second Fleet, the base technical specifications of the Protectorate's new missiles and a rundown of the capabilities and vulnerabilities of the dreadnoughts, I wouldn't mind."

She wanted to hate him. She *did* hate him, in fact—this man had ordered Project Prometheus, with all of the deaths and murder of children involved in that—but in person, his ready warm charm was almost overpowering.

"Roslyn Chambers. Mage-Lieutenant. KB-One-One-Nine-Eight-Seven-D-Three-L-Five," she recited.

"Name, rank and serial number," he concluded. "Unimaginative, but fair enough."

The cell was silent for a few seconds, and then one of the walls changed slightly, a "window" that hadn't been there appearing.

"I hadn't realized this room was quite so lacking in amenities," Solace said. "A window is the least we can do. I'll have someone bring you some books. They'll have to be physical, I'm afraid; we have security concerns."

"I'm one woman, denied my magic, in the center of a sixty-megaton fortress that hosts five hundred parasite warships and over a hundred missile launchers," Roslyn pointed out drily. "This station has, what, a thousand armed soldiers aboard? I'm not certain my boot-camp martial arts and basic technical skills are up to threatening you with a datapad."

"I've been surprised before, Mage-Lieutenant," Solace replied. "And I hesitate to underestimate a young woman who has been present at many of the turning points of the war—a young woman generally credited with being the reason any RMN ships escaped our trap at Nia Kriti to warn the Protectorate, and hence indirectly responsible for our defeat at Ardennes.

"We will take all of the precautions we must," he concluded. "There will be no violations of your rights as a prisoner of war, Lieutenant. Like the Protectorate, we regard ourselves as bound by the principles of the

Geneva Conventions even if we are not technically signatories to that ancient document.

"You will be interviewed by officers trained to learn as much as they can from you," he admitted, "but I would prefer that you come to regard yourself as our guest, not our prisoner. There is much you could do for us, in helping us bring this war to an end.

"You are, after all, something of a protégée of the Lord Regent, aren't you?"

Roslyn had nothing to say to any of that. She sat in silence as the fist of fear closed around her heart.

"We are not your enemy, Lieutenant. The government you serve espouses the very values of the monsters who murdered tens of thousands to create Mages. Surely, you must see that it is only in the dissolution of the separate castes of Mages and mundane and the disruption of enforced monarchies that we will finally see the end of the Eugenicists' horrific ideals and crimes."

He was so earnest, so calm and concerned...but Roslyn knew what he'd done.

"Tell me, Lord Protector, were you so determined to see the end of 'horrific ideals and crimes' when you ordered the murder of thousands of your own people's children to fuel your war machine?"

Solace shook his head at her and rose from his chair.

"Sacrifices must be made," he told her, his voice still warm and calm. "In time, I hope we can convince you of the truth of things. Until then, our security precautions will remain."

He bowed, a chubby little man with a warm voice and a heart of iron, and then he and his guards left Roslyn Chambers alone with her nightmare.

CHAPTER 34

THE APARTMENT'S SILENCE wore down on Roslyn after that. She remained on the couch, slowly curling into a fetal position as she struggled with her fears. She wasn't even sure what to do with herself.

Eventually, her fugue was interrupted by the sound of her next meal arriving. It took her a few minutes to force herself to unfold and eat the food. It wasn't bad, but she had little enthusiasm for any of it.

She found herself staring at the virtual window. Now that it was turned on, she could see that the screen had always been there, built in as part of the wall. The designers had done a good job of recessing it so that it vanished into the metal when turned off.

If the window was actually showing the view from Styx, it would be... *there*. Roslyn found the thin arc of the accelerator ring beneath them. Studying the view through the window, it was definitely a feed of the gas giant they'd passed to reach Styx.

Without the guards around her and with more time than she knew what to do with, Roslyn distracted herself by analyzing the various sparks of light. The window didn't have the zoom commands it might have had outside of a cell, but it was clear enough for her to slowly begin to identify, if nothing else, larger and smaller ships.

She could definitely tell the difference between gunships and capital ships, though the gunships were mostly also running fusion engines there. Presumably, standby wings were equipped with antimatter drives, but most of the production of that substance was clearly being used for missiles.

Roslyn started counting. If she ever made it out of there, the knowledge of what was present in Chrysanthemum would be critical. On the other hand, the numbers she was counting up were terrifying.

The Protectorate believed the Republic had started the war with between sixteen and twenty carrier groups, somewhere between one hundred and twenty and one hundred and fifty Promethean Interface–equipped warships.

Between military defeats and desertion, intelligence said the Republic was down to six or seven carrier groups after the Battle of Nueva Bolivia, with two to four unaccounted for. They'd figured that was around sixty warships, maybe as many as seventy.

Intelligence had confirmed the locations of five carriers and forty-three cruisers and battleships with some certainty, especially with the scouting missions by the *Rhapsody*-class ships.

That meant they'd believed the Republic had a maximum of twenty or so ships left unaccounted-for...and Roslyn was counting almost *seventy* major starships in the region around Styx.

For every ship she could see, there could easily be another one she couldn't—though at least some of these ships had to be transports and freighters to support the logistics of an operation of this scale.

There were shipyards visible as well. They were close enough to make out in some detail and she could see the shapes of dozens of the Republic's cylindrical hulls taking form as well.

This fleet *couldn't* have been ready a few months earlier. Even a handful of those carrier groups could have turned the tide of many of the battles of the war so far—and yet there were more warships in this system than the Protectorate had believed their enemy had left.

After taking a shower to try and wash off the last of the shock from meeting Lord Protector Solace—and the queasiness from just how personable the man turned out to be—Roslyn emerged to find that a set of books had been delivered to the room.

Somehow, she was unsurprised to find that the paper books were a collection of histories and political treatises on the hundred-year-long Eugenicist Wars between Earth and Mars, and the formation of the Protectorate at the end of them.

Even without opening them, she could guess the point of view they'd espouse. Boredom would drive her to read them sooner or later, she knew, but she needed to keep the reality in mind.

No matter how much the Republic wanted to convert her to their point of view, *they* were the ones who'd ordered thousands murdered to fuel their fleets. They weren't *wrong* in that the Protectorate inherently had some connections to the Eugenicists. The Mages had built structures in self-defense that resembled the castes their mad creators had imposed on Mars, but the *intent* mattered.

Roslyn could even admit that the Protectorate was flawed and in need of reform—exactly the kind of reform, in fact, that she understood was being negotiated on Mars right then.

None of that justified the Republic's actions. The Secession would have been allowed to stand if the Republic hadn't chosen war. *They'd* started the fight with the Protectorate in the end, rather than simply walk away.

If Roslyn was where she thought she was, several systems had even lied about whether they were joining the Secession, using the Protectorate's willingness to trust their members against them.

That was a truth that needed to be exposed. The existence and location of the accelerator ring needed to be exposed. The RMN needed to know that the Republic had ships and shipyards no one was accounting for, concealed in systems the RMN regarded as friendly and safe.

Somehow, Roslyn Chambers needed to escape. She had *no* idea how she was going to do that, but she needed to make it happen—and if at all possible, she needed to find Mage-Admiral Alexander and bring her out as well.

Her only actual hope of *getting* out might hang on the Mage-Admiral's power, anyway. Roslyn couldn't fight off a fleet on her own.

The Crown Princess of Mars? The Rune Wright, as ad Aaron had called her?

Jane Alexander might just be able to fight a fleet herself.

If she couldn't, she and Roslyn might well be doomed.

CHAPTER 35

THE BOOKS turned out to be a much less effective conversion tool than Roslyn suspected Solace had hoped. Skimming through the abstracts to begin with, she was surprised how many of the writers recognized that so much of the Protectorate's pro-Mage structure was born of fear.

Some didn't, but she left those on the bottom of the pile. The one boredom actually brought her to read was almost pro-monarchy in its level of neutrality, suggesting that the best answers were to find a balance between dealing with anti-Mage prejudices while slowly reforming the Covenant.

The Covenant was what defined much of the rules that kept Mages a separate caste from the rest of humanity. It was under the Covenant that Mages had separate courts and Guilds, rules that called for Mages to be tried by Mages and similar protections.

That had been the trade, after all. The Mages took the protection they felt they needed, including control of the Kingdom of Mars and the Protectorate the Mage-Kings had forged—and in exchange, they gave humanity the stars.

Roslyn laid the book down and stared at the "window" on the wall blankly. The books were the only distraction she'd been given, and she could *tell* that they had been selected carefully. If she wasn't careful, each book would make her more likely to buy into the spiel of the next one.

It was an old trick, one she recognized, but that didn't mean it wouldn't *work*.

In a convulsive moment, she swept the books off the table. She tried to kick the entire table over as she rose, but it was bolted to the floor. Only the lightweight chairs weren't.

After a moment's thought, Roslyn kicked the table again, harder. The spike of pain up her leg was almost welcome, a distraction from the awful situation she was in.

She paced over to the window and looked out at the accelerator ring again. That flimsy-looking construction stretched for tens of thousands of kilometers, surrounding an entire world and producing enough antimatter to fuel a fleet.

Roslyn could see the key to ending the war from her prison cell, and she had no way to communicate that with anyone.

Someone knocked on her door, interrupting her thoughts, and she glared at the entryway. There was no real way for her to deny entry to anyone. Despite the comforts of her cell, it *was* a cell.

Whoever was on the other side of the door waited a minute, knocked again, and then calmly entered the room. Roslyn glared at the familiar older man, but Colonel Othmar McLain simply shrugged at her.

"If you do not answer, I'm still going to come in," he told her gently. "I am mostly giving you a chance to make certain you are decent."

"What, you can't check on the cameras to be sure?" she asked.

"I could, but I choose to leave you some privacy," McLain agreed amiably. "Republic policy says those cameras can only be regularly viewed by personnel of the same gender as the prisoner. We provide what securities we can."

"Am I supposed to be grateful?" Roslyn demanded.

She should probably be more careful in how she addressed the man. Her best chance to find any way out of this mess probably involved befriending or seducing someone, and McLain was the first person to be alone with her in her cell so far.

"No," he allowed. "We are trying to make you comfortable, Lieutenant, but we must also see to our security."

Roslyn shook her head at him and dropped onto the couch, spreading her arms wide.

"As you can see, I'm no threat to anyone's security from this room," she told him. "You might as well have me naked in chains on the main thoroughfare, for all I can impact your *security*."

She managed to surprise a choked snort of amusement from the Colonel.

"What do you want, Colonel?" she finally asked. "I can't imagine you're here for conversation."

"That's not a bad interpretation of my instructions, actually," McLain said. He hooked one of the chairs over to him with the back of his ankle and sat on it backward, facing Roslyn with a small smile.

"The Lord Protector asked me to check in on you and see if there was anything you needed. Or, of course, if you had any questions on the books."

He gestured at the pile of books on the floor.

"It seems you've made up part of your mind already."

"Just because the Lord Protector wants me to read those books doesn't mean they're worth the paper they're printed on," she said sweetly. "Tell me, Colonel, which of these books actively calls for genocide?"

He sighed.

"None of them, I believe," he told her. "While I understand your point of view, I don't think anything that has happened could be called genocide."

"If not, then only because you were *stopped*," Roslyn replied. "Unless you want to hand me a jump-ship and a free pass out of the system, Colonel, I'm not sure I can help you."

"I'd say we don't have the Jump Mages for that, but you wouldn't need one," he said, glancing at her hands.

Roslyn clenched her fists. The plain fatigues she'd found in the apartment closet fit her well enough, but they didn't come with the gloves generally preferred by Protectorate Mages. If she turned her hands palm-up, the inlaid silver of her jump runes was clearly visible.

"I can get you a lot of things to make your stay more comfortable," McLain told her. "If you have a preference for clothing, food, drinks, et cetera, I can have that delivered or the meals changed. My understanding is that our file shows you have no food allergies or medication requirements, but if we're missing something, please let me know."

"I'm *fine*," Roslyn insisted, then paused. "Actually...I want to see Mage-Admiral Alexander."

"That's not on the list of things I can get you," the Colonel admitted.

"Then talk to someone who can, maybe someone *without* a hook on their collar."

He laughed and tapped the insignia.

"If it was a hook, Lieutenant Chambers, I think it would be the other way up. This is a shepherd's staff, the tool used to guide the flock," he explained the obvious to her. "It is the personal emblem of the Lord Protector and I am one of the Protector's Guard, his personal security force.

"Like the Royal Guard on Mars, we speak with authority beyond our formal rank, but Mage-Admiral Alexander represents the single most dangerous prisoner we have ever taken," McLain warned her. "I will *ask*, Lieutenant. It seems a small-enough concession to maintain your comfort, but that decision is out of my hands."

"Ask, then," Roslyn said. "I don't think there's anything else you can do for me, Colonel."

He rose and bowed.

"I will do what I can," he promised. "My task is to remind you that we are your hosts, Lieutenant, but until *you* accept that you were on the wrong side of this war, there is only so much we can do."

"I'm a long way from thinking I am on the wrong side of the war," Roslyn told him. "And I don't think I'm going to be on the losing side, either."

Despite the hole-digging Roslyn had done, McLain returned several hours later. When he arrived, she was amusing herself by building a tower out of the collection of books the Republicans had given her.

The knock on the door made her twitch in surprise, and the two-story construct she'd built promptly collapsed onto the table in a clatter.

"Come in," she declared loudly. There wasn't much point denying anyone entrance, and she didn't really care if they saw her treating the books as toys.

The Protector's Guard Colonel stepped through the door with a wry smile, looking at the spread-out pile of books that had been Roslyn's tower.

"Am I interrupting something?" he asked.

"Only testing the structural integrity of these books as construction materials," she said. "I am unimpressed. Can I help you, Colonel McLain?"

He produced two sets of manacles from inside his jacket, the cuffs hanging from his hands by their linking chain.

"I have permission to take you to see Mage-Admiral Alexander," he told her. "I do have to ask you to submit to full Mage-cuffing for you to leave this room, though. That isn't optional."

"I'm not surprised," Roslyn admitted. She looked at the manacles and chains in McLain's grip and swallowed. It was one thing to be trapped in a room that blocked her magic. It was quite another to voluntarily allow herself to be chained with a device that did the same.

"Fine," she ground out. "I don't have much choice, do I?"

"You can remain here," McLain said. "So long as you're in this apartment, we don't need to cuff you."

"That's because the apartment might as well *be* Mage-cuffs. *Fine,*" she repeated, rising and presenting her hands. "I will do what I must."

"Very well."

Two more Protector's Guards, the collar insignia familiar to Roslyn now, entered the room in response to a silent call. Both of them were women, she noted as they took the cuffs from McLain and began to restrain her.

For a nation willing to embrace mass atrocities, the Republic was being surprisingly respectful.

The chains attached to the manacles were longer and looser than those used when Roslyn had been a prisoner on the ship, allowing her to move more freely and keep up as McLain and their two escorts guided her through the warren of tunnels and corridors that made up the interior of Styx.

Roslyn's sense of direction was good enough to know that she was being led in circles, but with the confusing nature of the interior of a space station, she wasn't comfortable thinking she could cut time *off* the roundabout route McLain was taking her.

When they reached their destination, she was reasonably sure she could find her way to Alexander's cell *and* find her way to the shuttle bay—but she could only do either from *her* cell and via the route they'd shown her.

Since she was very sure that route was as inefficient as possible, that memorization wasn't valuable yet—but Roslyn was grimly determined to keep doing it until she had enough of a mental map of the station to perhaps find an efficient way out.

The entrance to their destination looked much the same as the entrance to her own cell: a security door flanked by Augments from the Protector's Guard in a hall that otherwise looked like a normal residential accessway.

One of those Guards—both women again, Roslyn absently noted—stepped forward to stop them as they approached.

"We have permission for the prisoners to meet," McLain told her. "You should have the authorization from Solace's office already."

"Let me double-check," the Guard replied. "Hold your position."

McLain was almost certainly senior to the woman, but it seemed the Republic had picked its most determined soldiers to guard the Crown Princess of Mars—it was what Roslyn would have done.

"Your authorization is confirmed," the Guard admitted after a moment. "I think this is a terrible idea, Colonel."

"Argue it with the Lord Protector," McLain replied. "It is *his* plan we follow, after all."

"It's too late for that, it seems," she said. "Take her in. We'll be watching."

"Of course you will," McLain agreed. He gestured for Roslyn's guards to lead her forward as the woman who'd remained next to the door pressed her palm to a reader.

Roslyn was watching and paying attention to *everything*. There might be a secondary authorization she couldn't see, but the main control seemed to be either a palm-print lock or a chip imbedded in the Guard's hand.

Either could be worked with given the opportunity.

The door slid open while she was focused on the lock, and she found herself shuffled forward into an apartment *identical* to hers. Even with the Mage-cuffs on, she could tell that it was warded in the same way as hers as well.

That kind of ward was rare enough in the Protectorate, but Roslyn was one of the small group of people who knew the Republic had made an alliance with a rogue Mage of unusually powerful gifts—now that she knew the term, she guessed he'd been a Rune Wright. Presumably, Finley had helped the Lord Protector make these cells—and once assembled, the wards could be maintained by any Mage.

For all Roslyn knew, the Republic was even using a Prometheus Interface for the recharging. At least theoretically, a Mage trapped in the Interface wasn't limited to the jump spell.

Her plotting and analyzing were interrupted when she fully stepped into the room and spotted the woman sitting on the couch. Jane Alexander was awake, which Roslyn hadn't seen since Sucre, and she rushed to the Admiral's side as quickly as she could with the manacles.

"Admiral, Admiral, are you okay?" she demanded.

Alexander moved her head slowly, her languid change of attention entirely out of character for her, and leveled an almost-entirely unfocused gaze on Roslyn.

"Roslyn?" she asked, her voice slurred. "It's...good to see you. Are you... Are you..."

Whatever Alexander had meant to ask seemed to escape her, and she lowered her head slightly with a sigh.

"Foggy," she said softly. "Drugs. Food. Water. All drugged."

Roslyn turned an angry glare at McLain.

"What the hell is this?" she snapped. "This isn't appropriate treatment for a prisoner of war!"

"We're doing the best we can," he said flatly. "Yes, Mage-Admiral Alexander is a prisoner of war, but she is *also* a walking weapon of mass destruction. We have some idea of what a Rune Wright like Admiral Alexander is capable of.

"Unfortunately, it's impossible to suppress her magic without some level of sedative," he continued. "Here, unlike aboard the transport that delivered you, we can at least keep her conscious and capable of some self-care, but the security of this facility and the tens of thousands of people aboard it requires her state."

He shook his head.

"I don't like it, Lieutenant, but it is necessary."

"Prick."

Only Roslyn was close enough to hear the Admiral's slowly muttered word, and she forced herself to conceal a grin. Despite the amount of sedatives the Republic was clearly feeding Jane Alexander, she was definitely still in there.

"You wanted to see her, Lieutenant," McLain said. "You have. I can permit you to spend a few minutes together, but I must remain with you."

Roslyn ignored him, kneeling in front of Alexander and taking the older woman's hands.

"Your Highness, have you been hurt?" she asked gently.

"Don't think so," Alexander slurred. "Har' to say with...this...*shit.*"

The Mage-Lieutenant's heart ached to see her mentor like this, fury burning away the last of her own fear. She wasn't sure how she was going to do it yet, but she was going to get her boss out of his mess.

"We have no reason to harm the Mage-Admiral," the Guard Colonel said behind her. "She is a legitimate POW. We are taking extreme precautions because of the danger level she represents, but we do not want to hurt her."

"Just interrogate her?" Roslyn snapped. Her own "interviews" had yet to materialize, though she knew they wouldn't be held off much longer.

"Of course," he confirmed. "We are at war, after all. I am tasked to find the best ways to protect *my* people, Mage-Lieutenant, just as you and the Admiral were tasked to protect yours."

Roslyn squeezed Alexander's hands hard, hoping the befuddled woman got the silent message: *I'm coming for you.*

"You missed the easiest way to protect your people a long damned time ago," she told McLain. "The Protectorate didn't want this fucking war. All you ever needed to do was nothing."

The apartment cell chilled as she turned to face the Colonel. His smile had slipped, and a momentary snarl marred his face before he regained his composure.

"The Protectorate was never going to leave us be," he said. "I think we're done here, Lieutenant. Time to go home."

Home was a dirty word to Roslyn right now. It meant Tau Ceti or her quarters on *Durendal,* not that forever-cursed cell that blocked her magic.

She needed to find a way out. She was *going* to find a way out.

CHAPTER 36

"JUMP COMPLETE," Shvets reported on *Rhapsody in Purple*'s bridge. They stretched. "We are now on the final jump of the New Berlin–Alignment route."

"Milhouse, get me a scan of the area," Kelly LaMonte ordered. Jumping into an area that *should* have traffic to it was a risk, but it was a risk that potentially gave her opportunities. "Is anybody home?"

"Taking a look," her tactical officer agreed.

As the scanners worked, Kelly leveled a gaze on the video link to the simulacrum chamber. Xi Wu was leaning against the railing of the platform holding the simulacrum itself, smiling wanly against fatigue in the spy ship's magical gravity.

"Go *rest*, love," Kelly told Xi Wu. "We want you all ready to go when we jump into Alignment. It might be nice and happy and friendly, but it might not be, and we need to be ready for that."

"I know, I know," the Ship's Mage replied. "Just waiting on Liara."

"We've got a customer," Milhouse snapped. "Big-ass bird, fifteen megatons. Beacon makes her *Gentle Rains of Summer*. She's a long way out in the middle of nowhere."

"Does the beacon have any details on cargo or contract?" Kelly asked. The ship name sounded familiar, but she couldn't place it. Hopefully, the Captain was feeling patriotic...or bribable. She could work with either.

"Lists them as under contract to Starward Shipping in the New Berlin System," Milhouse told her. "MISS files say Starward Shipping has a near-monopoly on shipping to Alignment, one of those sweetheart deals we *really* should do more about."

"But she's big enough for us to hide in the shadow of," Kelly replied. For a moment, she considered just doing that—her crew might be able to match their jump to make sure they emerged in the shadow of *Gentle Rains of Summer*'s jump flare even if all they had was the destination and the timing.

It would be *much* easier to do it with the freighter's cooperation and a full set of their jump calculations.

"Time lag?" she asked.

"Thirty light-seconds, sir," Milhouse replied. "Andrew Michaels is listed as the skipper of record."

"Thank you. We'll transmit a recording, then," Kelly said. A few careful commands brought up the recorder. She checked herself in the image, tugging the braid of her newly ocean-green hair to one side and making sure her not-quite-civilian shipsuit looked more military than usual.

"Captain Andrew Michaels of *Gentle Rains of Summer*, this is Captain Kelly LaMonte aboard *Indigo Melody*," she greeted the merchant skipper. "While I understand that this is a bit of an odd request, I need an hour of your time to discuss a critical, potentially financially lucrative-for-you matter.

"I suggest our ships accelerate toward rendezvous and you and I speak in person."

She checked the message and hoped her body language and shipsuit sent the right image. She *could* insert a uniform into the recording, but that would be too obvious. Kelly was hoping to catch this Michaels's attention *without* outright admitting on a recording that she worked for the Protectorate.

A minute passed in silence as *Rhapsody* accelerated toward the civilian ship. She was going to feel *very* silly if the big ship jumped without her.

"Transmission incoming," Milhouse reported.

Kelly had the file opened, scanned for viruses, and playing before her tactical officer had finished speaking. Every day the war dragged on was another day people like Mage-Admiral Alexander were ending up dead.

She was rapidly running out of patience.

"Captain LaMonte, I received your invitation with some...interest, let's say," the gray-haired man in the recording told her with a twinkle in his eye. "I'm always interested in financially lucrative opportunities.

"I've instructed my navigator to begin a rendezvous course for your ship, though I calculate we will be some hours before we are close enough to meet. May I invite you aboard *Gentle Rains of Summer* for dinner, Captain?"

Kelly smiled. It appeared her *entire* message had been received and understood.

"Mike," she pinged her husband on the communicator. "Get one of the shuttles rigged up to look all civilian and then see if you can find yourself a nice suit.

"I'll let Xi know in a bit, but it looks like we're going out for dinner."

And if bringing her spouses meant she brought a pilot, one who'd trained as a hand-to-hand expert with the best teachers the Martian Interstellar Security Service could find, and a fully trained combat Mage with her as potential bodyguards, well, wasn't that a coincidence?

As they exited the shuttle, Kelly took a deep breath of *Gentle Rains of Summer*'s shipboard air. She'd been an engineer before she'd been a spy and a starship captain, and one of the things she'd learned was that the air of a ship told you a lot of things about it.

There was just a hint of must in *Gentle Rains*'s air, enough to make the ship's age obvious—but only a hint. Someone was spending a lot of time and energy babying the old vents to keep them clean.

The shuttle bay gave off a similar impression. Her glance at the freighter's file had told her that *Gentle Rains of Summer* was forty-eight years old. By the standards of the container ships that traveled the

Protectorate's spaceways, that was about middle-aged, but it was old enough that care needed to be taken.

The shuttle bay showed every year of its age, but it was impeccably clean as Captain Michaels strode across the bay to shake her hand, two of his officers in tow...one of whom Kelly *knew*.

"Captain LaMonte, welcome aboard *Gentle Rains of Summer*," Michaels told her. "I'd like to introduce you to my Ship's Mage, Evelyn Nguyen, and my executive officer, Bran Wiltshire."

Evelyn Nguyen had the ambiguously brown features of a Martian native and bowed slightly to Kelly, but everyone was expecting the main focus of attention to be Wiltshire.

Wiltshire was a sandy-haired older man who'd been working his way up in administration on basically every civilian ship Kelly had ever served on. He'd been on *Blue Jay* under Captain Rice with her and then on *Red Falcon* with the same Captain. When *Red Falcon* had been lost, Wiltshire had returned to civilian life with a glowing series of recommendations and referrals from his now either wealthy or MISS former superiors.

They seemed to have done him good.

"Kelly," he greeted her with a broad grin. "It's good to see you again."

"The galaxy is way too damn small," Kelly replied, pulling the man into a quick embrace. Letting him go, she stepped back to nod to Captain Michaels.

"Wiltshire knows me and my spouses, but this is my wife, Ship's Mage Xi Wu, and my husband, First Pilot Mike Kelzin."

"Greetings to you all," Michaels told them. "While I don't believe Bran broke any confidences, he *did* suggest that if you were asking for help, it might be more important than you were letting on."

"It might be, yes," Kelly said carefully.

"Come, let's talk in private over a good meal," the freighter's captain said firmly. "That always seems the best plan for me!"

The meal was good. Kelly had no argument with the quality of the handmade pasta Michaels's staff produced for the six of them. It was delicious and it occupied the first twenty minutes of the dinner without interruption.

Once the plates were cleared away, the steward brought coffees, and the freighter Captain leaned forward over his, studying Kelly.

"Between one thing and another, I'm guessing it's not a coincidence that your ship is loitering near a Protectorate-loyal UnArcana World. What do you need, Captain LaMonte?"

"Cover," Kelly said bluntly. "We have reasons to feel that a more-detailed scouting run on the loyal UnArcana worlds is needed. My ship is capable of that run, but we can't jump into a system undetected."

"You want us to haul you in with our cargo?" Michaels asked. "That might take some doing."

"That shouldn't be necessary," she admitted. "If you can provide us a full copy of your jump calculations and we jump at the same time, my crew can make certain we emerge in your shadow. No one will ever be the wiser about our presence."

"That seems easy enough," he told her. "I assume that you didn't want to risk anyone on my ship telling the Alignment government about this?"

"Exactly. The less you can reveal, the less trouble you can possibly get in," she told him. "Dinner with a stranger this far out? Easy to justify, especially since it turns out we *aren't* strangers. Transmitting your jump calculations? Harder."

"If the Captain is on board, I can provide the calculations before you leave," Nguyen said in a soft near-whisper. "It is easy enough."

"We can pay for this," Kelly told them. "It's the least I can offer for the help we're asking for."

"I won't turn down the money," Michaels admitted, "but we'll do it. I don't jump to Alignment often, and I like the folks I deal with there, but I know where my loyalties lie in this damned war."

"Thank you, Captain," she said. "It's appreciated. Hopefully, all of this is unnecessary, and I will learn only that Alignment is doing everything they say they are and are truly loyal members of the Protectorate."

"But you wouldn't be going through this rigmarole if you thought that was going to be the case," Wiltshire said grimly, the XO looking thoughtful.

"No," Kelly conceded. "I don't think Alignment is entirely out of the fold just yet, but I think they're hedging their bets."

She'd check them anyway. Her suspicions still rested mostly on Chrysanthemum—and that system was enough farther out that she wasn't expecting to find a ship to hide behind there.

CHAPTER 37

"JUMP COMPLETE. *Gentle Rains of Summer* is exactly on target and so are we," Shvets reported. "Well done, Liara."

The junior Ship's Mage bowed her head on the video feed, looking utterly drained. Xi Wu was already stepping up beside her, gently guiding the other woman out of the way as she took over.

"Stealth spell active," Xi Wu reported. "We are invisible."

"Shvets, get us out from *Gentle Rains,*" Kelly ordered. "Captain Michaels has earned his money today; let's not put him at any more risk.

"Our destination is Mesa, the innermost gas giant."

Alignment had five rocky worlds, one comfortably habitable, and three gas giants. The usual arrangement of the rocky worlds on the interior and the gas giants on the outside was in play, with Mesa, Parallel and Angular all orbiting well away from Plateau, the habitable world.

"Angular has been in the data from the freighters," she explained as the spy ship's engines woke up. "Mesa and Parallel haven't, but Mesa is closest to Plateau and to us. We'll investigate Parallel before we leave the system, but I'm hoping we can do a fast sweep of them both and call it a day."

"Course is in, engines are active," Shvets replied. "We're on our way. ETA eighteen hours, assuming nothing comes up that calls for us to cut the engines."

Rhapsody in Purple had the same magical gravity as every RMN warship. The faster they accelerated, the harder it was for them to hide their presence, but the cloaking spell was sufficient to cover about ten gravities from their antimatter engines at any significant distance.

Kelly nodded and glanced over at the icon for *Gentle Rains of Summer*. Like most big civilian ships, *Gentle Rains* resembled nothing so much as an eggbeater. Six ribs extended from the front of the ship, sweeping back to connect to the engine module and rotating to provide gravity when the ship wasn't under thrust.

Their course was heading directly toward Plateau and taking them well away from *Rhapsody in Purple*, and she mentally saluted them.

"Fly safe, Captain Michaels, Wiltshire," she murmured. "Don't let me have got you in trouble. This is going to be a messy enough day as it is."

"Captain to the bridge, Captain to the bridge."

The carefully pitched alert cut through Kelly's quarters and she jerked awake, only avoiding banging her head against the wall because her husband got a hand in the way in time.

"Careful, love," he told her. "Go," he urged, kissing her forehead. "Conrad wouldn't wake you if it wasn't critical."

They were taking careful shifts right now, keeping an eye on things while letting everyone get some rest. Kelly was sleeping in her shipsuit to be ready, but she still took a moment to make sure she looked presentable before rushing to the bridge.

Milhouse and Shvets had the watch, and they were waiting for her as she came into the command center.

"What's going on?" she demanded.

"Had to cut the engines to three gravities," Shvets told her. "Adds two hours to our ETA at this point, but..." They waved at the screen. "Did Alignment have gunships before the Secession?"

The familiar bullet-like shape of a RIN gunship danced across her screen, fusion engines lit as the ship followed a standard patrol route.

"They did," Kelly confirmed, her voice hard, "but they were *Crucifix*-class ships, not *Accelerator*-class. I don't see rotational gravity pods on that ship, do you?"

The *Crucifix*-class gunships had four living pods on extended arms. Designed for long-duration patrols, they could rotate to provide pseudo-gravity to anyone in the pods. Under acceleration, the pods would swing behind the ship to have the thrust provide gravity in the same direction—usually called "squid mode."

The gunship on their screens was accelerating and there was no sign of squid mode anywhere.

"We picked her up first because she was accelerating, but we've IDed several more as we've kept moving," Milhouse told her. New red icons glistened on her display. "Once we had one, the other five were easy to find. They're running a standard security pattern around Mesa. Keeping their engines low-ish to avoid detection from Plateau, but I'd say they've got a base at the gas giant."

"We need more than supposition," Kelly said with a sigh. "We're talking about treason by an entire star system government, people. Even the *Accelerators* might have been delivered before the actual war.

"That means I need sensors on either an RIN starship or a major base that the Alignment government hasn't told the Protectorate about. We need smoking guns, unfortunately."

"So long as they're following the pattern it looks like they're following, we should be able to cut through Mesa's space at about thirty light-seconds without detection," Shvets told her. "That will require shutting down the reactor and running heat sinks at full. Barring similar tech and magic to ours, though, they won't hide anything from us at that range."

"We do what we have to do," Kelly replied. "I'll take turning the ship into a sauna over missing something. If there's a Republic base in this system, we need to know."

"Any chance it's the accelerator ring?" Milhouse asked. "We're still pretty far out."

"We might be missing the accelerator ring itself from this distance," Kelly agreed. "But if *you* were defending the most critical piece of infrastructure left to your nation, would you do it with six gunships in a standard patrol pattern?"

"Shutting down the reactor," Kelly murmured, as much to herself as anyone else, as she tapped through the screens on her command chair. *Rhapsody in Purple*'s Engineering section was small and self-contained. She *could* have a chief engineer, but the four-person team running the section was small enough that Kelly ran Engineering herself.

"We're cold," Milhouse announced. "Heat sinks filling. Containment active."

"Current velocity seven thousand one hundred and fifty kilometers per second," Shvets announced. "We will make our pass at nine million kilometers in eleven minutes from...mark."

Mesa was growing on the screens as their sensors focused on the gas giant and its orbitals. From almost a full light-minute away, even *Rhapsody*'s scanners could only pick out so much. Ships with active engines, major space stations, that kind of thing.

"Last official reports say that Mesa has a civilian extraction complex anchored on an inner moon," Milhouse said aloud. "Unless I miss my guess, that's this here."

The tactical officer highlighted a "moon" that was little more than a midsized captured asteroid. It was probably smaller than Phobos or Deimos back on Mars, even.

But it had a permanent stable orbit, which made it a good place to anchor a space station on. Milhouse's highlight picked out the mix of deep-space and surface infrastructure that made up the facility—relatively easily identified, given the five-thousand-kilometer-long cloudscoop tubes that dipped into Mesa's atmosphere to pull up hydrogen and other gases in immense quantities.

"And if that is the only station that's supposed to be here, I'll give everyone one guess on what contact bravo is," Milhouse continued, highlighting a different section of space. "Bravo appears to be entirely artificial, no anchoring. She's lower down, which makes her cloudscoops harder to pick out, but...I think I've got her."

The cloudscoops were the most obvious part of any fuel-extraction operation. It was hard to conceal a thousand-kilometer-plus magnetically charged pipe, after all. The 'scoops on "contact bravo" were a fifth of the length of the official refinery's version and had been clearly designed to be stealthier as well.

But there were also twenty-three of them to the official station's eight.

"Got a confirm on that, Milhouse?" Kelly said softly.

"Major refueling depot, sir," he replied. "I'm estimating a hundred million tons of fuel storage and what looks like at least twenty million tons of warehousing. Probably munitions and provisions, at a guess."

Kelly whistled silently.

"I imagine the RMN doesn't have a major logistics depot they forgot to mention to the MISS," she murmured. "But do we have anything else?"

"Hold one; I have new contacts," Milhouse snapped. Vague orange icons blipped onto the screen around the depot...and then the entire complex flashed bright crimson.

"I have a Republic cruiser in a defensive position," the tactical officer barked. "Beacon is shut down, but nobody else flies a twenty-megaton cylinder with rotational gravity. Installations *here, here* and *here* appear to be missile and gunship bases, ten megatons apiece.

"Lighter platforms than the Republic has used elsewhere, they're probably local builds, but I'm seeing at least twenty more gunships as we're getting closer. Plus, the cruiser."

Kelly nodded slowly, focusing her own screens on the Republic warship.

There was no mistaking it. A *Benjamin*-class heavy cruiser was built around a single cylindrical hull, five hundred meters long by one hundred and seventy-five meters across. That twenty-megaton hull was also used as the basis for the Republic's bigger battleships and carriers, but this was its most basic form.

And it was a ship that had *no* business in a Protectorate system.

"Any sign from Plateau that the planet has been occupied since our last reports?" she asked quietly.

"Nothing," Milhouse replied. "Everyone there seems to be acting like business is as usual."

"Bastards." There was no real heat in Kelly's epithet, just faded exhaustion. The minds behind the Republic had *known* the Protectorate would use kid gloves with any UnArcana World that didn't secede—that several of those worlds had stayed was a huge moral victory for Mars, after all.

And they'd used that against the Protectorate.

"Maintain course," she ordered. "Xi, get one of your people ready," she continued. "I don't care if these bastards know they're caught. We jump as soon as we're clear and safe. There's no accelerator ring here, which means even money is on Chrysanthemum and New Madagascar— and *we*, my friends, are heading to Chrysanthemum."

If she was very lucky, this little trip might mean the end of the war.

CHAPTER 38

WHEN SOMEONE knocked on Roslyn's door at noon, two days after her visit to Alexander's apartment, she was expecting it to be McLain
again. She intentionally fumbled a book she was fiddling with, collapsing
the structure of books she'd been building.

If she'd guessed the location of the camera correctly, it would look
like she was still building a house of cards to her captors. If she hadn't,
well, McLain might be coming to ask her just *why* she was using the
books they'd given her to build a rough map of Styx Station.

The knock repeated a few seconds later, and she realized it didn't
sound like the sharp and confident rap of the Protector's Guard officer.

"Come in," she instructed.

The door swung open, allowing two of her usual female guards to
step in. They did a quick survey of the room, then stepped farther inside and out of the way. Behind them followed a man she was unfamiliar
with. He wore a civilian suit in dark burgundy but had the same golden
crook on his lapel as the Protector's Guard.

He was a golden-haired young man with expressive blue eyes, at
most a few years older than Roslyn's own early twenties. He saw her and
bowed deeply.

"Mage-Lieutenant Roslyn Chambers," he greeted her in an unfamiliar slow accent. "I am Alecto Gil."

"Is that supposed to mean something to me, Mr. Gil?" Roslyn asked.
He smiled.

"Not really," he admitted. "I am one of several junior aides to the Lord Protector, though I have the distinction of hailing from *this* star system. Our esteemed leader has asked that I give you a tour of the reasonably unclassified portions of Styx Station and answer any questions you have about the Republic and, well"—he gestured to the books scattered across the floor—"the reading material he provided."

"That sounds more interesting than staring at walls," Roslyn told him. It would also give her a chance to add to her mental map of the station. She had a *good* memory and was focusing on remembering her way around. Enough silly tours trying to win her over might give her an opportunity.

She wasn't sure what that opportunity would even look like, but she knew she had to find it.

"She can't leave the room without Mage-cuffs," one of the guards noted, producing the silver manacles from inside her uniform. "Those were the Lord Protector's direct orders."

"Of course," Gil agreed. "I think we can dispense with the actual chains, though. You will be with us every step of the way if the Mage-Lieutenant decides to try something silly."

The guard did a good job of looming at Roslyn as she clasped the Mage-cuffs around her wrists and ankles. Roslyn wasn't going to tell them that they only needed one set—wrists *or* ankles would have been enough to block her power—even if she thought they'd believe her.

Once the cuffs were attached, the guard stepped back. She accepted her carbine back from her compatriot and checked the stungun attachment before leveling it on Roslyn.

"We need you alive," the guard noted. "But SmartDarts are pretty reliable on that count. You read me?"

"I read you," Roslyn agreed.

"Please, ladies, please," Gil interjected. "We have no need for threats and displays today. Lieutenant Chambers is a guest, even if not entirely by her choice.

"Come, let me show you our station."

Roslyn wasn't sure if Gil was as brightly naïve as he seemed or if he was just an idiot. Both were options, she supposed, though the most likely scenario was that it was a façade.

After all, if she read between the lines correctly, he was a politician.

The tour began in the gardens, the last thing that Roslyn expected to find aboard what was supposedly a military station. Massive panels above her head created enough artificial light to support close to an acre of growing plants, with paths weaving through them that Gil happily led her along.

"This was my people's insistence," he told her. "Every plant in here is edible. We bred them specifically to be both high-nutrition and attractive, allowing us to create multipurpose spaces like this.

"Styx has multiple gardens like this, to help soothe the souls of the people who serve on her. She's large enough to be able to spare the space, after all."

"She's, what, three standard twenty-megaton hulls linked together?" Roslyn asked. That was why there was no natural light in the garden, after all. Styx wasn't a rotating ring station that could have theoretically had *some* windows. The rotational gravity hulls used in Republic warships had zero-gravity transfer tubes at their centers, not a gap that would allow sunlight in.

"Four, actually," Gil told her. "Assembled into a pair of one-kilometer long sections connected together at the mid and end points. Each hull has separate rotational gravity, power and weapons, just in case something goes wrong."

"Like your secret base being found by the Protectorate," she said sweetly.

"That is unlikely to happen," he replied, pulling a flower down to smell its fragrance. "We will be safe here from the Protectorate. For long enough, anyway."

"Because we're in Chrysanthemum, which never officially seceded?" Roslyn asked, testing.

The politician theory definitely won out. Roslyn was looking for it and the young man barely flinched before regaining his composure.

"I can't speak to that," he told her virtuously. "We don't want to give you *all* of the Republic's secrets just yet. Come," he instructed with a nod. "I'm not going to show you the *entire* station—I just explained how large she is—but we can take a look at a few spots. Anything in particular you'd want to see?"

An escape route wasn't something he was going to show her, Roslyn knew. Command centers, weapons, shuttle bays...those all fell into the same kind of category.

"I'm a tactical officer by training, but you're not going to show me the guns or control centers," she said aloud. "I don't know, life support?"

He laughed.

"There are a few things I can show you," he told her. "Styx is as large as she is to permit her to *also* be a civilian station, Lieutenant. Come. Let me show you the promenade."

Either the hull that Roslyn was imprisoned in was the main civilian center aboard Styx, or there was a lot more civilian life aboard than Gil was implying. The promenade he took her to was basically a mall.

She wasn't allowed *into* the mall with its general civilian population, of course. Gil took her to a balcony that looked out over the promenade. The area stretched for several hundred meters in front of her, rows of shops organized into neat sections around decorative fountains and gardens—presumably part of the water- and food-supply systems like the larger garden Gil had shown her already.

Roslyn's rough count put the crowd in the mall at about six or seven hundred. Her study suggested that most of them were in uniform...and the ones that weren't wore clothing that just screamed *bureaucrat* and *politician*.

"So, where does what's left of the Republic Assembly meet?" Roslyn asked after watching the crowd for a few minutes. "This *is* the continuity-of-government facility, isn't it?"

"The Lord Protector is here. What else matters?" Gil replied lightly. "The Assembly voted him full executive power for the duration. Once this war is over, we'll make sure proper elections are held—both for us and the Protectorate."

"Because the Protectorate's elections aren't proper?" she said. "That seems a rather large assumption to make."

"No election made under a formal and imposed caste system can be regarded as free and fair," Gil explained, as if she were a dim child. "So long as the Protectorate continues to uphold its fundamentally flawed system, no election held in their territory can be regarded as valid."

Roslyn held her tongue. The Protectorate Charter and the Covenant of Mars *did* give Mages certain rights and advantages others didn't have—she wasn't going to deny that—but she'd never heard of even *one* world where voting rights were remotely different for Mages.

And both the Charter and the Covenant were being replaced with a new Constitution. The Protectorate had recognized its problems on its own, without needing the Republic to start a war to fix them.

The fact that the Assembly seemed to have been completely shoved aside in favor of the Lord Protector didn't exactly make the Republic look like a democracy to her, either.

"Unless someone wants to give me a credit chip and loose me in those stores, I figure we've got as much as we're going to get out of the promenade," Roslyn finally told Gil. "You seem to have a plan, Mr. Gil, despite asking me for suggestions. Where to next?

He smiled again. He had a *nice* smile. Shame it was attached to a prick.

"I had some ideas," he conceded, "but I am prepared to hear what you want to see."

"I want to see the accelerator ring," Roslyn said. That was probably a risky ask, but she *did* want to see the accelerator ring—and to find out just what the Chrysanthemum native guiding her around thought of a project that must have consumed his entire star system for years.

"All right," Gil told her, pride in the accomplishment leaking through. "There's an observation deck designed for just that. Are you all right in zero gravity, Lieutenant?"

"I am an officer in the Royal Martian Navy, Mr. Gil," Roslyn reminded him. Titles or not, he seemed to forget that. "I am entirely capable in zero gravity, yes."

"She means she can snap you like a twig in zero-gee, given a single handhold," the guard beside her muttered. Roslyn wasn't sure she was supposed to hear that—but she was quite sure Gil *hadn't* heard it. Or been supposed to.

It seemed she wasn't the only one who found him an annoying-but-pretty prick.

CHAPTER 39

ROSLYN AND GIL might have been pushing off and drifting through the zero-gravity portion of Styx, but her two guards had turned on magnetic boots as the transfer pods delivered them to the exterior hull.

In theory, Roslyn had an opportunity in that. She could, without much difficulty, move much faster than the guards could. On the other hand, she *couldn't* outspeed SmartDarts or bullets. She was quite sure her guards would choose to shoot her over letting her escape.

Plus, she was curious as to just what she was going to be shown. The microgravity part of the station looked similar to where she'd been brought aboard, which helped her close part of the loop on her mental map. It wasn't a full closed loop, not with the fact that the transport pods could go to any number of stations on the exterior hull, but it was a start.

Instead of heading into what she was reasonably sure was *a* shuttle bay, if not the one she'd arrived through, Gil led her along the hull and into an unexpected open space. At some point, this had probably been slated for the delivery of a weapon of some kind.

Instead of that weapon, it had received massive transparent-aluminum panels and opened out into deep space. Control panels on those windows allowed visitors to apply zoom factors and look more closely at whatever caught their eye.

Roslyn drifted out to the window and stopped herself next to one of the control panels, looking out at the massive construct of the accelerator ring. From there, she could see other stations wrapped around it.

A tap on the controls zoomed in on what turned out to be shipyards. Row upon row of refit yards—each of them holding a Republic warship. She counted dozens of ships in orbit, and there were probably half as many as that here.

"We built all of this in five years," Gil murmured. "Legatus sent us engineers, schematics, money...but we still did in five years what took them forty. A million workers have been out here for half a decade."

"Those ships are still under construction?" Roslyn asked. "There's an entire fleet out there."

"Only some of them were built here," he admitted. "We've only had yards capable of building starships for about a year. They were used for ring segments prior to that and proved easy to repurpose once we had the ring itself complete.

"The ring's only been online for six months. We barely managed to get it running before Legatus fell...but we did." Gil waved his hand at the window.

"The Protectorate surprised us with a secret fleet, with the dreadnoughts and the new missiles," he admitted. "But soon...soon, we'll return the favor. This was in motion before, to make sure we had a second string to our bow."

Roslyn barely kept herself from nodding. If this fleet had joined the first waves, the Republic would have carried the war by sheer numbers and surprise. Instead, they'd only had the fleet they'd brought to the fight—a fleet that might have been enough if the Protectorate's system militias hadn't rallied to Montgomery's call and the dreadnoughts hadn't already been under construction in the shadows.

"But the yards are online now. We've only built a dozen ships ourselves, but the yards have been busy with refits," he said proudly. "We received one of only a handful of Prometheus Interface manufactories and installation facilities. These ships were built elsewhere, delivered here by larger transports, but it falls to us to make them true starships."

A chill ran down Roslyn's spine and she forced herself to silence. It was *pointless* to challenge these people over the Prometheus Interface and its costs. Wasn't it?

"So, these ships aren't actually starships yet?" she asked.

"They are becoming starships," Gil said slowly, realizing he might have said more than he should. "We will be ready soon to deploy the second wave, to drive your invasion fleet back and rescue our worlds from the boots of Martian conquerors. This war is far from as over, as your people seem to assume."

"Despite half your fleet deserting or defecting?" Roslyn demanded, her anger getting the better of her. "You lose a fleet built by murder and murder more people to build another one? Where did these Mages come from, Gil? Were these *your* children or the ones your fleet *kidnapped* from Protectorate worlds?"

It was probably a good thing she was Mage-cuffed. It was taking every scrap of self-control she had to keep herself from lunging at the prick. If she'd had her magic, he would have been dead where he stood.

"Do you even understand just what your fucking *starships* entail?" she snarled.

"I understand the propaganda and lies the Protectorate spreads about the martyrs of the Prometheus Program, yes," Gil said stiffly. "You claim they are fueled by children and Mages, and I assure you, all of that is lies. Your Montgomery put together a neat piece of deception, one that worked on fools, but we are not deceived anymore."

"Really," Roslyn said. "Really. Lies. I've *met* Damien Montgomery, Alecto Gil. The man doesn't know how to lie. He doesn't know how to fake anger. If you trust George Solace over Damien Montgomery, you are the blind fool.

"And you have chosen death and hatred over your humanity."

The observation deck was silent.

"I think we're done here," Gil ground out. "If you will not listen, I will not be propagandized to."

"One of us is deaf and blind," she told him. "And I don't think it's the one of us who was kidnapped and imprisoned."

"Guards, take her back to her cell," the aide snapped. "This little excursion is *over*."

Roslyn considered resisting as the guards approached her with the chains for her Mage-cuffs, but there was no point. She'd just tried to push every button she could find on Alecto Gil—and she'd learned a few interesting things along the way.

The Republic had to have an answer to the accusations leveled at them, and it seemed their chosen one was that the brains in the Prometheus Interface were volunteers and non-Mages. It wouldn't hold up forever—it couldn't, not if the Republic wanted to keep building ships—but it might last until they'd launched this new fleet at the Protectorate's throat.

She stared at the yards and ships as her guards chained her hands and wrists together, until they attached the lead to the chain between her wrists and pulled her after them. Floating in zero gravity, she had no way to resist.

Gil stayed in the observation deck as the guards pulled her away, leaving her alone with the two women responsible for keeping her contained.

"You going to give us trouble?" the older guard asked as they reached the transit pod.

"What's the point?" she replied. "Let's go."

"Smart kid," her escort replied.

The pod delivered them to an unfamiliar set of corridors. Her escorts clearly had maps in their implants that they were following. Roslyn kept track of the walls around her, hoping to link it up with her mental map sooner or later.

Their route took them through a less public-facing part of the station, with far more utilitarian sections. Open spaces stretched around them, with large sectors containing piping and cables, and boxes and tubes suggesting the rooms and corridors she was used to seeing.

They were in the maintenance sections of the station. Given Styx's scale, the builders had clearly just left a two-meter-high empty gap between each floor, giving them open space above and around most of the usual working spaces of the ship to fix and repair systems as needed.

Her guards were clearly taking the fastest route possible, dragging her up stairs, over corridors and ducking under cabling and piping. If

Roslyn wasn't fast enough to keep up and pay attention, she was going to crack her head on something.

That meant she almost missed the "box" covered in silver inlay. It took a moment to place the set of three rooms from the outside, but she realized she was looking at an apartment warded against magic. Unlike most of the other rooms she could see from the maintenance space, which were linked together in rows of twelve at least, this one stood alone with three meters of space on all sides.

As they passed by, Roslyn tried to study the exterior of what was either her space or a near-duplicate as closely as she could. It was a later addition, she realized, added into a space that had been left empty for future upgrades.

And as a later addition, it hadn't been welded into place with the big machinery that put ships together. Some of the corner welds looked almost spotty...

She was yanked forward by her guards, *hard*, as she realized she'd slowed.

"Keep moving," the woman barked. "*We're* not giving you a fucking tour."

Roslyn trotted forward obediently. She might have learned what she needed to. The only question now was if she was strong enough for what she needed to do—and if the room she'd just seen was *her* room...or Alexander's.

They entered normal corridors shortly afterward, her guards leading Roslyn back to her room. That was in the wrong direction for it to be the one she'd seen, and she went along, linking bits of her mental map together as best as she could on the run.

Finally, the guards took her inside and pulled off the cuffs.

"*I'd* shower after having Gil slobber all over me for an hour," one of the guards observed drily. "Just don't cause trouble."

The door slammed shut behind Roslyn, leaving her trapped in a space that prevented her use of magic. Trapped in a box she'd seen the outside of…and with a mental map she had to put together as best as she could.

She dropped to the floor, pulling the books and treatises to her and trying to reassemble her mental map in a somewhat three-dimensional shape.

If the room she'd seen was Alexander's, then it was almost certainly *here*, barely twenty meters away. The route she'd been taken along to get back from the transfer pod led through the maintenance voids *here*. Depending on whether she could give the pod a destination, it could at least theoretically link up to the shuttle bay and deliver them to a spacecraft.

Roslyn was confident that she could fly anything. That was part of her training, after all. *Unlocking* a Republic spacecraft and getting clear of the station, though…that would be harder.

Unless she made someone do it for her. The Republican personnel responsible for running the situation had to be *terrified* of Mages. They'd spent so much effort trying to keep her contained and restricted from her power that the thought of a fully unleashed Mage would probably make most of them crap themselves.

She could force someone to get her off the station. She knew how to get to Alexander's quarters. The guards had been half-annoyed by Gil, half-aggravated by Roslyn's own prodding on the Prometheus Project, but their rush had been their undoing.

If she could escape.

If.

If the corner of her bathroom wall was as weak as it looked like the corner of Alexander's was…there might be a chance.

If she was strong enough.

CHAPTER 40

BEFORE SHE DID anything else, Roslyn spread out the books on the floor again. Positioning herself between the camera and the map she was assembling, she hoped that it looked like pure chaos to the observers. Just a bored prisoner entertaining herself.

The map was promising. The guards should never have brought her back on the direct route through the maintenance tunnels—they had clearly been twitchy over the tours and requests she was being granted, and her attempt to hammer Gil's buttons had rattled them.

They'd rushed and they'd revealed her way out. She moved books together, linking the two apartments—hers and Alexander's. If she could avoid her own guards, the first place she'd face opposition would be when she reached Alexander's cell and faced the Admiral's guards.

Shuffling the books around to remove the map, Roslyn carefully undressed, stacking her clothes on one of the chairs to make them easier to carry into the bathroom—and to give her an excuse to bring the only mobile furniture she had into the bathroom with her.

She turned on the shower, looking around the room and trying to match the interior of her prison to the exterior she'd seen of Alexander's. *There*. That corner—the one *in* the shower, where heat and warmth might have weakened the weld even further than she dared hope.

Roslyn knew that what she was about to attempt might be impossible. She was in good shape, but she was going to be trying to break welds and bend metal walls. If she was Alexander or Montgomery, she might have been able to pick the weak spot in the ward and focus on that.

As it was, all she could do was try to break open a wall and hope she could get it to work. The water was hot now and she took a deep breath. If she was lucky, the cameras were at least a bit fogged up now.

She knew she was still watched in the bathroom. Fogged-up cameras and a chair with her clothes on it were her only hope.

Tossing the clothes onto the floor, she threw a towel into the shower to give her footing and then stepped into the stall, carrying the metal chair. She judged the angle as best as she could and then *slammed* the furniture into the corner of the wall.

Nothing. She repeated the gesture, hammering futilely against the wall with all of her strength for several seconds.

She stopped, standing in the hot water and considering her results so far. She might have made a dent but not much of one. She certainly hadn't broken the welds.

So far, no one had reacted. Either they hadn't noticed, or they thought she was taking her frustrations out. That lucky reprieve wouldn't last, not with guards like these.

This time, she picked up the chair and placed it more carefully, slowly wedging the top of the chair's back into the corner and putting her full body weight against it. Water slicked over her, covering her efforts but impeding the grip her feet could get on the now-soaked towel.

Roslyn wiggled the chair, pushing into the gap with all of her might. She wasn't trying to bash through anything now. She was trying to lever the corner open, to break the mediocre welds she'd seen on the outside... or at the very least, apply enough pressure to temporarily sever the links of silver that made up the ward matrix.

There was a bang in the other room. Someone was knocking—her guards were probably opening the door.

She was out of time and she threw herself full-force into the chair, trying to create enough pressure to do something. *Anything.* She wasn't going to get a second chance.

For one moment, one physically painful moment that tore through her like a burning blade, the matrix parted. The walls were intact, but Roslyn had magic. Just a tithe of her usual power and only for a moment.

It was enough.

Roslyn Chambers *stepped*, a teleport of only a couple of meters at most—the critical meters that put her, naked and dripping wet, outside her cell.

For a few seconds, Roslyn fell into a defensive crouch, looking around her as she poked at her power. Then she exhaled, straightening as her magic rushed back into her for the first time in weeks. A blade of force answered her call as she turned, and she looked at the weak weld and silver ward that had almost defeated her.

Force and magic did what leverage and determination had failed to do. The corner split apart under the blow, revealing the still-steaming shower. Most importantly to Roslyn at that moment, however, was that the split broke the ward—and *also* revealed her clothes.

She'd mastered the art of teleporting her clothes onto herself at the RMN Academy. It was discouraged, but the trainers turned a blind eye when it made sense.

That party trick meant she was dressed in the plain black fatigues the Republic had given her when her two guards broke into her bathroom and came to a stunned halt, staring both at the hole in the wall and at the angry Mage on the other side.

Water could disperse electricity, but not as much electricity as Roslyn blasted through the ten-centimeter gap she'd opened in the wall. Both Augmented guards went down in a heap, cybernetics and flesh alike twitching as they overloaded.

They'd been sufficiently kind that Roslyn vaguely hoped she hadn't killed them, but her priority had to be escaping. Her guards were down and out, and they hadn't had a chance to report her escape.

Hopefully, they'd also been the people watching her security feeds. With their implants, that was easily possible. Roslyn would have had the cameras going elsewhere, though, so she doubted she was that lucky.

Someone almost certainly already knew she'd escaped. Her time was limited, and she took off toward Alexander's apartment. Twenty meters away—and she could see a door that looked like it was in the right place.

The hallway she burst into *looked* like the right kind of residential hallway to be the one Alexander's prison was on, but there was always the risk she'd guessed wrong. She was certain she could get to the other warded cell she'd seen.

What she *wasn't* certain of was whether that cell was *Alexander's.* There might well be other Mages held prisoner on Styx. If nothing else, there was a Prometheus Interface facility around somewhere. *That* station would have Mage prisoners, but those prisoners were likely kept separate.

The sheep held for slaughter weren't kept in the same place as the ones you wanted to interrogate.

Roslyn's fear that she was in the wrong place meant that she greeted the appearance of the two armed guards as she came around the corner with relief. Whatever warning they'd received about her escape, the women hadn't been expecting her arrival.

Augment cybernetics meant they reacted anyway. They moved like lightning, carbines snapping up as they saw Roslyn—but they weren't fast enough. Fire flashed from the Mage's fingers, bolts of white-hot plasma that hammered through armor and flesh and implants alike.

Roslyn strode toward the bodies she'd created, letting her anger and fear carry her. Her guards might have survived, but these two women were definitely dead. She'd killed before, she knew that, but that was a matter of lights on a console and sparks in the void.

This was the first time she'd killed with her own magic face-to-face. She knew that if she slowed down, if she let that sink in, she would be doomed.

Instead, she forced herself to lean down, to pick up the woman closest to the door and lift the corpse's hand to the scanner. She pressed the dead guard's palm against the control panel, hoping it didn't require some kind of mental command from the guard herself.

Nothing happened.

"Fuck," Roslyn cursed, and let the body fall. That would have saved some time and definitely some attention. She stepped back and considered the security door. The wards would have a gap in them for the door, and destroying it wouldn't break them—and Roslyn really didn't know what breaking the ward matrix would *do* to the Mage inside it.

The door was probably sturdier than the rest of the cell, but she didn't have much choice.

Blasting the door down would risk Alexander, so instead, she teleported it. One moment, it was in front of her, blocking her way. The next, it was falling to the ground several meters up the hallway.

Or most of it was at least. The inner several millimeters appeared to be inside the antimagic ward and remained in Roslyn's way. Carefully, ever so carefully, she stepped forward and pushed it.

The lock had been in the chunk she'd teleported. The fragment of door fell inward, hitting the ground with a loud clatter, and Roslyn looked across the threshold of the prison.

Mage-Admiral Alexander looked up from her couch, still looking vague and dazed.

"That doesn't sound like knocking," she said slowly.

"Admiral, it's Roslyn. We have to go," Roslyn told her. "I need you."

"Okay," Alexander said dreamily, rising and walking languidly over toward her. "This place was comfortable, but I trust you."

"What the fuck do they even have you *on*?" Roslyn demanded.

"No one was so kind as to explain," Alexander answered, her voice still slow and vague. "But leaving sounds nice."

Roslyn took a moment to make sure that she was actually rescuing her Admiral and not some doppelganger. She wasn't sure how to do that beyond inspecting Alexander's face closely, and she ended up just shaking her head.

"Come on," she told Alexander. "Hopefully, whatever's in your system works its way out fast. I need your power if we're going to live through this."

"I hope so," Alexander agreed, her words a relief even if her tone remained worrying. "I'll follow; don't worry."

The drugs might be making Roslyn's Admiral vague, but she seemed to still be in there. That was the best she could hope for, she supposed.

CHAPTER 41

WHATEVER SECURITY lockdown protocols Styx Station had didn't account for the maintenance voids wrapped around her decks. She wasn't *designed* to be a prison—she was designed to be a heavy defensive fortress, with ease of regular maintenance far more critical than internal security.

Roslyn and Alexander crossed the maintenance section unopposed except for cleaning robots that Roslyn blasted to scrap as a matter of course. The robots' destruction was probably an obvious trail, but their cameras would have been just as effective.

There *was* going to be resistance at the transfer pods; she was certain of it.

"Can you fight?" she asked Alexander. "There's going to be Augments at the next stage and they're trained to kill Mages like me."

"I... I... No." Alexander's tone was still dreamy, but there was a frustration in it, too. "No strength. No magic."

"It's all right, sir; the drugs will fade," Roslyn assured her boss. "We'll both get out of here."

That was going to leave dealing with an Augmented and armed security squad waiting for them up to her, and Roslyn wasn't feeling *that* confident. She focused on her mental map as she considered the access she could see ten meters away.

If she went through *there*, she could hit the squad from the side. That assumed they were waiting for her at the door—but even if they were expecting her to go through a wall, they would never know *where* she was coming through.

"Wait here," she told Alexander. "I'll be back for you, I promise."

"Okay." The Admiral nodded, her eyes unfocused again. "I hate this."

"Join the club," Roslyn hissed. She gave her boss one firm nod, then stepped up to the wall.

Force answered her call, her magic even more eager than usual after weeks without it.

The wall *exploded* away from her in a spray of metal shards that cleared any possible threat—and Roslyn's magic snatched up that shrapnel into a whirlwind of power that went ahead of her as she charged down the hallway.

The security alert was working perfectly, just as she'd feared. A dozen soldiers in black armor, half of them even in combat exosuits, had taken up positions around the door she'd been planning to charge through. Several were positioned to cover their backs, clearly anticipating exactly the trick she'd pulled.

Her swarm of metal slammed into the Augments waiting for her. The ones covering the ambushers' backs went down first, metal tearing through lightly armored flesh and spraying blood across the others.

Gunfire answered her approach, but Roslyn held a second shield of force in front of her, deflecting the blind-fired bullets that reached her as her storm tore into the enemy. The metal shards hit exosuits and failed to penetrate, the armor resisting even those projectiles as Roslyn faced them.

Even in exosuit battle armor, Augments moved with a speed no unmodified human could match. They were charging her now, heavy battle rifles echoing in the corridor as they slammed high-speed penetrators into her shield.

The walls around her disintegrated under misses and ricochets, and Roslyn's power spoke once more. A lance of superheated plasma answered her call, air compressing into a line of intense heat and flame that cut through the leading exosuits like butter.

Two attackers went down. A third. Two more reached Roslyn through everything, vibroblades snapping clear of their armor as they swung for her with speed augmented by implants and armor alike.

Her training was clear: if an Augment has you in arm's reach, *be somewhere else.*

Instead, she summoned a blade of force, stepping deeper into the lead Augment's reach and removing their vibroblade at the elbow. As the other trooper tried to swing their blade to hit her and miss their compatriot, she threw the blade of force at them and conjured another one to stab through the chest plate of the trooper she was next to.

Both soldiers went down, and Roslyn was alone with the wounded and the dead. Some of them would live, she hoped, but none of them were going to get in her way now.

Triumph warred with nausea, and the young Mage forced down both as she went to collect her Admiral.

They wouldn't be triumphant until they were back with Second Fleet.

The transfer pods were locked down to prevent anyone using them, but the controls for the system were surprisingly simple. Roslyn parked Admiral Alexander in one of the seats and opened up the panel.

She had to chuckle. Inside one of the most secure stations in the galaxy, the controls for the transfer pod looked almost identical to those of the cars she'd stolen as a misfit teenager. Hotwiring the pod was a matter of moments, the vehicle starting to move along the track under its own internal power.

"We're going to lose gravity in a few moments," she told Alexander as she rose from the panel. Her own magic was already generating a gravity field to keep her feet on the ground. "Can you keep yourself down yet?"

"No." Alexander's voice was more stable now, but that only made the frustration stand out more clearly. "No magic."

"All right," Roslyn said gently, poking through the emergency supply cabinet in the pod. She found what she was looking for quickly enough—a portable oxygen mask and a tether. She gave the mask to Alexander and then tethered the other woman to herself.

Alexander was sufficiently present now to put the mask on on her own, smiling gently at Roslyn.

"I'm still here, Lieutenant," she murmured. "But...the world's a haze still. I don't know what they did but I...I know they did it, now."

"That's an improvement," Roslyn admitted. The pod came to a slow halt, sending Alexander drifting up into the air until Roslyn grabbed her by the tether. "We're going to hit trouble. Stay behind me.

"We need a shuttle, which means we need to get someone to unlock one for us."

"Didn't you just hotwire the pod?"

"I can hotwire ground and aircars," Roslyn confirmed. "Apparently, transfer pods use groundcar control systems. I am a hundred percent certain I cannot hotwire a military shuttle."

"Then...convince someone?" Alexander asked.

"That's the plan. We just have to get out this door first," Roslyn said grimly. She adjusted the tether, making sure Alexander was behind her, and then summoned her most powerful shield.

The door slid open and a superheated blast of plasma hammered into it. Plasma blasters were rare as hen's teeth, but Roslyn was aware of their existence—and of the fact that they were one-shot weapons.

She pushed her shield out through the door as gunfire and shrapnel rockets burst against it as well. Pulling Alexander behind her, she stepped out behind the shelter of her barrier of impenetrable air...and into hell.

They'd been hoping to catch her unaware. The Augments had to have known what was going to happen if they fired those kinds of weapons against her shield, but she'd been ready—and the backblast from the plasma bolt had been bad enough.

The Republic force's own weapons had gutted their front line, and the second had dumped their heavy weapons in horror. Gunfire smashed into Roslyn's shield and she trembled. She was reaching the end of her own limits now; she could recognize the feeling.

The RMN Academy made *very* sure their Mages could recognize that feeling.

Roslyn charged forward into the chaos, pulling Alexander with her as gunfire battered her shield uselessly. She wasn't even trying to strike back now, just to get past them. She didn't have the strength left to do both.

Finally, she was clear enough to spare some strength. There was a gap as the defenders tried to swing around to catch her from behind—and she pulled the walls in behind her. There was no real "floor" or "ceiling" there. Roslyn's spell let her walk wherever she liked, and the Republic troops had mag-boots to do the same.

So, she pulled all four walls in toward the center and crushed them together. No one was getting through after her and Alexander.

"Now the shuttle bay," she muttered.

The blast door to the shuttle bay was closed, but that didn't slow her down. It took most of the last of Roslyn's strength to blast it apart, but she did it. She barely managed to hold a shield long enough to get into the massive void where the shuttles waited, but thankfully, no gunfire echoed against it.

There was no time for calculating or even guessing. She ran for the closest shuttle, what looked like an armored assault shuttle. There was a man hanging in the ramp, gaping at her as she charged. He probably *had* mag-boots, but he must have missed the security alerts.

From the warmth of the deck, the shuttle had just landed in the last ten minutes or so. It was *probably* empty, but Roslyn didn't have time to care.

She used her magic to pin the man to the shuttle and studied his uniform for the insignia she needed to be there.

She barely managed to conceal a sigh of relief when she spotted the pilot's wings.

"You're going to unlock this shuttle for me to fly out of here," she hissed at him.

"Not a bloody chance," he snarled. "Who the fuck are—"

She pulsed electricity into him. Not a lot—she wasn't sure she could still *conjure* a lot of lightning—but enough to hurt.

"I will electrocute your nerves and implants to death one piece at a time until you unlock this shuttle," Roslyn told him, her voice determined and cold. She wasn't sure she *could* do it, but she was certain she *would* do it.

There was no other way off Styx Station.

"You're insane," he told her. "Fine."

"Go."

Roslyn pushed him ahead of her, clinging to the last of her strength to keep the gravity spell up as they made their way to the cockpit.

"This station is in the middle of a fleet in the middle of a Republic system," the pilot told her. "The shuttle doesn't even *have* interstellar charts, let alone a jump system. You're *fucked.*"

"My problem, not yours," Roslyn pointed a glowing finger at him. "Unlock it."

He typed in a code on the console. The screens she could see used the same operating systems as the Protectorate version, which gave her a chance.

"Thank you very much," she told him sweetly—and then grabbed him by the shoulder. All of the accessways inside the shuttle were open, and she could hear exosuited boots approaching the bay.

For now, though, she threw the pilot backward. The shuttle was big—but not *that* big. The pilot flew down its full length and out the end in the seconds it took Roslyn to take the pilot's seat and take control of the systems.

She closed the door behind the departing pilot and brought every one of the shuttle's systems online. She spared the extra second to make sure she didn't vaporize the pilot, and then brought the thrusters online.

The safety interlocks wouldn't let her bring up the main engines inside a shuttle bay, but the craft had specific thrusters for just that purpose.

"The bay door is closed," Alexander observed behind her, the Admiral's voice having lost most of its dreamy undertones. "Do you have a plan, Chambers?"

"Yup," Roslyn agreed. They were accelerating toward the door, slowly but surely, as she flipped a set of commands. "I just armed six nukes. Their scanners can see that. Either I get out into space or a good chunk of Styx Station gets blown to itty-bitty pieces.

It was a gamble—but it was all she had left. She'd had to let the gravity spell go now, strapping herself into the pilot's seat. As she blazed toward the bay doors, she felt Alexander release the tether, the Admiral pulling herself into the other seat.

"This, I think I can do now," Alexander noted, her words still slow but firm and certain now. "I have weapons control. I confirm six one-hundred-megaton warheads armed."

"You have weapons," Roslyn confirmed. "Four. Three. Two...there we go!"

The bay doors slid open with the speed of perfectly maintained systems. Roslyn's speed was rising quickly, but she was still at velocities better measured in kilometers per hour than kilometers per second.

"Clear, clear!" Alexander confirmed. "Gunship incoming...well, that works."

Roslyn didn't even need to ask. The red icons marking that she'd armed all six of the assault shuttle's nuclear missiles flashed green and then blank as the weapons blasted clear of the spacecraft.

The missiles weren't supposed to be ship-killers. They were designed to clear landing sites or threaten merchants, with ranges, warheads and accelerations that were anemic compared to real warship missiles.

The gunship was barely a hundred kilometers away. They didn't have time to realize something was going on before all six missiles hammered into the thirty-thousand-ton spacecraft.

The explosion helped cover Roslyn's escape. She dove the shuttle next to the nuclear fireballs as the main fusion thrusters woke up.

"Where now?" Alexander asked. "Threat display is getting very full."

"I'm not sure," Roslyn admitted. "I figured you'd have your magic back by now and we could swap off."

"I don't," the Admiral said grimly. "I don't know why, I need time...but I don't have my magic, Chambers. I don't have *any* magic. We need...cover."

There were over fifty *capital ships* maneuvering to try and get a shot at their tiny shuttle. Styx was the largest fortress, but it wasn't alone in Hyacinth orbit—and the gunships were starting to deploy toward them in their dozens.

Hyacinth.

The gas giant.

"This might suck," Roslyn admitted. "But it's the only chance I see."

The shuttle flipped in space, dodging several laser beams as Roslyn danced her through a half-forgotten evasive pattern toward her target.

Then several large angry men sat down on her chest as she pushed the assault shuttle to its maximum acceleration toward Hyacinth.

"How deep do we need to get to be undetectable?" she asked, her tone surprisingly calm to her own ears.

"Three atmospheres," Alexander said after a second. "Not sure how deep that translates to. Can this ship take it?"

"The alternative is to test if she can take antimatter warheads," Roslyn replied. "I know the answer to *that* question."

With an entire fleet trying to pursue them, she drove their stolen assault shuttle into the upper tiers of Hyacinth's atmosphere.

Somewhere in the depths of the planet was at least a momentary safety.

CHAPTER 42

ROSLYN KNEW she was a competent but not spectacular pilot. Dodging and weaving her way through the incoming fire and into the storms of a gas giant's upper atmosphere was far beyond anything she'd ever practiced—and flying was an occasional training exercise for her, not a regular task.

Somehow, she did it. Alexander worked the shuttle's weapons as they plunged, expending the rest of their missiles, the non-nuclear ones intended for ground targets, as decoys and counterstrikes.

The silence when the threat detectors stopped going off was a shock.

"We're clear of targeting radar and incoming fire for the moment," the Admiral told her. "How deep are we?"

"Two point eight atmospheres," Roslyn said. "I'm taking us deeper and pulling...seventeen degrees west of north."

It was a random angle, and that was exactly what they needed. It wouldn't take long for the Republic warships to find some way to blindly bombard the layer they thought the shuttle was in.

They were at three atmospheres when the shuttle's systems warned them they were exceeding maximum recommended pressure. Roslyn shared a long, silent look with Alexander...and then went deeper.

"Listen," the Admiral said a moment later. The shuttle hull was *creaking* around them.

"Leveling out," Roslyn confirmed. "We are at three point four atmospheres. Not sure of our actual depth, to be honest. Deep."

"Okay." Alexander exhaled. "We can go deeper if we use magic to reinforce the hull."

"I'm out," Roslyn said. "I need to rest. Eat. Something…everything. Can you?"

"No." The single word hung in the shuttle cockpit like the sword of Damocles. "My magic is gone, Lieutenant. I don't know what they did, but most of the drugs have worn off and I have *nothing*."

Roslyn didn't know how to respond to that. If the Republic could take the magic from someone as powerful as Jane Alexander, they were in serious trouble. Her entire plan, such as it had been, had relied on the Mage-Admiral being able to get them out from there.

"I need to eat," she decided aloud, rising and leaving the cockpit, grimacing against the gas giant's gravity.

They'd stolen a full-size Space Assault Regiment assault shuttle. While its primary purpose was to deliver a platoon of soldiers to a planet or starship, it was designed for a lot of potential emergencies. The seats in the walls, designed to strap in assault troopers during a high-speed drop, could fold down to act as cots, turning the spacecraft into an impromptu barracks.

It had bathrooms, a tactical command center…and a section of storage that could be rotated out into the main area to open up a large kitchen. From the design, Roslyn figured the only way *all* of those features were expected to be used at once was if the shuttle was on a planet.

But she was able to get into the kitchen area and access the food storage. There were supplies aboard for actual meals, but most of the food was exactly what she'd expected: military ration bars and drinks. Electrolyte-laden high-calorie ingestibles to maintain a unit in a high-threat environment.

She grabbed two sets of a drink and a ration bar and reentered the main hold. Alexander had left the cockpit as well, but she hadn't made it as far as Roslyn had. The Admiral was showing every year of her almost-complete century, her face ashen-pale as she sat on one of the drop seats and looked up at Roslyn.

"Here," Roslyn said, passing one of the drinks and ration bars to the Admiral. She tore open her own drink and drained half of it in a single long swallow.

"I think the fuckers did more to me than I was afraid of," Alexander admitted. "Painkillers are starting to wear off. Too stiff to move much."

She slowly followed Roslyn's example and drained her drink pouch. Even that motion caused her to wince.

"I need you to help me," she told Roslyn. "I need the jacket off; I need to see my arms."

Alexander sounded terrified. Roslyn would have helped anyway, but the tone of her boss's voice accelerated matters. She took a single bite of her ration bar and set to carefully removing the outer layer of the clothes the Admiral was wearing.

There was a black tank top underneath—the fatigues were identical to the ones Roslyn was wearing and a far cry from a proper shipsuit—but removing the jacket bared the Admiral's arms and the glittering silver runes that marked her forearms and biceps.

"Those aren't anything I'm familiar with," Roslyn murmured.

"Montgomery has them too," Alexander told her. "Proof, I guess, that the recurring rumor you slept with him to get his help is bullshit. As if I *needed* any proof of that."

Roslyn couldn't help herself. She laughed aloud at the thought.

"I'm not sure Montgomery would see me as anything other than a kid *now*, let alone when I was seventeen," she told Alexander. "He's not my type, anyway. Too skinny. Too intense."

"That he is," Alexander agreed, studying her arms. "So, if the Runes of Power are still there, they did something else."

Runes of Power. That wasn't a phrase Roslyn had heard outside of bad thrillers and extremely sketchy rumors. Apparently, they were real.

Now that she looked more closely, she could see the divisions between the individual runes. There were two on each of Alexander's arms, one wrapped around her forearm and one around her bicep.

"What do you need, boss?" she asked, taking another bite of her ration bar. She was ravenously hungry, she realized, and she kept eating while she waited for the Admiral's response.

"To not hurt," Alexander snapped, then stopped. "A lot of this is... stiffness," she murmured. "Probably from being sedated to fuck for weeks on end. But..."

"Sir?"

"Help me turn this into a cot," Alexander ordered. "They couldn't have...but... *Fuck*."

Roslyn had a better idea. She folded down the seat *next* to where Alexander was sitting, extending it to create a narrow but serviceable bed.

The Admiral tried to rise, only to spasm halfway up. Roslyn took her arm, helped Alexander over to the bed and watched as she lay down, face first.

"They did something to my lower back," Alexander told her. "Help me take this shirt off."

Roslyn obeyed, helping lift the tank top off and then moving Alexander to settle her more comfortably. As the Admiral lay back down on the bed, what had been done became blatantly, obviously, visible.

The Rune Wright's upper shoulder blades were marked with a similar rune to her arms, the organic silver whorls of a fifth Rune of Power. The rune wasn't in Martian Runic, its lines and connectors not even resembling the seventy-six characters and fourteen connectors of the language that defined magic. It was more refined, more natural—more true to magic even in Roslyn's eyes.

The *new* rune, the one hacked into Alexander's lower back with something close to a stencil rather than the proper tools, was in Martian Runic. Roslyn was no Rune Scribe, and deciphering runes was hard for her, but she could make out key components of a matrix she hadn't even known *could* be made.

"It's a new rune," Roslyn told Alexander softly. "A modified form of the ward on the cells. The fuck?"

"Can you take a picture and show me?" the Crown Princess of Mars asked, her tone determined.

It took Roslyn a few moments to find a portable computer. Her wrist-comp was somewhere on Styx Station, but like their Marine cousins, space assault troopers didn't land with their personal wrist-comps.

She took a picture of the rune and passed the tablet to Alexander.

"Fuck." There was a depth of despair in the single word that Roslyn had *never* heard Jane Alexander use.

"Sir? Admiral Alexander?"

"That rune is almost as classified as my Runes of Power," Alexander told her. "*We* wouldn't carve it on the surface of the skin, though. We make sure it can't be undone by inlaying it inside muscle, usually the left thigh."

Roslyn had never even *heard* of anything like that in the Protectorate. "What the hell is it?" she demanded.

"It's the Rune of Nullification, Lieutenant," her boss said. "It's what we do to Mages who break the highest laws. It's how we take someone's magic."

CHAPTER 43

THERE WAS NOTHING in the particular patch of empty void that *Rhapsody in Purple* was drifting in to mark it as special or dangerous. There were no ships there other than them, no enemies hurling missiles and lasers, nothing.

It was just a patch of empty space that happened to be one light-year away from the Chrysanthemum System, and Kelly LaMonte stared at the galactic map silently as she considered her options.

"Xi, send all your people to bed," she finally ordered. "We won't jump until all of you are rested up and ready to go."

"That's—"

"The best way to make sure we can jump the hell back out if things go wrong," Kelly cut off her wife. "This ship already carries enough information to potentially turn the tide of this war. We need to see what's in Chrysanthemum. If our enemy is waiting there, the Protectorate needs to know.

"We also need to make damn sure we survive. We won't be playing risky games for detailed data in Chrysanthemum."

"We also won't be able to hide our arrival," Shvets warned her. "Not unless someone has a civilian freighter in their back pocket they haven't mentioned."

"Not that I've noticed," Kelzin replied, flashing a grin across the conference table. "I *think* I'd notice that. Freighters are a tight fit in my pockets."

The senior officers were gathered in the meeting room next to *Rhapsody*'s bridge. A hologram of the map of the space around them hung above the table, the map a stark explanation of their position.

They were technically in Protectorate space now, but Chrysanthemum was a Fringe world at the far end of nowhere. The fastest route to most of the Protectorate was *through* the Republic, which had helped keep the supposedly loyal UnArcana World even more isolated through the war.

"Even if we moved to the regular jump lines into Chrysanthemum, the odds are that we wouldn't see anyone," Kelly reminded her people. "The system has seen an average of one freighter a month for the last three years. That's given us quite a bit of data to work with, but it also points out our target."

She tapped a command, replacing the hologram of human space with an image of the Chrysanthemum System itself.

"Peony and Dandelion are both a bit too large to host an accelerator ring," she noted, highlighting the innermost and outermost of the system's three gas giants. "Both are also currently nearly aligned with Chrysanthemum itself, which means we actually have decent scan data on them.

"Hyacinth is our joker," she continued, highlighting the last gas giant. "As planets go, she's basically the same size as Centurion. If they took the schematics for the Centurion Ring, they could duplicate them on Hyacinth without much work."

She shrugged.

"Of course, there are seven gas giants we can say that about in official Republic space, so that's not a selling point all on its own, but with everything else we've run into...well, I want to take a *real* close look at Chrysanthemum-Six, AKA Hyacinth."

Her officers were nodding as they looked at the map.

"The good news is that she's basically on the opposite side of the star system from Chrysanthemum right now, which gives us a nice clear run to the planet without the locals seeing us," Milhouse said.

"Except if she's hosting the accelerator ring, there's going to be a damn *fleet* guarding her," Kelzin replied. "The easiest way to tell if we've found our target is to count how many battleships start coming our way!"

"Mike hits the nail on the head," Kelly agreed, yanking on her braid gently as she looked at the map. "The geometry says we can jump in relatively close to Hyacinth and get a decent scan shortly after arrival.

"But we saw in Republic space that the RIN is getting better at reacting to the possibility of scout ships. We covered our tracks in Alignment. We can't do the same here, and if Hyacinth is what we think it is, we're going to be looking at a hunting swarm to make what we ran into in Gygax look like kids out playing."

There was a grim silence in the room. The carrier that had come out after them at Gygax had been operating to a clearly developed doctrine, and the Republic still had a communication advantage over the Protectorate.

A doctrine deployed in one place was readily available to every *other* place as well.

"So, does anyone have any clever ideas?" Shvets asked. "The only one that comes to mind for me is to jump in, hurtle toward the planet at maximum acceleration, get everything we can and jump out."

"Between Xi, and her team, we can do that," Kelly agreed. "But our timeframe would be short. *Very* short. Remember that they're just as capable of microjumping as we are."

"But we have four Mages," Kelzin suggested slowly, her husband's perpetual grin turning thoughtful. "Turn that around, my love. We're just as capable of microjumping as they are."

The silence was more thoughtful than grim now, and Kelly returned her husband's grin.

"Normally, we'd jump in and have one of them hiding us," she noted. "But if we're not planning on hiding, then we have the option to make at least one jump around the system."

"That will drain whoever does it just as much as a full-scale jump," Xi Wu warned. "And if we jump in close to a gravity well, there's risk to both the Mage and the ship."

"I wasn't thinking jumping in any closer than the first jump, actually," Kelzin said. "Civilian ships jump in at, what, three light-minutes from a gas giant like this?"

"Give or take. We can do ninety light-seconds. Maybe eighty," Xi suggested. "What are you thinking, love?"

"We jump in at five to ten light-minutes, a long-distance scoot 'n snoop," Kelly's husband told them all. "We act like we're being sneaky; we get their attention and we wait for the hunting swarm to jump out to track us down.

"If we run the heat sinks but not the stealth spell, that should keep them guessing enough to get their ready force out to our position—and then as soon as they arrive, we jump to the other side of the gas giant, ninety light-seconds out.

"Burn for Hyacinth at high speed while we have the bastards looking for us in the outer system. Get our scans in, then jump the hell out and head for home. They're no better at tracking jumps than we are."

It was *possible* to track jumps. The people, the Trackers, who could do so were immensely rare, however, and the Protectorate only had a handful in their employ. One had been supposed to join the MISS contingent running scouting missions in the Republic but hadn't arrived yet.

Kelly didn't have a Tracker, and she was reasonably sure the Republic didn't either.

"This does sound like the kind of stunt an aggressive assault shuttle pilot would plan, yes," Charmchi noted, the big cyborg grinning from ear to ear. "I like it. Skipper?"

"I like it as well," Kelly admitted. "We're never going to successfully sneak in past a fleet. They might not have one, in which case the whole game is unnecessary, but...if they don't have one, this isn't the place we're looking for, anyway."

She met her husband's gaze and smiled.

"I like it," she repeated. "But remember that if we're right and this is the accelerator ring, they're going to pull every stop out to catch us. There will be more ships that they can microjump after us."

"Yes, but can they microjump ninety light-seconds starting in a gas giant's gravity well?" Mike asked. "Xi? Could you?"

The Mage snorted.

"Probably," she allowed. "It would suck and all I'd want to do afterward is sleep for a week. Though I guess that's why we have four Mages aboard."

"Whether the Prometheus Interface can achieve that is an open question," Kelly admitted. "I guess we'll find out—but we'll have one of our Mages standing by to get us out of Chrysanthemum if they do.

"Let's be honest, people: if there's *that* much of a Republic presence in a system that's supposedly loyal to the Mountain, we already have our answer!"

CHAPTER 44

THE FIRST SHOCKWAVE jolted Roslyn awake. She hadn't expected to actually fall asleep when she'd lain down on the uncomfortable cot, but she'd managed it regardless.

Now the entire shuttle shook around her as she rolled off the hard surface and rose against the heavy pull of the gas giant's gravity.

"Admiral?" she asked aloud.

"We're trapped on a thirty-meter-long shuttle inside a gas giant surrounded by an enemy fleet," Alexander replied calmly. "I think you can call me Jane, Roslyn."

"What's going on...Jane?"

"Not sure," the older woman admitted. "I was meditating."

Alexander had put the fatigue jacket back on and was still moving slowly, with a level of pain and despair that tugged at Roslyn's heart. It *hurt* to see her mentor and commanding officer this close to the edge.

"Here, eat." Alexander shoved a ration bar over to Roslyn. "We're going to need your magic to get through this, I'm afraid."

A second shockwave rippled through the shuttle, lurching the sturdy spacecraft to the side. Both women traded glances and set off for the cockpit.

Alexander was slower, and Roslyn had the systems up by the time the Admiral joined her.

"Nukes," she told the older woman. "Ground-bombardment weapons like the ones we used on that gunship. They're firing them randomly into the gas giant with timed detonations."

Two more explosions rocked the shuttle, and a warning light popped up on one of the screens. Roslyn checked it and sighed.

"And it's going to work," she admitted. "They're still detonating them too high up to really cause us damage, but they'll work on that. The shockwaves are traveling hundreds of kilometers in this mess. They don't need to be perfect. They just need to get close."

This time, four warheads went off simultaneously. The zone was expanding, and Roslyn shivered, almost in time with the shockwave that rippled through her ship.

"We have to move. I thought I'd taken us far enough away, but I wasn't sure *what* they'd do."

The shuttle's engines were more visible from orbit than the shuttle herself, but the shockwaves themselves would eventually make the shuttle's presence clear if the RIN ships were paying attention.

"Are you refreshed enough to protect us?" Alexander asked.

"I think so," Roslyn admitted. "For a while. But they can keep this up for longer than I can protect the shuttle."

She suited actions to her words, reaching out with her power to forge a small bubble of even thicker atmosphere around the ship to absorb the shock before it reached her. As the waves of several more nukes washed over them, she grunted at the effort—but the shield stayed up.

"I'm taking us deeper now that I can shield us," she told Alexander. "I'm going to cut the curve and bring us back up to three and a half atmospheres farther away."

"Good plan," Alexander agreed. She shook her head. "What I'd give for Second Fleet right now."

"Second Fleet might be outgunned by what they've got here," Roslyn warned. "They have something close to three-quarters of the strength they started the war with concealed in this system. Not all of it's jump-capable, but still...seven or eight carrier groups."

"And they're installing Interfaces here," Alexander said grimly.

"They've got a propaganda answer to the accusations around the Interface, too," Roslyn continued. "They told *me* that the brains were non-Mage volunteers. Called them martyrs."

"Makes sense," the old Mage agreed. "We know damn well the brains were Mages, but if they can sell their fighting force on that lie...they can fight. And given that their fighting force will want to believe they aren't fighting for monsters, well."

"It's an easy sell," Roslyn confirmed. "What do we do, Admiral? All I can think of is to squirm around their depth charges and try to survive as long as possible."

She was deep enough and far enough away now that the shockwaves weren't a critical threat anymore. Her shield was even *more* critical now, though. The shuttle was showing pressure of around two atmospheres, but that was only because her magic was keeping it that way.

The true pressure around them was closer to five atmospheres now. Armored as the shuttle was, it was designed to withstand *impacts*, not constant pressure. Roslyn suspected that if she dropped the shield now, the shuttle would crumple like it was made of paper.

They were moving faster than the depth-charge pattern was expanding, but more ships were joining the bombardment now. Most likely, the only nuclear missiles in the fleet had been aboard shuttles like the one they'd stolen, and it had taken some hours to fabricate fusion warheads for weapons the starships could deploy.

Nobody was going to fire antimatter warheads at a planet they were planning on using later.

Now the RIN clearly had that fabrication going at a steady rate, as what had been one bomb became ten, twenty—a hundred warheads at once over an ever-expanding area.

"We're not going to survive on that plan, Roslyn," Jane Alexander half-whispered. "You can't fight a fleet with your magic, especially not if you use yourself up just keeping us alive. They're not going to give up until they have reason to believe we're dead.

"We were valuable as prisoners, but as escapees, we're too dangerous to let live."

The flash of the warning signs on the shuttle screens was the only interruption to their silence.

"What do we do?" Roslyn finally asked.

"We run as best as we can and we..." Alexander bit her lip. Roslyn could see tears of anger in her superior's eyes. "I want to fight these bastards," she ground out. "I want to demonstrate to them the full power of Mars, to demonstrate why their ilk has always feared the Mountain.

"But so long as this *thing* is in me, I have no power. They have stolen my Gift, and for that, I would burn them all to ashes."

"What if it wasn't in you?" Roslyn said. Alexander's gaze snapped on to her like a hunting hawk and she quailed under the Admiral's eyes. "If we removed it, what would that do?"

"That's why we bury it deep when we nullify criminals," Alexander admitted slowly. "In theory, if the Rune of Nullification is removed, my power would return. But...you're not a Rune Wright, Roslyn. If you broke it, without knowing exactly where to cut it, you could trigger a release of my own power that would rip this shuttle apart like a teacup in a storm."

"So, we need to remove it in one piece," the younger woman replied, feeling ill as she contemplated what she was suggesting. "I need to get us to somewhere away from their bombing, somewhere that gives us an hour or two of time."

"There could be no mistake or slip, Roslyn," the Admiral said quietly. "You'd need to remove the entire rune from my back in one piece. You're talking about *flaying* me."

"We have painkillers, plastiskin, surgical tools—this is an assault shuttle, Jane," Roslyn countered. "It should have a full trauma bay somewhere. If we can get away from the bombs, we should be able to do it."

"That's madness," Alexander whispered. "And yet...it's no crazier than inlaying a Rune of Power on your own arm with magic."

Roslyn blinked, looking down at Alexander's forearms.

"Who the hell did that?" she asked, feeding slightly more power to her engines.

"Who do you think?" the older woman asked. "Damien Montgomery. This plan of yours is his kind of crazy. It always worked for him, I suppose."

Roslyn *heard* Jane Alexander swallow.

"Get us to safety, Roslyn," she ordered. "I'll go find the trauma bay. We won't have a lot of time."

CHAPTER 45

"JUMP COMPLETE," Liara Foster announced.

"Stealth systems engaged, engines online," Milhouse reported in turn as *Rhapsody in Purple*'s scanners began to sweep the Chrysanthemum System.

"We are on a course for Hyacinth under maximum nonmagical stealth," Shvets confirmed. "Current range, nine point two light-minutes. ETA if we don't do anything...uh, a day-ish?"

"And somehow, I don't think we're going to be taking that long," Kelly murmured. The initial sensor sweep of Hyacinth, even from this range, was showing massive energy signatures. "What the *hell* is going on over there, Milhouse?"

The bridge was silent for at least ten seconds as the tactical officer went through the data.

"What we're seeing is the aftermath of at least five or six hundred fusion warheads," he concluded. "Looks like fifty warheads a minute in an expanding pattern." Milhouse fell silent for a moment, then shook his head.

"They're being fired *into* the gas giant, sir," he said. "Like...depth charges. What the hell could be inside a gas giant that's making them that angry, sir?"

"I don't know, but I'm not going to complain about the distraction," Kelly replied. "Keep an eye open for their response. Even if they're busy nuking the gas giant, I expect them to find a carrier to send out after us. I'm seeing a *lot* of ships over there."

"We wouldn't if their drives were cold," Milhouse said. "I'm not getting anything resembling exact numbers, but I'd say we're looking at dozens of ships and hundreds of gunships. We're too far out for me to resolve anything without active engines like, say, an accelerator ring, but..."

"If there's a goddamn *fleet* in orbit of Hyacinth, that's a bloody good sign," Kelly agreed. She looked over at the video link to the simulacrum chamber.

"Xi, are you ready?" she asked her wife.

Xi Wu was the least experienced of her Mages in many ways, with Liara Foster and Melanie Droit both being secondees from the Royal Martian Navy. She'd been run through an accelerated version of the same training as her subordinates, however, and was also a more *powerful* Mage than either of her subordinates.

Today, for this mess of a microjump, Xi wasn't leaving it to her subordinates.

"I have the simulacrum and I am prepared to jump us," Xi Wu confirmed. "Watching all the scanners. I make it at least eight minutes before we're likely to see anything."

"They might have Link-equipped sensor satellites to cut that number down," Kelly warned. "We found a few of those in Legatus after the fact—and while we haven't seen them since, if this was their fallback position, well. They'll be here if they're anywhere."

"Keeping our eyes open," Xi agreed.

"Numbers are getting cleaner as we resolve more data, sir," Milhouse reported, his voice strained. "It's not good. I'm reading at least fifty active capital ships. Whatever's going on inside the gas giant has them stirred the hell up, but...that's almost as many ships as the RIN is supposed to have left."

"And we've accounted for most of what they're supposed to have left," Kelly agreed. "These ships couldn't have been ready before the end of the Siege of Legatus, but...what a goddamn mess."

"Your orders, sir?" Milhouse asked formally.

"We proceed as per the plan," Kelly told them all. "We stand by to microjump closer in once we've drawn at least some of their ships out of position. We have enough to bring Second Fleet here, but I want to make sure the Fleet knows *exactly* what they're walking into."

There'd been enough traps and misestimations in this war already. Kelly LaMonte was not going to contribute to another one.

"Light from our jump flare should have reached Hyacinth ten seconds ago," Shvets reported. "Any guesses on how long until we have a carrier in our faces?"

"About a minute and a half," Kelly replied. "I'd say two to three minutes, except they've clearly already mobilized their fleet after whatever the hell is pissing them off."

"Should we be planning to try and extract whoever they're trying to bomb out?" Mike Kelzin asked. "Anyone who pisses the RIN off *that* badly...I kind of want to make sure they get away."

"They're on the wrong side of a fleet, Mike," Kelly pointed out. "I agree. I *want* to get in there and extract whoever has an entire battle fleet bombing a gas giant, but so long as that fleet is there..." She shrugged. "In an absolute best-case scenario, we can only conceal *Rhapsody* at about fifty thousand kilometers. We can't do any better for the shuttles—they don't *have* any stealth systems and would be entirely relying on a Mage."

"The planet is a hundred thousand kilometers across," Shvets noted. "If we came in on the opposite side from the fleet..."

"Do you want to bet our lives and the potential end of this war on there not being anything in position to pick us up as we did that?" Kelly asked. "There's almost certainly an accelerator ring around that planet, people. A half-million-kilometer space station. It *will* have sensors along its length, which means we can't sneak up on any side of the gas giant."

She watched the timer counting up from the moment the Republic ships would have seen their jump flare, and sighed.

"If it was just us, I'd take the risk," she admitted. "But right now, this ship is carrying enough to end the damn war. We're taking *one* more chance, people. One more dive into hell to make *certain* we've found the enemy. But we can't do more than that. We have a plan to do that as safely as possible.

"We cannot risk that knowledge being lost. I wish I knew who they were chasing, and I wish we could save them, but we can't. This war has to *end*."

The count was at ninety seconds and rising. The RIN hadn't responded as quickly as Kelly had expected, and she yanked on her braid in frustration. She didn't want to jump until they'd moved out of position, but...

"We're probably not going to get a major disruption out of them today," Milhouse noted as the count continued to rise. "Should we just jump in? We know there's going to be a fleet there, no matter what we do."

"I still want them focused out here," Kelly told them. "We give them five minutes, at least."

"We're ready," Xi Wu said. "Whenever they come."

"They seem distracted, at least," Milhouse agreed. "Two minutes. We're into a regular response time."

"I'm not complaining, but I do wish that they'd—"

"Jump flare!" Milhouse snapped. "Multiple jump flares; I'm reading at least five ships at two hundred thousand kilometers!"

"Well, at least we got their attention after all," Kelly replied. "I was starting to think we were being ignored. Xi?"

"We're already gone," the Ship's Mage said flatly. Even as Kelly turned her attention to the display showing her the incoming battle group, the world *twisted* around her.

"Jump complete," Xi said, her voice far more exhausted than it had been a moment before. "Passing off to Mel."

"Shvets?"

"Emergence on target; we are twenty-seven million kilometers from Hyacinth, and I am vectoring in at maximum power."

"That was a full carrier group, Captain," Milhouse reported. "*Courageous*-class carrier, two *Combination*-class battleships and four *Benjamin*-class cruisers."

"Always nice to be respected and sent the best," Kelly agreed. The Republic had sent over two hundred million tons of warships after her little two-hundred-*thousand*-ton stealth ship.

"I think they're just paranoid," her tactical officer told her. "Because this is our El Dorado, Captain. I can confirm we are looking at an accelerator ring in orbit of Hyacinth. Accompanying shipyards, fortresses and a goddamn multiple-carrier group fleet."

"Then I think we need to get out of here," Kelly said in a sharp exhale of breath. "We can pray for the poor bastard whose distraction bought us the time for this, but we've got to take advantage of it and *go*.

"Mage Droit, are you ready to jump?"

Many of the ships nearest to them were starting to adjust course toward them. They weren't an immediate threat, but Kelly had no intention of pushing the limits of her time. A *Martian* squadron wouldn't risk any microjump under five light-minutes, but the RIN might have different protocols.

"We're ready down here," her third Mage confirmed.

"Milhouse, get me a count on those hulls," Kelly ordered. "You have sixty seconds. Droit—the count is sixty seconds."

"Understood," both of her subordinates replied.

"That's a lot of damn ships," Milhouse said after a few seconds. "I've definitely picked out six carriers and eighteen battleships, but the gunships are making it hard to be certain I've got them— Status change!

"*What the fuck?!*"

Even on *Rhapsody*'s casual bridge, that was a useless report, and Kelly was about to turn it back on her tactical officer when she looked at the screen herself.

CHAPTER 46

"THESE SUPPLIES SUCK," Roslyn said grimly as she laid out the limited tools available to her. The shuttle was running on autopilot, but that could only buy them a few minutes for this process.

"They're what we've got," Alexander said, though she sounded nervous to Roslyn. "They've got a local anesthesia spray, right?"

"I'm not sure that's going to be enough," the young woman replied. "I think I've got the dosage worked out for a general."

"A general anesthetic isn't an option," the Mage-Admiral said. "We need me able to act as soon as this damn thing is out of me."

"I'm about to cut a twenty-centimeter-square layer of skin off your back," Roslyn pointed out. "I *really* don't think a local anesthetic is going to—"

"The one the Marines use is rated for similar insanity," Alexander cut her off, lying face-down on the cot with her shirt off again. "It will work. It will *have* to work."

Roslyn swallowed and looked at her tray of sterilized tools. The trauma bay on an assault shuttle was designed to be used by a medic instead of a doctor, but it was still intended for someone with a *lot* more medical knowledge than she had.

It also wasn't intended to be used for surgery outside of emergencies. Dedicated hospital shuttles would come down in any major landing. The trauma bay and the medic were intended to keep troops alive long enough to get them either to a hospital shuttle or back to a mothership.

But she had what she needed. She *needed* to find the stomach to cut open a friend and mentor. She *had* the scalpels for it.

With a long, slow exhalation, she picked up the local anaesthetic spray and checked over its instructions. Calibrating it was simple enough, and she slowly ran the spray over the Rune of Nullification and the skin around it.

"Well, given how fresh and painful that thing is, that helps all on its own," Alexander told her. "Do what you have to do, Roslyn."

Roslyn very carefully tried not to pay attention to the Admiral's putting a rag between her teeth, focusing on the task to hand.

Everything in the trauma bay was automatically sterilized, but the scalpels were also stored in a miniature autoclave that flash-sterilized them before use. The metal was warm under her hand as she picked it up and swallowed.

"Can I use magic to steady my hands?" she asked slowly.

"No," Alexander said in a muffled voice. "Don't know how the Rune will react. Magic that close to it is dangerous."

"Thought so," Roslyn admitted. "I'm about to—"

"*Don't* tell me," her mentor snapped. "Just *do it.*"

Roslyn cut. The anesthetic hopefully helped, as Alexander didn't immediately start screaming, but it wasn't a fast process. Sharp as the blades were, they lost that sharpness quickly enough. She got through one long, twenty-centimeter cut, and then she had to swap scalpels.

They'd anticipated that, though. The scalpels were self-sharpening when heated—the autoclave served two purposes—but Roslyn had collected *all* of them in the shuttle. She swapped to a new scalpel and began the second cut.

Alexander was definitely biting down on her rag now. Roslyn couldn't notice, didn't *let* herself notice as she finished the second cut. The third. The fourth.

Now the most terrifying part. A fifth scalpel slid into the flesh and began to lift up the skin as Roslyn made sure she was removing enough flesh to lift out the Rune of Nullification.

It went slowly, with her spraying plastiskin as she lifted up sections of skin and tried to hold down her nausea, but it went surprisingly smoothly. When it was done, an entire section of Alexander's back glistened with the pale pink medical membrane, a contrast to the faded brown skin of one of the Martian royal family.

"Admiral?" Roslyn asked. There was no response, and she dumped the Rune of Nullification into the bag she'd had to hand for it, and moved to check Alexander's breathing and pulse.

"Admiral?" she demanded. She checked the vitals. Alexander was breathing. Her pulse was steady. Her eyes were closed...she'd passed out from the pain, without ever screaming loud enough for Roslyn to even realize how bad it was getting.

"I need to move the shuttle," she told the unconscious Alexander. "I can't... I..."

She trailed off.

"I don't know what to do," she admitted. "So, I'm going to let you rest and go move the shuttle."

Nuclear bombs at least made one level of priority *very* clear.

Roslyn didn't even know if they'd succeeded. All she knew for certain was that Jane Alexander was unconscious and the Republic Interstellar Navy was starting to close in on her. If they hadn't initially been using the shockwaves from the bombs as sensor tools, they definitely were now.

A hundred-thousand-kilometer gas giant had a lot of surface area, but the RIN had a lot of ships and a lot of bombs. Gunships were doing most of the work now, it looked, with cruisers and battleships backing them up.

Her view out of Hyacinth was better than the RIN's view into the gas giant, but that wasn't by much. She had a rough idea of where the enemy ships were, and she knew *exactly* where the nukes were going off.

And she was running out of places to hide. The shuttle was only actually in danger from warheads that went off within ten kilometers or so—but she estimated the RIN could use the vibrations to detect the shuttle at five hundred kilometers at least.

The pattern of the explosions told her *they* were estimating four hundred. The bombs were going off in a perfectly sequenced mesh of detonations spaced eight hundred kilometers apart. Their timing was tight enough that there was no way she could dodge through after the bombs went off.

She was staying ahead of it so far, but the net was closing. Best case, she figured she could keep them safe for another thirty minutes.

"Roslyn?" a tired voice said from behind her. "I'm sorry; I didn't expect that."

She turned to see Alexander leaning against the cockpit door, struggling against the gravity. Her fatigue jacket was back on, but she hadn't fully done it up. She was fighting with exhaustion and pain and looked utterly shattered...but...there was something there.

"Jane? Are you all right?"

That spark spread into a smile as the Crown Princess of Mars held up her hand and conjured a tiny, dancing sprite of light on her palm.

"More than all right, my young friend, my savior," Jane Alexander told her. "You did it. I need to sit for a minute or two and drink another of those godawful ration drinks, but...the Nullification is broken, and my Runes of Power are answering my commands."

"Sit and drink, then," Roslyn instructed. She had a stockpile of the rations in the cockpit now and passed a drink over to the Admiral as her superior carefully took the copilot's seat.

Roslyn returned her focus to the deadly dance on her display.

"We don't have much longer before they use the shockwaves to detect us," she told Alexander. "Ten minutes, maybe twenty."

"I need those ten minutes, so let's take them," Alexander replied, closing her eyes as she drained the ration drink and grabbed a second one. "Fuck those bastards for that Rune," she said conversationally.

Roslyn smiled, her boss's returning strength their only real hope of surviving this mess. Her attention slipped away from the screen for a moment, and she blinked. Her view wasn't great but it wasn't *that* bad.

"A bunch of ships just disappeared," she told Alexander urgently, running the data back in time on a second screen. "Looks like seven ships just jumped somewhere. From high orbit of a gas giant?"

She shook her head.

"They've *lost* ships pulling stunts like that," Roslyn observed. "What are they playing at?"

"What did they *see* is probably a more important question," Alexander said. "Can we tell?"

"We're a thousand kilometers deep inside a gas giant," the Mage-Lieutenant pointed out. "We can barely see what's in orbit, let alone what's in the rest of the star system."

The two women exchanged a long look, then Alexander took a deep breath and looked down at her hands.

"Take us up," Alexander ordered. "Can this cockpit do a three-sixty-by-three-sixty view?"

It took Roslyn a moment to confirm that the shuttle *couldn't*. What it could do, though, was provide a fully functional surround view to a helmet and headset, which they set up as quickly as they could.

For Alexander to use her magic effectively, she had to be able to see outside the ship.

"Don't we need an amplifier to do this?" Roslyn asked as she lowered the helmet onto Alexander's head.

"The amplifier provides power and distance," Alexander replied. "*You* would need an amplifier to use magic for this at all. I need it mostly for range…and everything we care about is in Hyacinth orbit. The range is damned short by space-combat standards."

"You can do this?" Roslyn asked. She knew she was repeating herself, but they were about to commit suicide if Alexander was misjudging.

"I can. Now bring us up out of the gas giant, Roslyn. We have an escape to pull off and a war to end."

Roslyn focused on her controls, pointing the shuttle upward and bringing the engines on at full power. In a blink of an eye, they went from hiding in the bluish gasses of Hyacinth's atmosphere to rising from the depths like a homesick meteor.

"I have sensor data from outside the giant," she confirmed as they continued to rise. "Ships are definitely moving; they've picked up something... I have a jump flare! Jump flare at ninety light-seconds; RIN is maneuvering to intercept."

"I think that might be our ride, Roslyn," Alexander said brightly. "ID her!"

Seconds ticked away as they blazed skyward. The RIN would locate *them* quickly enough. They had no time, but...

"She's not hiding. It's one of our spy ships," Roslyn snapped as the image resolved. "She's heading toward Hyacinth at fifteen gravities. They found the bastards!"

"And now they've found us and get to be our ride," the Admiral told her. "Hail them and let them know who we are. *I* am going to clear us a path—and see what I can do about this accelerator ring."

They burst clear of the gas giant's atmosphere in a final explosion of loose hydrogen, and half a dozen gunships swerved to try to engage them.

Half a dozen gunships died in a blink of an eye, vanishing in balls of ice-white fire unlike anything Roslyn had ever seen. The pair of cruisers behind them blew up in fireballs she at least *recognized* as Alexander tore apart their antimatter-containment systems.

An expanding sphere of dying ships surrounded Roslyn's assault shuttle as they blazed into the stars, and she brought up the shuttle's com systems.

"Protectorate ship, this is Mage-Lieutenant Roslyn Chambers and Mage-Admiral Jane Alexander," she said quickly, desperately. "We have commandeered a Republic assault shuttle and are en route to your position at our maximum acceleration. Please make rendezvous for extraction; we cannot escape this system on our own.

"I repeat, this is Mage-Admiral Jane Alexander and Mage-Lieutenant Roslyn Chambers. We were taken captive by the Republic and have escaped. We are en route to your position. Please rendezvous for extraction."

She turned her attention back to the close-range sensors in time to watch Alexander's magic tear a battleship into its two component hulls and fling those wrecked pieces into Hyacinth's upper atmosphere.

Roslyn was still flying evasively, desperately trying to avoid as much of the incoming fire as possible, but she wasn't sure that was even *necessary*. A spray of twenty-gigawatt beams from a trio of closing battleships resulted in four direct hits. Any one of those four should have obliterated the shuttle. Instead, they dissipated harmlessly—and three battleships blew apart as magic tore through their antimatter-containment systems.

"I have the fleet but they're damned determined," Alexander said aloud, her voice distracted and a little strained. "The ring is yours, Roslyn. Can you break it?"

Roslyn wasn't a Rune Wright and didn't have five Runes of Power inlaid into her flesh. Very little of her training had ever focused on dealing with things on a starship scale without using an amplifier—she'd learned *one* spell to use as an antimissile defense, but even that was supposed to have a civilian simulacrum to work from for targeting.

Instead, she pointed the shuttle directly at the accelerator ring. The Hyacinth Accelerator Ring was more fragile than its Centurion predecessor, lacking heavy armor, defensive installations or any of the other things that made the Centurion Ring a world in the sky.

It handled a massive amount of power and it wasn't thirty thousand kilometers ahead of her. It was barely *three* thousand kilometers ahead of her, and the shuttle's screens were enough for her to locate it in her mind.

She summoned her power, that deceptively simple spell that could detonate an antimatter missile's fuel tanks, and slammed every scrap of her magic into that station. She didn't know where to find an antimatter tank, so she slammed a single blade of force through the entire station.

Against a missile, the spell used a spark and a five-meter force blade. With the simulacrum and the three-sixty-by-three-sixty view from a simulacrum chamber, she could be accurate enough to do that.

Against the Hyacinth Accelerator Ring, she dropped the spark and panic-summoned a force blade a *kilometer* long. In the end, she didn't detonate a fuel tank.

She carved a gash halfway through the ring. The sheer amount of force inherent in a ring over a hundred thousand kilometers in diameter did the rest. The wrecked ring snapped away from her with awe-inspiring force, crashing into a carrier attempting to evade Alexander's wrath and triggering a massive explosion that wrecked carrier and station segment alike.

Roslyn suspected Chrysanthemum could rebuild the ring. Eventually. But not today—or this week or next week.

Not before Second Fleet could get there—and all around her, the reserve fleet of the Republic, their secret second arrow that should have turned the tide of the war, collided with the power of the Crown Princess of Mars.

And died.

"Lieutenant Chambers, this is Captain LaMonte aboard *Rhapsody in Purple*," the radio messaged greeted her. "We are inbound on your position and preparing for rendezvous."

There was an awed, hushed tone to LaMonte's words.

"If you can maneuver to match our velocity at a midpoint and the Mage-Admiral can keep us safe while we make our approach, we will pick you up in approximately six hours." The message paused. "Please... make sure the Crown Princess doesn't accidentally mistake us for a hostile."

"No risk of that," Alexander murmured. "Everyone else is running for the hills."

And they were doing so from the opposite side of the gas giant, too. Not even a *gunship* remained in line of sight of their tiny shuttle as they accelerated toward the stealth ship.

"Are we safe?" Roslyn asked.

"That depends on whether they find their gumption in the next six hours or so," the Admiral admitted. "If they come out after us once we're well on our way, I can only hurt them from within a hundred thousand klicks or so.

"On the other hand, I'm pretty sure I can stop their missiles...and I think I made an impression."

The assault shuttle's computers had no concept of softening the blow. They were happy to show Roslyn how many ships had died around them as they fled the gas giant.

There had been seven carriers and over sixty starships gathered around Hyacinth. One carrier group had left earlier to try and capture *Rhapsody*. They had wisely chosen not to return.

Of the rest, at least thirty starships and five or six hundred gunships had died before the rest had fled. The accelerator ring's destruction was a more slow-motion process now, but it was shedding segments and descending into its gas-giant host.

The last major fleet of the Republic Interstellar Navy was debris and corpses—and the shuttle computers were perfectly happy to give Roslyn their estimate of over a million dead from Alexander's power.

If anyone had assumed the power that had ended the Eugenics Wars had rested entirely in the Olympus Mons Amplifier, today had proven them *very* wrong.

"*An impression* is one way to say it, I suppose," Roslyn murmured. "I guess we just reminded everyone why they need to fear Mars."

"And we need to get back to Second Fleet and return here," Alexander said. "Because we *also* need to demonstrate that the power of Mars is a *shield*, not a sword."

CHAPTER 47

THERE WAS a sharp tension to the air as the Republican assault shuttle descended to a halt in *Rhapsody*'s shuttle bay. Its coloring and lines were ever so slightly wrong compared to the spacecraft already waiting aboard the scout ship, clearly marking it as a stranger in this space.

Part of the tension, Kelly knew, was the potential that the shuttle was still somehow a trap. She wasn't entirely sure *how* the Republic could have pulled that off, but it was still technically an enemy ship that they were taking aboard.

The rest of the tension was due to the reason she knew that was a silly concern. She might have commandos from Charmchi's platoon stationed around the bay, and Shvets at her left hand just in case, but they'd all seen the Republic's fleet driven into retreat and the accelerator ring broken.

There was *fear* in the space right now, and Kelly wasn't sure how to lift that tension. She felt it herself. She'd been vaguely aware that Damien Montgomery and the Alexanders were far above ordinary Mages, but she'd never expected to see *one Mage* take down a battle fleet.

Cooling jets sprayed the exterior of the shuttle and the pad around it with water that turned instantly to steam, buying a few precious minutes, and a light near the pad turned from red to amber.

It would now be merely extremely uncomfortable for a human to leave or approach the shuttle instead of almost certainly fatal. A door opened and a ramp extended from the spacecraft, allowing two women to step outside.

The taller and older woman was leaning on the other, radiating a bone-deep weariness that Kelly could see from ten meters away.

"With me," she murmured to her escorts, setting off to meet the Mage-Admiral. Kelzin kept pace with her on the other side from Shvets, the three of them entering the unnatural sauna around the landing pad.

"Captain LaMonte," Roslyn Chambers greeted them, the young Mage looking only barely less exhausted than her Admiral. "You have no idea how good it is to see a friendly face."

"I can only guess," Kelly admitted. "Admiral Alexander, how are you?"

"Alive," Alexander said in a tight voice. "In a lot of pain... I need to rest."

"Mike, get the Admiral to the medbay," Kelly ordered as she took in the Crown Princess of Mars's state. "We'll take care of you, Mage-Admiral. It's not every day someone single-handedly wins a war after dying."

Alexander was clearly too exhausted to take that in, readily accepting a transfer from Chambers's shoulder to Kelzin's. A commando was there a moment later, the two men propping up the Admiral as they led her away.

The younger Mage waited until Alexander was on her way, then turned back to face Kelly and drew herself up to attention with a perfect salute.

"Mage-Lieutenant Roslyn Chambers reporting, sir," she stated. "I'm assuming that Mage-Admiral Alexander and I were presumed dead. We were kidnapped by an Augment infiltration cell that had managed to remove and replace Her Highness's Royal Guard detail.

"I'm not certain what measures they took to cover their mission, but we were brought here to be interrogated by the Lord Protector himself." Chambers shivered. "I think Alexander was a prize, but he was hoping to *turn* me."

"The evidence suggests he failed, Lieutenant," Kelly replied, trying to process everything the younger woman had packed into a handful of sentences. "Is there any reason you know of why we should remain in Chrysanthemum?"

"No," Chambers said. "It will take them some time to recover from the body blow the Admiral did to them, but we'll want to return to Second Fleet as soon as possible." She swallowed. "I suppose Alexander should be in contact with Mars ASAP as well."

"Fortunately, Second Fleet has mostly returned to Legatus," Kelly told the young woman. "Which is where we're headed, no matter what."

She tapped her wrist-comp.

"Mage Droit? We've got everyone and I don't think there's anything left for us in this system. Get us out of here."

"Yes, sir!"

Kelly wasn't a Mage, but she could tell when a ship jumped. Some of the last tension in the shuttle bay released as magic rippled through the starship.

"And we're clear," she murmured to Chambers. "You got yourself and the Admiral out, Lieutenant. That's not shabby."

"She did most of the work at the end," the young woman admitted. "I...broke the accelerator ring, but she was dealing with an entire *fleet*. It was awe-inspiring. And terrifying."

"Those tend to go together," Kelly agreed. "Can you jump, Mage-Lieutenant?"

"Once I've rested a bit, yes," Chambers said. "I know even one Mage can make a difference, but I've already run up to my limits."

And a bit beyond, Kelly judged. The young woman's eyes were blood-shot and there were light streaks of red on her upper lip. She suspected Chambers hadn't even realized she'd been bleeding, but Kelly was familiar with the signs of early thaumic burnout.

"Rest was part of the plan, Lieutenant," she told the young woman. "At least a day, but even then, you'll cut twenty-four hours off our run to Legatus."

"If there is any way I can help, I will," Chambers said, her tone determined.

"Right now, Mage-Lieutenant? You need to go join Admiral Alexander in the medbay and let my husband and our doctor check you over," Kelly ordered. "You've had a hell of a few weeks, from the sounds of it.

"We'll take care of it from here; you have my word."

"Thank you," Chambers said, visibly sagging around her bones as *her* tension slowly released. "I... I..."

"Medbay, Lieutenant," Kelly repeated.

Roslyn Chambers was going to need some long sessions with a therapist, but that wasn't Kelly LaMonte's call or job. *Her* job was to get the two women who'd probably won the war home in one piece.

CHAPTER 48

RHAPSODY IN PURPLE had been enough of a relief that Roslyn had thought she'd let go of all of the tension she'd accumulated in her weeks in Republican hands. She realized she was wrong when she completed the final jump into Legatus and saw Second Fleet on the screens.

Dreadnoughts, battleships, cruisers...a Martian fleet over a secure world. A safe haven with friends and allies.

There had apparently still been tension left in her shoulders to release, and she nearly collapsed before being caught by Xi Wu.

"I was waiting for that," the dark-skinned Mage said with a chuckle. "We're still a few hours out, but the Captain will report in. Get to bed; we'll wake you when we know more."

"I don't think I can sleep at this point," Roslyn admitted.

"That wasn't a *suggestion*, Lieutenant," Xi Wu said pointedly.

Roslyn wasn't entirely clear on what ranks, exactly, anyone aboard the stealth ship had. She could treat LaMonte as a Captain without hesitation, but the rest of the crew seemed a mix of RMN hands, who weren't using ranks, and civilians.

Right now, though, the important part was that Xi Wu was the senior Ship's Mage.

"Yes, sir," Roslyn confirmed, saluting and slowly making her way out of the simulacrum chamber.

She could see dreadnoughts. That meant she'd won.

Four hours later, she was woken up by one of the cyborg commandos that seemed to be everywhere on the small ship.

"Mage-Lieutenant? The Admiral is asking for you," the man told her. "We've made contact with *everyone*, I think, and we're heading for the Link. Fast."

"Thank you," Roslyn replied, pulling herself out of bed.

The commando saluted and stepped outside, leaving her to get dressed and check in on the situation on her new wrist-comp.

The Link the Protectorate had claimed for their use in Legatus was aboard an orbital station that had been stripped of everything else. It now served entirely as a com relay linking the former capital of the Republic of Faith and Reason to Mars itself.

Rhapsody was burning at her maximum fifteen gravities of deceleration toward a rendezvous with that station. Roslyn could eyeball the intercept at about twenty minutes, which meant she really was short on time.

Thankfully, she finally had access to proper fitted shipsuits again and was able to dress in the single-piece garment quickly. Her cyborg alarm clock was waiting for her outside her room with a smile.

He was roughly her age and attractive in a clean-shaven-but-rough-hewn way. That Roslyn was even noticing that suggested she was finally getting over the base level of exhaustion that had consumed her since the Republicans had delivered her to Chrysanthemum.

"Looks like we're running short on time," she told the man. "Lead the way."

Mage-Admiral Jane Alexander had finally received proper medical attention for both the cocktail of chemicals the Republic had put her on as well as for the massive chunk of skin Roslyn had removed from her back. She was seated in a briefing room with Captain LaMonte and looked mostly free of pain.

Roslyn could see the places where new lines had been carved into the old woman's face from her ordeal, but Alexander seemed on top of things. She wasn't going to assume weakness on the Mage-Admiral's part.

The fate of the entire *fleet* that had collided with her was a counter-indicator to that idea!

"Roslyn, come in, sit down," Alexander instructed. "We'll be reporting to a shuttle in a few minutes. Is there anything aboard *Rhapsody* you'll need?"

"No, sir," Roslyn confirmed as she took a seat next to her boss. "Didn't bring much aboard except an assault shuttle I don't need to keep."

"That's good," LaMonte said with a chuckle. "My husband will be flying you over to the Link Station, and he point-blank refuses to fly that thing. We'll be handing it over to some friends of ours who will dissect its computers for anything we can learn about Chrysanthemum, but the shuttle itself is relatively useless to us."

"And much of what we might learn about Chrysanthemum will be background details now," Alexander noted. "The shuttle was assigned to the accelerator ring, which...won't be a problem anymore."

There was a satisfied tone to Alexander's voice that made Roslyn conceal a shiver.

"My niece is aware that we're alive and has leveled the full authority of her office to demand to speak to me the moment it is physically possible," Alexander continued. "I'm imposing on my authority to bring you with me for now, Lieutenant. At this point, I trust your judgment over just about anyone else alive."

"Yes, sir. Thank you, sir," Roslyn said quickly.

"You saved my life, Roslyn," the Admiral reminded her. "That is not an act or a debt that I will forget or permit others to forget. If they want to hang glory and victories on me, I'm hanging them on you, Mage-Lieutenant. You are a heroine of the Protectorate. Don't forget that."

Roslyn swallowed. She knew what she'd done had been *difficult*, but all she'd really been doing was enabling Alexander. Any victory was the Admiral's, really.

Alexander didn't look like she was going to buy that argument, though.

"Yes, sir. Thank you, sir," she repeated—earning herself a laugh from both of the older women in the room.

"I know damn well you're not that self-effacing, Mage-Lieutenant Chambers," Alexander told her. "Remember that unlike the rest of your fellow officers, *I* got the full story of how you got the Lord Regent's recommendation letter. Petty-thievery skills are useful when assisting in covert ops and escaping enemy bases, but they weren't acquired by a wallflower!"

"No, sir," Roslyn admitted. "I'm sure at *least* a quarter of the Mages in the Navy could have done what I did, though, sir."

Her false humility got her another laugh.

"Better," the Admiral told her. "All right. Is our shuttle ready, Captain?"

"It should be, or Mike is sleeping on the couch tonight," LaMonte replied. "I'm glad we were there at the right time, Admiral."

"So am I. If you'd been much earlier or later, you'd have brought Second Fleet in to finish the job and avenge us, but I do prefer this whole *living* business."

CHAPTER 49

UNTIL THE MOMENT the video feed from the Link showed the faces of the two women he'd seen reported dead, Damien Montgomery didn't truly believe that Jane Alexander and Roslyn Chambers had survived.

Too many people had died around him and around the throne of Mars for him to trust that some of those deaths had been a lie.

Once the two women, one old, one young, appeared on his screen, he *had* to believe it. Next to him, he could tell that Kiera Alexander was fighting back tears, the Mage-Queen of Mars's carefully managed façade disintegrating.

"You *are* alive," the Queen whispered through her tears.

She and Damien were once again in his office, taking advantage of the now-permanently-installed standalone com console relaying from the Link at Deimos. Both of them sat in front of the big stone desk, facing the video camera concealed above the wallscreen.

"I am," Jane Alexander confirmed. "Despite the best efforts of our enemies, my beloved niece. I am alive and the Republic already regrets that. I..." She sighed. "What happened to my actual Royal Guards, Damien? They were replaced before they arrived in Nueva Bolivia."

"We don't know yet," he admitted. "The investigation I started was focused on the shuttle. We'd confirmed it was destroyed by a bomb, and we were trying to focus on how *that* happened."

"That's fair," the old Admiral conceded. "I've already sent orders to *Durendal* to arrest the supposed Mountain catering team, but it turns out they'd 'returned to Mars' after my death."

"What catering team?" Kiera Alexander demanded. "We sent a platoon of the Royal Guard. That was all."

"So I'd guessed from the fact that team was feeding me different pieces of multi-part poison," the Mage-Admiral said. "Fuckers." She shook her head. "We can confirm that the Republic fallback position and the accelerator ring are in the Chrysanthemum System, if that part of the report hasn't percolated upward yet."

Damien nodded, exhaling his breath in a long sigh.

"I personally ordered LaMonte's scouting mission, so I'm not surprised," he admitted. It felt, now, like they should have seen that one coming. "We'll also send a task force to investigate New Madagascar, just to be certain. I would prefer to keep the kid gloves our subordinates wanted, but..."

"Two of their compatriots betrayed Our trust," Kiera Alexander said next to him, and he *knew* that tone and use of capitals. "They will suffer Our distrust."

"The situation in Chrysanthemum requires immediate attention," Mage-Admiral Alexander told them. "The accelerator ring is no longer functional and their fleet was heavily reduced, but we'll need to move on the base there before Lord Protector Solace has any more clever ideas."

"What...happened?" Damien asked. Then he realized. He, of all people, knew how deadly a Rune Wright could be—and most of his involvement in space combat had been at real combat ranges, hundreds of thousands or even millions of kilometers.

"Mage-Lieutenant Chambers broke me out of my cell," the Mage-Admiral told him. "As we escaped, we realized the bastards had put a Rune of Nullification on me, but Chambers successfully removed it.

"They faced the wrath of a Rune Wright at ranges of under ten thousand kilometers. I broke them, Damien. Now we need to make certain we *finish* the job."

Damien nodded slowly and focused on the young woman who'd been silent so far. Roslyn Chambers wore an unmarked shipsuit and looked surprisingly well for someone who'd been through everything she had been.

"It seems the Protectorate owes you a great debt, Lieutenant," he told her. "It seems I chose well on Tau Ceti back then."

"You gave me a chance that others might not have," Chambers said quietly. "Everything I do is in repayment of that."

"I think that debt is paid ten times over," Damien replied. "It was repaid in ships saved at Nia Kriti, in the victory at Ardennes—and now, in the life of the Crown Princess of Mars. I think we owe *you*, not the other way around."

"This doesn't change your addition to the line of succession, Damien," the Mage-Queen pointed out with a chuckle beside him. "You're now *second* in line, but you are still a Prince of Mars."

"Let's keep any public announcement of that quiet until you're no longer my ward, shall we?" Damien asked. He was uncomfortable enough with that as it was—and so far as he was concerned, the fewer people who knew about it unless it became necessary, the better.

The only person who absolutely needed to know was Grace McLaughlin, and she was on her way to Mars as they spoke. Part of him was looking forward to the inevitable confrontation between his girlfriend and the Mountain's medical establishment over the concept of Rune Wright children.

The rest of him was dreading it.

"You put Damien on the list, did you?" Mage-Admiral Alexander asked. "That's a good call, Kiera. We need that extra certainty. God alone knows how much time is left to me."

"Enough, we hope," Damien replied. "If nothing else, if Chrysanthemum is in the shape you think it is, I agree that we need to move. Second Fleet should be fully resupplied. Admiral Marangoz will surrender command to you; I don't think we need to worry about that."

"How'd he do as fleet CO?" Jane Alexander said. "I know he rubs some of my officers the wrong way." She snorted. "*I'd* have given command to Medici."

"That was my inclination, but I'm biased in Medici's favor," Damien noted. Medici had saved his life once—and Kelly LaMonte's, for that matter. The man had commanded the cruiser squadron that had saved the freighter *Blue Jay* from the pirates that had hunted her down to capture a Rune Wright.

"So, you decided against him because you know you're biased?" Jane Alexander asked, shaking her head. "Sometimes, my dear friend, I think you are perhaps too determined to only do the right thing."

"There is no such thing," he replied. He smiled and shook his head. "Your mission remains what it always was, Jane: reduce the Republic by whatever means necessary. Do we need to give specific orders?"

"No," she told him. "Inform Protectorate High Command that Second Fleet will be moving as soon as physically possible. We will proceed to the Chrysanthemum System and we will reduce whatever remains of the Republic fleet.

"And if we are only moderately lucky, we will finally end this fucking war."

CHAPTER 50

ROSLYN CHAMBERS was nervous as she approached the primary conference room on *Durendal*. The space was designed to hold hundreds of officers, and she was almost always aware of meetings taking place in it well ahead of time—as the Admiral's Flag Lieutenant, she was one of the only people with the ability to even book meetings and presentations in the space.

The event she was attending had appeared on her schedule overnight, requiring her to be in the conference room at oh nine hundred hours. There were no further details of the event, though a quick check had shown that Admiral Alexander's schedule was also blocked off for it.

They'd been back in Second Fleet for three days and were only a handful of jumps, less than a day's travel, from Chrysanthemum. Those three days had been a whirlwind of activity of meetings and calls and virtual conferences, all coordinated by Roslyn Chambers and Indrajit Kulkarni with the ease of long practice.

It was all normal enough to restore some of her calm and balance, but this appointment was weird enough to throw her completely off her step. She had no idea what was going on—and she stopped dead in her tracks at the sight of two of *Durendal*'s Marines standing on either side of the door to the conference room...in full dress uniform.

"Mage-Lieutenant, hurry up," the Sergeant on the right told her. "Everyone is waiting."

"Everyone?" Roslyn realized she'd squeaked, and the two Marines chuckled.

"Go on," the Sergeant repeated, reaching over to hover their hand above the door panel. "It's safe; I can promise you that."

The other Marine chuckled again at that comment, but it was surprisingly reassuring to Roslyn. No matter what, she was still going to trust the Marines.

She stepped into the amphitheater-style room and swallowed. *Everyone* definitely seemed to sum it up. There were at least a dozen flag officers in the room—and just how the *hell* had whoever had organized this got a dozen flag officers onto *Durendal* without her knowing?!—as well as an equal number of senior Captains and what looked like ten percent of the dreadnought's crew.

All of them were looking at her. There was a clear path down the steps to the main stage, whose only occupant was Mage-Admiral Jane Alexander, the old officer standing straight-backed but smiling as she made a small gesture for Roslyn to approach.

Roslyn obeyed the gesture, walking in stunned silence under the eyes of hundreds of her fellows. She stepped onto the dais and came to attention, saluting her boss.

"Admiral."

"Kneel, Mage-Lieutenant Roslyn Chambers," Alexander ordered.

Swallowing hard, Roslyn obeyed. There was just the two of them on the stage, and Roslyn realized the recording equipment was active as well. Off to one side she could see Mage-Captain Kulkarni—and the operations officer's grin told her *exactly* who had organized all of this around her.

"Officers and Spacers of the Royal Martian Navy and the Royal Martian Marine Corps," Alexander said loudly and clearly. "There are many duties, responsibilities and tasks laid upon us all. To serve faithfully and truly. To master the tasks before us. To wield our skills justly and well. For those of us with magic, to master our Gift instead of be mastered by it—and to wield our power in the service of all mankind.

"Tradition and treaty lay further responsibilities on prisoners of war. To remain silent in face of interrogation. To learn what we can about the enemy. To escape, if possible. These duties are regarded as ideals as much as true tasks, especially in a modern era where prisons can strip even the most powerful of Mages of their power."

The room was silent except for Alexander's words, and Roslyn shivered under the attention of those hundreds of eyes.

"When captured in a covert operation by the Republic of Faith and Reason, Mage-Lieutenant Roslyn Chambers lived up to *all* of those duties," the Admiral said. "She resisted interrogation and attempts at co-option. She learned enough about her enemies to engineer her own escape despite being trapped inside a guarded cell that negated her magic.

"All of this, perhaps, we would regard as the duty of an officer in Her Majesty's Navy."

Alexander paused, letting that sink in to her audience.

"But. From there, Mage-Lieutenant Chambers proceeded to rescue myself from similar imprisonment and steal an enemy shuttle, taking us both to safety. When we discovered that the Republic had found a means to block *my* power as scion of Mars, she found a way to undo that block— allowing me to engage the Republic Fleet.

"Her actions led directly to the destruction of the second Republic antimatter accelerator ring, the crippling of a major Republic Interstellar Navy combat formation, and to Second Fleet learning the location of the enemy continuity-of-government facility. They also led, quite directly, to my own freedom."

Roslyn was still kneeling. She was reasonably sure of what was going on now, though she wished someone had *warned* her that there was going to be a ceremony to go along with the medal she figured she was going to get.

"While we hope that no officer or spacer of the Navy has to face an entire battle station with nothing but their wits, we can all hope that we would rise to the challenge as you did," Alexander told her. "My own involvement in the situation was such that I felt it wasn't my place to decide on your rewards, Mage-Lieutenant.

"One half of your reward was decided by a panel of your superiors, twelve Admirals and Commodores of this fleet who are present today.

The other was decided directly by Her Majesty, Mage-Queen Kiera Alexander.

"It is in *Her* name that I act today. Bow your head, Mage-Lieutenant," Alexander instructed.

Roslyn obeyed.

"In the name of the Mage-Queen of Mars, Kiera Alexander, the fourth monarch of our Protectorate, I bestow upon you, Mage-Lieutenant Roslyn Chambers, the Mage-King's *Ruby* Medal of Valor."

The gold star with its carved ruby planet dropped around Roslyn's neck before she could even process. *The Medal of Valor?!* She knew she'd gone above and beyond, but the *Medal of Valor?* She'd received that once already, but that had been for stepping up as a tactical officer when she'd been a mere *Ensign*...and she didn't know of *anyone* who'd received it twice!

The room exploded in applause as Roslyn knelt there in stunned silence, but Alexander waved them all to silence.

"Any senior officer here could do the rest," she said loudly to a chorus of chuckles. "But I don't think anyone will begrudge me this. Take this, Chambers."

Roslyn's head was swimming and she was still kneeling as she took the jeweler's box. She recognized it. She knew what it had to be before she even opened it.

"I checked the records," the Mage-Admiral told her. "You are the *second*-youngest officer ever promoted to the rank of Mage-Lieutenant-Commander in the Royal Martian Navy." She paused thoughtfully. "Well, discounting posthumous promotions, which seemed like a good call."

Roslyn removed her Lieutenant's bar in a stunned fugue, slowly fumbling with the new paired bars until Alexander chuckled and took them away from her. The Admiral pinned the new bars to Roslyn's collar with a quick, practiced hand and then lifted the young woman to her feet.

"Officers, Spacers and Marines, I give you the *third ever* holder of two of the Mage-King's Royal Martian Medals of Valor: Mage-Lieutenant-Commander Roslyn Chambers!"

This time, no one attempted to calm the applause.

CHAPTER 51

MAGE-LIEUTENANT-COMMANDER Roslyn Chambers expected to be transferred to a new role sooner rather than later, but for the moment, she remained Mage-Admiral Alexander's Flag Lieutenant, which meant her place was on *Durendal*'s flag bridge as Second Fleet erupted into the Chrysanthemum System.

There were no games or maneuvers today. Three dreadnoughts led six battleships, twenty-six cruisers and fifty-two destroyers into the system in a single massive bloc of firepower. All eighty-seven ships accelerated toward Hyacinth at fifteen gravities while their sensors swept up every scrap of data they could find.

"The wreckage of the accelerator ring has been stabilized," Kulkarni reported. "It looks like they could trigger a separation of the segments, so they split it into two sections and pushed them into orbits."

She shook her head.

"Fixing that looks like it's going to be a nightmare," she admitted.

"If they let us, we'll help them," Alexander said brightly. "If they don't, well, they built it in five years. I guess they can fix it."

"Even with transmuter Mages, there might be value for those rings if we can build them in five years instead of forty," Kulkarni noted.

"If I understand what I was told correctly, they basically took complete control of Chrysanthemum's economy to pull it off," Roslyn told the operations officer. "I don't think anyone else is going to manage it—but then, the value I can see is in building a ring around an inhabited world as an industrial platform."

"That's about what I was thinking, I have to admit," her superior agreed. "Still a massive project but not a half-million-kilometer project."

"All of this is germane to future matters, but what kind of defenses have they mustered?" Alexander asked.

"It looks like they've reinforced from what you left behind, sir," Kulkarni reported. "They're back up to what looks like seven carriers, fifteen battleships and forty cruisers. That's...something like eighty or ninety percent of what we figure they've got left."

"They sent out the call the same time we did, but *they* have instantaneous communications," Roslyn concluded. "They figured we'd come here with everything and, well. Without an antimatter supply, their only hope is to knock out Second Fleet."

"Not much of a hope," Alexander replied. "Are they maneuvering?"

"Yes, sir," Kulkarni confirmed. "Range is just under one light-minute and they have seen us. They are adjusting their positions to put the fleet between us and the stations above Hyacinth."

"But not coming out to meet us?" the Admiral asked.

"Not yet, sir. Any change to our orders?"

"No. Proceed as per the operation plan. Let me know the moment they've launched their gunships."

"There are about two hundred in space and forming up on the fleet, but they haven't launched anything new," the operations officer reported. "Analysis is expecting two thousand from the carriers and a similar number from defensive platforms."

"Understood. Advise when we see gunship launches," Alexander repeated.

Thirty minutes passed. Forty. An hour—one in which Second Fleet continued to accelerate toward Hyacinth, their sensors drinking deep at the well of light and radiation to learn as much about their enemies as they could.

"Still no gunships," Alexander murmured. "ETA to Samurai range?"

"One hundred seventy-three minutes," Kulkarni reported. "Fifty-five minutes after turnover."

"Hmm."

Alexander's wordless noise echoed in the bridge as the fleet hurtled toward the battle that would end the war, one way or another.

"Your assessment, Mage-Captain?" she finally asked.

"They're holding the gunships back to rest the crews and preserve fuel," Kulkarni replied instantly. "They're operating inside a hard limit on antimatter availability. They don't want to give up the advantage of having AM engines on the gunships, but their production without a full-scale accelerator ring isn't up to the demands of a war."

"Even if they win today, they lose the war," Alexander said aloud. "We can court a long-range engagement, force them to expend missiles and antimatter, and come back next week. Then the week after. And the week after.

"They can't win this."

"But they can hurt us and hurt us badly," the operations officer replied. "If they've got six thousand gunships over there instead of four—or eight, or ten—they can still hit this fleet with enough missiles to end us."

"We have to allow for that possibility, yes," Alexander agreed. "Fleet will adjust course," she ordered. "We will commence deceleration early to bring us to zero velocity at maximum Samurai range.

"Let's see what they do."

A light flashed on Roslyn's console, and she blinked as she stared at it for a moment.

"Sir, we're receiving a recorded transmission from Hyacinth," she reported. "It looks like it's coming from Styx Station."

"Interesting. Isolate it from the main systems and play it, Lieutenant-Commander," Alexander ordered. "Let's see what the Lord Protector has to say for himself."

The message had already gone into an isolated buffer to keep it away from the dreadnought's computers. It ran through a series of scanners into a separate buffer that allowed Roslyn to play it on a screen in the flag deck.

The woman who appeared on the screen was *not* Lord Protector George Solace. She was older than he was, with long pure-white hair that hung to her shoulders with a flow and elegance many younger women would kill for.

The stranger wore a black skirt-suit and stood behind a transparent podium marked with the stylized hammer and cross of the Republic of Faith and Reason. She was in some kind of briefing room, though if there was anyone else in the room they were out of the camera's view.

"I am Melissa Stormgast," she greeted them. "I am the duly appointed Speaker of the Assembly of the Republic of Faith and Reason. Under the Constitution of the Republic, I am third in the line of succession... which, today, makes me Acting President of the Republic.

"Vice President James Connors was killed resisting arrest three days ago. President George Solace, the Lord Protector of the Republic, has been impeached and arrested."

Stormgast was silent for several seconds.

"While I won't pretend that we would have moved if the result of the war had not become clear, I will also not pretend ignorance of Solace's crimes. We *were* ignorant, once, but we bought into his propaganda because we chose to.

"We no longer choose to, and Lord Protector Solace is on suicide watch to make certain that he lives to stand trial for grand crimes against humanity."

Durendal's flag bridge was silent. Roslyn felt like the entire *ship* was silent as they waited for the words that they hoped Stormgast would say, the words she *had* to say, given how she'd begun.

"I am charged, Admiral Alexander, by the surviving Members of the Republic Assembly, to negotiate the terms for the surrender of the remaining forces and worlds of the Republic of Faith and Reason."

ABOUT THE AUTHOR

GLYNN STEWART is the author of Starship's Mage, a bestselling science fiction and fantasy series where faster-than-light travel is possible–but only because of magic. His other works include science fiction series Duchy of Terra, Castle Federation and Vigilante, as well as the urban fantasy series ONSET and Changeling Blood.

Writing managed to liberate Glynn from a bleak future as an accountant. With his personality and hope for a high-tech future intact, he lives in Kitchener, Ontario with his partner, their cats, and an unstoppable writing habit.

OTHER BOOKS
BY GLYNN STEWART

For release announcements join the
mailing list or visit **GlynnStewart.com**

STARSHIP'S MAGE
Starship's Mage
Hand of Mars
Voice of Mars
Alien Arcana
Judgment of Mars
UnArcana Stars
Sword of Mars
Mountain of Mars
The Service of Mars
A Darker Magic
Mage-Commander
Beyond the Eyes of Mars (upcoming)

Starship's Mage: Red Falcon
Interstellar Mage
Mage-Provocateur
Agents of Mars

Pulsar Race: A Starship's Mage Universe Novella

DUCHY OF TERRA
The Terran Privateer
Duchess of Terra
Terra and Imperium
Darkness Beyond
Shield of Terra
Imperium Defiant
Relics of Eternity
Shadows of the Fall
Eyes of Tomorrow

SCATTERED STARS

Scattered Stars: Conviction

Conviction

Deception

Equilibrium

Fortitude

Huntress (upcoming)

Scattered Stars: Evasion

Evasion (upcoming)

PEACEKEEPERS OF SOL

Raven's Peace

The Peacekeeper Initiative

Raven's Course

Drifter's Folly

Remnant Faction (upcoming)

EXILE

Exile

Refuge

Crusade

Ashen Stars: An Exile Novella

CASTLE FEDERATION

Space Carrier Avalon

Stellar Fox

Battle Group Avalon

Q-Ship Chameleon

Rimward Stars

Operation Medusa

A Question of Faith: A Castle Federation Novella

SCIENCE FICTION STAND ALONE NOVELLA

Excalibur Lost

Made in United States
Orlando, FL
26 June 2022

19163630R00190